"A swashbuckling adventure that will appeal to fantasy fans as well as mystery fans." —*The Denver Post*

"A fun read. Provides new insight into familiar characters." —Margaret Frazer, author of the Dame Frevisse Mysteries

"A gifted writer who brings new life to our friends, D'Artagnan, Athos, Porthos, and Aramis." —Victoria Thompson, author of the Gaslight Mysteries

"A cracking good book that succeeds on many levels . . . The evocation of early seventeenth century France is just as Dumas had it. A round of applause, too, for writing a book set in a period not already overdone and in packing a teasing plot, well-loved characters that spring to life, and plenty of authentic background into a book of just the right length. Waiting until the next book is going to be hard . . . Highly enjoyable!" —MyShelf.com

"Dumas fans eager for further details of the lives of his swashbuckling heroes may enjoy this first in a series of historical mystery novels that transforms those men of action and intrigue into the king's detectives." —*Publishers Weekly*

"A fun swashbuckling historical mystery . . . filled with action." —*The Best Reviews*

"The author captures their adventurous spirit. Her prose is thick with description and grandiose dialogue that pulls readers into the era of King Louis XIII. It takes some attention to keep track of all the intriguing characters in this mystery, but if you're looking for something out of the ordinary, this is a fun read." —*Romantic Times*

The Musketeers Mysteries by Sarah D'Almeida

DEATH OF A MUSKETEER
THE MUSKETEER'S SEAMSTRESS
THE MUSKETEER'S APPRENTICE

The Musketeer's Apprentice

Sarah D'Almeida

BERKLEY PRIME CRIME, NEW YORK

THE BERKLEY PUBLISHING GROUP
Published by the Penguin Group
Penguin Group (USA) Inc.
375 Hudson Street, New York, New York 10014, USA
Penguin Group (Canada), 90 Eglinton Avenue East, Suite 700, Toronto, Ontario M4P 2Y3, Canada
(a division of Pearson Penguin Canada Inc.)
Penguin Books Ltd., 80 Strand, London WC2R 0RL, England
Penguin Group Ireland, 25 St. Stephen's Green, Dublin 2, Ireland (a division of Penguin Books Ltd.)
Penguin Group (Australia), 250 Camberwell Road, Camberwell, Victoria 3124, Australia
(a division of Pearson Australia Group Pty. Ltd.)
Penguin Books India Pvt. Ltd., 11 Community Centre, Panchsheel Park, New Delhi—110 017, India
Penguin Group (NZ), 67 Apollo Drive, Rosedale, North Shore 0745, Auckland, New Zealand
(a division of Pearson New Zealand Ltd.)
Penguin Books (South Africa) (Pty.) Ltd., 24 Sturdee Avenue, Rosebank, Johannesburg 2196,
South Africa

Penguin Books Ltd., Registered Offices: 80 Strand, London WC2R 0RL, England

THE MUSKETEER'S APPRENTICE

A Berkley Prime Crime Book / published by arrangement with the author

PRINTING HISTORY
Berkley Prime Crime mass-market edition / September 2007

ISBN: 978-0-425-21769-6

BERKLEY® PRIME CRIME
Berkley Prime Crime Books are published by The Berkley Publishing Group,
a division of Penguin Group (USA) Inc.,
375 Hudson Street, New York, New York 10014.
The name BERKLEY PRIME CRIME and the BERKLEY PRIME CRIME design are trademarks of
Penguin Group (USA) Inc.

PRINTED IN THE UNITED STATES OF AMERICA

10 9 8 7 6 5 4 3 2 1

To the memory of my grandmother,
Carolina Joaquina Marques,
who told me stories.

The Many Inconveniences of a Sin of Vanity;
Flying and Fighting; Murder Done

∽

MONSIEUR Pierre du Vallon—a huge man with broad shoulders and a wealth of red hair and beard—knew that his besetting sin was vanity.

Oh, he wouldn't put it that way, though his friend Aramis often put it just that way. If pressed, Monsieur du Vallon, whom the world had known for years as the Musketeer Porthos, would say that he knew himself to be a well set man, twice as broad, twice as strong, twice as valiant as all others. Pushed further, he might admit he had a fine taste in clothes and that his swordplay was the best ever seen. This he did not consider vanity, as such, but a mere statement of facts. It only seemed to him odd that most people refused to acknowledge these truths.

That this made him particularly vulnerable to the admiration of those who did know Porthos's true worth, Porthos would be the first to admit. It had been Aramis's admission that Porthos was the best fencing master in Paris which had caused Porthos to try to teach the effete young man—then known as Chevalier D'Herblay—how to fence in time for an impending duel. It had, however, been Porthos's real worth as a teacher that had allowed Aramis to kill his opponent in that duel—in direct violation of the king's edict against dueling. And this in turn had forced both D'Herblay and du Vallon—his second in the duel—to go into hiding, as Aramis and Porthos in the King's Musketeers.

None of which, Porthos thought as he stood in the middle of the vast, empty room, explained why he found himself now waiting for a student who was a good two hours late.

The student, Guillaume Jaucourt had approached Porthos some weeks ago and had told Porthos that he knew Porthos's secret. He knew Porthos's true identity. Porthos had shrugged this off, because who would listen to a son of minor nobility, a young boy just turning twelve. And besides, Porthos was fairly sure that the King and Monsieur de Treville, captain of the musketeers, knew his identity. He was fairly sure, even, that it was an open secret in the court. It was only that—Porthos thought—as long as no one could prove it, the King didn't need to punish Porthos for du Vallon's trespass.

But then the young man—who had begged Porthos to teach him fencing—had said that du Vallon had been universally acknowledged as the best fighter and sword master in all of Paris—which is to say in all the world.

Porthos's inability to resist hearing the truth thus stated, had made him agree to teach the boy to fence. And he'd done just that for weeks. The youth—a stripling with promise of future sturdy manhood—had proven deft with the sword, capable of parrying and thrusting with the best of them, and with fast and deceptive enough footwork to rival Porthos's own.

Not that Guillaume was ready to fight duels. He was all of twelve, with dark red auburn hair, grey eyes and an intent, serious expression. He'd listened most attentively to Porthos instructions not to duel. After all, the Musketeers didn't take boy recruits. But he'd proven a willing student, ready and capable of great work.

He'd always been on time. Punctual like an Englishman. It was only today that he was late. Very late. And Porthos found himself worried against his wishes.

The room where Porthos stood was on the bottom floor of the lodgings he rented. Situated at the back, it faced the garden and the back gate. It had been—in the distant past when the house had been built and when this area of Paris had still held fields and farmers—the loggia of the building, the place where harvest was brought in and fruits and vegetables stored.

Vast and cool and windowless, it got all its light from the door when it was opened. Why the landlord hadn't converted it into rooms to rent, Porthos didn't know nor care. But when he'd found out that this room sat here, unused, at the back and bottom of the house, he'd made it his business to ask the landlord for the use of it.

Given the musketeer's size and girth, few men of normal size thought to say no to him. And so Porthos, and his friends—Aramis, Athos and D'Artagnan—had for some time commanded the use of this room for their sword practices. Musty and smelling of long-disuse and dried apples, it was nonetheless broad enough and secret enough that they could have mock duels without calling on them the wrath of the Cardinal Guards with their fanatical enforcement of the prohibition on duels. And here they didn't have to listen to comments and heckling from other musketeers as they did when they practiced at Monsieur de Treville's residence.

Aramis had snickered and said it was vanity that had led Porthos to line the narrow space with many mirrors. And though Porthos felt aggrieved by the accusation, he did not know how to defend himself.

For there was this in Porthos, able, accomplished giant that he was—that words scared him more than any foe whom he could meet in field of battle or duel might. Words slipped through his mind, where sounds and sights and senses resounded as clearly as church bells on a silent summer afternoon.

So he lacked the words to explain to Aramis the mirrors were there for two reasons—one to propagate what little light came through the open door. And another, to allow him to study his movements and those of his opponents when they practiced swordplay. If it allowed him to examine the excellent cut of his doublets, the fullness of his hat plume and the way his broad, ankle-long venetians molded his muscular legs, so much the better.

But now he looked in the mirror and did not see that. Instead, above the worn linen pants and tunic, in which he'd dressed for the lesson, he saw a pale, intent face with dark blue eyes staring in puzzled wonder.

Because Guillaume hadn't come.

And this, he told himself, might not mean any more than that the boy had been stopped by a zealous father or an officious mother. From things the boy hadn't said, from hints and notions and occasional mentions of his family, Porthos understood they didn't mean for him to learn to fight.

Why, Porthos couldn't hazard to guess. Who understood parents, anyway? Porthos's own father hadn't wanted his son to learn to read, being fully convinced that learning to read would soften and feminize his huge son. Porthos hadn't been able to master reading until he'd come to Paris in search of his fortune.

Perhaps Guillaume's father intended the boy for the church and perhaps he subscribed to the—not particularly popular—notion that churchmen should be men of peace. In which case, Porthos should introduce him to Aramis, who had once been a seminarian and who still considered himself in training for the habit, but who could wield the sword with murderous skill and intent.

Still, Porthos told his very worried-looking reflection— Guillaume's absence meant nothing. Absolutely nothing. Just that his family had caught him sneaking out of their lodgings. Or perhaps that the boy had changed his mind about wanting to learn swordplay. Which meant Porthos should never have agreed to teach him in the first place. Or not for free. At least if he'd demanded money the boy might have taken the whole thing more seriously.

The Porthos in the mirror ignored these rational reassurances. He bit worriedly at the corner of his lip. Porthos grumped, and smoothed his moustache out of his mouth and glared at his reflection.

The reflection glared right back, his eyes full of worry. Worry for what? The boy was fine. He'd missed one lesson. What was there to that?

Porthos's thick fingers pulled and stroked frantically at his luxuriant red moustache. What was there to it? Only this. That the boy had been so intent, so decided, so capable of hard work, that Porthos refused to believe he would give up on his lesson so easily.

And because Porthos had made sure the child understood that he wouldn't continue teaching him unless he showed for every lesson punctually, Guillaume would know that this one miss could mean the end of his apprenticeship.

The Porthos in the mirror looked triumphant, justified in his worry. And Porthos stomped. God's Blood! So, the boy was late. And so, perhaps something had happened to him. What was Porthos to do with that? He was not the boy's father.

And on this there was a sharp feeling of something that inarticulate Porthos would never find the words to describe. He had the sudden forlorn feeling that, had life been different—had his family lands not been poor and forsaken and inhabited by peasantry just as poor and forsaken; had his father known how to plant the land with newer, more fashionable crops—he would now be married and have half a dozen children clustering around him. The longing for that life that had never happened surprised him. He would have liked half a dozen broad-shouldered sons, clustering around him, learning sword fighting and horseback riding from him, and admiring their father's strength and courage.

He growled at the Porthos in the mirror, whose image was giving him these ideas, and removing his hat, flung it with force to the dusty stone floor of the room. Oh, curse it all. God's Death! What was he to do about this? And what did Guillaume have to do with these children that Porthos had never had and would probably never have?

What the frowning, worried reflection seemed to tell Porthos was that Porthos had enjoyed Guillaume's company as if Guillaume were a replacement for those sons Porthos would never have. And the boy had responded to Porthos that way too. He'd listened to him with full attention and learned to repeat his movements faultlessly.

No. Nothing short of a major disaster would have prevented such a determined and cunning boy from coming to his lesson.

Slowly, Porthos picked up his hat and dusted its plume. The devil of it was that he had no idea at all where the boy came from. Oh, the child had told him his name, but Jaucourt was not a name that Porthos knew. It must be the name of a family recently come to Paris from the provinces and probably renting lodgings meaner than Porthos's own from some landlord, in some part of town. What part of town, only God himself knew. That is, if He had paid any attention to such an unimportant matter.

Porthos hadn't bothered to find the family home because the child was clearly coming to his lessons in secret—but assiduously.

As a huge sigh escaped his lips, Porthos wondered how to track someone—how to find them and discover if a mishap had befallen them when you didn't know where they were coming from or what their route was?

He walked to the door and looked down at the garden, slumbering in the early morning cool soon to turn into heated midday of very late summer. Very well. So, he knew that the child came in through the garden gate at the back.

Without much thought, without much more than a need to move, a need to do something, Porthos walked impatiently down the garden path, past the kitchen garden with its parched-looking rows of herbs, and down, past an area where trees shaded the path, to the unpainted, rickety gate at the back that had been barely visible from the practice room's door.

He opened the gate, satisfied at its shriek, and looked out at the broad plaza back there. Back here, truly, you wouldn't know you were in Paris. This garden gate opened to a bucolic landscape—the back of several houses, narrow alleys running between the tall walls that encircled gardens.

There was a vague scent of roses in the air, and Porthos remembered that Guillaume had come in yesterday with a rose in his cap—a bright red rose with wide-spread petals, of the sort that often grew along the lanes of Porthos's native village. Guillaume had said they were flowering just up the lane from here.

Like a dog on the trail, Porthos followed the strong scent of roses across the plaza. Peering down a lane, he saw a straggle of nearly wild roses pushing over the top of a rickety stone wall. The roses were exactly the same color and look as the one Guillaume had worn.

Convinced he at least knew the boy had come this way, Porthos trotted down the narrow alley. It was barely wide enough for his shoulders and it was hemmed in by two very long, very high walls, both of which, from the noise and talks emerging from beyond them, probably hid communal gardens shared by several rental houses or houses filled with rental rooms.

At the end of the alley, another alley ran across it, forming as if the top of a T. Porthos frowned. Right or left? If he went right, and the boy was coming in, late, from the left, he would miss him completely. And then Guillaume would wonder where Porthos had gone.

What had Guillaume said about his route here? What that might give Porthos a clue as to where the boy came from?

Vaguely, because he hadn't been paying much attention, Porthos remembered that Guillaume had complained of the heat of a smithy he passed on the way here. It had been a couple of weeks ago, when August was at its hottest, the sun beating Paris to a red heat, as though it had been metal laying on Vulcan's own forge.

And now straining his ears, Porthos could hear as if hammers on metal. From the right. He hastened down the right side of the alley, till he came to a busy forge. It took up the bottom space of a tall house, but it had at least three doors, all of them open to the day. There were anvils with sweating men pounding on them, and there were boys working frantically at the bellows, and there was a nobleman—from the attire—in a corner, holding a nervous white horse who was being shoed by two muscular young men.

Porthos bit at the corner of his moustache. So—there was a forge. Pray heaven it was the right one. Now . . . from here . . .

Something about a fishmonger's. Just down the street. Porthos's nose led again, till he came to a fishmonger's in a huge plaza. From there so many roads led on that Porthos found himself quite at a loss. Until he remembered Guillaume admiring Porthos's new boots and saying that he'd seen some at the cobbler's on the way here, but that his father would never give him money for them.

Peering down the streets, Porthos found the cobbler's. From there, he remembered the boy making some mention of a tavern at the end of an alley and how musketeers sometimes drank there. The boy hadn't wanted to discuss the tavern much, but he'd told Porthos it was the Hangman.

From Porthos's foggy memories of being led by Athos to every tavern in Paris, when Athos was in one of his drinking moods, Porthos found the alley that led to the back of the Hangman.

He walked down half the alley before he saw the boy. At first, he thought it was just a pile of clothes, though the clothes were purple velvet and the hat had a plume uncommonly like Guillaume's. It was crumpled against a wall, on the muddy ground of the alley at the back of the tavern.

But when Porthos approached, his big feet raising dull echoes from the packed dirt, the bundle near the wall stirred, the hat went up, and a flushed, haggard face with bulging blue eyes stared at Porthos.

"Guillaume," Porthos said. "What is wrong, boy?"

The boy looked at Porthos. His eyes were wide and shiny, but didn't seem to see him. "The angels," he said. "The angels flying." He was very red.

"Oh, here, boy. How much did you drink?" Porthos asked, feeling annoyed with Guillaume and with himself. It was clear the boy had got hold of wine somewhere. Clumsily, Porthos reached for the boy and tried to make him stand, but he only flopped around like an ill-stuffed rag doll.

Guillaume's arms moved, outward. "Flying," he said.

And here, Porthos was momentarily confused. The boy was flushed, and he acted drunk, but there was no smell of alcohol about him. Could he have gone mad? Or was he ill?

"Here," Porthos said, trying to support the boy as he would one of his comrades when wounded or drunk.

But the boy twisted and convulsed.

"Thirsty," he said. "Very thirsty."

Porthos, despairing of holding him firm, finally lifted him up and threw him over his shoulder. He would take Guillaume back to his lodgings then call on Aramis. Aramis knew nearly everything and everyone. If the boy was sick, Aramis was the best person to find the boy's family. Sick or mad, they would need to know.

Porthos hurried back towards his lodging at a semi-run. The boy, thrown over his shoulder, talked constantly, but not of anything that Porthos could see. "Beautiful," he'd say. "Angels. Flying. Flying. Birds. The sky is so blue."

These words, as they walked through narrow, darkened alleys made the hair at the back of Porthos's neck stand up. It was as if the boy were talking of some reality only he could see.

Suddenly he stopped and convulsed, then again. There was a sound like a startled sigh.

It didn't surprise Porthos when he put the boy down on the floor of the practice room to find the boy had died. Still he checked it, with a finger laid against the boy's neck, a hand searching for a heartbeat that wasn't there.

At long last, he stood and slowly removed his hat in respect for the small corpse with his wide-open eyes, his expression of surprise.

Guillaume Jaucourt was dead. Who knew from what? Who knew how to contact his family? Who could break the news to them? And—if murder had been done—who could ensure the killer was found?

Athos, Aramis, D'Artagnan. The names of his friends, the other three of what all called the four inseparables, came unbidden to Porthos's mind. He never doubted it.

Slamming the hat back down on his head, he left the practice room, closing the door gently behind him. Athos, noble as Scipio and twice as wise, Aramis, learned in theology and the labyrinthine ways of Parisian society, D'Artagnan the young, cunning Gascon. Those three would know how to help Porthos seek justice for his apprentice.

Up and Down the Staircase; Alarm and Peril;
The Demands of Friendship

THE two men looked as different as two men could look. Early morning, on the marble staircase, that led from the antechamber of Monsieur de Treville's to his private office, they fought a mock duel for the right to ascend the staircase.

Defending it, on the higher step, was a dark-haired, pale-skinned man. His features would have made a classical sculptor weep and his zeal-burned dark blue eyes could have graced a mystic or a saint. But he stood, sword in hand, with the adept grace of the veteran duelist. His tight-laced, Spanish-cut doublet and knee breeches, now more than a decade out of fashion, lent him a timeless air and also the air of one who would have control over his own body.

His name was Athos and had been Athos ever since he'd joined the musketeers to hide who knew what shame or disgrace. Throughout Paris it was rumored that he came from the highest nobility and that his crime was such that, if named, it would cause the heavens to shudder.

The rumors were almost right. Before assuming the musketeer's uniform as other men take the penitent's cowl, the man had been Alexandre, Count de la Fere, descended from one of the oldest and most honored noble houses in the kingdom. And the sin for which he sought to atone was the execution of his Countess for what had then seemed to him sufficient reason—but which seemed more monstrous with each passing year and more unjustified with each new rigor of his chosen penance.

Facing him, on the step below was a man in his midtwenties. With his long blond hair, his soft, supple clothes that dripped with lace and screamed with edging and which gave him the appearance of a dandy, he might look soft and effeminate. No one who saw him would retain the illusion long and certainly not after seeing the feline leaps, the graceful falls, the seemingly careless lunges of his swordplay.

He called himself Aramis and said he was merely sojourning in the musketeers till he considered himself worthy of joining a monastical order. Indeed, only some years ago, as the young and naive Rene Chevalier D'Herblay, he'd been a seminarian in Paris, intent on taking the orders for which his pious mother had destined him from birth.

But D'Herblay's weakness was women. And unfortunately women showed the same propensity towards him. Which was why he'd been found reading the lives of saints to a lady of slightly less pure reputation than her family would wish. In the resulting duel he'd killed the lady's brother. Because dueling was illegal, ever since then he'd been hiding in the musketeers, under the name of Aramis.

Now he climbed the stair, pressing his friend close, his thrusts so carefully aimed that they did no more than slit the fabric of Athos's doublet.

"You really must learn to cover your right," he told Athos with a smile that might pass as a smirk. Athos frowned.

Aramis smirked more widely. There was an excitement in taunting Athos. Aramis had known his friend long enough and seen him in close enough situations that he realized inside Athos there was as if a wild beast, looking out and snarling in fury and held in check only by Athos's intellect and Athos's conscience. There was the feeling that at any moment the control might slip loose and the beast escape the confinement of the well-trained nobleman.

But not now, and not over a game. Instead, Athos smiled back, one of his rare smiles, this one tinged with the amusement someone might feel towards an impertinent child. He charged down the stairs, pressing Aramis close and making Aramis sweat in trying to parry all the thrusts.

The rules of this game, as it was played by the corps of musketeers—the best sword fighters in the reign of his Majesty Louis XIII of France—were that the first to be pressed all the way up the stairs to the landing in front of the door to the office of Monsieur de Treville, their captain, or the first one to be pushed all the way down the stairs and off the steps altogether would lose the game. The loss usually involved many jokes from all their comrades and, inevitably, a round of forfeited drinks stood by the loser and a round of celebratory drinks by the winner.

Aramis had no intention of losing. He'd lost the last three times he'd played this game with Athos, and the one he'd played with Porthos. He'd not yet succeeded in challenging the cunning Gascon, D'Artagnan, to this pastime. The sly newcomer to their group had a way of smiling and ignoring the best taunts and challenges from the rest of them. Unnerving when it had been so easy to challenge him to a duel on his first day in Paris. One must conclude either that the Gascon had grown prudent—something as unlikely as a fish growing wings—or that he valued his purse higher than his life. This last was quite likely, particularly as his purse, like that of the rest of them, was so often empty.

Aramis's was not exactly brimming with coin just now, and he knew while he might be able to forgo paying for drinks as a winner by pleading poverty, he could never forgo paying the forfeited drinks to the winner and any hangers-ons should he lose. And Athos could drink most men in Paris under the table, while showing no other sign of inebriation than a profound and growing melancholy.

On this thought, Aramis found himself on the very last step of the stairs, defending himself ineptly with his sword held too close to his body, while Athos charged down the steps, his lips curled in that curious snarl-look they got when he was near claiming victory. Seeing Athos like this, always raised the question whether the musketeer would remember in time that this was a friendly game and stop himself from spearing his friend through.

Aramis was fairly sure he would and yet he was not willing to lose the remaining content of his purse. Making use of his agility, which was his greatest asset in any duel, he made as if to leap down, then ducked under Athos's sword arm and came at him from the other side, pushing Athos's sword out of the way with his doublet-padded forearm, and physically forcing his friend to take three steps up hastily. This gave Aramis room enough to lope upwards two steps and reengage Athos in swordplay.

From beneath came the sound of shouted encouragements. "There's life in Aramis yet." And "For a priest, he doesn't fight badly." And, of course, "He is right, Athos does leave his right shoulder shamefully uncovered."

All of it followed by the clink of coins that indicated bets were being made and paid by the mass of musketeers down there, in the waiting room.

Aramis tried to ignore them, as he concentrated on pushing Athos up yet another couple of steps, an intention that Athos resisted with his not inconsiderable skill at parrying. In a way these mock duels were harder than the real duels, where Aramis could simply have tried to thrust his sword through his opponent's heart. But he would never injure Athos, or not voluntarily.

Together, Athos, Aramis, Porthos and even the newcomer, D'Artagnan, had dueled and bled. Their friendship had been cemented by a hundred instances of mutual defense, a thousand shared secrets. They could no more kill each other than they could commit suicide. One would feel much like the other at any rate. And not killing Athos while forcing him up the steps was harder than it would have been to kill just about anyone. After all, they'd practiced and fought together so long, each knew the other very well and every move could be anticipated.

It was easiest of all to fight each other to a standstill. To get through, Aramis must block every thought and move that didn't have to do with sword and footwork, and the unyielding body in front of him . . . He must forget it was Athos. Only remember he must not kill him. He must . . .

With swords clashing, in the sound of metal, and, with their swords gripped between them and held upright, with too little room to move, Aramis pressed forward with his body, forcing Athos up one step, two, another . . . Very quickly.

And then Athos recovered his balance. And on that balance came the ineluctable fact that Athos weighed more than Aramis—his rather solid mass of muscle and bone still looked lean enough but was by far more hefty than Aramis's gracile figure. Once Athos had firmly planted his feet, Aramis could not budge him.

Athos speaking through his teeth said, "Will you claim forfeit, Aramis?"

From his voice, it was hard to tell whether it was a taunt or he truly meant for Aramis to forfeit the game and concede defeat, even though the younger musketeer was nowhere near losing. From Athos's maddened dark blue eyes, too, it was hard to tell if he even remembered what humor was.

"*Sangre Dieu*, Athos," Aramis said. "Would I forfeit?"

"Well," Athos said. "Then I have no choice but to make sure you lose." And on that the larger musketeer gave his friend a shove.

Aramis caught himself quickly. A foot behind to recover his balance, and no harm really done, and then, from the door to the antechamber, a familiar voice calling, "Aramis!"

He turned, without even thinking. He turned, half ready to scold Porthos for interrupting him at his game, and then he saw Porthos.

The huge redhead whose ancestors, doubtless, had come to the coasts of France in long ships, was not dressed

in the style in which he usually permitted himself to appear
in public. That was the first thing strange about it all, because Porthos was vain as a peacock and his normal attire
in public was twice as bright as any bird's plumage.
Aramis could not remember his friend ever having appeared in public in this attire of worn linen breeches and
a tunic that looked like a beggar would disdain it. No.
Aramis had seen Porthos in these clothes, but only in the
practice room, in the privacy of Porthos's own lodgings.

In the normal course of things, Porthos would rather—
much rather—die than be seen in public in this shabby a
display. But, worse, the face above the clothes looked like
Porthos had already died. Pale and bloodless, with a grey-
ish tinge to the lips, Porthos's skin made his eyes look un-
naturally bright, his hair and beard a screaming scarlet
stain.

"Porthos," Aramis said. And thinking no more of his
duel or his potential forfeiting of money to buy enough
drinks to fill the Seine—or satisfy Athos—he jumped over
the elaborate railing of the staircase and landed, sword still
in hand, in a hastily cleared space in the hall below.

Too late he realized he had probably forfeited the contest, and was not reassured by the sound of Athos's landing
on the mosaic floor behind him. Not reassured as far as losing the contest, but at least reassured by Athos's support.
He heard Athos sheathe his sword and remembered to
sheathe his own.

The crowd was parting between him and Porthos.
Though they were all musketeers, battle hardened and
ready to defend themselves against many foes, few had the
body to obstruct Porthos's progress. The sheer bulk of
Porthos would clear the way. And few of them would stand
in front of Athos or Aramis either.

So as the crowd melted away and pressed out of their
path, on either side of the room, Aramis and Athos met with
Porthos.

Porthos was silent—which in itself was strange, after

demanding their attention so forcefully. He looked from one to the other of them, and then at the staircase and the railing over which Aramis had jumped. He frowned, as though trying to make sense of something particularly difficult. "Sorry I interrupted your game," he said.

"The game matters not," Athos said. "We can finish another time."

And, as Aramis let out a breath, relieved at not being held to forfeit, Porthos nodded. "It's very important, see? He's dead."

"Who is dead, who?" Aramis asked, his impatience tempered by concern. He would easily have been the first to admit that his friend was inarticulate and had a difficult time expressing himself. But today Porthos seemed inarticulate even for himself. As if he were in shock. And why would Porthos be in shock at someone's death? Death was their profession and their companion, walking by their side night and day.

"Who is dead? Who?" he asked, in alarm and, lowering his voice, as the horrible thought occurred to him that he'd not seen the young Gascon since last night. "Not . . . D'Artagnan?"

But Porthos's eyes widened in surprise, as if D'Artagnan's death had never occurred to him, and then he shook his huge leonine head. "No. Not him. The boy. My apprentice."

Apprentice? Frowning, unable to understand of what Porthos spoke, Aramis realized that other musketeers were listening in on their conversation and that a hushed silence had fallen in the room.

Before he could think what this meant, he heard a well-known voice yell, from upstairs, at the entrance to the captain's office, "Athos, Porthos, Aramis."

Aramis turned to see a musketeer—who had been in conference with the captain—skulk down the stairs. At the top of the stairs Monsieur de Treville stood, glaring down at them.

Though he was as olive skinned and as short as their friend D'Artagnan, who came up barely to Aramis's shoulder and no more than to Porthos's chest, there was not a man in the room that wouldn't swear Monsieur de Treville was at least twelve feet tall. And each and everyone of them would have allowed himself to be—cheerfully—cut into ribbons for the captain.

Which was why Aramis's breath caught in his throat as the captain said, "If the three of you, gentlemen, would come in to my office, I'd like to be a part of your conference."

Without a word, Aramis turned to obey. And found that Athos was already ahead of him, running up the stairs. But he had to reach for Porthos's arm and pull before the giant musketeer realized he must obey. That he hadn't jumped to the captain's order meant something was very wrong indeed.

Monsieur de Treville's Displeasure;
Secrets Kept;
Where Plots and Treason Lurk in Every
Corner

"**A**M I to understand," Monsieur de Treville asked, frowning, and rounding on Athos, as he entered the office, "that your young friend, D'Artagnan, got himself killed?"

Athos whipped his plumed hat from his head and inclined slightly. In the anteroom he never bothered to remove his headgear, but here, and in the presence of his superior, he had to. "I don't believe so, Monsieur de Treville. At least Porthos said no. Didn't you, Porthos?"

He looked sideways towards his redheaded friend, to see him standing there, beside Aramis, his mouth half-open and a look of confused thought on his broad features, as though Athos had just asked him an insoluble question.

Aramis who could be as impatient as any of them with Porthos's slowness looked shocked at Porthos's silence. He reached out and shook Porthos arm. "Porthos!" he said. "It is not D'Artagnan who is dead, is it?"

"What?" Porthos said, as though waking. He looked at the captain as though noticing him for the first time, and, whipping his hat from his head fanned himself with it. "No, it's not D'Artagnan." He looked around, and homed in on one of the three armchairs that faced a broad desk.

He dropped into one of them and only then seemed to notice the surprised look on the face of the captain who remained standing. "I beg your pardon, Monsieur de Treville," he said then. "It's been a hell of a shock."

For a moment it all hung in the balance. Athos's memory extended back over the years when they'd all gotten excoriated in this office for small offenses and big, ranging from having allowed themselves to be defeated in a duel by guards of the Cardinal to the recent and horrible time when Monsieur de Treville had been convinced that Aramis had murdered his mistress. For an offense like Porthos's—sitting down in the captain's office without the captain's permission—it could go either way. The captain could laugh it off or he could yell at the musketeer in terms that would peel the skin of an elephant.

The shrewd dark eyes of the captain narrowed as his gaze swept over Porthos. And perhaps because he noticed the musketeer's unusual pallor, his look of stunned shock, Monsieur de Treville sighed and shrugged.

"Who is dead, Porthos?" he said. "And why do you announce it in my antechamber, thus starting the gossip flowing?" As he spoke, he walked around his own desk, and sat down in his own chair. He waved to Aramis and Athos. "You may sit down as well, gentlemen, since Monsieur Porthos took the initiative."

Again there was the little surprised motion, as if Porthos hadn't fully woken till then. "I'm sorry," he said. "Shouldn't I have sat down? What . . ."

"No," Monsieur de Treville said firmly. "Never mind that. Only tell us who is dead."

"My apprentice," Porthos said. "The boy."

"What boy?" Aramis cut in impatiently, mirroring the impatience that Athos himself was starting to feel. "We did not have the pleasure of knowing that you had an apprentice."

Porthos shrugged. "I did not see any reason to tell you since it didn't involve you."

Athos waited for Porthos to go on and when nothing

issued from Porthos's lips, he prompted. "Well, will you tell us now?"

"I believe I must," Porthos said. He sighed. "Since otherwise I might never know who murdered the boy."

"Oh, so it is murder you've alarmed my antechamber with," Monsieur de Treville said, his voice just caught between amusement and impatience.

This Athos could understand, since Porthos often caused both feelings in him. The gigantic musketeer from Normandy was not, at the best of times, a master of rhetoric. In fact, many of the men who assembled in the antechamber right now took him for a simpleton and marveled that such men as Athos and Aramis associated with him. And most of them attributed their friendship to charity.

But the truth was that Athos—who'd despaired of heaven on that day when he'd left his wife swinging by the neck from a low branch in his domain of La Fere, and abandoned both title and lands to come to Paris and become a musketeer—had very little interest in charity and even less interest in those who were his intellectual inferiors. He knew that in Porthos's huge head, beneath the wealth of red hair, worked a brain at least as fast as his own and probably faster. Time and again, in difficult situations, it had been Porthos who had cut through the fog of confusion and theories to see the plain truth: a gift far rarer than seeing the complex truth.

It was just that Porthos—who had once been a dance master, who was unequaled with sword, and whose thought could follow complex puzzles—found his way to words difficult and barred, as though his words must reach the world, one at a time through a small slit in a thick wall.

Now, having declared that he must tell them about his apprentice he'd ground again into silence. His huge fingers played with the gold braid on the edge of his hat and he looked attentively down at them, as though hypnotized by their movement.

"Porthos, you must speak," Athos said, commanding his voice to gentleness. His life had schooled him little in such. His father had demanded much of him, from manliness to courage, but never tenderness and never charity to those weaker than himself. He'd been inclined to it at any rate, as a young man who read much and thought more. But he'd had to leave tenderness and finer feeling behind after his wife Charlotte's death. After Charlotte's murder. "Porthos," he said again, a little louder, as Porthos turned to look at him. "You must tell us who your apprentice is and why he's dead and why you're here."

Porthos shook his head as though to clear it. "He was Guillaume Jaucourt," he said. "And he came to me to learn sword fighting. And he died just a little while ago. He's in my practice room. I'm not sure he was murdered, of course. I think he was poisoned."

"He came to you to learn sword fighting?" Aramis asked. "In the name of all that's holy, why? Why would anyone come to you for sword fighting lessons?"

Porthos looked wounded, then shrugged. "You did. Once."

"You were a sword master then. It is different," Aramis said.

And Monsieur de Treville's voice cut in, cold and sensible and holding only the slightest tinge of that amusement that Porthos caused in most people when they weren't exasperated at him. "Did he know who you were, Porthos? Or suspect?"

Porthos shrugged, then nodded. "He came to me," he said. "And tried to blackmail me into teaching him," he said. "He was"——the huge hand was held up at about his shoulder height while sitting—"this tall. A stripling with barely as much width to his whole trunk as one of my legs. Redheaded. Freckled. With pimples starting. And he told me I had to help him learn to fight with a sword or he would tell the world my secret."

"And you taught him?" Athos asked.

Porthos looked up. Suddenly he smiled. For the first time since he'd come in looking dismal and cold and lost, he looked like himself. "Not because of the blackmail," he said. "Look, he was a child. Barely twelve. And all of us when we were children, we were subjected to our parents' whims. My father didn't want me to learn to read, and Aramis's mother didn't want him to learn to fight. And Athos—" he stopped. Their eyes met and Porthos's smile died away entirely and he shrugged.

Athos wondered what he'd been about to say. Porthos and Athos had never, that he knew, discussed Athos's upbringing. In fact, of all of them, he was the one who'd been least inclined to speak of his upbringing and background. They might know of the crime that had sent him into the musketeers, to flee his conscience more than anything else. But of the time before that, they knew nothing. Athos was not curious enough to ask. Porthos had an inconvenient habit of knowing the truth. He looked away from Porthos and at Monsieur de Treville sitting judgelike behind his desk.

"Well, I felt that sometimes parents don't know what's best for their child," Porthos said. His voice had lost some of its force but regained it as he went on. "And Guillaume's parents might not want him to learn to fight, and they might intend him for the church, but some of our best fighters have been men in orders and some of our best religious men have been fierce swordsmen."

"Indeed," Aramis said, not without irony. "His eminence Cardinal Richelieu, himself."

It was like Porthos not to take this for a challenge but to accept it as a comment, Athos thought. Because Richelieu had indeed been a fierce duelist in his youth.

Porthos clearly saw nothing wrong with the mention of him. "Like him," he said. "So I thought what harm does it do to teach Guillaume a little swordplay, if he can get away from his parents to learn? What ill does it do? Who cares?"

"His parents perhaps," Aramis said, his voice cutting cold.

"Well, perhaps," Porthos said, and shrugged. "But I figured somehow, and soon enough, that boy would be out on his own and he would do as he pleased. And if he was so desperate to learn that he went through the trouble of finding out who I was and coming to me . . ." He spread his hands across the top of his hat. "I thought the least I could do is teach him."

"And did his family find out?" Athos asked sharply. "Are you sure he died by poison and not from a beating? Some parents . . ."

Porthos shook his head. "No marks on him. Almost for sure poison, unless someone hit him on the head. He was talking about angels and flying."

Aramis, facing Athos over Porthos's inclined head quirked an eyebrow. Athos shrugged. It could be anything. The boy's father might have found out and punished him severely. But why should he? "Wouldn't it have been easier for the parents to prevent the boy from coming to lessons?" he said.

"Exactly," said Monsieur de Treville. He brought his hands up, with his wrists resting on the polished desk, and touched the tips of his fingers together. "Exactly what I was thinking, Athos. I was also thinking that no matter how determined to devote the child to the church, few parents would view this delinquency as little more than a show of spirit."

"And if they were determined to send him to the church," Aramis said, "they were more likely to punish him by making him repeat maxims of the Testament or study his theology." Somehow he managed an audible shudder in his disciplined, well-bred voice.

Porthos raised his eyebrows but said nothing.

"Exactly," Monsieur de Treville said again, and then, looking straight at Porthos. "Jaucourt, you said? Not a name known to me. A noble family, you think?"

"He referred to his father as the gentleman Jaucourt," Porthos said.

"I've never heard of them," Monsieur de Treville said. "Of course there are many families come from provincial domains in search of fortune or royal favor in Paris whose names wouldn't be known to me. But usually, if a family is at court, some rumor of their presence, some reference to one of their retainers, reaches my ears." He wiggled his fingers against each other and seemed immersed in black thoughts. "Did he ever tell you how he found out your true identity, Porthos?"

"Sir?" Porthos asked, puzzled.

"If he was truly twelve," Monsieur de Treville said. "Or thereabouts, surely he can't have done a great deal of searching out the truth on his own. How would he come by it?"

Porthos shrugged. "It's . . . People know it, Captain. I lived in Paris before I joined the musketeers." He opened his hands and if to signal the obvious. "And I'm not exactly one of those people who pass unnoticed in a crowd."

Monsieur de Treville nodded, but his long, thin-fingered hand stroked at his well-trimmed beard. "Doubtless," he said, and smiled a little as if to acknowledge that the thought of Porthos passing unnoticed in any crowd was ridiculous. "But it's been many years, Porthos, and how would the boy know?"

Porthos shrugged again. "Perhaps his father knew?"

"From a noble family so newly arrived to Paris that we've never heard of their name? Unlikely, my friend," the captain said.

"But then," Athos said, "what do you think is behind all this?" As for himself, he couldn't anymore have articulated a coherent theory than he could have hazarded a reasonable-sounding guess, but something was working at the back of his mind, something that made the hair stand on end at the nape of his neck.

Monsieur de Treville shook his head. "I hesitate to say it," he said. "Since it is possible I am wrong and just of habit attributing the worst of villainy to a foe. But the Cardinal bears you some ill will—has born all of you some ill

will for a long time, for being the fiercest fighters in his
Majesty's Musketeers. And since these past two recent in-
cidents in which you foiled his plans . . ."[1] Monsieur de
Treville drummed his fingers on the desktop. "Well, his animosity for you knows no bounds. I would say, Porthos my
friend, it is quite likely the boy was sent to you and told
who you were. That his death owes something to the Cardinal. And that things are set to accuse you of murder, in an
attempt to defend yourself from blackmail. What—" The
captain stopped. Porthos was shaking his head violently.

"No," he said. "Guillaume was sincere and sincerely
seeking instruction in sword fighting."

The captain shrugged. "Perhaps. I did not say he wasn't.
Only that the Cardinal was behind sending him to you and
that the Cardinal is behind his death. Or might be. Just because Cardinal Richelieu is the greatest power in France,
more powerful even than the King, it doesn't follow that
every plot and every evil should be laid at his door. However, a lot of them can be, and it also doesn't follow that he
is innocent in this one."

"And," Athos said, feeling his uneasiness answered by
the captain's theory, "the truth is that it would be all too
easy for him to find a young boy of small nobility, dissatisfied with his lot in life, and to arm him with the means to
approach you. It would be no more unlikely than his finding an orphan and putting her in a position to impersonate
the Queen, all without the poor young woman knowing she
was being used at all.[2] It could have happened that way,
Porthos."

"But . . . a child?" Porthos asked.

"If the Cardinal thought it fit his views of what is good
for France, I think he'd willingly kill a newborn dauphin in
his swaddling clothes."

---

[1] *Death of a Musketeer; The Musketeer's Seamstress.*
[2] *Death of a Musketeer.*

Porthos looked at Athos, intently, his eyes focusing seemingly with all his will. "If the Cardinal has anything to do with Guillaume's death, he shall be called out, Cardinal or not."

The captain looked alarmed. He came out from behind his desk and put his hand on Porthos's shoulder. "Porthos, my friend. The important thing right now is for you—all four of you, including your friend D'Artagnan, who was privy to the other crime investigations—to find out who the boy truly was, how he died, and if there's a culprit. If it turns out to be the Cardinal, I shall take it upon myself to seek vengeance. I shall present proof to his Majesty himself. Meanwhile, I would say you must hide this crime. And you must promise me that you'll do nothing rash."

"Captain," Porthos said, sounding bullish.

"Promise me Porthos. Haven't I saved your life on more than one occasion?"

"Monsieur de Treville, you have, but—"

"Then promise me."

There was a long silence. Athos could almost imagine the cogs turning inside his friend's head as he weighed the best course of action.

At last Porthos sighed heavily. "I promise. I promise I shall do nothing until I know. If the Cardinal is guilty though . . . I will demand my revenge."

"Then we shall talk again," Monsieur de Treville said. "Meanwhile, I would send for your Gascon friend and start your enquiries."

The Disadvantages of a Pious Servant;
Yet Another Conspiracy;
Not the Expected Murder

ꞪENRI D'Artagnan had arrived in Paris four months ago and so far his experience of the city was both better and worse than he could have anticipated. This mixed result could be directly traced back to the influence of Monsieur D'Artagnan's two parents.

An only child and just barely out of adolescence at seventeen, Monsieur D'Artagnan looked very much like his mother—a small Gascon with olive skin, straight dark hair and piercing, intelligent eyes. From her, beyond appearance, he had inherited a certain hardheadedness of mind and manner and an unwillingness to let any perceived event rest till he'd ascertained the cause behind it.

From his father, a veteran of the religious wars, Monsieur D'Artagnan had received a more romantic inheritance, to wit, an old sword which had broken in two in his first skirmish; an orange horse of uncertain parentage which Monsieur D'Artagnan had seen fit to divest himself of; a letter of introduction to Monsieur de Treville which had been stolen from Henri on his way to the capital; and the advice to fight often, fight much, and not to tolerate any disrespect except from the King or the Cardinal.

The letter having been stolen had made it impossible for

D'Artagnan to get a post in the musketeers as he had hoped. He had instead been offered a position in the guards of Monsieur des Essarts, a sort of probation he was enduring with all the determined stubbornness of a not very patient man.

However, the advice to fight often had led him—on his very first day in Paris—to challenge all three of the best duelists in the musketeers. Such his luck, when Athos, Porthos and Aramis made good on their planned confrontation, they had been interrupted by guards of the Cardinal. In a moment—one of those sudden moments of youthful enthusiasm that can and often do decide a man's whole life—D'Artagnan had thrown his allegiance with the musketeers and against the guards of the Cardinal. Even better, his fighting had been material in turning the duel in favor of the musketeers.

This had set seal to an unlikely friendship in which the trio of inseparables was transformed into a quartet. And four months, many fights, many duels and countless drunken revels together later, D'Artagnan was not sure he would trade his three friends for a shiny, new uniform of the King's Musketeers.

At any rate, he thought, as he sat in his quarters, eating a sparse meal of bread and cheese—having just come off his guard duty and preparing to sleep before whatever revels or duels his friends might have planned for this afternoon—this friendship had earned him the confidence of Monsieur de Treville and it bode fair to win him, also, a place in the musketeers, should one open up.

A sharp knock on the door startled him and woke his servant, Planchet, who had been asleep on a nest of blankets on the floor. Since D'Artagnan had often heard that sleeping was like eating, and since food was often too scarce in these lodgings for the still-growing Planchet, he'd advised the young man to snatch a sleep-meal whenever he was not urgently needed. Having scarfed down his portion of bread and cheese Planchet had gone to sleep almost instantly. He now rose, rubbing his eyes, his thatch of dark red hair standing on end and looking like nothing so much as an uncertainly piled haystack.

D'Artagnan waved him towards the door, and, for his part, drank up the rest of the somewhat sour wine in his white ceramic cup, then wiped his mouth with the back of his hand. His lodging consisting of exactly two rooms— the inner chamber in which he slept and this outer chamber, with a table, chairs and a blanket in the corner for Planchet—this was where he must perforce receive all visitors.

The entrance door was down some stairs, at the same level as the door to the ground floor where D'Artagnan's neighbor, Monsieur Bonacieux—a worthy merchant— lived. But since D'Artagnan didn't hear any sounds of arguing and nothing that sounded like Planchet's heated avowal of his master's being asleep or on guard duty, D'Artagnan assumed this would not be the landlord in search of his overdue rent. And because he didn't hear any protests, he assumed also it was not either a merchant seeking payment or an enemy trying to find D'Artagnan.

Instead, there was a soft murmur of voices, and then the sound of two steps up the stairs. D'Artagnan rose, half expecting one of his friends to come into the room.

But the man who came in was Bazin. Bazin looked much like a particularly rotund medieval monk and dressed like a monk, in dark and dreary wool. His hair loss imitated a tonsure with some credibility and he walked in small and measured steps well suited to treading a monastery's hallowed halls.

That he was not a monk was not in fact his fault. From childhood, Bazin had attached himself to Aramis as Aramis's servant, reasoning that when the young man achieved the religious orders towards which he was being raised then Bazin could at the very least be a lay brother in the same order.

The interruption of this course through Aramis's impetu-

ous if successful duel, and Aramis's entrance into the musketeers were events which had shattered Bazin's world as
unexpectedly and surely as though a comet had struck
through the endless stratosphere and hit the Earth. He
couldn't fully comprehend what would cause his master—
whom he was used to thinking of as a well-mannered and
pious youth—to abandon such a sure course or to embark
on such violent ways.

Long ago, and through no particular course of thinking,
but more through the blind resentment of an animal who
must blame someone for his misfortune, he'd settled upon
blaming the other musketeers for Aramis's downfall. That
D'Artagnan was too late a comer to their friendship to be
in any way guilty for Aramis's present life did not in any
way change this resentment. D'Artagnan wenched and
drank and dueled with the other three, and therefore
D'Artagnan too was to blame. D'Artagnan too—should
Bazin be allowed to expound on the matter—encouraged
Bazin's master's fondness of a sinful world.

All this—which D'Artagnan had heard expressed in
voice once or twice—was written in the servant's sullen
expression as he bowed in D'Artagnan's general direction,
all the while glaring at him out of eyes that seemed too
small for the large and round face.

"Ah, Bazin," D'Artagnan said, seeking to appear
pleased. He should be pleased, because Aramis was—after
all—a good friend. And yet, why would Aramis send his
curdle-faced servant to D'Artagnan if he knew how Bazin
would resent it. Out of the corner of his eye, D'Artagnan
saw Planchet settle himself on his blankets to watch, smiling a little.

Planchet being who he was, and a genius in his own
way, D'Artagnan was never too sure what amused
Planchet more—Bazin's sullen dislike or D'Artagnan's attempt to disguise his own antipathy. Ignoring his own servant, he looked at Aramis's. "So, Bazin, what brings you
here?"

"My master sent me, sir," Basin said with that excess of humility that betrays someone very sure of talking to an equal if not to an inferior. "He would like you to come with me to Monsieur Porthos's house."

"What? Now?" D'Artagnan asked, because Aramis knew his schedule and very often one or the other of the musketeers would stand guard with him at Monsieur des Essarts. "But I just came off guard and was about to . . ." His words slowed down. "Is it a duel?" he asked, reaching for his sword on the table.

Bazin crossed himself and shook his head, and, as D'Artagnan moved away from the sword, sighed and said, "Not a duel, sir . . . and yet it might not be a bad idea to bring your sword. There are . . . It pains me truly, but my master seems to always end up setting himself against men of the church and the Cardinal . . ."

"The Cardinal!" D'Artagnan said, trying to reach for the sword and his hat at the same time and managing only to kick his chair out of the way—since his sword was on the table and his hat on a chair in the opposite direction. "The Cardinal. Is one of my friends in danger of arrest, then?"

Bazin started to shake his head, then shrugged. "Well, monsieur, the life you gentlemen live, are you ever more than a few moments away from being thrown in prison for one reason or other?"

D'Artagnan opened his mouth to retort, then closed it with a snap. Part of the problem was that Aramis made no attempt to control his servant's mouth, the other part was that Bazin was in fact not a real servant and certainly not a musketeer's servant. Rather, he was a monk playing at being a servant. And every chance he could possibly get to sermonize he would seize with the enthusiasm of a preacher on a mission through heathen territory.

Before he answered, D'Artagnan could see himself goading Bazin into a never-ending, spiraling argument, which would include the fate of those who lived by the sword as well as a plethora of details and curiosities on the lives of obscure saints and martyrs, at least one of which Bazin would—invariably—compare himself to.

So instead he inclined his head in less than an affirmative and reached first for his sword in its scabbard, which he fastened to his waist, and then for his hat, which he slapped on his head with grim determination. In doing so he caught sight of Planchet's mildly amused look. "Planchet," he said for no better reason than to spoil the young man's amusement. "Follow me."

He felt inner satisfaction in seeing the young man's startled and worried face, but didn't stay to savor it, nor did he wait for Bazin to take the lead. D'Artagnan knew his way to Porthos's place well enough. And besides, while Aramis and even Athos might think they needed a servant to walk ahead of them and cut a path through the Paris crowds for their impressive selves, D'Artagnan had no such great idea of himself.

Oh, his family was the wealthiest and noblest in their village. Which wasn't saying much. All told his father's land, all small inherited parcels put together, wouldn't equal the amount used for the children's cemetery in Paris. His father had been a glorified farmer with better pedigree, and the whole of the servants in their commodious farmhouse had been two—his father's valet and helper, and his mother's maid. A couple married to each other and inclined to treating D'Artagnan as one of their own children.

He was no more used to having a servant to separate him from the populace than he was used to regarding himself as a great lord. He ran down the stairs and opened his door and stopped.

Before him stood a vision of loveliness. She was blond and her features were of the sort young men dream angels might have. D'Artagnan stared at her, shocked, none too sure she hadn't come out of his own disordered dreams.

Oval faced, slim but with an ample bosom shown to great advantage in a well-cut gown of the sort worn at court, the sort that D'Artagnan had only seen from a distance while helping his friends guard the entrance to the royal palace. It was velvet and pink and . . . it pushed up where it should and it molded where it must.

Its owner was looking at D'Artagnan with the thunderstruck expression and the slight blush that made him absolutely sure that he was dreaming. Women—particularly women as beautiful and delicate as angels—never smiled at him and certainly not this way.

"I . . . I . . ." he said, and realized he had his hat still on his head and whipped it off with a flourish. "I'm sorry, madam. I'm not used to seeing duchesses in this neighborhood. My name is D'Artagnan and I lodge here. I am a guard of Monsieur des Essarts."

The woman smiled wider, a slowly widening smile that made D'Artagnan feel his cheeks heat as though in the full blaze of sun.

"I thank you," she said, inclining her head. "But I am not a duchess. My name is Constance Bonacieux and I live here too," and with her hand she indicated the door to Monsieur Bonacieux's dwelling.

D'Artagnan tried to imagine the wizened old man and this beauty and shook his head. "You are his daughter?" he asked. "His niece?"

But she only laughed. "His wife. Though most of the time I stay at the royal palace where I serve her Majesty." She blushed and looked down. "I am Madame Bonacieux."

D'Artagnan registered the disappointment that she was married at the same time that he thought she'd looked down as though embarrassed at being married. And he thought that Porthos's lover was married. And Aramis's lover had been. And then he couldn't think anymore because his mind was too full and his heart ready to burst and he could neither move nor speak looking at her.

A throat was cleared loudly behind him and he turned to see Bazin glare. "My master said—"

"That I should hurry, of course," D'Artagnan said, and

turned back to see Constance curtseying at him. Again his heart was full to bursting, but this time it compelled him to action. He ran to the side of the house where roses with broad satiny pink petals spilled over the garden wall. Late blooming roses, their fragrance intoxicating in the air. He reached for one, ignoring the bite of the thorns on his fingers, and pulled it free of the vine, then scraped the thorns off with his fingernail and, bowing, with hat held to chest, proffered Madame Bonacieux the rose.

She blushed as pink as the rose and for a moment looked as young as D'Artagnan's seventeen years of age. A glimmer of tears appeared in her eyes as she said, "You shouldn't, monsieur."

"The flower deserves to be ornamented by you, madam," D'Artagnan said, and bowed.

She blushed darker. "Thank you," she said. And she took it.

He bowed to her again then ran, since Basin and Planchet were already walking a bit down the street. It wasn't till he'd caught up with them and passed them, on the crowded sidewalk that he realized he'd given her one of her husband's own roses. And it wasn't till he was almost at Porthos's door that he realized that the way she had blushed she must not be used to such gallant gestures. Well. He'd never had too good an opinion of Monsieur Bonacieux and now this decided it all. The man was a low creature, not deserving such a wife.

With this thought in his mind he started towards the front door of Porthos's lodging.

"Not there, Monsieur D'Artagnan," Basin said. "The practice room. At the back."

"The practice room?" D'Artagnan asked. Basin nodded and D'Artagnan started down the alley towards the back gate, then trotted along the garden to the broad door at the back of the house which led to what he assumed was an abandoned cellar where the four of them often practiced sword fighting.

That they were meeting here must mean he was required for second in a duel that demanded extraordinary skill. He flung the door open and stopped, shocked.

The three musketeers were there, assembled around something lying on the floor of the room.

Not something. Someone. A corpse. But it was not a corpse as D'Artagnan was used to seeing them, after duels or brawls. It was smaller, more delicate. A child. It was a child.

"Sangre Dieu," he said. "What is this?"

Where Poison Might Be Useful
to a Churchman;
Pedigree and Ancestry

ARAMIS turned from where he knelt, on the stone floor by the child's body. So young a child. Somehow he didn't count on that, though he'd heard that he was only twelve. Perhaps Aramis had forgotten what he had looked like at twelve. Perhaps it was living all day, everyday amid rough men that made this small corpse seem more pathetic and frailer than it should have been.

He heard D'Artagnan's exclamation, he saw out of the corner of his eye as Porthos turned to explain the scene, helped now and then by Athos's single, prodding word.

Aramis, in his turn, was looking at the corpse. He wasn't sure the boy had died of poison. There was no way of knowing. It could have been poison or a sudden illness. But Porthos's description, and the child's fixed and dilated pupils, and the dry skin which seemed still too dry added up to a feeling in Aramis that there had been a poisoning done here.

There were other details about the body. The suit he was wearing was good. Or good enough. But though the violet velvet had been the best money could buy, and though it had once been well tailored, it was obvious to Aramis's considering eye—used, at any rate to examining form and fashion among all—that it hadn't been tailored for this boy but for another. One who'd been larger of shoulders and thicker of waist.

It might mean all or nothing. It might mean the boy's family was that sort of mean nobility hanging by their fingernails to the edge of their birth privilege, forever afraid of dropping off. They would buy the best thirdhand and be quite glad they could afford it. That would fit with a family just come to town to seek their advancement at court. But then, this level of wear, and the suit not tailored for the wearer would fit just as well a family of the highest nobility and careless of appearances. Those with many boys often passed the suits down the line as each of them grew out. And then, if Guillaume had been destined for the church, he was probably the second child or third. Often it was first to the land, second to the army and third to the church, though those last two were often reversed.

Aramis permitted himself a bitter smile that he was one of very few only children to be raised for the church. There were reasons for that, and at any rate, he was not dissatisfied with his vocation, such as it was. If he could control his immoderate fondness for the fair sex, he would be able to be a great churchman. A bishop or . . . he was aware of a smile sliding across his lips before his brain commanded it. Or a Cardinal.

"Is there anything to smile about?" Porthos asked. He'd walked around and planted himself near the child's head, looking down at Aramis. He was pale and he was sullen and he looked truculent as though he could barely wait to find someone on whom to take out his anger.

Aramis shook his head. Any man in this mood was scary. A man who knew how to use a sword in this mood was very scary. And a man Porthos's size was always very scary. "No. I was thinking of . . . my mother."

This got a sudden raising of the red eyebrows above Porthos's eyes and he said, "Oh."

Aramis hastened to change the subject. "Was he hot, Porthos? When you found him?"

"Hot?" Porthos said. "Yes." He nodded slowly, as though considering it. "Hot as if he had a fever, and scarlet as if he burned with it, and seemed to be hallucinating too. And he said he was thirsty." He paused for a moment and let out air in a sound that was neither sigh nor huff of exasperation but had hints of both. "Was it poison, Aramis? Or did something befall him on the way here? He seemed perfectly fine two days ago, when I saw him last."

Aramis shrugged. He looked into the child's eyes and shook his head. "I would tell you it was just a fever," he said. "One of those sudden fevers that kill in a moment. Except . . ."

He looked up and met with Porthos's concerned glance, and sighed because he very much suspected this was indeed murder and though a fever might have meant they were all now in peril, a murder was yet something else again. Together the three of them had unraveled two murders done by stealth. Neither of the murders had proven easy to solve. And both of them had brought far too many complications that none of them could have dreamed or anticipated. Even the murder that didn't pertain to him had involved the Cardinal. And each murder had come close to destroying the four friends or at least to chasing them out of Paris and out of the musketeers.

"What?" Porthos said. He squatted down, so that his face was as close to being on a level with Aramis as it was likely to get. "What do you suspect? What causes your suspicions?"

Aramis sighed again. "It is his pupils. They are wide and dilated. You said he talked of angels and of flying. I think he was poisoned and from the symptoms I would say it was belladonna, which the Englishmen call nightshade."

Porthos frowned. Athos and D'Artagnan, on the other hand, seemed to inhale at the same time and then to remain silent with what was more than just the absence of words, like certain nights are darker than merely the absence of light would warrant.

Aramis looked up and saw Athos's face set and serious. "You know much about poisons, Aramis," he said, slowly.

Aramis raised his eyebrows. Sometimes Athos's reactions were unaccountable, though the Gascon, too, was looking pale and drawn and suspicious.

"You don't think I killed the boy," he said, heatedly. "What reason would I have had to—"

Athos shook his head. "I never thought that," he said. "But I wonder what part of your upbringing had to do with learning poisons and why this was thought necessary."

"When I was a very young man," Aramis said. He avoided looking at his friend because if he did he would have to take offense and he didn't want to call Athos for a duel. "In fact, about the age of this poor child, I was, for six months, apprenticed to a Benedictine monk who believed in the practice of charity by more visible means than the disbursement of wealth. He treated illnesses through herbal remedies and at his knee I learned the use of herbs to heal, and their counterpart, the ill effects they could have if misused." And, unable to repress his malice, he looked up at Athos's chiseled features set now in mild surprise. "Why did you think I'd learned, Athos?"

The older musketeer colored, a rare event and a striking contrast between the blood flooding his cheeks and his normally marble-pale skin. "The Vatican," he said, not making much sense. "And power within the church. One hears . . . stories . . ."

Aramis grinned, suddenly. He never knew from whence Athos's fears and suspicions came, but unlike D'Artagnan's or Aramis's own, they usually echoed from some deep well of suspicion learned from a book in some library in forgotten childhood. "Indeed, one does," he admitted to Athos's murmur. "But the stories one hears aren't meant to apply to everyone who enters the church. It has never been said that the men in the hierarchy of the church are better than other men, only, one hopes, aided by grace. And, Athos, when I take the habit, if I become hungry for temporal power, I'll have better means to advance than poisoning those in my way."

"That I believe," D'Artagnan said, with the sound of an exclamation that escapes the speaker unawares.

Aramis nodded at the young man. "And that you might. But the thing is, I have reason to believe, from his skin still being very dry, that he died of belladonna. This can't be sure, but I'd wager it." As he spoke, he started looking through the corpse's attire.

"Aramis!" Porthos said. "Surely you don't mean to search him."

"Surely I do," Aramis said.

"But his family!"

"We must find his family. And there is no one to tell us who they are or where they live."

"He said his name was Guillaume Jaucourt."

"A name none of us has heard. Porthos let me look. A letter, or some trinket with a coat of arms will get us that much closer to restoring this child to the relatives who, for all we know, search for him in vain even now."

But the doublet had no hidden pockets. It wasn't till Aramis patted the corpse down—gently as though some part of him feared waking the child—that he found, beneath the edge of the doublet a leather purse. And within the leather purse . . .

Aramis removed the purse and the tie that held it at the child's waist, and went through its contents.

There was only a sheaf of pages, looking like paper that had been scavenged a bit from everywhere at random and cut or torn into random sheets. The top of the first one read in the uncertain, scrawled handwriting of a child just learning to write, "The genealogy of Monsieur Pierre du Vallon."

This was enough to raise Aramis's eyebrows and peak his attention because if very few people in Paris remembered Porthos's family name, even fewer had ever known his first name. Aramis knew it only as the result of long and close friendship. He scanned the pages. It was damning indeed.

Oh, Aramis knew very well that Porthos wasn't of as long or noble a line as his own or Athos's. From his father's refusal to let him learn to read or any other book learning—which Porthos had only remedied once he'd come to Paris and been on his own—to Porthos's broad shoulders and the way he approached life, all bespoke a family so close to its own peasants that they were only above them by reason of birth. Or perhaps not even that.

Aramis frowned at the pages. If this was true, if the words on this page were copies of old records or recordings of old gossip, then Porthos's ancestors had been born plebeian and grown rich through trade until, having enough money and having purchased enough lands, they had declared themselves noble and stopped the payment of the feudal labor tax and claimed ancient noble ancestors. In all this they had been aided by the great plague that had swept the land.

There were notes referring to the monasteries and village churches where the supposed originals of these records were kept.

"Porthos," Aramis said and, without explanation, passed the sheets of paper to Porthos.

Porthos frowned at them, squinting, and flipping through the pages. Then he let the pages fall from his hand as if he'd lost all interest in them. He looked at the small corpse, his brow knit in incomprehension. "He had a recording of my family line? What does that mean? Is that how he found my true name."

"Not unless the recording came with a drawing of you," Aramis said acerbically. He repented it immediately as Porthos shook his head. Porthos wasn't stupid, but he was, at the best of times, too literal. And now, in shock . . . "No, Porthos, think. He couldn't have known it from that . . . What concerns me is what it says. About your ancestors. Did he tell you he knew that?"

"What?" Porthos asked, still frowning in confusion.

"That your ancestors had ennobled themselves more or

less on their own fiat," Athos said. He'd picked up the pages and was looking through them. "By stopping payment of the labor tax and claiming noble ancestors. Before that they were bourgeoisie engaged in . . . horse trade?"

Porthos smiled. It wasn't an expression of joy but an almost sardonic pull of the lips in a face not accustomed to reflecting subtle emotions. "Ah. Yes. My ancestors were bourgeoisie. Does that make you despise me, Athos?"

Athos frowned, then sighed. "Porthos, we've been friends for years. There's nothing that would make me despise you. I'm just saying that society at large might view your—"

"I don't give a horse's ass for society at large," Porthos said, visibly startling Athos. Then sheepishly, added, "I'm sorry. I know I'm not as noble as you, Aramis. I'm probably not as noble as D'Artagnan and no one is as noble as Athos." He said it without irony and probably did not mean the sting that made blood surge, visibly, in Athos's face. "But why would this child have those papers? Who cares? Who, unless it is someone considering a marriage alliance with my family."

Aramis gave up on finding anything else on the small corpse. No jewelry, no coin, nothing—nothing he could find, at least without a more thorough and tasteless search than he was willing to undertake. He stood up and looked at Porthos who, in turn, rose slowly to his feet, as though half aware of defending himself against an accusation none of them was going to voice.

"Porthos, any other nobleman, or almost any other nobleman would consider it a great shame to be known as having bourgeois blood. And you are known in the land for being a proud man who romances princesses and duchesses."

Porthos shrugged. "All this"—he held up the pages— "can be found in our parish records, if you're willing to dig. And it was two hundred years ago and more. Since then my ancestors have married women descended from noble families. In all, we probably have as many noble ancestors as anyone else, Athos always excepted, of course."

"Porthos—" Athos said, a hint of warning in his voice.

"No, Athos, no. Truly. I can't imagine your family marrying anything less than women with as full a pedigree and as great a noble background as yourself. You're probably descended several times over from Caesar and Hercules and Hannibal and them all."

A smile—one of the few, rare, untroubled smiles to grace Athos's face—slid over the older musketeer's lips and, his voice showing amusement and not offense, he said, "I doubt Hercules and Hannibal, but if I understand your meaning, you do not mean to give offense."

"Not at all," Porthos said. "And that"—he pointed at the sheaf of papers now in Athos's hand—"doesn't offend me, nor would it offend me if the word got out. Who in this land can point with certainty to a pedigree longer than two hundred years. Princes have less, if the mother line were investigated."

"You're missing the important part," D'Artagnan said. He'd stood in the background, half in shadows, holding his hat to his chest as if he were at a funeral service. Now he spoke, his voice trembling a little and his dark eyes looking haunted by something he couldn't quite name. "You're missing the whole thrust of this, all of you. The thing is not whether Porthos is noble enough or not." The young Gascon smiled, a sudden sardonic smile. "Coming from Gascony and from a family scarcely wealthier than the farmers around it, I can't promise I'm even as noble as Porthos, so I'd be the last to condemn our friend's ancestry. And I don't know how the dead boy found it out, and that, too, is perhaps important but not now. The most important thing, right now, is what he hoped to gain by having it. It is clear . . ." D'Artagnan looked over Athos's shoulder at the scribbled pages. "It is clear at least to me that this was written in a boy's untutored hand. So chances are great he copied it himself. But why? And what did he hope to gain from it?"

As usual, D'Artagnan had gone straight to the heart of

the matter. Aramis felt as if the ground moved under his feet, tilted, turned upside down. He did what he usually did when an idea was unbearable and he could not readily cover it in theological reasoning. "Are you suggesting," he asked D'Artagnan, "that the boy tried to blackmail Porthos with this knowledge?"

D'Artagnan looked surprised. "I wasn't suggesting it," he said. "Merely asking why he would want to have Porthos's genealogy in his pocket."

"I was suggesting it," Athos said. "Porthos, did he?"

"Athos, are you saying you suspect Porthos of killing the boy?" Aramis asked, his hand at his sword.

Before Athos could answer, Porthos did. "Don't be a fool, Aramis. No one could accuse me of killing a . . . child. I like children." He rubbed his huge fingers on his nose as if it itched. "Once, seems long ago, I wanted to get married and have many children. I don't know how it got so far and me without children." He seemed to fall in deep thought. "What I mean is, this life we live . . . what's the future in it?"

Aramis, not daring to say more, still clenched his hand on the grip of his sword and glared his defiance at Athos.

But Athos only shook his head. "I never meant that. I would no more suspect Porthos of murdering a child than I would suspect any of us. No. What I mean is, was the child supposed to be found dead? Porthos says he found the boy collapsed behind some tavern. What if he had been found dead like that, and this the only thing in his pocket? Think you not that, to someone who doesn't know Porthos, this"—he waved the written pages in the air—"might be believed to be enough cause for murder?"

Aramis opened his mouth, then closed it. He shook his head in turn. "Someone might think it was. Porthos, did the child ever talk to you of your family?"

Porthos sighed. "No. I might have told him things my father once or twice said while he was teaching me to use my sword, but that was about it. Other than that, my family was never mentioned."

"So," D'Artagnan said, his voice brisk, as if even he didn't want to dwell too long on what he was saying, "what if someone else planted these pages on the boy and then poisoned him? So that when the boy was found everyone would think that Porthos did it?"

Possible Poisoners;
The Impossibility of Tracing a
Noble Boy in Paris;
The Advantages of a Young Lady's
Accomplishment

"IT's a mare's nest," Porthos said, his mind thinking through everything that had happened. The boy being ill. His death. Then those papers. What could the papers mean? And what could they have to do with the boy's death. "It has to be. None of it makes sense. Who would investigate my family line and copy it and put it in the boy's pocket? And why would anyone kill him just to reach me?"

Aramis sighed. He looked tired. Truth be told, Porthos thought, Aramis hadn't been the same these last couple of months, since his lover, Violette, had died. But he was starting to be more like himself, more . . . at ease with the world and those in it. Now, looking at Porthos, Aramis seemed haunted and hunted, like a man who sees something horrible pursuing him. It always worried Porthos when Aramis looked like this, because it was as good as betting that with any little push, anything gone the slightest bit wrong, Aramis would start talking of joining a monastical order again. And then for weeks he would stop drinking and wenching and swearing and wax all pious every time fighting was mentioned.

There had been several of these episodes, and usually they didn't last longer than a couple of weeks, but however long they lasted, they were a great trial to Aramis's friends. And it was best to stop them before they started. Only this time Porthos was not sure how to stop it.

"Aramis, I know you're scared by something. I know you're thinking something that frightens you, but I don't know what it is nor how to make you stop thinking it."

Aramis nodded. "I know. It is this—who would want to hurt you so badly that they were willing to use the boy? Who would want to get you condemned for murder so badly that they'd study your ancestry."

"The Cardinal," Athos said. "Only to be honest, his eminence normally targets heads higher than ours."

"There are other people that Porthos might have made enemies of," D'Artagnan said. "There are many he's bested at duel. And there's the husband of his . . . Duchess."

Porthos caught the slight hesitation before D'Artagnan called Porthos's lover a Duchess and of course D'Artagnan knew she was no such a thing. In the time he'd known the musketeers surely he'd caught on that Porthos's loved lady, Athenais, was nothing but the wife of an accountant. Still, Athenais's husband, Monsieur Coquenard, old and definitely not noble as he might be, did have power of a sort. Though he kept Athenais very short on the purse, it was rumored he had deep chests of coin somewhere. Which meant he could have bought conspiracy as surely as the Cardinal could have ordered it.

"All of these," Aramis said, "are not so much a worry as his eminence. I do know there's little chance of his being involved, but if there's any chance at all, that means we must be very careful about all our movements in this matter. Twice already, by a bare thread, we've escaped coils that his eminence meant should kill us or stop us. Now . . ." Still looking too old and too worried, he hid his eyes with his hand for a moment, then let his hand drop. "We might not be so lucky."

"So we investigate," Porthos said, briskly, quickly, not wanting to give Aramis any chance to fall prey to that deep melancholy that, in him, could only be cured by sermonizing and the clinking of rosary beads. "We investigate as we must. Who better than us? It's not as though it were the first time."

On some level, he was aware of feeling grief and loss for the boy. For a moment, for a few weeks, the boy had supplied the illusion of having a son. He had made it less obvious what Porthos had sacrificed to the life of a musketeer. But now he was gone. Oh, Porthos wouldn't and couldn't pretend to the grief of a father. But grief it was, and no use denying it. "I want to find out who killed him, anyway. For his own sake," he said. "Guillaume was . . . a good boy and would one day have been a great duelist. He didn't deserve to die like this, with all of life untasted."

It was the most eloquent condemnation he could manage, of the unknown person who'd killed the boy. He knew that Aramis or Athos, even D'Artagnan could have made a more moving speech, a more decisive case for catching the boy's murderer.

But such as it was, it sufficed. It seemed to move the others to action.

"First," Athos said, briskly, "we must find a place to put the body. It is no longer as hot as it was in the peak of summer, but it is still too hot to just leave him here. We might find his family quickly enough, but then we might not find it for a long, long time. The priest that Aramis knew, who could put coffins in his cool basement is himself dead[3] and therefore we can't avail ourselves of his charity. My own cellar . . ." Athos shrugged. "Is cold enough for wine and at this time of the year it will do, if we can procure a coffin."

---

[3]*Death of a Musketeer.*

"A coffin I can still arrange," Aramis said. "I can direct Bazin to beg one from a monastery in town, and we can store the body in it."

Athos nodded. "Good. That's one problem taken care of. Of course, we'd better find the boy's parents quickly nonetheless."

"But how are we going to find his parents?" D'Artagnan said.

"By his name," Aramis said. He flashed a superior smile. "We can ask around. D'Artagnan, we know you are a newcomer here, but the rest of us have many contacts in Paris and many people of whom we can ask the whereabouts of this family."

D'Artagnan didn't seem impressed, Porthos noted. In fact, one of the reasons he liked D'Artagnan, he decided, was that the young man seemed as little impressed with Aramis's or Athos's pronouncements as most other people were with Porthos's.

"What if the boy used a false name? What if his family is truly not who he said it was? If the Cardinal is involved . . ." D'Artagnan said.

Aramis looked about to dismiss the comment out of hand. He got that fighting light to his green eyes that normally meant he was about to dismiss something as a piece of idiocy. But something seemed to come to his mind that stopped the protest on his lips. The mouth he'd opened, closed with a snap, and he frowned at D'Artagnan as if the boy had done something to annoy him. For a while he was quiet, glaring. Then he said, "Well, what do you suggest then?"

D'Artagnan shrugged. "I don't know what to suggest," he said, opening his hands in an expression of helplessness. "I'd say describe him, but description alone might not be enough. How many boys of eleven or twelve do you think there are, running around Paris? And how many who might have red hair, or wear a good violet velvet suit?"

Aramis glared more. Porthos wondered if D'Artagnan

was intimidated by the glare. Himself, he had long ago learned that Aramis glared like this when he was thinking. Or rather, when he was forced to think along lines he did not wish to pursue.

After a long while, Aramis looked away, then raised his hand, slightly folded and, seeming to look intently at his impeccably manicured nails, said, "I do have some ability to sketch. I could draw the boy's likeness, and copy it, so that each of us would have a quick drawing of him, to be used in asking people if they have seen him."

"You're a painter?" Porthos said.

Aramis looked up, a defensive expression in his gaze. "Not a painter," he said. "I merely do a little sketching. In pen and ink or in coal. A very quick likeness. My mother . . ." He blushed and cleared his throat. "It is a pastime of my mother's and she taught it to me when I was very young."

"No doubt," Athos said, drily with just a hint of humor in his voice indicating that he was joking. "Thinking that like all well-bred young ladies you'd need the art."

Aramis blushed, the color coming to his face in a tide. He reached for his sword, but never allowed his hand to touch it, making himself drop his arm straight alongside his body, instead. "Do you wish me to do it, or not? Whatever you think of the ability, or even of how I came by it, doubtless it would be useful, would it not?"

"Please," Porthos said, before Athos could open his mouth. "It would be very useful, yes. In fact, I don't know how we can do it without your help."

"Indeed," D'Artagnan agreed, seemingly catching on. "It would be very useful to all of us."

They both glared at Athos, who only nodded and said, "Very useful."

Bazin was sent to Aramis's lodgings for paper and the sort of charcoal used for this work. While he was gone, the four friends debated what to do.

"The best we can do, I think," Aramis said. "Is to ask at any lodgings around here where a noble family might be who has a son who looks like this. How far do you think he walked, Porthos?"

Porthos shrugged. "I got the impression he didn't walk very long," he said. "Half an hour at most. He sometimes said he had run the whole way and while . . ." He felt his throat close at the thought of how young the boy was. "He was very young and therefore full of energy, I don't think he could have run much more than a quarter league, perhaps?"

"So it would have to be lodgings hereabouts," Athos said, thoughtfully. He'd placed himself at some distance from the corpse and leaning against a wall, looked at all of them detachedly. "Within the area that we, ourselves, live."

"His suit is not very good," Aramis said and, before Porthos could protest that it was fabric of the best quality, he added. "It is good velvet, I'll grant you, and well cut. But it was not cut for him. It is too big in places and too small in others, and the breeches are much too short."

"Sometimes," D'Artagnan said. "Families of minor nobility do buy—"

"Used suits," Aramis said, levelly. "Indeed, I am not a fool. I know that families do try to save money, particularly when the boy is young and still growing. But mind you, if they are minor nobility, or even"—he waved away an objection none of them had attempted to make—"if they are the highest nobility but he is the youngest of many boys and inherited his brothers' clothing, then this would be a child who would be sent for errands everywhere. Everyone in this area would have seen him—from wine merchants to laundresses. In the country the youngest son would get charged with minding the livestock or exercising the horses. In the city, he'll be sent for a bottle of wine for his father and a silk kerchief for his mother."

"And so you suggest?" Athos asked.

"That we go out," Aramis said. "I shall take Porthos, and we shall go to the palace. To the people we know there." He allowed himself a quirk of the eyebrow. "From maids to noblemen, I'm sure if the family has gone to court at all someone will have seen the boy or heard of him. I'll ask around, also, to theology professors and monks and see if anyone had taken him on to teach him, since his family intended him for the church. And I think you and D'Artagnan could perhaps ask around here? Within the distance a boy might run here? Porthos, where did you find him?"

"Down the alley," Porthos said. "Past the smithy and the flowering roses that spill over the wall. There's an inn there, or at least the back wall of it. The front door faces the street on the other side. He was sitting against the wall and he seemed to be dreaming with his eyes open." He wished he knew, if it truly was poison, how long it would take to act, and how far the boy might have come. He didn't know how to put these thoughts into words.

Looking down at the boy hurt. Though he'd been dead a little while now, and though he looked pale, it was not so much the look of one dead as of a child on the verge of falling asleep. The eyes looked up at the ceiling, blankly, and there was no sign of anguish. If one looked at him long enough, there was the feeling he would presently get up and smile and say wasn't it a good joke, and hadn't he fooled them all.

Porthos was used to his corpses having more blood on them, or more signs of violence. The boy looked like he'd been stunned, not killed. And yet Porthos was not a child. He knew what dead meant. This was no prank. There would be no waking up, no talking, no more fencing lessons. There would be nothing, now, for Guillaume.

With a pang, Porthos realized he would miss the boy, and let a heavy sigh escape him. As Aramis looked in his direction, he said, "*Sangre Dieu*" and for once Aramis did not scold him for the blasphemy, just inclined his head and said nothing.

At that moment, Bazin came in, with a wooden box which, upon opening, contained several sheets of paper and some dark sticks of what appeared to be charcoal of different tones. Porthos moved nearby to watch Aramis work. The younger man's fingers moved quickly over the page, drawing a likeness of Guillaume with what appeared to Porthos like divine ability. The boy's sharp nose emerged, and his slightly too square chin. You could tell if he'd grown to his full size and maturity he would one day have been a square-jawed man. You could see his face would have gained bulk and a certain solidity.

Porthos looked away as the scene had become inexplicably shaky. It was possible his eyes were full of tears, but he'd refuse to admit it. Instead, he swallowed hard, and swallowed again, and looked at the door, which was ajar, allowing only a sliver of light in.

Presently, he heard Aramis close his box of drawing materials, saw Bazin take it, and heard, without being fully able to understand it, Aramis give instruction to Bazin on where to find a coffin and Athos give instructions to the ever-silent Grimaud, his servant, on where to put the coffin in the wine cellar.

He wasn't aware of the servants leaving, but they must have left because when Aramis tried to hand Porthos one of the pieces of paper with the boy's picture, the servants were no longer there and D'Artagnan and Athos were standing by the door and looking back at Porthos with the worried expressions of people standing by a sick bed.

Porthos disciplined his face to show no emotion. So the boy was gone. So he would never grow up into the brave, determined man he'd promised to be. How many boys had died too young since the world had begun? It didn't bear thinking about.

One glance at the picture Aramis had drawn showed him, as it were, Guillaume brought to life momentarily, with an expression of self-confidence in his eyes and the slightest of smiles on his lips.

Porthos rolled it carefully and held it in his hand. It didn't bear looking at too much.

The Differences Between a Pedigree and a Baldric; The Differences Between Murder and Friendship

ARAMIS knew Porthos well enough to be alarmed at his friend's reactions. Grief for the boy, he could understand or almost understand. But there was a seething rage in Porthos's look; a sense of fury being held barely in check.

It was not natural in Aramis, the turn of mind that rejoiced in the company of children or young adults. Rather, he considered them as yet not fully formed humans who must by the action of society and the guidance of a caring adult become polished exactly like a pebble becomes polished by the action of the sea. And while there were those who might value unpolished pebbles for their natural charm or their interesting surfaces, Aramis, with his elegant appearance, his careful education would take his jewels properly faceted or not at all.

So he didn't understand, first of all, why Porthos would choose to associate with a juvenile of the species, rough and ready and unable to share interesting court gossip, or comment on Porthos's choice of fashion. Part of this, of course, made him wonder if Porthos valued Aramis's friendship quite as much as Aramis thought. And another part made him wonder if Porthos was the man he thought he was. Which, of course, bore an important weight on this subject, because his certainty that Porthos had *not* murdered the boy rested primarily on his knowledge of Porthos.

All this was in Aramis's mind as—after waiting for what seemed like much too long for Porthos to change into his usual gold-hedged and gaudy musketeer's uniform—he and Porthos left Porthos's lodging through the garden and the back gate and started to the left towards the broad street that would take them to the royal palace. To the uneasiness of such thoughts, he must add the fact that Porthos was looking at Aramis out the corner of his eye and twirling his moustache now and then, not in the way he would when he was showing it off for maid or duchess, but in the way he did when deep in thought or faced with a puzzle he couldn't decipher.

Aramis was ready to accept Porthos's grieving over the boy—though the whole thing confused him. What he was not ready to do was accept that Porthos was also suspicious of Aramis. Suspicious of what, in God's name? And why? Surely Porthos didn't think Aramis had snuck up on the boy early morning and filled his confits with belladonna juice because the boy was a juvenile and therefore more trouble than profit in the world? If Aramis were to turn to that for reason, he'd be busy strangling babes in their cribs the whole livelong day.

They walked up the crowded street side by side, in the heavy foot traffic of late morning. Men and women either rushed home for a meal or hastened out and about their pursuits, assignations and meetings, duels and celebrations. Now and then the sound of horses' hooves from behind made passersby rush onto the side of the road and flatten themselves against the wall—or against other passersby already flattened against the wall—while carriages with coats of arms on their doors, or horses' rushing under the impulse of the riders' whips passed them by.

It was after one of those moments of immobility, flattened side by side against the stone wall of what appeared to be a house of ill repute, while perfumed ladies in scant attire and their wine-soaked customers pressed against them, that Aramis decided he could take it no more.

"Porthos," he said. "Why do you keep looking at me as though you suspected me of unnameable crimes?"

Porthos looked startled. He blew out breath under his abundant red moustache. "Me? Suspect you of crimes? Forbid the thought. I would never suspect a friend of a crime." He rubbed the bridge of his nose. "It is that my friends think other people would believe I was a criminal. That is what puzzles me. Not angers me, mind, for I'm not a wrathful man. But it astounds me."

Porthos being subtle and trying to subtly give hint of offense would cause the same disquiet in most bosoms as a rabbit, its muzzle stained with blood, chasing a lion around. Aramis was human enough to be disquieted but even more human in feeling amused at Porthos's attempts at hinting something.

"Porthos," he said at last. "I don't suspect you of anything. You know that! But you're looking at me as if I'd killed your favorite hound and had designs on your horse."

Porthos harrumphed, another behavior that didn't come naturally to him. "You and Athos both surely sounded like you thought everyone at large would believe I might kill an innocent child to prevent my pedigree from being divulged. As though I could care less who my ancestors were, other than the most recent ones." He made a sound in his throat as if spitting. "I didn't know nobility, even of birth, much less nobility of mind and behavior, could be measured by how many noble ancestors a person could count. I always thought it was just what it was at the moment of birth."

Oh. So that was what was working at Porthos. At least this, Aramis was prepared to understand. "I've always considered you noble enough," Aramis said. "At least . . ."

Another *harumph* and Aramis hastened to add, "I mean, I'm not sure I look at nobility the same way others do.

Look at me, I let my servant run on and on at me about my misbehavior and how I should long since have entered the church."

This elicited a chuckle from Porthos, which, at least, had the advantage of sounding like natural Porthos. "We all think Bazin would be made far more acceptable by a regular thrashing, or at least the liberal use of a muzzle."

This was such a common complaint, that Aramis smiled, for a moment, and forgot he was aggrieved with Porthos, before coming back to his main argument. "The point is," Aramis said, "that though Bazin is no more than the son of tenants on my parents' land, I know he was brought up for the church as I was, and his mind is, if not the equal of mine—" Did Porthos truly need to snort? "If not the equal of mine, at least close enough to it that what he says might illuminate my path as I try to make myself worthy enough to enter the church."

Porthos made a sound again. "So you're not sure what's noble and what isn't, but you believe this could be a plot to implicate me? That people, strangers and people who've talked to me, would think I killed just to prevent it being known that not all my ancestors were noble? And killed a child, yet?"

Aramis shrugged. "We all know you to be proud, Porthos, all of us."

"Indeed? In what way am I more proud than any of you?"

Aramis felt blood rush to his cheeks. There was nothing for it but he would have to list his friend's defects of character, or at least the visible outward marks of those defects. The truth was that beneath his quick gossiping tongue and the eye that was ever ready to apprehend and mock a fashion faux pas, Aramis was more tolerant than he would wish anyone to know.

His maxim, or at least one of the maxims that cluttered his religiously brought-up conscience was "Judge not lest you be judged." He knew how often—particularly in sins of the flesh—he fell short of the Christian ideal. Particularly the ideal of the Christian bound to a religious life of chastity and obedience. He didn't like to throw Porthos's vanity, or Athos's drinking, or D'Artagnan's more than eager wish to view everything as a challenge to a duel into his friends' teeth. And he hoped and fervently prayed they wouldn't throw in his teeth his inability to resist any beautiful female who set her mind on dallying with him.

But now he would have to and there was nothing for it. He waved at Porthos. "There is the way you dress," he said, stiffly. "I don't find anything wrong with it, mind," he lied. Truth was there were a hundred things wrong with it, but mostly the fact that a well brought up gentleman wouldn't dream of mixing stripes with dots or adorning his person with three different shades of gold trim and a bit of silver thrown in just in case. It wasn't the sort of wrong he meant, anyway, he told himself. "But there are few musketeers who, on a musketeer's pay, wear that much good quality velvet and such a profusion of gold and silver."

"What is wrong with wishing to appear nice?"

"Nothing," Aramis said. And floundered. "Nothing at all. You know what care I take with my own appearance. But then there is . . . and mind you, I mean no offense about your most excellent Athenais."

"You leave Athenais out of this," Porthos roared causing a few people near them to turn and stare and others, farther up, to run out of their way, possibly convinced that Porthos's noise was a carriage at full trundle coming up behind them.

"I did say she was most excellent."

"Indeed she is, and you should abstain from mentioning her name at all, except in praise."

"I am praising it," Aramis said, at his wits end. "I have nothing against the lady or her mind, even if she sometimes thinks it fair to make sport of me." He lifted a hand to stop another outburst from his friend. "But is it, or is it not true that you tell everyone around that she's a duchess or a princess, or another of the high heads of the realm."

Porthos sulked at this, setting his lips in a taut line and

glaring at Aramis. "She should be. And she is noble born. And by nobility of mind and capacity of thought, she should be . . ."

"Oh, I'm not disputing that," Aramis said. "But still, if you think so highly of her you could just say that—that she's as good as any princess. Not tell all and sundry that she is a princess."

Porthos shrugged. "I know what people think of me. Musketeers. Courtiers. They think I'm rough and dumb. And I . . ." He shrugged. "I don't want them to think themselves justified and to assume I can't aspire to the highest ladies in the court. I can, you know? When I first came to Paris, and even when I first became a musketeer, I bedded my share of them. Only they are all so incredibly boring, all full of their own magnificence and beauty and never wishing to talk of anything else. So I have . . . Athenais. But I don't think that's what people would believe. They would think Athenais's station in life is the best I can aspire to."

"Yes," Aramis said patiently. He considered pointing out that the hole in Porthos's pedigree was of the same kind, but then he thought Porthos would point out that he'd never threatened to kill anyone who discovered that Porthos's lover was nothing but an accountant's wife. So he sighed. "And then there's D'Artagnan."

"Eh? What is wrong with D'Artagnan? Oh, yes, I know what he's said. His father is a younger son and the whole of their property is so small that the area of the cemetery devoted to children is larger than their entire holdings, but Aramis . . . He's clearly nobly born, taught to use his sword at an early age and . . . Aramis, he at least was taught to read at an early age. He understands you even when you are full tilt in one of your theological speeches and I suspect he understands Athos's quotations too. At least sometimes he smiles when Athos says something that makes no sense to me. So I don't see what D'Artagnan has to do with your thinking everyone could believe I would kill a child to hide some imaginary shame over my ancestors."

"I didn't mean any of those things," Aramis said. "But cast your mind upon your first meeting with D'Artagnan. Did you or did you not challenge him to a duel for having got enmeshed in your baldric and thus showing people that it was not gold on the other side?"

Porthos's eyes went very wide, then he frowned as though trying to understand what Aramis might mean by all of this. "In public," he said. "He did it in public, and when I'd been showing off the new baldric too. What was I to do? Oh, I understand now that he didn't do it on purpose. He was just in such a blessed hurry to catch up to Rochefort. But at the time it seemed to me that his entire purpose in life was to show the world that my baldric was not nearly so fine as it looked."

"See, and you challenged him to a duel."

Porthos raised an eyebrow as though pondering the matter—again an unaccustomed expression and one that would have looked more natural on Athos. "So, I challenged him to a duel. As did you, if I remember, because the pup tried to return to you the handkerchief of a lady you didn't want it to be known you associated with. And Athos—Athos of all people—challenged the young Gascon to a duel because D'Artagnan careened into him and failed to apologize enough for the hurt he caused Athos's shoulder. I believe at the time apologizing enough would have consisted of slitting his own throat then jumping into a roaring fire." Porthos smiled, sheepishly. "The truth, my friend, is that none of us was himself that day. We'd just had the very unpleasant experience of being arrested by the guards of the Cardinal, followed by the even more unpleasant experience of having Monsieur de Treville flay our flesh from our bones with sarcasm. Surely you don't think any of us is normally that thin-skinned?"

Aramis couldn't help but grin. "Well, D'Artagnan is."

"Indeed," Porthos said and grinned, and twirled his moustache in a more accustomed manner, probably at a young woman who was standing in the doorway of a tavern ahead and smiling at him through the gathering gloom. "But still, I challenged him for a duel. I did not poison him or knife him in the back, did I? I'm not a villain. And D'Artagnan wasn't and isn't exactly a child. Kindly recall what he did to Chausac and de Brisarac on his very first confrontations."

"Yes, but . . ."

"No buts about it. Just because I'm willing to challenge someone over exposing my baldric, it doesn't mean I would poison someone else for exposing my pedigree. And I'm sure all other musketeers would know that."

"Ah, yes, but does the Cardinal know it also?"

Porthos sighed. "They say he's shrewd and that he has spies everywhere. Surely he knows I would no more kill someone by stealth than I would spread gossip about someone behind their back. If someone makes me aggrieved enough to wish to kill them or even to say anything unpleasant about them, I say it to their face or call them out to a duel. I do not, and never have, done things by stealth. I'm not good at it, at any rate."

"Indeed," Aramis said.

"So if this were the Cardinal's plot, he would have known it wouldn't work."

"Porthos." Aramis was sure the edge of impatience in his voice was now making people stare at him. "His eminence might know you'd never do it. But he would think people believe you vain and proud, and that your being vain and proud, you'd be a logical suspect for this."

"Oh," Porthos said. His expression cleared for a moment, then became charged again. "I hope he's wrong. If he does think that. Because . . . because I hope most people know I'm honorable, also."

"Indeed," Aramis said.

Porthos nodded. And then with that inconsequence full of meaning of which only Porthos was capable, he added, "But you know, we're all now friends with D'Artagnan."

To Aramis's blank look, he explained as if it were the

most obvious thing in the world. "So the duel wasn't that important. Perhaps you're wrong. Perhaps most people realize that I wouldn't kill a child because of my ancestry. Perhaps even if there is one person out there evil enough to commit murder for that reason, perhaps even if all this came out, no one else would believe it."

"Perhaps," Aramis said, though secretly he suspected that this was no more than wishful thinking on Porthos's part. "And yet, I would not wish to risk it. So I hope we find who murdered the boy quickly, if indeed he was murdered. Which means, too, finding his family, through them we'll know any contacts he might—or might not—have had with the Cardinal. And we'll be prepared to avenge Guillaume."

"We are agreed on that," Porthos said.

And so, while having a fascinating discussion about baldrics and pedigree, they left behind the noisy and bustling areas of town and walked now along a street lined with mansions, most of them with guarded gates. Aramis thought it best to keep his council.

A Propinquity of the Heart;
When Everything Adds to a Good Impression;
Athos's Amusement

"**W**HY is it logical?" Athos asked D'Artagnan, "that we should go to your landlord's first? Surely not that many noblemen lodge nearby?"

D'Artagnan couldn't seem to remember why it was logical at all. His home was within walking distance, but it was hardly in the best part of town. Rather, it was in an area frequented by the bourgeoisie and not particularly wealthy bourgeoisie at that. The Rue des Fossoyers where the young guard of Monsieur des Essarts lodged, was broad and lined on both sides with tall buildings that sheltered shops on the bottom floors. Some of the merchants lived on the bottom floors, too, while other lived above their shops. But usually all or part of the houses were rented to people very much like D'Artagnan—young men seeking their fortunes in Paris and with their foot on what could be considered the first rung in the ladder of success.

In D'Artagnan's case, his new uniform of the guards, almost indistinguishable from that of the musketeers save for a slightly lighter color, marked him as noble born. Other young gentlemen wore the garb of clerks or apprentices in various professions ranging from law to blacksmithing.

D'Artagnan knew, or at least suspected that some of them might be noble . . . and if they were noble . . . He felt Athos's stare on him and shook his head. "I thought," he said, his desperate cunning saving him as it so often did. "That if they're not too wealthy a family and not too well known at court, they might have had dealings with my landlord who is, among other things, a grocer. I suspect he has all kinds of other businesses too, though, from lending on security of some sort, to perhaps selling used clothes or appointments that such a family might need. Since Aramis said the suit didn't fit well . . ."

And on this, D'Artagnan ground to a stop and shrugged. Athos nodded. "And since the suit didn't fit well you thought that of all the possible shops in Paris, the boy must have been seen by your landlord." He cleared his throat. "I thought you were several weeks in arrears with your rent, though?"

D'Artagnan shrugged. "If we do it properly we will not need to see my landlord," he said. "His wife, who normally stays at the palace is visiting and she . . ." He felt the blush climb to his cheeks and heat there, like a blazing furnace beneath the skin. He shook his head, as he thought of the beautiful woman and wished that he wasn't quite so transparent about his interest.

But Athos must have been in a kind mood. He inclined his head slightly. "Ah. Sometimes even the logic of seventeen is right, or at least leads one onto the right path. Don't worry about it, D'Artagnan, as I see no evil. We might as well ask. In a place like this, full of merchants and clerks, you're right that someone might very well have seen the boy who was almost certainly not high nobility."

"Why not high nobility?" D'Artagnan asked. "Aramis said that he might just be the youngest of a very noble family."

Athos shrugged. "Because I don't know the name. I'm not going to claim to know every noble family in France. However, I do know most of the high nobility by name or surname at the very least. I know all of them to Aramis's level at least. Not . . . I might not be able to tell you where their domains are or who their children are. I certainly might have no idea what they look like—but I have at least heard the name once. And Jaucourt is totally new to me. So, I suspect that they are either recently ennobled or very small and provincial nobility."

D'Artagnan, who had for sometime been aware that a gulf lay between nobility such as his own and the type of nobility that Athos embodied, only nodded. "Why didn't you say this before?" he asked. "In Porthos's practice room?"

Athos shrugged. "What, after the great discussion about pedigree? To what end? It would only have annoyed Porthos and accomplished nothing. Besides—" He shrugged again. "Who knows? Even families of low nobility have important cousins, second cousins or friends. If it's a noble family recently come to court, it could very well be that what drew them here were just such contacts. If anyone at the palace has seen them, then surely Porthos and Aramis will find out, between the kitchen maids and the duchesses. And as for us, why shouldn't we canvass your neighborhood? It has at least the advantage of being well-known territory."

If Athos was being facetious, D'Artagnan could not detect it. But as they approached D'Artagnan's lodgings, its bottom floor occupied by Monsieur de Bonacieux's shop and lodgings, D'Artagnan forgot all about what Athos might think of him and of this errand.

Behind the panes of the lower window, he distinguished, as though half in shadow, a feminine shape. And before his mind could assure him of any such thing, his heart sped up and his mouth went dry.

From the other side, perhaps because of the woman distinguishing a like shape, there was movement, and then the opening of the window, creaking slightly—and there in the opening stood the lovely Madame Bonacieux. She'd changed her clothing. The gown she now wore was not exactly high court fashion, but a simpler, looser garment. And yet, it outlined her heavy breasts just as tightly, and the plunge of its low-cut neckline displayed a fair amount of white and rosy skin.

D'Artagnan's thoughts stopped in their tracks when he realized she was wearing his rose—the rose he'd given her—on the very end of that neckline, the stem between her breasts and the petals peeking above. He struggled for words like a drowning man might struggle for the proverbial straw, but none came to a tongue that seemed, suddenly, thick and unyielding.

He forced sound through his lips, but what came out was a stammered, "Ma–Ma–Ma–" and no end to the word "madam," no matter how he endeavored to pronounce it. She smelled like roses, a soft scent, like summer at full bloom, like . . .

"Madam," Athos said very correctly, from just behind D'Artagnan. D'Artagnan turned to see Athos, hat drawn, bow with more flourish than he normally accorded any woman.

Athos was always correct with every woman and often more gentlemanly than anyone else around, yet he was always somewhat reserved and fearful, like a child who once burned will stay away from the fire.

Looking at Athos steadied D'Artagnan who was able to draw his hat more clumsily than Athos had, and to stammer, finally, "Madame Bonacieux."

The beautiful woman was looking at both of them now, including Athos in her welcoming smile. Her fingers, though, were playing, as though she didn't realize what they were doing, with the petals of D'Artagnan's rose.

"Sirs," she said, and smiled at them. "I saw you from behind the window, and saw you hesitate and thought that perhaps you . . . perhaps you . . ."

D'Artagnan started wondering if Athos was right and if his logic was seventeen-year-old logic or if, perhaps, there was something else, other than logic at work here between himself and Madame Bonacieux.

"We did," he said. "Have a question, but I don't know if . . . since you don't spend much time here, I don't know if . . ." He floundered again, all his thoughts fleeing him, as he realized her eyes were the exact color of the summer sky when he'd been a young boy and left his father's house to go and lie out amid the grass fields, looking up at the cloudless, sun-bright sky of Gascony.

"We'd like to know if this boy has been seen in this neighborhood," Athos said, pulling his drawing of Guillaume from his sleeve, where he'd secreted it, and displaying it to Madame Bonacieux. "He's given his name as Guillaume Jaucourt, but we're not sure it is his true name . . ."

Madame Bonacieux took the picture, opened it and looked at it for a moment, with a little wrinkle of puzzlement between her eyes.

"Have you seen him?" Athos asked.

"No," she said. "I'm sure I haven't. But I'm also sure I've seen a face very much like his at court . . . Though I'd be at a loss to tell you precisely whose it was. I can assure you that it is not someone who is much in her Majesty's circle and company, where I reside, but . . . someone I've seen before, and my mind tells me it was at court."

"At court," D'Artagnan said, jumping in. "How much did this person look like the boy? Could it be his brother or his father?"

Madame Bonacieux shook her head. "I couldn't tell you any clearer," she said, and her voice seemed to say she regretted not telling D'Artagnan anything at all he wanted to know, and some more besides. "I just . . . There is an air of family to it. Same cut of the chin, same tilt of the eyes, perhaps. Can't tell you who it was, though, so it is probably not someone of the highest nobility."

"And you've never seen him here? On this street?"

Madame Bonacieux sighed a little—a sigh of confusion

and exasperation. "I spend so little time here. If I . . . would you wait a moment?"

Athos nodded, and so did D'Artagnan. At least he hoped he did. The fact was that around Madame Bonacieux he felt as if his head were floating several meters above his neck and could only be felt at a distance, as if in a dream.

Just before coming to the capital—and perhaps it had been at the back of his mother's mind when she'd recommended that he go and make something of himself—he'd developed a sort of smoldering passion for his cousin, Genevieve. He'd loved her desperately and passionately. Her image had filled his mind during the day and visited his dreams at night. She'd allowed him one kiss, and that kiss still seemed to linger upon his lips, in mingled sweetness and pain.

Pain because Genevieve was the daughter of his father's older brother and betrothed from before she could even speak to a Spanish lord whose lands, on the other side of the border, delineated the limits of D'Artagnan's uncle's domain. Even had she not been pledged already, the chances of her father, who'd inherited the larger portion of the lands that fell to the family, accepting the suit of his penniless nephew were not very high.

But even at the height of his infatuation with Genevieve, D'Artagnan had not felt quite so out of his depth and as if he were walking in an unreal world. No. To hark back to a time when he felt this confused, he needed to go back all the way to when he was seven and had caught the small pox and lain feverish, between life and death, for many days.

As if from outside a fog that surrounded his mind and thought, he heard Athos. "Ah, D'Artagnan," the older man said. "Women are dangerous. Better play with fire than with a woman. Fire will only burn your body."

D'Artagnan, startled out of his reverie, looked back at Athos. The musketeer appeared both concerned and amused, an expression that made him look at once younger than he was and somewhat sickly, as if he too were burning with a fever, or at least remembering a time when he was.

"I don't know what you mean, Athos," D'Artagnan said from the height of dignity conferred by his unfinished adolescence. And if his cheeks flamed, let them. He felt embarrassment at being caught in his admiration of this woman—this married woman. But is also took effort to refrain from telling Athos that it would help if Athos did not choose women as others played with unguarded flame. Being attracted to women that were less than murderous might have made the older musketeer's experience with love very different.

The problem was that D'Artagnan actually didn't know anything for sure about the musketeer's life. All he knew had been inferred and could not be spoken of in the full light of day. The other thing was that he, himself, had no idea what type of women attracted him. It was easy to pass judgement on another man's taste when he knew so little of females that he had no idea how his own love life would unroll. So he contented himself with saying, "I'm simply making a search for this boy, on Porthos's behalf and to find the boy's family."

Athos made a sound in his throat. It might have been suppressed laughter.

Madame Bonacieux was gone some moments, before coming back, carrying the drawing. She handed it to Athos.

"No one seems to know him," she said. Her fair, high brow was knit in puzzlement beneath a straggle of blond hair. "No one. And no one knows a Guillaume Jaucourt. Only . . ." she hesitated.

"Only?" Athos asked.

"Only my husband's clerk who takes care of large-volume orders says he remembers the boy vaguely in something connected with wine, sometime back. I really don't know if I'd put much faith in it, though. His memory seems to be like mine—he remembers the boy or a face like his."

"Well," D'Artagnan said. Her absence had given him time to clear his head, time to get his thoughts in order. "Since we're looking for his family, I would like to know if you think of anyone who might resemble him."

For the first time Madame Bonacieux looked curious. "You are looking for his family? Why? What has he done? Has he stolen something or . . . ?"

D'Artagnan shook his head. "No," he said, thinking fast. "It's just that a friend of mine has undertaken to teach the boy swordplay and the boy has missed his last lesson." That much was true. "My friend is worried and would like to make sure nothing untoward has happened to the child."

The woman's expression changed. D'Artagnan couldn't quite say how, but it shifted, softened. He realized, suddenly, that she was probably younger even than he'd first estimated. In fact, though she was married, she couldn't be much older than he was. Twenty-one, maybe, or twenty-two. He also become aware that in her mind he'd just gone from a law enforcer attempting to capture a thief to a man worried about a child.

Even D'Artagnan was not so inexperienced or so innocent that he didn't know how appealing that would be to a young female. He felt warmly rewarded for his efforts and hoped he never needed to inform the lady that the child was already, in fact, dead.

As they walked away, D'Artagnan said, "At least we've heard he looks like someone that she knows, so he's probably truly related to someone at court. You know, Athos, there's something you haven't taken into account."

Athos looked at him, raising both eyebrows.

"That the child might indeed be the son of a nobleman, but not of a noblewoman."

Athos's lips trembled into an almost smile that was, in him, a sign of extreme amusement. "Oh, D'Artagnan, I've thought of that. The existence of bastards of noble houses is not something totally unknown to me."

D'Artagnan recalled, with a pang, that some trouble before had involved what was almost certainly a bastard of Athos's very noble house. "I didn't mean—" he said.

"No, of course you didn't," Athos said. "Forgive me if I seemed to overreact. It's just . . ." He frowned. "I too have the impression he resembles someone, but it's not . . . I cannot place my finger on it." He shook his head as if to clear it. "Let's go ask around some of the places in town better known for lodging noblemen."

The Advantage of Moving in Different Spheres; Maids and Duchesses; Knowing People Who Don't Know You

"IT would be best if we separated," Aramis said, as soon as they were past the gates of the palace. "And meet here again once our enquiries are done. If you encounter trouble, send me word by someone. If I run into trouble, I shall send you word."

Porthos nodded. He didn't resent Aramis's suggestion. Oh, perhaps Aramis was embarrassed to be seen with Porthos—it wouldn't be the first or the last time. Porthos was aware that his clothing was too loud, too brash, too brazen for his carefully attired, groomed and perfectly mannered friend. He knew that most people wondered why they were friends at all.

But he also knew that under normal circumstances Aramis would be taking Porthos along. These weren't normal circumstances. The two of them needed to find out as much as possible about the boy, Guillaume, and his family in as short a time as possible. That meant going where their strengths were greater. Porthos knew some people among the servants, notably the girlfriend of his servant, Mousqueton. And Aramis . . . who knew who Aramis might know? But they were all probably too high in the instep for Porthos to approach.

"Aramis," he said, instead, as his friend turned to leave.

Aramis looked back and Porthos struggled with the thought that had been bothering him since they got through the gates. "What if we never find his true name or his family?"

Aramis frowned. "What makes you think—"

"There are so many twelve year olds in Paris. And if he was working for the Cardinal, he might be hidden. He might . . . The Cardinal might have muddied the trail . . ." He shrugged.

Aramis tilted his head sideways, as if in thought, then threw the mass of his blond hair back with a careless hand. "We'll find them, Porthos, don't worry. We'll show the picture and ask questions. And if someone doesn't know him by that name, they might know him by another one. And if they don't know him by any name, they might yet look at the picture and think they know someone who looks like him. We'll trace him. Paris is a very large town, but when it comes to the nobility it is like a small family, gathered in and bickering. We've all run into each other. Or our ancestors have."

Porthos nodded. Sometimes when Athos and Aramis spoke of the nobility of France, he felt very much the plebeian. They seemed to assume all French nobility was related and that they all counted in the numbers of their close relatives three assorted dukes and five kings. Porthos's family had nobility enough in its ancestry, even if some long-lost ancestor had fudged the point. But that nobility consisted of minor seigneurs and small land owners, not people who normally went to court. Not people who normally cared to go to court. That he knew, he'd been the first in his family to even come to Paris.

But Aramis spoke as if he were so sure that Porthos hated to question him. Instead, he said, "But what if we can't find his family? What if no one will know who he is?"

"Oh, don't worry," Aramis said with airy impatience. "Don't fret. One way or another we will find him. You forget that I know a lot of people. I even know people who don't know me."

"You—?" Porthos asked, confused.

"I mean there are people of whom I've heard, who almost surely have never heard of me." Aramis turned and awkwardly tapped Porthos on the shoulder. "Really, don't fret. I'm sure we'll find out. If four good men, with working heads on their shoulders and ready swords, can't find the parents of a lost child in Paris, the world has come to be a complex thing indeed. You go and talk to whomever you know in the palace and I'll pursue my own acquaintances. We'll meet here. Can't be more than an hour."

Porthos watched Aramis turn and head up a staircase at a fast pace. Sometimes he wondered who Aramis knew, and how. Oh, until recently Aramis's main center of information at the palace had been a Duchess, Spanish by birth, who allowed Aramis to call her Violette, and allowed him to call on her very frequently.

But Violette, once Duchesse de Dreux, was gone. What other contacts did Aramis have? To whom did he talk?

From things the musketeer didn't say, Porthos suspected that Aramis was deep in intrigues in the palace. All of Paris knew, or at least surmised, that their Majesties—not liking each other and keeping separate courts and separate favorites—the King favoring—at the whim of his grey eminence, the Cardinal—Germany, and her Majesty favoring Spain and Austria, meant that their interests and opinions, their policies and desires, were often at cross purposes. The royal palace—Porthos vaguely felt, though it was rarely given to him to be in on the secrets and convoluted calculations—was like a swiss cheese, tunneled through with myriad plots.

Porthos suspected that Aramis navigated amid all those plots and made all his plans, and knew everything there was to know. And watching Aramis's agile figure run up the staircase barely visible through the door opposite, Porthos shuddered in relief.

He would hate to be where Aramis was, to be caught in the cross threads of multiple plots, to always have to watch his mouth and what he said. He liked to blurt out the truth and nevermind what people might think.

Of course, he wasn't absolutely sure where to go in the palace, himself. He knew a lot of people here—but mostly by sight. He'd seen the servants, talked to them, flirted with the maids for all the years he'd been serving guard at the palace. And now and then a maid brought him a warm drink—or an alcoholic one—on a cold night and stayed to flirt.

These weren't friendships, as such, but they were the kind of acquaintances that would normally allow him to go along the hallways, showing the picture of the boy and asking if anyone had seen him. The easiest thing to do, the thing he'd do at any other house, would be to go to the kitchen and install himself there, with his tales of war and his charming smile to every woman who came near him. And then he'd flash the picture, and soon, between one mug of wine and the next, he'd have talked to every servant in the palace and found out all he wanted.

Even in the royal palace, that would be the best strategy. The kitchen was huge, sure. And filled with people of all descriptions going about their disparate tasks. But Porthos was well known enough, if by sight only, that he might get some attention.

Only now . . .

Standing in the hallway, he twirled his moustache. Only now, he didn't dare. The thing was that last time he'd needed to investigate the servants in the palace one of the female cooks had got very friendly with him. Very, very friendly. And she wanted to be more than friends, in fact. So much so, that Porthos had felt he could not comply with her wishes without betraying his own, longtime lover Athenais.

So if he went into the kitchens . . . The cook would be on him, in anger and lust, and he wasn't sure which he dreaded more.

In an agony of hesitation, he stood in the courtyard and twirled his moustache, trying to think of another way. There was the girlfriend of Porthos's servant, Mousqueton. Her name was Hermengarde, and she was maid on the third floor of the palace. It might be easier and ultimately quicker to have brought Mousqueton with him, but Porthos had neglected to do so. Instead, the servants had stayed behind to manage the small corpse and the coffin.

But he thought if he stood in the stairwell between the kitchen and the third floor—the back stairwell used by the servants—he would sooner or later see either Hermengarde or someone who looked likely enough to take a message to her. As far as he understood the lives of servants at the palace, most of what they did was fetch food for their lords and ladies, and sometimes filch it from the kitchen if they didn't have the seniority to get it by fair means.

In fact he got very lucky. No more had he made it to the back staircase—steep, made of stone and haunted by persistent smells of old meals that lingered like the ghosts of dinners past—than, climbing two steps, he almost bumped into a slip of a blond girl, walking down. And the blond girl, in the attire of the King's servants, looked up with a smile and said, "Monsieur Porthos. How come you are here? Is everything well with Bonif—With Mousqueton?"

Porthos pretended he didn't hear Hermengarde—for it was she—ask him about Boniface, Mousqueton's birth name, which Porthos had changed for the more bellicose one of Mousqueton. Instead, he smiled at her. "Nothing wrong with Mousqueton at all, only he's busy with a small task for me, and I came here in search of you." And, as the girl's eyes widened in alarm, he hastened to say, "Because I need some information about someone who might have been to the palace."

The girl nodded. "If you'll only wait, Monsieur Porthos. I have an elderly Countess, arrived from the provinces last week, clamoring for roast chicken and threatening all and sundry with a beating if it is not promptly fetched for her."

"Where . . ."

"Just wait here," the girl said with a flash of teeth that could be a smile or just a grimace of impatience. She squeezed past Porthos, down the farther flight of steps towards the kitchen which was at a lower level than the patio through which he'd entered.

Moments later she came back carrying a tray with a plate covered by a smaller plate, and a small cup of wine on the side. "This should do," she said smiling, as she went by him. "I had to filch it from the old devil, the chief cook." She smiled over her shoulder. "So I daresay I'll be in trouble next time, but not in as much trouble as you'd be if you crossed her path, monsieur."

"Does she still remember me?" Porthos asked, twirling his moustache nervously as he followed Hermengarde up the stairs.

"Oh, yes," Hermengarde said. She laughed a little, musical giggle. A rich smell of chicken and wine rose from her tray, and she moved as if her feet and her body, whole, were all part of a mechanism that somehow, effortlessly, kept the tray stable and the food upon it from tilting or spilling. "Oh, she remembers you." She looked over her shoulder and her animated face looked impishly happy. "You see, she really had her sights set on you. She has now been listening to palace gossip, and she heard that you're carrying on with some princess. She says if she finds out who the crowned trollop is, she shall poison her."

Porthos twirled his moustache some more and thanked all divinities that Athenais was neither a princess nor lived anywhere within the confines of the palace. "She doesn't live in the royal palace," he said.

"So Mousqueton told me. He says she is a foreign princess, and he's very sure that she'll never be in danger of the old devil. And meanwhile my friends and I shall amuse ourselves by laughing at her fits."

Porthos wondered if Mousqueton had told Hermengarde

the truth. Somehow he doubted it. After all, demeaning his master was no part of Mousqueton's self-interest. He depended on the glamour of his noble master to help him keep Hermengarde hypnotized. Unless, of course, he was so serious about Hermengarde that keeping her in thrall of him was no longer necessary and in that case—Porthos not being stupid—he knew his secret was as safe with the girl as it was with Mousqueton.

They had reached the third floor of the palace, where were normally lodged the highest members of the nobility, and where Aramis's girlfriend had lodged. Hermengarde ducked from the stairwell onto the little landing, and from it tried to open a door with her dainty slippered foot to allow herself into the hallway. Porthos reached past her, grateful for his bulk and his long reach, and held the door wide open, until she slipped past.

"Thank you, monsieur," she said. "If you'll follow me now to the door, I'll take the food in and then I'll be at your disposal to answer any questions you please."

Porthos followed her. Five doors down and they got to a small door that seemed to have been especially fitted to get into the space between two normally spaced doors. From its size and mean construction—appearing to be built from various planks of wood that someone had found lying about and nailed together with half-splintered strips of wood and bits of leather—it might have been the servants' quarters door in a mean provincial house, or else the door leading to a closet or a back hall.

Hermengarde knocked at it, and a voice within made some indistinct—but sharp—sounds. Hermengarde opened the door and went in, admirably juggling her tray. Porthos, thinking that in this case discretion was definitely the best attitude to take, waited beside the door with the same attitude of indolence and patience as he had learned to assume while on guard duty.

Hermengarde went in. From within came the clink of

the cutlery and some muted talk. Then a sharp, aged voice, not Hermengarde's said something accusatory, and Hermengarde said something apologetic. And then something hit the other side of the door. Hard.

Porthos jumped and was about to open the door when Hermengarde opened it, and came out, without her tray, with her cap disarrayed over her blond hair. She closed the door behind her and stood aside a little, arranging her hair and her cap.

"Did she throw something at you?"

Hermengarde nodded. "She did, the old witch. She threw a shoe at me." Suddenly, the grave little face broke into a smile. "Well, at least it wasn't the chicken or the wine. That would have been a waste of good food, and besides it would have made me wash my hair or my cap." She walked towards Porthos, and, grabbing his arm, pulled him down the hallway away from that door, with a finger on her lips to indicate he should be quiet.

When they got almost all the way to the landing, where it was unlikely that their voices would carry back far enough to reach the old woman in her small room, Hermengarde said, "Honestly, these provincial nobles. They come to the palace, in search of royal favor or sometimes of pensions they think are owed their relatives for some great deed of the past. Or sometimes it's money for a daughter's dowry or convent fee, or a place in the musketeers or guards for their sons. They come and they're assigned some mean room, because the King has never heard of them and has scant heard of their domain. And then they . . . stay. And they engage in petty plotting with other noblemen to overcome the plots of yet other noblemen, until they're driven so mad by their conceit and self-importance that you can never please them. She was upset at me because the chicken was only a breast and had no wing attached, if you please." She shook her head. "Boniface tells me that I'm lucky to serve in the royal palace, but I tell you, monsieur, I think he's lucky to have a decent master who respects him."

Porthos supposed that was his cue to offer her a post, but really—his life was no life for a married pair of servants. There would be the campaigns in which he and Mousqueton—for all he might wish to call himself Boniface—would go, without warning, or with very little warning. There would be the months when they ran out of money and had very little to eat, though something to drink could always be managed. It was no life for a beautiful young woman and certainly no life for the children that might follow.

And children made Porthos think of the children he'd never have and that, in turn made him think of Guillaume. He was aware of his features acquiring a grave cast.

"Monsieur, what's wrong?" Hermengarde asked, her voice gentle and almost tender.

"I . . . It's just that . . . I'm concerned . . ." He didn't know what to say, then sighed heavily. "You see, I have had an apprentice . . . er . . . someone to whom I was teaching fencing. A young man."

"Have had?"

"He . . ." Porthos considered rapidly. He could tell the girl a lie, but chances were Boniface-Mousqueton would only tell her the truth. And besides, the girl had proven trustworthy in the past. "He showed up late and very ill today, and then he . . . he died. When he died I realized I had no idea where he lived or who his parents were."

"Didn't his parents contract the lessons with you?"

"No," Porthos shook his head. "His parents didn't want him to learn to fight. They probably destined him for the church."

"Oh," she said. And then, "But then they don't know he is dead."

"No," Porthos said, and for the first time felt a pang at the thought of having to tell them. What would they think? And what feel? What could he say to ease their pain, he who wasn't a parent?

He pulled the picture from his sleeve and passed it on to

Hermengarde. "I am trying to tell them as soon as possible," he said.

She unfolded the picture and looked at it reverentially, like someone would look at a saint's relics. "Beautiful young man," she said. "But I've never seen him." Folding the picture again, she handed it to Porthos. "I would answer for his not having been anywhere near the palace," she said. "People would have noticed otherwise. Handsome boy. I can count in both hands the number of boys that age around the palace who are not already in someone's employ. Most people who come to court are older."

Porthos nodded, but pushed the picture back at her. "Can you ask around?" he said. "Just in case. I can't because of the cook. But . . . I'd truly like to know for sure."

Hermengarde looked dubious but then nodded. "Yes, I'll ask. You'll wait here?"

"No," Porthos said. "I'll wait in the courtyard by the south entrance. If you'd be so kind."

She nodded. "I will be as quick and thorough as I can. I do wish to help you in your errand of mercy. Better than the fetching and carrying I do all day."

Porthos managed a smile of encouragement and a full-hearted bow at her, hat in hand. But in his heart he felt she would find nothing.

Somewhere, Guillaume's parents were worrying over his absence and Porthos had no way of even finding out who they were. And, if perchance he did find them, he would be able to do nothing but cause them more grief.

Where Porthos is Missing;
Where Information is Missing;
Where One Thinks the Unthinkable

WHEN Athos arrived at Porthos's home, he found D'Artagnan and Aramis already there. As a worried Mousqueton led him up the stairs, and Athos emerged into the spacious room where they met at Porthos's, the other two rose from their seats at the massive table, and turned to look.

"Oh," Aramis said. "I thought . . ."

"You thought?" Athos asked.

Aramis sighed. He looked tired and drained, more so than he had looked for many a week now. Aramis normally managed to look perfectly groomed, perfectly attired and not at all affected by any situation no matter how unpleasant. It had taken Athos sometime to realize this was not because he did not, in fact, care about anything, but rather because he was in his way almost as stoic as Athos. Even if his way required perfectly manicured hands, a wealth of lace and silk and the latest in plumes for his hat.

"I thought you might be Porthos," Aramis said, and allowed himself to slump back into his chair, in a distinct un-Aramis-like slump. "Here, Bazin, fetch us some wine. I think the tavern down the street has some that might be less than vinegar." He tossed Bazin a coin that the servant plucked overhand from the air.

"You have money?" D'Artagnan asked, not accusatorial, but more curiously as a man for whom money has become one of those marvels often heard about but never seen with ones own eyes, or by anyone one knows.

Aramis looked at D'Artagnan, and shrugged a little. "I sold some theology books," he said.

Athos was amused to note a hesitation in Bazin's step, but the servant seemed to have decided against warning them on the evils of drinking holy books. To stop the risk altogether, Athos moved forward, pulled his chair and sat. "Why would you think I was Porthos?" he asked. "Where is Porthos?"

D'Artagnan shook his head and Aramis sighed.

"But you were with him," Athos said, looking at Aramis.

"And you were with D'Artagnan," Aramis said.

"D'Artagnan and I separated, so we could talk to twice as many landlords and tavern keepers," Athos said, sternly. "We didn't see any reason to meet again until we met here with whatever intelligence we gathered."

"And did you gather any?" Aramis asked.

Athos shook his head and looked at D'Artagnan who opened his hands in a silent show of helplessness.

Athos leaned forward. "And you, Aramis? You separated from Porthos, and—?"

"I separated from Porthos at the palace," Aramis said, hotly, as though he expected one of them to accuse him of snobbery. "His acquaintance and mine at the palace are different and we thought we'd get more information by going to our separate sources. We were supposed to meet in the courtyard where whoever arrived first would wait for the other."

"And he didn't meet you?" Athos asked.

Aramis shook his head. "Not only that, but as I waited there, I was overtaken by a palace maid, Hermengarde, whom I gather is a good friend of our Mousqueton."

Aramis nodded towards the servant. "She had the drawing of Guillaume with her. She said she had been asking around the palace, to all other servants and no one had seen him." The long, well-manicured finger drew a circle on the polished wood of Porthos's massive table. "Which accords with the witness from the noble ladies to whom I spoke."

"So, no one at the palace has seen him?" Athos asked.

"None," Aramis said. "We asked, as I said, between us, to most servants and most noblemen, and no one had seen the boy. No one knew, either, of a family by the name Jaucourt. And you know, even if they are the smallest of minor nobility, I don't think it's possible for them to be in Paris and be in such splendid isolation. Surely, if they came to court, they have to have met with some distant cousin, or some lost friend from their homeland. Somehow, someone at least who has some hold on the court and who knew who they are."

"I've thought of that too. I didn't find any anything among the landlords to whom I spoke, either. And surely someone would at least have heard of them, or seen them visit relatives or friends."

"Unless they are truly so isolated, or from some godforsaken province where they have no contacts with the court," D'Artagnan said. "Look at myself. When I came to Paris, my best chance of making my fortune and my name was the letter my father gave me for Monsieur de Treville with whom he'd served so many years ago." He smiled a little. "If I hadn't been foolhardy enough to arrange a duel with three of the most notorious duelists in the corps, I'd doubtless have ended up lost and forgotten in some corner of Paris."

Aramis cleared his throat, the way he did when impolite laughter arose and must be suppressed. "Three duels, D'Artagnan. You attempted to start three duels."

"But see—I only got myself known and noticed because I'd brought with me the notion that fighting early and often was my way into the musketeers and perhaps into fame and fortune."

"Yes," Athos said. "But you came alone, a single young man, seeking to make your fortune at the tip of your sword. It's not that way, is it, when one comes with children? When families come to the capital they have to come with the belief—no matter how deluded—that they know someone or that someone will help them get favor with the King. They can't afford the weeks of starving or living off chocolate or—" He allowed his gaze to slide slyly towards Aramis, who, he was sure, had been given coin by some lady of his acquaintance, and had not, in fact, sold his theology books. "Or theology books."

"So we have nothing at all on any Jaucourt family, and we do have a young boy's corpse in my cellar," Athos said. "To whom we cannot even give decent burial."

Aramis shook his head, violently, not a negation, but more as if to call attention to something else. "More importantly," he said, impatient. "Porthos is missing. He'd told the maid that he'd wait in the courtyard to hear of her investigations, but he did not. So, there must be something that called him away . . . something important."

"Did you . . ." Athos coughed and looked at Mousqueton, then back towards Aramis. "Did you go to the home of his Duchess, and ask if perhaps . . ."

"If perhaps she was hiding him under her skirt?" Aramis said. "Oh, that would have pleased her husband very much, wouldn't it? And besides, how could I?" He looked towards the window. "When he left the palace, it was early afternoon. Why and how would Porthos gain admittance to the Coq—" A sharp glance from Athos, and Aramis stopped short. "To his Duchess's palace? And how would he remain hidden there till now? He does not pass easily for a clerk. And I doubt he would fit anyone's green dress."

The last, said with feeling, and alluding to Porthos's mistress's attempts at hiding Aramis in the past, made Athos smile. To be honest, he was sure that Mousqueton knew very well that his master's lover was not a duchess.

He would even wager that Mousqueton knew who she was and where she lived. Porthos had hired Mousqueton when Mousqueton was little more than an undernourished urchin accustomed to living by his wits on the streets of Paris. Though Mousqueton now had admittedly respectable employment, he still used his wits quite well. And it didn't take great cunning to penetrate the deceptions Porthos wove. Porthos always despised deception enough to not do too good a job at it.

"Wouldn't that be the most likely place for him though?" Athos asked. "Surely they have their arrangements." He'd rather burst than share with the other two the rope ladder that he knew Athenais kept in her room and which she used to let Porthos up on occasion.

Aramis shrugged. "You always assume all of us are weak enough for any woman, that we'd be most likely to run to any woman at a time of trouble, but tell me, what rational sense does it make?"

"It makes no rational sense to me," Athos said, speaking slowly. "That any of you get involved with these women and that you give them power over your lives and over your safety."

Aramis's eyes burned with quick offense that made Athos wonder if the blond musketeer was well on his way to replacing his seamstress. With Aramis, he dared say, they'd find out only when he was ready to let them find out, unlike the young Gascon whose partiality for his landlord's wife flared in blushes, and showed itself in stammers, and whose thought was so dominated by the woman that he would bend the entire investigation around the need to see her.

"I think, Athos, that you, too, have done this in the past. You have behaved irrationally and given power over your life and your safety to women."

Athos felt the cut, but it was an old wound and one that no longer bled. One that, like old battle wounds, flared only under very precise conditions and whose dull, aching venom could be ignored the rest of the time. "I never said, Aramis, that I was a saint. Only that I saw the error of my ways and I no longer follow my animal impulses when they could endanger my life and sanity."

Aramis opened his mouth, as though to answer, but before he could speak, D'Artagnan said, "All that is very well, but granted, Athos, the rest of us are fools for women, still, where could Porthos have gone? The two of you have known him much longer than I have. What could have prompted him to forget his appointment with Aramis and to disappear?"

"A message," Aramis said, and half rose. "A message saying it came from one of us, and demanding he meet us somewhere."

"But none of us sent him a message. At least I didn't, did you D'Artagnan?" Athos asked.

"Athos, I didn't say one of us had sent it, only that someone came to Porthos and said we had. And thus . . ."

"Convinced him to go to an ambush?" Athos rose in turn.

"Sirs," Mousqueton said, speaking quietly from where he'd been, near the fireplace, engaged in disposing wood upon it, against—Athos supposed—the time when nights became cold again. A corpulent young man, he looked most of the time like a simpleton disposed to smiling too much. But his dark eyes were shrewd and as full of cunning as Aramis's green ones. "Sirs, I beg your pardon, but my master is no fool and—"

"I never said he was," Athos said coldly.

"No, sir," Mousqueton said, facing up to Athos's displeasure with more aplomb than many a nobleman would have managed. "However, you believe that he would leave his post and go in search of whoever he believed had sent him a message."

"All of us would," Athos said. "If it came from one of the other three and said they needed help urgently."

Mousqueton shook his head. "No monsieur. I hate to

disagree with you, but . . . You see, my master is a modest man." He saw Athos's cocked eyebrow and responded to it. "He's modest where it counts. Not perhaps in his attire or in the flair with which he displays his sword handling, but he is modest where it counts. He would never trust himself, by himself, to untangle whatever problem the others of you might be facing. So if that were the case, if someone had called him and told him that another of you needed rescuing, he would have gone in search of Monsieur Aramis. Or else, he would have sent someone in search of him. Hermengarde or someone else he could command."

Having kept his countenance steady and his gaze straight on Athos all through this, Mousqueton now betrayed his nervousness by wiping his broad hands to the front of his doublet—a carefully refashioned old one of Porthos's. "I hate to contradict such a noble person as yourself, Monsieur Athos, but the truth is I know my master."

The man's nervousness and his humility combined with his stuborness granted him one of Athos's rare smiles. "You might be right, Mousqueton, but granting you that you are, would you tell me, please, where your master might have gone, and what he might be doing?"

Mousqueton shrugged. "If he went of his own accord it could be anywhere, sir. He . . . He was suffering shock from the death of the boy, was he not? And when he's in shock or otherwise worried, my master is as likely as not to walk aimlessly for hours. He's done it before, monsieur, before he decided to throw his lot in with Monsieur Aramis and to become a musketeer."

"You say if he went of his own accord. You mean, you consider he might not have?"

Mousqueton shrugged. "It would take a half a dozen men. You know how my master fights, sir. But it is possible, yes. I'm not stupid, Monsieur Athos—"

"Not at all," Athos said.

"Then credit me with having heard that you are afraid

the Cardinal has something to do with this, and if he does . . . It's likely as not my master is in the Bastille, is it not?"

Just on those words, from downstairs came the sound of someone knocking hard on the door.

Devotion and Worship;
Comfort and Hunger;
Where Some Women Are Infinitely
Superior to Duchesses

PORTHOS had left the palace before he realized he was doing it. It was his absolute certainty that Hermengarde would come back with no new discoveries, with nothing—in fact—that Porthos didn't know already.

She would not know who Guillaume's parents were. Porthos tried to remember all that Guillaume had told him about his family, as he walked. Strangely, for a boy who'd said his father didn't want him to learn swordplay, he'd never mentioned his father at all. There had been no comments about something his father had done or said. Truth be told, there were no comments about his mother even. The only person the boy talked about was his sister Amelie.

Porthos remembered the name because it had tender associations for him. When he'd been a young man, younger by just a little than D'Artagnan was now, there had been a young woman named Amelie.

Porthos's father said she was a peasant with her feet in the muck, but to Porthos she'd been kind and gentle, her voice ever pleasing. And though most people in the village treated Porthos as they treated his father—as creatures to avoid at all costs and to lie to when they couldn't avoid them—Amelie had treated her giant, redheaded future lord as she would have treated a village lad her age.

In the fields, beneath the overspreading trees and behind thickets of berry-heavy bushes, Porthos had learned the first steps in the love of women. And Amelie had learned right along with him, he supposed.

It had come to a bad ending. It was bound to. Porthos's father didn't like the idea of his heir being involved with a peasant girl. If Porthos married at all, Porthos's father had told him, it would have to be later, and it had better be to a girl of some worth. Later, because first Porthos must endeavor to raise the fortunes of a miserable rural backwater of a domain that could hardly support many more generations—what with its peasants leaving, generation by generation, and going to the cities in search of fortune. And to a girl of some worth to increase the chances that Porthos's grandchildren could still support their title.

Porthos had raged and stormed and his father—just as redheaded, just as large and far more brutish, hardened by a life on the land, a life of seeing his prestige diminish—had raged. They'd clashed and fought and for a time Porthos had entertained running away with Amelie and marrying her somewhere secret. But then Amelie's father had said he'd send her to a convent and lock her away on bread and water, a penitent the rest of her life. Or, if Porthos would simply leave her alone, they would arrange a suitable marriage for her, and she would be able to go on with a normal life.

And Porthos's father had threatened to turn her family out unless Porthos left for a while and thus broke the affair off completely.

Threats to him, Porthos could withstand and laugh at. But threats to Amelie made him quake and regret his rash and foolish attachment.

He'd left for Paris before the end of October, and in Paris . . . Walking along the streets of that town, as evening spun to night and the smell of cooking and of family dinners enjoined around a thousand humble tables mingled on the street, he rubbed the bridge of his nose. In Paris, he'd found his avocation with sword—first teaching sword fighting, and then as a musketeer.

And in Paris he'd met Aramis and Athos and D'Artagnan. Few men, he knew, were so fortunate as to have such friends, brave and capable and as close to him as his own hand or his own arm. But . . .

But he wondered what would have happened if his father had let him marry Amelie. They would be poor as church mice, doubtless. One of those families with little more to pride themselves upon than the noble ancestors of at least one of them. And heaven knew, even his ancestors weren't that noble.

They would have gone without food as often as he went without food now. And doubtless, many a time he would have had to work the fields alongside his peasant farmers, clearing land and seeding it. Doubtless his children would be little more than farmers. His children . . .

He bit at his tongue hard to stop that train of thought, which brought with it a thought of Guillaume and of the parents who would, even now, be worrying about him, the parents to whom Porthos could bring nothing but bad news.

Shaking his head, he realized he'd walked across half the town and that he was now in a neighborhood that was very familiar to him. It was a bourgeois neighborhood of houses that stood shoulder to shoulder, their closed facades keeping behind them the private lives of the residents and their private economies and presenting nothing but solidity to the world.

Up that street and down another, he would come to the garden of Monsieur Coquenard, accountant. And behind the house, the third window on the left was Athenais. A carefully aimed shower of pebbles upon her shutter would bring down the rope ladder through which Porthos could ascend to the closest thing to heaven he was likely to know in his life.

Only . . . It was too early for that. It was afternoon and everyone would see him.

But his need drove him. It was, like most things that caused him to act and act quickly, something he could neither think clearly through nor even attempt to put into words. Just a feeling. A feeling that Athenais would know what to do. She would make sense of this all. He must go to Athenais.

Because going into her garden and throwing pebbles at her window was out of the question, instead, he went into the alley at the back of her house. He had some vague idea of waiting there for hours, till darkness fell, till the movement in the house stopped, but when a girl came out, headed for the alley, he recognized her as Athenais's maid, who had seen enough of their meeting in public and private that, if she didn't know they were lovers she was a worse fool than Porthos was willing to credit.

When the girl saw him, she widened her eyes. Of course, even if he was known, meeting a musketeer in an isolated alley would be alarming for any woman.

Porthos hastened to remove his hat, hold it to his chest and bow.

"Mademoiselle," he said. "Mademoiselle. I'm sorry to surprise you like this. I meant you no harm."

The girl smiled and batted her eyelashes at him. She put her hand to her relatively inconsequential bosom with more theatrics than real alarm. "Oh, Monsieur Porthos," she said. "You scared me."

He bowed again, deeper. "Pardon me, mademoiselle, only . . . I wanted to know if you could take a message of mine to your mistress."

"My . . . mistress?"

"Madame Coquenard," Porthos said. Just last week he'd visited and this chit of a girl had seen him. Granted, he'd visited via the rope ladder and his time with Athenais had been scant. Still, he didn't think anything could have happened to

Athenais in a week. At least nothing he would not have heard about.

The maid shook her head. "Oh, the mistress isn't here," she said, making Porthos feel as though his heart had just dropped out of his chest and to the muddy ground of the alley.

"Where is she?" Oh, let her not have gone to her parents, who were minor nobility somewhere in the wretched countryside.

"At church," the girl said. "Only, they had a Mass for a friend of Monsieur Coquenard's that died last week, and she has gone to attend."

"Oh," Porthos said, and hesitated for a moment, not sure how to ask which church.

"St. Magdalene's," the girl said. "Just down that way and up the street."

Porthos followed it before he thought what he was going to do. After all, what could a man do in those circumstances? It wasn't as though he could barge into the church and there, in the incense-scented decorum of saints and sermons, pull Athenais away for a cozy little chat on murder and the horrors of the lonely life of a musketeer who'd never have children, could he?

When he got to the church, it was worse than he'd thought. For one, it was packed. And packed with the sort of upper-middle-class people who prized themselves on dressing well but in as dull a manner as possible. His musketeer's uniform, his plumed hat clutched in a sweaty hand, all called attention to him. The gold trim on his coat and hat was matched only by the gold decor of the church and the deep blue velvet of his clothing echoed only in the deep blue of a cloak on the statue of the virgin, in its wall niche to the right of him. All the rest of the church, all of it, was thronged with people in black and brown or somber and boring grey.

He looked at that massed dullness, trying to see his

Athenais, trying to spy her reddish gold hair—to speak the truth fast going white—amid the many people in the room. But he couldn't see any woman's hair. All of them were swathed in cunning hats and veils.

And the air was thick with incense, and the priest, standing at the podium and speaking, had a rolling, thunderous voice as he spoke of carnal sins and of the death that waited even the most proud man, the most beautiful woman.

Porthos sweated and prayed. His relationship with God was very simple. He asked only that God take care of those things that Porthos could not take care of for himself. Oh, Porthos would try to get food for himself. And Porthos would fight valiantly against those who were his foes, or simply against those who were willing to fight when he was bored. And he didn't seek God's help against what he considered the greatest evils in his world—the lack of good wine, and uppity guards of the Cardinal hell bent on enforcing the edicts against dueling.

In return, he asked only that God play fair with him and be a gentleman—that God not allow him to get killed by accident when he was fighting as well as he could, that God not strike him or his friends with some shameful debilitating disease, and that God not take in account Athenais's wedding vows, for what did they mean? Athenais had been as good as sold off by her father, a penniless nobleman who'd betrothed her to a wealthy accountant in return for having his own debts forgiven. And the accountant was seventy when Athenais had married him, and who could expect him to live another ten years as he had already, preserved in venom and vinegar.

And if Athenais's marriage had been consummated, well it had been long ago, and it had been done in a way that neither formed her expectations nor marred them. It was left to Porthos to show her the pleasure that could be obtained between a man and a woman. And her heart was as truly knit to his and his to hers as if they'd been married.

And it was no one's business at all, and Monsieur Coquenard's least of all.

The preaching of the priest made him nervous nonetheless. It twined with Guillaume's death and with his own feelings that his life had taken a wrong turn somewhere, and left him bereft and wondering if he was indeed in the hands of a vengeful God.

He was still sweating and praying, when a lady's voice said, from nearby, "Monsieur? Could you move? I cannot reach the holy water with you standing there."

Porthos recognized the voice as Athenais's and opened the eyes he'd closed to pray, to see her standing near him, in a very fetching brown dress, matched with a sort of brown veil which made her look paler and younger.

Immediately, with a feeling like his prayer had been answered and his faith in the gentleman renewed, he dipped his huge paw in the fountain, and brought out a handful of water, into which Athenais dipped her fingers, crossing herself. She left, with two attendants following her. One of her husband's clerks and a maid. Porthos waited a few breaths, and crossed himself in turn, before going out, amid a throng of people leaving the church.

Outside, on the covered portico of the imposing building, Athenais was speaking sharply to her attendants.

"But Madame Coquenard," the young and pimply clerk was saying, "the carriage is waiting. With the horses. You cannot mean to walk home."

"No," Athenais answered, imperious. "Not that it would be any concern of yours if I did, but I just recalled that my friend, Armandine, is ill and she lives just a few doors down. I will go and see if I can help her in any way. And then I will ask her husband to have a carriage take me home."

"But madam," the clerk said. "Why can't we wait?"

"Because I have asked you not to wait," Athenais said. "I don't want Armandine to feel that she has exposed my people to inconvenience or that I have gone to great trouble to visit her. Go home, boy. You too Catherine."

"But, Monsieur Coquenard—" the young man said.

"Is my business and not yours. My husband knows of my works of mercy. He has yet to object to them."

Finally the two attendants left. Athenais turned and walked slowly down the steps, and then started down the street. Porthos waited to see the Coquenard carriage—unmarked and probably bought used, or else received in security for a debt—drive by, with the two befuddled attendants riding in front with the driver. And then he waited a little longer before taking off in pursuit of Athenais.

With his long stride, he caught up with her shortly enough, just as Athenais took a sudden turn into an alley. He went after her and, a little while in, in the darkness of evening, he caught up with her, clutched at her arm. "Athenais," he said.

"Shh," she said, without turning. "Just a little while farther on, Porthos."

A little while farther on turned out to be five minutes of hard walking, after which Athenais stopped at the door of what looked like a very small, modest house. Fishing in her sleeve, she brought out a key, and opened the door. She went in and closed it, but not all the way.

Porthos followed. Inside it was a one-room dwelling, of the sort that most working men in Paris lived in, save that this one was freestanding and not a part of a larger room. Like many such dwellings—such as the one in which D'Artagnan lived—it was let furnished and therefore it contained a small wooden table and two chairs, and a bed with a thin mattress and a blanket. There was no fire in the hearth and the place smelled cold and unused, if also very clean.

Athenais turned, and removed her wrap. By the abated light of day coming through the single window which looked onto what seemed to be a small, walled garden, she appeared very beautiful and far younger than Porthos knew her to be. He felt as if he were looking at Athenais as she'd been when she'd married Monsieur Coquenard—seventeen-year-old Athenais, devoid of artifice or fear.

"Athenais," he said, as he flung the door shut, and pushed the bolt to close it. He advanced towards her, and crushed her in his arms, feeling her blessedly warm and alive in his. He lowered his mouth to hers and kissed her, his hunger for her body augmented by his feeling that he was living a life that was no life and that he needed . . . something he couldn't even name. Warmth or nourishment or life itself.

They were carried on the wave of his hunger, Athenais letting him do as he pleased, until the wave crested and ebbed, and they found themselves on the thin mattress, almost naked—he was wearing only his shirt and she a sort of petticoat for which he didn't know the proper name—and sated, in each other's arms.

It was then that the little house and its furnishings bothered him. "Athenais," he said. "Whose home is this?"

She sat up so slowly that she didn't break his hold on her and started, composedly, as though this were the most logical thing to do, to comb through her disarrayed hair. She removed the pins, then rebraided her hair. Holding the hair pins in her mouth, she spoke nonetheless clearly enough. "Mine," she said. And then. "Or Monsieur Coquenard's. We acquired it in a deal some time ago, and it's been leased, but the occupant moved out. I had the key with me, as I meant to inspect it before leasing it again. I didn't mean to come here today, but I'd put the key in my sleeve-pouch and meant to come here maybe tomorrow. When I saw you in church, it seemed . . . providential."

"Um . . ." he said, and leaned forward to kiss the neck she'd bared in pulling her hair up to braid.

She giggled at being tickled with his beard. "I'll never get my hair braided properly this way," she said. "And the servants will wonder how I got so disarrayed in looking after Armandine."

"Is your friend truly ill?" Porthos asked.

"She gave birth this week," Athenais said, her hands moving very rapidly and braiding her hair by touch more accurately than many a woman could do it in front of a mirror. "A boy."

"Athenais . . ." Porthos said.

Athenais turned, concerned. One of the things that Porthos liked about her was that even when he couldn't put what he felt, or what was bothering him, into words, she nonetheless seemed to catch the edge of his worry, the crux of his sadness. She turned to look at him, and she let go of her hair, as her gaze softened. She took the pins out of her mouth and kissed him, a quick, concerned peck on the cheek. "Porthos, we can't. You know we can't. How would I explain it to my husband? He no longer can . . ."

Porthos shook his head. "I know," he said. "But I wish we could. I wish we could get ourselves . . . well . . ." He shook his head again, as if to clear it, but the images only came rushing into it more—the images of a life that could never be his. "I wish we could have our own home," he said. "Even if it were as modest as this. And two boys and three girls." He thought about it a minute. "No, too many girls. What would we do with them all? How would we find them all dowries. Four boys and a girl."

Athenais giggled. "I see you've given the matter a great deal of thought," she said, her eyes wishful and grave. "Pray tell, why must we have girls at all?"

"Well," Porthos said. He chewed on his lip with concentration. Right then that imaginary family seemed the most important thing in his world, and it blocked out his thoughts of the dead boy. "I want at least one daughter who will be as beautiful as her mother."

"Oh, Porthos," she said, in the soft tone women use when they don't believe a compliment, and yet know that the speaker means it. Her hair, which she'd never pinned, had flowed free of the braid and now covered her shoulders in red gold waves.

With the petticoat, which was a skirt only, leaving her top completely bare, the lose waves of her hair looked like the veil of a saint. No. Not a saint. A pagan goddess. No saint would go about bare breasted. "Not unless there were swords in it."

Athenais blinked. "Swords?"

"On the saints' breasts," Porthos said. "It's the only time bare breasts are allowed in church."

This brought a peal of throaty laughter from Athenais. She grabbed his hand and forced him to open it, palm up, and put her hair pins in it, while she started braiding her hair again.

"Madam, do I look like your vanity, or your maid?"

"You look like a man with great big hands, who can hold my hair pins," she said, and helped herself to a hair pin to hold her hair in place.

Porthos sighed. Athenais looked over her shoulder. "What is wrong? None of this is like you—coming to see me before dinner time, nor being so oddly sad and concerned."

Porthos sighed again. "It's the boy," he said.

"A boy?" Athenais looked genuinely surprised, then nodded, as if she'd finally understood. "The Gascon?"

"No, no. A real boy. Twelve. He approached me, months ago, and . . . he knew my true name, Athenais! And he asked me to teach him sword fighting."

"And you," she said. "Very promptly thrashed him for thinking you were a proscribed nobleman and then refused to have anything else to do with him."

"Athenais!"

"No. Of course not." She looked as if she were about to say something else, but had stopped herself in time. "You gave in to his blackmail."

"It wasn't blackmail, Athenais. He was just a boy. Twelve. A stripling. And what he wanted was to learn sword fighting. What did I lose by teaching him? And he was good too."

Athenais sighed. She retrieved the last hairpin from his hand, and put it in her hair, and rose. "Was good? *Was?* Porthos . . . what happened?"

It all came spilling out, simple descriptions of what happened because Porthos had never learned the knack of embellishing a story and so told things sequentially, as they'd occurred. When he talked about his genealogy in the boy's pocket, Athenais had been reaching for her dress. She let her hand fall. "It was blackmail, Porthos."

"Why? Why would it be blackmail?" Porthos asked. "I'd already given in to what he wanted, which was to teach him to fight. Why else would he have my genealogy in his pocket? What could he make me do with it?" Porthos shrugged. He'd told Athenais about the genealogy and about what it revealed. "You see, I know my family is not as noble as yours, but—"

Athenais laughed. "Porthos. My father married me to an attorney of no nobility at all. As his third wife. Porthos. Don't speak of genealogy and papers and traditions."

"Yes," Porthos said. "But the thing is that I never cared. There's Athos, noble as Scipio, and he doesn't care if my ancestors were merchants, does he? He's as much my friend as he's Aramis's."

Athenais had thrown her dress over her head and now looked firmly trapped by it. Porthos knew that she normally had a maid or two to help her dress. He hastened to fulfill the role of the maid, and she let him lace the dress up her back. He'd never done this job, but he'd done its reverse often enough. He told her how they'd looked in the palace and Athos and D'Artagnan were canvassing the neighborhoods for someone who might know the boy's family. "Only, no one ever heard of Jaucourt as a family name and, Athenais, what if we don't find them? What if they're in agony looking for their boy, and he's lying dead, and they'll never know it? And what if I find them and I have nothing but this dismal news to give them?"

Athenais was grave. She turned around and looked seriously at Porthos. "He told you he was noble," she said. "And that his family name was Jaucourt?"

Porthos nodded.

Athenais pursed her lips together and looked at him, with that expression she had that made him feel like he was a small child under the serious scrutiny of a stern governess.

She turned away from him and reached for her veil on the table and picked it up, then put it down again. "Porthos, have none of your friends considered . . ."

"Oh," Porthos aid. "Aramis thought the boy might have been sent to me as a ploy of the Cardinal's, that the papers in his purse, and his having been killed might all be part of a ploy to get me taken for murder."

Athenais turned around. She looked more serious than ever. "Yes, all that might be true, and more besides, but has none of you considered that he might have given you a false name?"

"A false name?" Porthos said. "Oh, yes, we considered it. That is why Aramis made drawings, when we went to ask for him, in case he had a different name."

"But you're looking for him in the palace?" Athenais said. "And where noblemen lodge? It has not occurred to you, my dear, that he might not be a nobleman at all? Just a street urchin the Cardinal employed in this? Or someone did?"

"But he . . ." It had never occurred to Porthos. And now it did, he felt cold and lost. Curse it all. If Guillaume wasn't even a nobleman, then it meant he could be anyone at all in Paris. How were they to find his family. "But he behaved as a young gentleman," he said.

Athenais nodded. "Manners are a thing anyone can pick up with just a little observation."

"But . . . Athenais! How am I to find who he is, then?"

Athenais tilted her head a little. "I would go near where you found him. And start looking there."

"Near where I found him . . ." Porthos said.

Athenais wrapped her veil around her head. "And now if you'd escort me to Armandine's home, so I don't have to brave the streets of Paris alone, I'll make up something to account for my delay. That I was moved to go back and pray, perhaps."

As she locked the door behind them, and he waited beside it, she said, "You know, I could hide the fact that this house hasn't been let. I could hide it in the accounts. My husband would never know. And we could have it."

"Why?" Porthos asked. "We have the rope ladder."

"And every servant waiting for the bed to creak. This could be ours, just ours."

He nodded saying nothing. He wished it was really theirs and their true home. Aloud, he said, "I found the boy lying against the back wall of a tavern."

"Then that's where I would look first," she said. "That tavern and the immediate neighborhood."

News at Last;
The Strange Knowledge of Porthos's Mind;
Suits and Genealogy

D'ARTAGNAN stood up at the sound of running steps on the stairs. In his mind, he formed a picture where some intruder had pushed past Mousqueton and was now rushing up the stairs to do them who knew what mischief.

He noticed that Athos and Aramis had put their hands on their swords, and he, in turn, let his hand drift towards his. Only then did he think that he'd not heard anything from Mousqueton who'd gone down the stairs to open the door on the pounding.

And there was only one person that Mousqueton would let climb the stairs without at least making some remark . . . He thought this, just as Porthos, red hair in disarray, face almost as red from running as his hair, climbed the last step and emerged onto the broad room.

"I've found—" he said, and stopped, breathing hard, and bending over, hands on knees, as he recovered his breath.

"What?" Athos asked.

"Have you found the murderer?"

"Have you found the boy's family?" D'Artagnan asked, while he thought that Porthos, who rarely breathed hard after duels, must have run all the way to tell them this.

Porthos looked at D'Artagnan and nodded, as he straightened. "I found where the boy came from. Not his family." He frowned. "At least I don't think so. I didn't go in and ask. But I found where he . . . lived. And worked."

"Worked?" Aramis asked. He stood frozen, as he had risen from the table, his hand now fallen beside his sword and he looked shocked at the thought that the boy might have worked.

"We were all fools, you know?" Porthos said. "I thought we were missing something, but it never occurred to me what it might be till I spoke to Athenais."

"Athenais!" Aramis said.

And along Athos's lips, a smile slid, as if wordlessly affirming he'd been right after all.

Porthos looked at Aramis and frowned. "Of course, Athenais. Where else would I have gone like that, without warning?"

"I didn't know where you had gone," Aramis said. "And I half suspected you might have been killed or kidnapped, or . . . somehow tricked into leaving the palace. You told me you'd wait for me in the courtyard."

Porthos's face fell. He looked remorseful and also upset at himself. He slapped his own forehead with some force. "Indeed I did, Aramis. I'm sorry. Did I worry you?"

"I knew you were too evil to die that easily," Aramis said, and looked intently at his nails, as if examining them for imperfections. As if Porthos's disappearance had left him quite unmoved.

Porthos smiled, not at all taken in, then frowned, in obvious contrition. "I'm sorry. I really didn't mean to wander away. I didn't realize I'd done it until I was almost at Athenais's home, and then it seemed a little silly to go back. I didn't even know why I was doing it, you know, except, as Hermengarde—your excellent Hermengarde, Mousqueton—" He nodded to his servant who smiled. "As she was going about the rounds of making sure no one in the palace had heard of the boy or seen him, all I could think of was that she wouldn't find anything. I just had a feeling. And such feelings in me usually mean my mind knows something I don't know."

"Your mind cannot know something you don't know," Aramis said, giving up the examination of his nails. He sounded irritated, which—D'Artagnan thought—was the way Aramis normally sounded around Porthos. "Your mind is yourself."

Porthos shook his head. "No, Aramis," he said. "*Your* mind is *yourself*. My mind . . . Well . . . Sometimes I think I do half my thinking with my elbows or perhaps my toenails. And they don't always talk to my mind, you see?"

"Nonsense. No one can think except with their mind and—"

"Well, Aramis," Porthos said. "Sometimes I know things my mind can't put into words. And sometimes I'm not even sure what I know until I have talked it over with someone."

"So you went to speak to Athenais," D'Artagnan said.

"Yes."

"And what did the incomparable Athenais reveal?" Athos asked.

Porthos turned towards Athos quickly, as if suspicious of irony in the older musketeer's tone, but on looking at Athos, and, apparently, finding only honest curiosity in his gaze, he sighed and shook his head. "The incomparable— and she is that, Athos—" he said, as Athos nodded, "Athenais told me that we'd been overlooking a very important chance that the boy might have lied to us."

"Nonsense," Aramis said. "You're losing your wits. I told you from the beginning that it was possible he was lying to us. That was why I thought I should do a drawing of him. So that we were not dependant on the name Guillaume Jaucourt to find him. I thought there was a good chance the name was false."

"Yes, but none of us thought of looking beyond the name," Porthos said.

"What do you mean?" Aramis asked. "You speak in riddles."

"It is plain."

"I don't see how," Athos said.

"Really, Porthos," D'Artagnan said, trying to sound more reasonable than his two aggrieved and older friends. "You've told us nothing except that we should look beyond the name. In what way do you mean?"

"Well," Porthos said. "What else could be false?"

"I knew it," Aramis said. "He was a plant by the Cardinal."

"No," Porthos said. "Or at least . . . I don't know so yet. But he was not what he said he was. Athenais said that any plebeian boy can learn to act noble with a little wit and a little practice. And that started me thinking . . . And she said I should go and ask near where I found him. Just ask people in the neighborhood. That they were more likely to give me an answer than anyone else was."

"So, what was the boy's real name?" Aramis asked.

Porthos shrugged. "Guillaume. Just . . . Guillaume. No one seems to know a family name for him. He doesn't seem to have a family. He lived with his sister in the tavern down the street, the tavern against whose wall he was leaning. The Hangman. We rarely go there because—"

"The wine is overpriced," Athos said.

"And the proprietress could glare a hole in a stone wall," Aramis said.

Porthos nodded. "That. And that's why we failed to know the boy. Apparently he and his sister help at the tavern. Fetching and carrying and picking up things . . . you know, as young people do."

"So he was in fact a street urchin," Aramis said.

Porthos shrugged. "Something like it, though the tavern keeper seemed to give them a place in his stables to sleep and at least some food." He frowned. "Everyone seemed to think they worked too hard, everyone told me how hard they worked." He looked disturbed by the thought.

D'Artagnan nodded. Of course, work was the normal state of childhood. In his own father's domain, the farmer's children started helping in the fields as soon as they could. And he, himself, though it couldn't be called exactly working, had been taught to hunt as early as he could be trusted to sit astride a horse and hold a bow. And in a way, that was a nobleman's work. At least the part of it that involved keeping beasts from the fields his peasants tended. And he knew girls learned to cook and tend house from the moment they learned to walk.

He'd grown up with all that and it seemed to him quite normal, but it wasn't till he'd come to Paris that he'd seen true work among children. Children who rose early and worked all day and were only allowed a respite from the work late at night and for a few hours, till dawn brought another round of work.

He saw them everywhere, stoking the fires at forges and holding horses for people, and running errands for various masters through the streets of town. He saw them, seemingly, always working. Never resting. And all of them had a hungry, restless look. But hungry most of all.

He'd heard from Porthos that Mousqueton had been one of those children—a skinny street brat, driven by hunger to try to steal from the then fencing master. Looking at the large young man it was hard to believe. And Mousqueton himself had told him a confused story of being left orphaned so young he didn't remember his parents, only fending for himself on the streets of Paris.

This urban poverty and the children who endured it seemed to D'Artagnan far more wretched creatures than his working, but contented neighbors in Gascony. At least most children there lived with relatives. And at the peak of winter, when nothing grew, they got to sit by the fire with their parents and while away the dark days in peace.

Coming out of his thoughts, he realized that the others were well away into discussing something.

"So, we'll go to the tavern," Porthos said. "And ask."

"It's not that easy, and you know it," Aramis said. "If it were that easy, you'd have braved it yourself, going into the tavern and asking questions on your own. But it is not. We can't walk in and start asking about the boy without their suspecting that there is something wrong and some reason for strangers to ask."

"We'll say that some stranger asked us to look," Porthos said. "We can hint it was the boy's father without saying it."

"What if they know who the boy's father is?" Athos asked.

"Unlikely," Porthos said. "Boys who work like that, at that young an age . . ." He shrugged. "If he had a living father, somewhere, he'd have gone to his father, or given him the money. There would have been some . . . presence of his father in his life."

"He might have run away from the provinces to come to the city," Aramis said. "His parents might still be there, somewhere, in the country."

"Indeed," Porthos said. "But if so, it is unlikely the tavern keeper will know of it. And if he ran away bringing his sister with him, then surely there was some great reason to run away. Which means that he would not have told the tavern keeper of his parents."

"True," Aramis said. "First of all we must use tact in asking."

"And that," Porthos said, "is why I didn't go in on my own. I thought I'd need tact, and immediately thought of the three of you."

Sometimes, D'Artagnan thought, it wasn't easy to tell if Porthos was being serious or ironic. But he guessed at serious, in this case, because Porthos seemed genuinely pleased at the thought of his friends coming with him to the tavern and helping him ask questions.

"There's only one thing," Athos said. "We can't quite eliminate the chance that the Cardinal is involved in this."

"But if the boy is a simple tavern boy," Aramis said. "Surely—"

"There's nothing sure in this," Athos said. "Yes, he's just a plebeian boy, but how many times has the Cardinal not reached into the lowliest ranks to get his spies, his agents, his enforcers? Granted, Rochefort is as noble as I am, if perhaps poorer. But there are others . . ."

They all nodded. They'd run into others. Grocers and prostitutes, beggars and wine sellers who, surprised by the condescension of the Cardinal in even speaking to them, were more than willing to do the great man's bidding. It could almost be bet that the lower the origin of the recruit, the more slavishly he'd do everything that the Cardinal asked.

"But . . ." Athos said. "Whether the Cardinal's or someone else's, the truth is that he must have been in someone's pay."

"Why?" Porthos asked, frowning.

"Two things. If he were not, there is no possibility he could have—on his own—afforded such a nice suit as the one he had on. And neither would there be any reason for him to have a list of your ancestry in his pocket."

"Right," Porthos said. And frowned. "At least no reason we know."

"If you're going to tell me again that your mind knows things you don't know . . ." Aramis said.

Porthos shrugged. "Not anything that defined, no. It's just that . . . well . . . there might be more complex reasons than we know now." He frowned. "Or at least . . . We usually end up finding that there are, don't we?"

As he spoke, he turned and started down the stairs, followed by Athos and Aramis. D'Artagnan followed, thinking that Porthos was right about that. Around the four of them, particularly when murder was involved, things were usually stranger than they seemed to be at first.

The Hangman; Another Nobleman;
A Young and Quiet Girl

As soon as they entered the Hangman—its name represented by a leaping man holding a noose and looking almost maniacally inclined to mirth—Athos knew why they didn't frequent it much. It wasn't so much that the wine was overpriced. It was more like the whole tavern was out of the musketeers league.

While the Cardinal, in a fit of passion, had been known to declare that no drinking spot or bawdy house in town was free of the scourge of the drunken, brawling, whoring musketeers, he was in fact wrong. The more expensive bawdy houses were very free of them, as were the more expensive taverns, like the Hangman, with its clean tables, its well-scrubbed walls, the candles that burned wax and not some smoky mixture of tallow, and its sour-faced proprietress behind the bar, looking menacingly at the four men with their uniforms and swords, as they came in.

A jovial fat man—possibly her husband—scrubbing one of the nearest tables, looked up at them as they entered, too, and his face did a quick succession of expressions, from surprised to worried to frantically jovial, the last the expression of a man who does not wish to see a brawl start in his tavern. "Sirs," he said, looking up. "Glad to see you. Find yourself a place to sit. Amelie!" This called over his shoulder towards the shadows and definitely not in the tone he would dare address his imposing wife. "Amelie, where have you got to, girl?"

A girl of about ten, stick thin, with dark eyes and lank brown hair came out of the shadows. She was attired in a clean, probably third- or fourthhand dress and other than her thinness could have been the couple's daughter. But Athos doubted very much that any child of the couple would have been allowed to grow so thin. Also, the woman behind the bar looked on the girl as though she were something that had crawled from beneath a rock, and moved her lips as though muttering something under her breath.

The musketeers and D'Artagnan sat at the nearest unoccupied table, and the girl approached, hesitantly. Athos's phobia towards women did not apply yet at this age, when girls were more children than anything else. He felt towards the girl as he felt towards boy children the same age—as he would view something young and in distress. A vague feeling that he should protect her crept over him, and his voice was kinder than it would be to any adult as he said, "Hello, Amelie."

He fumbled in his almost empty purse—it was getting so tallow candles would soon look good for dinner—and brought out a coin, which he tossed in the middle of the table and to which Aramis, silently, added two more. "Get us what wine those will buy, would you? A mug for each of us."

The girl bowed and scrambled towards the bar and the woman behind it. Soon they could hear her whisper and hear the woman answer in harsh tones.

Athos ignored the exchange. No matter how tempted, it was neither possible nor desirable for him to save every stray waif in Paris. For one, there was a good chance he'd end up killed if he tried. And for another, his duty was somewhat more immediate. He'd sworn to serve king and country. And, in this particular case, he'd sworn to defend Monsieur de Treville, and to find out who'd killed this boy so that the boy's death could not be used in a plot against the musketeers. Then there was his loyalty to his friends, and to Porthos, most of all, who was suffering from shock and grief at the death of the boy he'd considered some sort of apprentice.

"*Holá*, host," Athos said, towards the tavern keeper.

The round-cheeked man looked up from the table which, to own the truth, he seemed to be only pretending to polish while he kept an eye on the four newcomers.

"Yes, Monsieur Musketeer?" he said, looking up, his hand still on the rag with which he'd been polishing the already gleaming table with some sort of oil he kept in a clear bottle by his side.

"Could you come here for a moment," Athos asked, giving his whole countenance, his whole speech that tone of command that he knew other people resented but obeyed in equal measures. Porthos called it putting on his noble airs, and Aramis looked on enviously, whenever Athos did this, as though he wished he, too, could command people by assuming a natural superiority of look and manner. D'Artagnan merely watched, which was perhaps the boy's greatest quality.

The tavern keeper hesitated and glanced towards his wife. But as his wife was very busy setting cups of wine on a broad tray, he shrugged and approached them.

"How may I help you?" he asked.

"You may tell us if you know this boy," Athos said and pulled, from his sleeve, the picture of Guillaume as drawn by Aramis.

There was recognition in the man's eyes, as soon as they fell upon the drawing. Then there was a frowning, momentary look, as though the man were considering whether he could lie and have his lie believed. He looked up and, in Athos's dark blue eyes must have read the certainty that his first expression had been detected.

The man scrunched the rag he still held in his right hand, and frowned, then sighed. "It's Guillaume," he said.

"Guillaume who?" Porthos asked.

The man looked at him and opened his mouth, then

closed it again. He shrugged. "Just Guillaume, sir. He was born in our stables and I guess he grew up here. I never heard of his having a family name."

"His . . . mother's, perhaps?" Athos asked.

The man shrugged. "His mother was a . . ." He looked at Amelie who approached with a tray laden with mugs. She sagged under the burden which was clearly too heavy for her. The tavern keeper's eyes softened, and he looked back at the table. "His mother arrived here with child. She came, she said, to find her fiancé. She never found him. She stayed and helped serve." He shrugged. "Amelie was born a few years later, and then a few more years later, Pigeon— as the clients called her—their mother, died of a fever. We let the boy and the girl stay in the stable, but other than that, know nothing about them." While Amelie put the mugs of wine on the table, the man gave Athos as clear and untroubled a glance as ever man bent upon customer. "Has the boy done anything that has got him in trouble?"

"No," Athos said, and that much was true, since Guillaume could now be said to be past all trouble or at least all trouble a mortal body could find. He thought fast. If he claimed he knew the boy's father he was only likely to excite the curiosity and perhaps the venality of the tavern keeper. Easier, much easier to claim the boy had been trying to find better employment. "It's only," he said, "that the boy talked to my servant Grimaud, some time ago. It seems he was interested in being a fighting man's servant himself. At the time I didn't know anyone looking for a servant and I didn't have enough employment for him, myself. But since then I've heard of a young musketeer who comes from a house with some . . . some substance behind it. He has a servant already, but wants someone to look after his horses, and I thought perhaps . . ." Athos rallied. Since the man didn't know the boy was dead and didn't seem to be concerned about him, there was little point in telling him of the event. Easier, much easier, to find out something about the boy's life from this man and maybe from that deduce the killer. Easier to find if the boy might have been in the employ of someone else—like the Cardinal. "Is he about?" Athos asked, and saw a flinch from Porthos who sat catercorner from him on the table and for just a moment feared that Porthos would remind him the boy was dead.

But Porthos, strangely and unaccountably, seemed all concentrated on what the girl, Amelie was doing, walking back with the tray, setting it on the bar. This was unfathomable since Porthos didn't usually even notice children much. He probably hadn't paid any attention to a child since the time he'd adopted Boniface under the guise of hiring him, and made him into the more bellicose-sounding Mousqueton, and the day that Guillaume had asked for instruction in the plying of a sword.

But perhaps Guillaume had made Porthos think about all children. Now and then, in the privacy of his own thoughts, Athos, who had left thirty behind, thought of an heir—someone who would inherit his domain and his title after his death. Unfortunately to beget an heir he'd need a woman. And Athos's experience of women had neither qualified him to trust them nor to trust himself.

Athos looked back at the tavern keeper, who was looking at Porthos, also, with some concern. He now transferred his glance to Athos, "No, sir. I haven't seen the scapegrace in some days . . ." He shrugged. "The thing is, you see, that he's been talking for some time now about leaving my employ and finding himself a patron who is wealthier and better able to look after him. He's not stupid, Guillaume. Cheeky, undisciplined and often infuriating, but not stupid." He smiled a smile that made him seem more human. "He taught himself to read and write when he was very young, begging one letter of a customer, another off another. People taught him because he had winning ways. And so, he knows how to read and how to write, and he's got ideas in his head . . . I don't know what he means to do at any time."

"Is it normal for you not to see him for days?" Athos asked.

The man shrugged. His unconcerned face seemed to show absence of guilt. "Oh, he's been gone, now and then, for two or three days. Never more than that because, you see, he's not really a bad boy and he cares for his sister, and comes back to see her. Amelie, she's good and she's always here and always helpful. But Guillaume . . ." He shrugged again. "Young boys will be young boys. In my own day, I used to dream . . ." For a moment his eyes unfocused, as though he were looking back at a lost time. "I used to dream many things. But the thing is . . . He's not a fool, and he will look around till he finds something that suits him. He worked for a nobleman for a short time, but he didn't like it, and they thrashed him, so he came back here and ran errands for me awhile longer."

"A nobleman?" Athos asked. "Would you happen to know his name?"

"I don't rightly remember. Why?"

"Because I'd like to know if perhaps the boy has already found employment with this nobleman, in which case my searching for him is in vain."

"No, no," the tavern master said. "He didn't find employment with the man. He left him. Something about the man giving him a thrashing."

"And yet," Athos said, making his face as impassive as possible. He was vaguely aware that somewhere near the bar the woman was muttering at the young girl. "And yet, I think these things are sometimes not as clear as they seem. Young boys, particularly, get angry at a master for an unkind word and leave as though this were the end of the world . . . only to come back later and make it up and seek employment again."

The tavern keeper sighed. "It is possible," he said, but in the tone of a man who concedes a point so as to avoid an argument more than because it's true.

He looked as though he were thinking things through

and Athos would have bet what he was thinking was that it wouldn't do any harm at all to send the men to the noble-man. At the worst, it would be a wild goose chase, and it would get them out of his hair.

Because Athos was sure the man didn't know the boy was dead—either that or he was the world's best actor—he would be thinking if he could forestall the whole thing a while Guillaume would show up and take care of his own business.

"Amelie," the tavern keeper called. "Amelie, if you would please . . ."

Both woman and girl looked up. The girl was crying. There were marks of tears on her cheeks. The woman was lowering a hand that had been raised either for a slap or for another slap. She pushed the girl rudely, in the middle of her back. Her lips moved. She whispered, but it was clear she was saying "Go then."

None of the men around the tavern seemed in the least concerned with this scene and Athos, himself, didn't know why it made his hair stand at the back of his neck and why it made him feel less desirous of drinking the very appetiz-ing wine in front of him.

It was the nature of human beings—though perhaps not the best part of their nature—to abuse those over whom they had power. This, writ large, had led to the tyrannies of the Roman emperors. Writ far smaller, it commanded a myriad smaller tyrannies, from the father who imposed his every wish on his terrified sons to the master who abused a helpless servant. It was nothing new. Nor could Athos, with the best intentions in the world, stop humans from behav-ing as humans.

He was not a child, charging out at the world, ready to right all wrongs and correct every injustice. He was not even a young man like D'Artagnan full of illusions and hope for the world. He was older, and tired, and sure of nothing except that he too could commit horrible acts. So why was he bristling at the treatment of this young girl who now approached, her eyes full of tears, wiping her face on the back of her hand.

She managed a little smile for Athos, and a pretty curtsey.

And Athos who knew very little about how not to scare people—Athos who could make strong men quake and who had been known to intimidate the most evil hearted of villains—forced a smile at her. He was afraid it looked either like a sickly expression or like a display of teeth in menace. From the girl's little startled jump, he was afraid it looked like that to her too. But he modulated his voice and tried to speak sweetly, gently, as his nursemaid had once spoken to him. "Amelie," he said. "This man—"

"Martin, monsieur," the tavern keeper said.

"Martin tells me that your brother was briefly employed by a nobleman, but Martin does not remember the name. Do you?"

Amelie nodded, her grey eyes still overflowing with tears and very attentive and grave. "Yes. Yes, I do. It was Monsieur de Comeau."

"Comeau . . . and where does he lodge?" Athos asked. He had a vague memory of having heard the name and the association was not pleasant.

"Guillaume said he was down that street awhile and that he rented the two floors over a bakery. He did not tell me any more."

Athos nodded gravely. The girl had pointed down the main street on which the tavern was located and finding a place down the street atop a haberdashery wouldn't be all that hard. That a nobleman was lodging in this part of town meant he probably wasn't very wealthy. Then again, renting two floors would require more income than any of the musketeers could command. "Thank you, Amelie," he said trying to keep his voice even and low, in the same way as before and hoping—very much hoping—it didn't come across as a threatening whisper.

"Monsieur," Amelie said, eagerly. "Is he there, then? With Monsieur de Comeau? He said he would come back and he would have a lot of money, and that he would take me with him and I'd live like a lady. Is he there? Did he get employment with Monsieur de Comeau again?"

Athos was saved from answering by the tavern keeper's putting his hand on the girl's shoulder and saying, in a much better gentle voice than Athos was sure he could command, "Now, Amelie, don't bother the gentleman. He is trying to find your brother to offer him employment. I'm sure we all want to see your brother employed in a position he enjoys. Whether he'll ever make enough to take you with him, much less to have you live like a lady . . ." Martin shrugged. "You must not believe all the crazy dreams your brother spins."

Martin turned to Athos, "The boy means well, and, as I said, who did not entertain a crazy dream as a young man. I assure you he is normally reliable, at least when properly employed. Of course, we never quite employed him, just told him he could get some food in return for a bit of work. So he never had a real job here, but he helps our stable boys look after guests' horses and I'm sure—"

Athos realized the man was doing his best to repair any impression he might have given that the boy, Guillaume, might be unreliable. He was doing his best, and a bit besides, to convince Athos that the boy could be hired and that the boy was worth hiring.

Picking up his cup of wine and taking a quick swallow of the wine, Athos thought of Porthos saying that the boy had always been exactly punctual. An amazing virtue in a young nobleman, as they had thought him at the time, but even more laudable when it involved a young peasant boy who could, at any time, be commanded to some task that might interfere with his time and his plans.

From his description, too, having acquired his letters early and without any real instruction, Guillaume must have been a smart boy. Perhaps Porthos was right in lamenting him. Perhaps he would have become a man worthy of being called friend.

And thinking of Porthos, Athos realized that Porthos had grabbed young Amelie's arm and was talking to her, in hushed tones. He wasn't absolutely sure what Porthos meant by it, or what he was trying to find out. With Porthos it could be intensely important and absolutely all that needed to be known on the case, or something so strange as to have no bearing whatsoever on events.

In case it was the first, though, and suspecting that the tavern keeper might interfere with the talk, should he notice, Athos endeavored to keep the man from noticing.

"Does Guillaume ride?" he asked. "My friend might have need of a young man who can ride messages to his father's domain a few hours distant."

A Name Well Remembered;
Porthos's Guilt;
A Girl's Shame

"**A**MELIE." Porthos grabbed at the girl's arm, as she was about to go away, and she turned from the table to stare at him, her eyes half-afraid and half-hopeful. "Amelie, what was your mother's name?"

It had been working at him for a while. It was probably nothing. How many women were there in France named Amelie? Dozens. Hundreds. So why should he imagine, looking at this girl, that she was the daughter of the woman—no, the girl—he'd loved as a young man? Amelie didn't look a thing like that other Amelie of time's past. She had lank mousy-colored hair, where Porthos's Amelie had blond hair. And her grey eyes had no echo of Amelie's dark ones.

And yet . . . Perhaps it was Porthos's guilt working at him. He'd left in the dead of night, without so much as saying good-bye to the girl who'd given him everything, the girl who'd shown him what the love between a woman and a man could be.

He'd thought at the time that if he just left, she could continue with her life without thinking about him. After all, what had Porthos been in her life but a distraction and a nuisance? What good was he, or dreaming of him—of marrying the gentleman's son—to a simple farm girl? If he left, he thought, she would marry someone else quickly. And her life would go on as if nothing had happened between them. Let him carry the sense of what he had lost, but let her not suffer.

That had been the idea, but was it the truth? Horrible ideas rose in his mind, ideas he didn't want to dignify with full thought. He didn't want his mind to know what he thought. He didn't want his mind to even suspect it, truth be told. But he knew . . . he knew all too well.

The grey-eyed little girl looked back at him. "My mother?" she asked.

"Do you know what your mother's name was."

"They called her Pigeon," she said.

"Who did?" Athos asked.

"Men."

His heart clenched. There was no reason, really, none at all to imagine that Pigeon could ever have been his girl-friend, but what if she had? She had been someone's girl-friend. And there was Guillaume with Porthos's genealogy in his pouch. But he'd never tried to blackmail Porthos, and why else would it matter to him?

"But that was not her real name, was it?" he asked. He kept his voice even, sweet. The girl looked scared and he didn't want to scare her. First, he knew well enough that his towering height and his red hair scared most people. And second, he could well imagine that being interrogated by Athos would scare practically anyone. He didn't need to induce more terror in Amelie. "Do you know what her real name was?"

Amelie nodded, once. "Amelie," she said. "Like my name."

"Ah," Porthos said. "And did you know . . . Did your mom ever talk of her fiancé, that she came to Paris to find?"

Amelie shook her head, then shrugged. "Not to me, but she must have talked to Guillaume, because he said he'd found him."

Porthos's heart clenched within his chest. "Guillaume

found him?" he asked, unable to keep his panic from his voice. "Guillaume found his . . . father?"

The girl nodded. "He said his father was a nobleman and he had found him," Amelie said. "And then he said that he was going to get me money, lots of it, and that he would come get me and I would live like a lady."

Porthos's brain had gone numb. His father was a nobleman. He had found him. He was going to get money and take his sister to live like a lady. *Sangre Dieu, he was my son*, Porthos thought. And on the heels of that. *And he was going to blackmail me.*

In the surge of these conflicting emotions, his mind and heart seized and he trembled.

Seeing him tremble, Amelie surged forward, put her hand on his shoulder. "Monsieur? Are you well? Only you look so ill."

And out of nowhere the tavern keeper's wife descended, hard of face and harsh of voice, grabbing at the girl, pulling her away from Porthos, raining a hail of blows on the girl's face, on the little frail body. "Whore," she screamed. "You're a whore like your mother. It's all you'll ever be. Tempting men. You're not even a woman and you're a whore."

Porthos rose, grabbing for the woman's arm, and found the tavern keeper, Martin, holding his arm. "No," he said. "No. Let her be. If you come between you'll only make it worse. If you come between she'll kill the girl or turn her out which is the same as killing her. No. This will blow over, it always does." He spoke, fast, low, in a whisper that could be heard by Porthos, but not by anyone else over the woman's scream. The other diners looked on the thrashing as a spectacle. The other musketeers and D'Artagnan rose from the table, hands on their swords, but they didn't move, while the tavern keeper stood there, holding Porthos's arm and whispering. "If you go for her, I'll have to defend her," he said. "And then your friends will kill me, and Amelie will have no protection. Please, Monsieur

Musketeer I beg you to believe I do not want the girl hurt or thrown out."

His voice was so earnest, his expression so urgent that Porthos believed him. Quite without knowing what to say, he felt as if he were back in his youth, back in the time when his father had laid his choices before him and sent him from du Vallon rather than letting him elope with Amalie.

A bargain with the devil, he thought. *I'm making a bargain with the devil.* But sometimes all choices are bargains with the devil and seeing the girl get beaten—very still, without crying—he realized that for Amelie these beatings were nothing new and that he couldn't in any way help her. Not by interfering. Bad as her situation was, it would be worse out on the streets.

And what could he offer her, if she were thrown out? It was possible that Aramis knew of some charity, some house that took in girl children of uncertain parentage and no means. But almost for sure, there, too, she would be beaten. And it was not as if he could take her home and adopt her. Had she been a boy and known how to cipher, he could have handed her over to Athenais. However, even in Athenais's care, he knew the clerks often starved, on the meager money her husband allowed for their feeding. Oh, not starved to death, but went about famished and disconsolate. That was where they had found D'Artagnan's servant, and Porthos remembered how Planchet preferred even the irregular food he got now to the continuous privation of an attorney's clerk.

He could do nothing. All this went through his mind, as he slowly lowered his arm and allowed the tavern keeper to turn him around and say, "Leave, sir, leave, please, and I shall deal with it all. I'll take care of the girl."

Like an overweight sheepdog herding wolves, he hounded the musketeers to the door and out of it, till they stood outside in darkness, blinking.

"It was damnable, that," D'Artagnan said, rubbing his face with his hand, as though trying to remove the memory of the scene they witnessed. "Why was she attacking the girl?"

"I think," Athos said, slowly. "That the girl is her husband's daughter."

This had never occurred to Porthos. He'd been busy holding himself accountable for Guillaume's existence and, somehow, in his mind, thinking that if Amelie was his sister, then she must be Porthos's daughter also. All of which was nonsense because the child had been born a good two or three years after Guillaume and therefore could not be his. He stared at Athos in shock saying, "How? How? How?"

Athos sighed. "I imagine in the normal manner of such things. The woman, Pigeon, was fulfilling much the same function the children would later serve, helping with serving and running errands in return for some food and a place to sleep in the barn. She was probably a handsome woman, or at any rate more accomodating than his wife . . ."

"I wasn't . . ." Porthos shook his head. "Athos! I am not a child. I wasn't asking you how it came to pass. I was asking you why you thought so, how you deduced that."

"Oh. She has his eyes," Athos said. "Clearly. And also clearly he cares for her as a daughter, more than just a childless man would care for any orphan."

"Oh," Porthos said. His head hurt. He'd drunk the cup of wine from the tavern and he knew from the taste that it was good wine, but it felt heavy in his stomach, like lead. "I think . . ." he said in a whisper. "I think that Guillaume was my son."

"Why?" Aramis asked. "Why would you think that?"

"She said . . . The girl said that her mother was also named Amelie and that her brother told her he'd found his father and that his father was a nobleman."

"The nobleman!" Athos said. "I knew it."

Porthos didn't know it. He looked, confused.

"The nobleman who thrashed him," Athos said. "It had to be him. I thought it was a little strange that he was seeking work with a nobleman but left after a thrashing. Surely a thrashing would be nothing strange for a waif born in a stable."

"But . . . he was my son," Porthos protested.

"Why would you think that?" Athos asked.

Porthos ticked off the reasons on his fingers. "First," he said. "He came to me and I'm a nobleman."

"He'd be more likely to think of you as a musketeer," Aramis said. "He would say, he'd found his father and he was a musketeer, not a nobleman."

Porthos shook his head. "I am a nobleman." He lifted another finger. "Second, he did have my genealogy in his pocket, and of what interest could it be to him, if he was not my son?"

"He could have been intending to blackmail you with it," Aramis said.

"He never spoke a word about it."

"He might have been waiting, or he might just have acquired it. Or it might have been put in his pocket by someone else who wished to make it look like you killed him because he tried to blackmail you."

Porthos sighed. All of that was true, and yet. "The girl, back home, the one my father didn't want me to marry, the one he told me to leave, which is how I came to Paris, was named Amelie. And the girl there, she said her mother was Amelie. And when I left would be . . . thirteen years ago. So Guillaume . . . Guillaume could be my son."

"Porthos," Athos said, sounding as gentle as he'd sounded to the child in the tavern. "Porthos, do you know how many Amelies there are in France? Does that child look at all like your lover?"

Feeling defeated and miserable, Porthos shook his head. "But—" he said.

"Porthos, my friend," Athos said. "It is not reasonable for you to think this. It is not . . . right. You feel guilty over your girlfriend that you left behind. And you feel guilty about poor Guillaume, and the two of them have come together in your mind so that, somehow, you think they must be related, but they are not, Porthos."

Porthos's head whirled. He tried to think, as he had before, of Amelie fat and happy, a farmer's wife with many children clustered around her. But he couldn't. The image in his mind now was of her working in that miserable inn. Of her giving up on finding him. Of her finding consolation with the tavern master and eventually . . . He shook his head. "I don't know Athos. I'm still afraid that is the only reason Guillaume would come to me, that he knew something . . . Amelie in there says that her mother talked to Guillaume about his father. He must have known something. And why did he come to me?"

"To learn to duel?" Athos asked. "He'd meant to be a gentleman and live like one, and so he wanted to learn to fence? So he could uphold his end in a duel?"

Porthos opened his hands, in a show of helplessness. "The thing is," he said. "That I can't imagine why he would find me of all the fencing masters in Paris. Oh, yes, it's very good to hear anyone say I was the best, and perhaps I was. I know I was very good, but—"

"Chance, my friend," Aramis said. "And you were good. Chance, is all."

"At any rate," D'Artagnan said. "This is not the place for us to have this discussion. The hour grows late. If we must discuss this, and discuss where we will go from here—and I believe we must—let's adjourn to my home."

"Mine," Porthos said. "It's closer."

He set out, in the direction of his lodging. Oh, he knew that Athos's mind was better than his. And Aramis knew Latin and Greek and rhetoric and had a mind that might be better than anyone's. Even Porthos's head told him it was foolish to assume that because the girl-waif had the same name as his Amelie they were the same person. Foolish. Idiotic.

But his heart ached over it. He felt it must be true. Guilt. It was what Athos had said. Guilt over Amelie and guilt over Guillaume. It didn't make them mother and son. But it made them both victims of Porthos's abominable pride.

He should never have left Amelie behind. A peasant she might have been, but how could Porthos, back then, an illiterate provincial lord's son, think he was better than her? And Guillaume? Why had Porthos so easily believed that he was a nobleman's son? A used suit of decent make. Was that all it took for Porthos to think that he was a nobleman?

Porthos hadn't bothered find out where he came from because he didn't want to know. He enjoyed the boy's hero worship of him. He enjoyed the fencing lessons. And he'd not wanted to know more.

Had he known more he could have . . . offered the boy a post as a servant. He could starve as well as Porthos and Mousqueton. He could have rescued him. And Guillaume would not now be lying dead in Athos's cellar.

Things Known and Unknown;
A Discussion on Poisons;
The Beauty and the Plot

"**W**HAT do we know, then?" D'Artagnan asked. They were seated in the front room of Porthos's lodging, the one just up a flight of stairs from the street. It was the most spacious and grand of any of their lodgings, and right now the bits of marble decoration on the wall and the elaborate painted ceiling—all of which had once graced a much grander house, which was now divided into lodgings—felt oppressive in its grandeur. That, and the advanced hour, probably explained why the four friends had been sitting around Porthos's table, looking sullen and quiet, each lost in his own thoughts and concerns.

Even D'Artagnan's words didn't bring the immediate storm of conversation it normally would bring. Instead, they all looked at one another, and Porthos looked solemnly back at D'Artagnan and blinked. "That Guillaume is dead," he said.

D'Artagnan nodded. And then he tried to briskly move the subject away from the obvious fact of the dead child, a fact he understood caused Porthos to mourn and lament, to something more rational, more clear cut, less steeped in grief. He tried to get them to think of it as a puzzle. "The thing is," he said. "Who killed him?"

"Did anyone kill him?" Aramis said.

As they all turned to look at him, the blond musketeer shrugged. "It must be said."

"But . . . you were the one who told us he had symptoms of poisoning," Porthos said, his voice dull.

"Yes, but . . . Poisoning need not be murder. Children eat things by accident all the time. Or out of curiosity. Or simply because they're hungry." His green eyes looked into D'Artagnan's and seemed troubled by one of those rare expressions of concern that didn't relate to Aramis or to whatever lady held Aramis's attention at the moment. "Peasant children did, sometimes, when I was growing up. Ate the wrong berry. Or picked the wrong mushroom. It always scared me. Not that I thought it might happen to me, but because some children like me out there . . ." His voice trailed off, he shook his head, and then when he spoke again it was with his old confidence and self-assurance. "But the truth is that we don't even know for sure what the poison was. If it was poison." He raised a hand to stop an objection from Porthos, though none seemed forthcoming. "I think it was nightshade, but I'm not sure, and until I'm sure, we'll not know how much was needed to kill him, or when it was administered in order to kill him by the time he got to Porthos, or . . . where nightshade can be got, other than the bushes, or . . ."

"So, how do you propose to know?" D'Artagnan asked.

Aramis linked his hands and rested his chin upon them. "I know a man."

Porthos normally reacted to this announcement with an exclamation of surprise, saying that usually Aramis knew women. But Porthos was not in good enough spirits to say it. Instead, he shrugged. "And what would this man of yours know about it?"

"He's a monk, Porthos," Aramis said. "Here in town. He works with poisons."

"You know a poisoner?" Porthos asked, frowning.

"No. He works with poisons to find those helpful qualities

which they might have. For you must know that there is no
substance so wretched that it does not, somewhere, serve
to cure an ill, as well as to cause one. Brother Laurence is a
Benedictine and he works indefatigably to improve the lot
of man." Aramis looked up. "You can come with me,
Porthos, when I go to speak with him."

"Well, then," Athos said. "I shall take D'Artagnan with
me tomorrow and go find Monsieur de Comeau and find
out how his story accords with Guillaume's, shall I?"

D'Artagnan opened his hands. "I have guard duty in
early morning, but I shall be quite free midday. And I suppose if tomorrow is going to be consumed with such investigations, I should take myself to bed now." He looked
suspiciously at the sky, where the high moon announced
the hour as close to midnight. "If I hurry I might get a good
four hours of sleep."

"I'll leave now, also," Aramis said, rising. "And keep
you company part of the way."

They walked together down to the front door where an
ever-vigilant Mousqueton opened the door for them.

Outside, they walked for a while in silence, before
D'Artagnan said, "You don't believe then, Aramis, that the
boy was Porthos's son?"

Aramis shrugged. "I wouldn't know one way or another.
There are so many children . . . I don't think we have any
reason to think he was. But then, we also have no proof that
he wasn't. Porthos is old enough to have fathered him,
mind . . ." He seemed preoccupied with something for a
long while. "Sometimes I wonder . . ." He shrugged and
rubbed his face with his spread fingers, as though seeking
to remove an obstruction to his sight.

"If you have any children out there, forgotten?"
D'Artagnan asked.

Aramis smiled unexpectedly. "None that would thank
me for claiming them," he said. "If I have sired any child, it
was when I was very young and surely his mother's husband can better look after him than I can. Also, if that ever

happened, the lady never saw need to inform me. No, D'Artagnan. I was thinking of Violette. If she had lived and had my child, I wonder what the child would have been like." He was silent a while longer. "You know, it's funny because until now I never thought I'd want to be a father. It's obvious that Porthos wishes to be one, but I never thought of it. And then Violette . . . Well . . . I'd have liked to see what kind of child we'd have had together. I would have liked . . ." He shrugged again. "But what is life without some regrets? And, after all, in consigning myself to holy orders and the church, I shall have not one, but a hundred spiritual descendants."

D'Artagnan was so surprised, he let the words burst forth before he could stop them, "You are sincere about wanting to take orders."

"Oh yes," Aramis said, looking a little surprised. "I thought you knew? What would be the point of shamming?"

D'Artagnan shook his head. Having blurted out his feelings without thought he now had to concentrate to attempt to make sense. "It's just that I knew you wanted to enter the church, but I wasn't sure it was a real spiritual pursuit. So many people take orders . . ."

"I know, I know," Aramis said. "His eminence the Cardinal, for instance. But . . . This is not for me. I do intend to devote myself to the church. I have given it much thought these last few months, since Violette . . ." He shrugged. "I don't think I'll ever feel for anyone what I felt for her. At the same time . . . I am a fallible man. I don't feel I'm ready to dedicate myself fully to the church yet. And so I shall wait. Besides, our friends need me."

D'Artagnan interpreted Aramis's speech to mean that Aramis was not ready to give up on the fair sex. But perhaps here, too, he was doing Aramis an injustice. At least Aramis meant to take his orders seriously when he took them.

Meanwhile they'd arrived at the Rue des Fossoyers, and D'Artagnan's mind wandered away from Aramis and Aramis's concerns. He found himself scanning the front of the house anxiously, looking for the shape of someone watching from the windows. Oh, he knew it was ridiculous at this time of night. What would she be doing up? Waiting for him? She was a married woman and worked for the Queen as one of her favored maids. And he was a seventeen-year-old guard, not even a musketeer. What could she ever see in him?

He realized he'd been silent for a while and that Aramis was watching him curiously. D'Artagnan blushed dark and said, "I must go. I really should get some sleep before I stand guard tomorrow at Monsieur des Essarts."

"Yes, you probably should," Aramis said, but he still looked curious. When D'Artagnan didn't say anything, Aramis said, "Good night my friend." And turned to leave.

No sooner had he taken three steps away, than D'Artagnan heard an urgent "Pssst" out of the shadows.

He barely had the time to turn before one of the windows in the bottom floor opened and something came sailing out of it. By instinct more than by design, D'Artagnan caught it, in the dark.

It was a rose. Not the one he had given her, but another, for it still had its thorns upon it. To protect his hands upon catching it, she'd wrapped a silken handkerchief around the stem. It was lace bordered and the initials worked upon it were CB.

He lifted it to his lips and kissed the initials. From somewhere up the road, he'd swear he heard Aramis chuckle.

But when he turned, Aramis was walking away, in the dark night, and didn't look like he'd ever turned back or witnessed the scene.

D'Artagnan looked back, towards the window, from which rose and handkerchief had dropped, and saw her looking out. *Her.* Or at least enough of her to recognize: a hint of blond hair, the curve of a cheek, two intent blue eyes. His heart sped up and blood thundered in his ears like an oncoming summer storm.

He bowed deeply and removed his hat, while bowing almost to the ground.

As he straightened, he saw her smiling at him, a smile full of intent and meaning and at the same time, she lifted her hand, as though telling him to wait.

D'Artagnan wasn't sure what she meant, but at that moment, he couldn't have moved no matter how much he wished it. He stood planted, on the street in front of her house, and presently—it seemed to him as though she were decanted from moonlight and roses—she opened the door and stood before him, dressed in her dress and a cloak with a hood. She was a little breathless, causing her chest to heave and putting pink on her cheeks. Which made her even more beautiful than she'd been before. And she plucked at his sleeve. "Monsieur. Would you render me a service?"

D'Artagnan was sure he was sleeping, then. The night had run too long and he must have fallen asleep, with his head on Porthos's table, and the others, feeling sorry for his youth and tiredness, had scrupled to wake him. That must be it, because it was only in D'Artagnan's dreams that beautiful women asked him this sort of question. In fact, it was only in D'Artagnan's dreams that beautiful women spoke directly at him.

However, this being a dream he enjoyed, he decided he would take it at the full and enjoy it to the end. Bowing deeply, he said, "Madam, you have only to tell me where I may lose my life in your service."

She smiled, and blushed darker, and said, "Oh, I hope that might not be needed, but you see . . . I have a friend . . ." When he didn't dispute this, she went on. "A friend who is married to a most suspicious husband, and there is a man she loves, but with whom she is too honorable to have any commerce. She wishes to send this man a message, to prevent his being foolish enough to appear at her door as he's been threatening to do. Only, she is constantly watched."

"By her husband?"

"And his minister."

"And his—" D'Artagnan took a deep breath. Until that word he had been, complacently, imagining that Madame Bonacieux referred to him in a round about way. "You mean she is the—" Her hand clapped on his mouth before he could finish the sentence.

"Yes," she said.

"And?"

"And this message to her gentleman friend she entrusted to me," Madame Bonacieux said. "Only I am a woman, too, and frail. I'm afraid of being attacked between here and the house where I'm supposed to deliver it. She believed my husband might protect me, but I don't think my husband will be much good against armed attackers, do you?"

Her hand still covering his mouth, all he could do was shake his hand.

"Would you escort me, then?" Madame Bonacieux said. "On my errand?"

"With the best will in the world, madam," D'Artagnan said, offering her his arm. She accepted it, and slipped her hand upon it.

"You are so brave, monsieur," she said. "I perceive with you, there will not be the slightest cause for alarm."

In fact, D'Artagnan found no cause for alarm, at any rate. As they walked along the deserted, darkened streets, everything was quiet. It seemed to him, for a long while, that he heard steps behind him, but after a while he was sure it was just the disordered beat of his own heart.

He was so far in this dream of love and romance that he didn't realize for a long while that they were going towards the Rue Ferou, where Athos lived. It was only as they stopped in front of a house, and Madame Bonacieux said, "Only go back now. I will get someone else to escort me on the way back," that he realized he was just across the street from Athos's home.

Bowing slightly, he turned away from her obediently. Some part of him reproached himself for leaving her without being absolutely sure she would be safely escorted on the way back, but the rest of him insisted he must obey her. This was, after all, the Queen's business and bigger than both of them.

He turned away and had gone only a few steps, when he heard, behind him, running feet. Turning he saw Madame Bonacieux at the door, raising her hand to knock, and six guards of the Cardinal bearing down on her, swords out.

"Ah, villains," D'Artagnan called out. "You'd attack an unprotected woman?"

He turned, sword in hand, and rushed back. "To me, villains."

The men instantly turned to accept his challenge and D'Artagnan, perceiving that he was far outnumbered and that these were old hands at the game of duel, called out in turn, "Athos, Athos, help me."

A window opened above, and presently Athos's front door was flung open and two men rushed out. Athos who joined the fray with ready sword and Grimaud who rushed away into the night.

Considerably relieved, but still hard pressed, D'Artagnan called out, "To me, musketeers, for the King."

Just at that moment—Grimaud doubtlessly having gone, providentially, to the nearest tavern, a crowd of musketeers appeared, following Grimaud. They fell onto the guards and the fight was joined with such enthusiasm, that D'Artagnan found himself on the periphery of it, looking at Athos.

"How came this to be?" Athos asked.

D'Artagnan shook his head. He knew if he talked of Madame Bonacieux Athos would call him a fool. He said, instead, "I was walking around, thinking, and I found myself here, and they fell on me." Even as he spoke, he made sure his beautiful landlady was nowhere in sight.

"How came you to be here? Near my house?"

D'Artagnan shrugged. "I don't even know. I was walking. I lost track of where I was."

From Athos's disdainful smile, D'Artagnan perceived that Athos thought he'd been thinking of Madame Bonacieux, anyway. And let him think that, for D'Artagnan had.

Leaving the still furious fight behind him, D'Artagnan started towards his house, feeling for her embroidered handkerchief within his sleeve.

An Odd Avocation; Poison in the World;
Belladonna

᪥

𝕴T was cool morning as Aramis headed for Friar Laurence's workshop. It was in fact one of those beautiful mornings where the world appears newly minted or recreated. The normal stink of Paris seemed muted, as a cool breeze blowing from the river brought with it freshness and untainted air.

Early morning, the city looked like a woman just awakened, Aramis thought, and not yet having put on her makeup or her public attire. Most windows were shuttered. From far off came the sound of a horse's hooves on cobbles. From somewhere else, in the nearer distance, the sounds of a woman calling out something, and of a child crying. Other than that, it was stillness, punctuated with birdsong, here and there.

If you closed your eyes, it would be possible to imagine that you were in a small village, somewhere, surrounded by bucolic solitude.

Only Aramis didn't close his eyes. He looked around, instead, at the tall buildings around him, at the shutters opening, here and there. Down the street, a woman threw open her door and walked out to sweep the street. Elsewhere, a man's voice rose in round, full singing.

It was this Paris that Aramis loved. Or perhaps, truth be told, it was one of the parts of Paris he loved, for he loved the evening Paris, too, shrouded in darkness and full of secret alleys and fraught encounters in the streets. And he loved Paris in the afternoon, languid under the sun, the streets filled with passersby.

The city was like a woman, and like any woman she exerted an hypnotic fascination over Aramis. In his heart of hearts he had to admit that was part of what held him away from the church, to which he always said he was destined. The truth was he could no more leave Paris than he could be truly celibate. Not yet.

He hastened away from the center of town and towards the suburbs, where there were more people awake and signs of life in the workshops and forges. Farther still, down beaten-dirt streets, he found himself standing in front of the Benedictine monastery—an imposing stone facade with small, deep windows that would allow the light in, but not the prurient curiosity of a glance out at the street to see who might be passing.

Again, as always when he approached such places, Aramis asked himself what it would be like to live within, in the sacred silence, with ordered days and specified times for every task. Oh, obedience didn't frighten him. He had to obey now. He obeyed Monsieur de Treville. He stood guard when he must and he went on travel for the captain when he must. He came when bid, and he fought whomever the King ordered. No, obedience was not a problem.

And poverty . . . well . . . Despite his lace and velvet, the well-cut clothes upon which he spent much of his money, the truth was that no musketeer was truly rich. The wolf of famine often rounded the musketeer's door and very, very often was admitted in.

No—of all the three it was only chastity that bothered Aramis. And not just the vow of chastity that would prevent him from touching female flesh again, but the vow of chastity that would bar him from looking at women, from taking a material interest in the day-to-day life of the city and of his neighbors and of the court too.

Chastity stood before the door of the monastery as a stumbling block stopping Aramis on his way to taking vows. And yet . . . He sighed and knocked at the heavy oak door.

It was presently opened by a cowled monk in a black habit. Upon seeing Aramis, he bowed and mumbled his welcome, as Aramis had been known at this house since he was just a young seminarian newly sent to Paris to be educated.

"I have come to see Brother Laurence," Aramis said, and was waved through, his presence here being customary and so well known that they wouldn't bother even to escort him down the long, cool hallways, the shadow-filled darkness of the monastery.

An ancient building, constructed of massive stone blocks, it seemed designed to keep the world out, though the Benedictines were not a cloistered order and indeed often worked within the world as teachers, physicians and other avocations. But within here, it was all fresh and silent and Aramis once more felt the tug to leave the world behind and consign himself to unvarying holiness. Only, he remembered the call of the streets outside too well to obey.

He hastened faster down the hallways, towards the back of the building where they'd set up Brother Laurence's workshop. The figures who met him on his way nodded to him and he nodded in response. That none of them remarked upon his presence nor even seemed to notice his rather gaudy—today a deep blue—velvet attire, nor the discrete bits of golden ornamentation upon it, which contrasted as much with their black habits as a bird of paradise's plumage would contrast with a crow's, only told how accustomed a presence he had become within.

Brother Laurence's workshop was open, and Aramis went in—into a labyrinth of shadows and shelves, of strange materials bubbling in glass apparatuses, and other, more difficult to understand vessels. Metal and clay and little contained flames were all around. From the ceiling of the workshop hung dried bunches of herbs and also a stuffed crocodile whose purpose Aramis was loath to enquire. On shelves, distributed more or less haphazardly, sat jars filled with odd fluids, or else with bits of animal and plant. Again, Aramis didn't ask about them unless they came up in some conversation or brought up in some discussion. He had a vague idea that most of them were unpleasant or at least unsavory.

"Ah, D'Herblay," Father Laurence said. He popped up around a set of shelves with every appearance of a jack-in-the-box coming forth from the confined space. Truth be told, he looked more than anything like one of those trained monkeys that court ladies kept around for show, only slightly bigger and slightly less hairy. His features were almost entirely simian, his nose just slightly more prominent than that of a monkey. And his eyes, like a monkey's, peered dark and preternaturally intelligent from deep sockets. The black cowl around his face made the whole look incongruous, like a child's prank or a lady's idea of a joke.

That he was grinning inanely with pleasure at Aramis's visit would have alarmed a man who knew him less well. But Aramis only smiled and said, "You know very well, Brother Laurence, that I have laid that name by and will not resume it until I think myself purged of my sin and capable—"

"You'll not resume it until you're done playing the musketeer," the little man said, waving the rest of Aramis's intended speech away. "Come, come, I am no fool. Aramis, then, if you insist on being Aramis. Glad to see you. It's been at least two weeks, and I haven't told you any of my new experiments. I'm almost sure I've found an herb to suppress cough. You know, in winter it is often the cough and the tiredness of it that kill our aged ones."

Aramis had never been able to understand why Brother Laurence assumed that Aramis had the same interest in his herbal medicines that he himself possessed, save that, he supposed, the little man got to speak with precious few people. His brothers, doubtless, not being fools, avoided the workshop if they could. Aramis always thought that had been the reason to locate it at the back of the house, facing the still sizeable backyard.

Oh, doubtless, it also made it convenient for Brother Laurence to tend to the herbs and trees and cultivate the odd plants that were part of his materials. But at the same time, it took him out of the main flow of the house, so that no one need pass by the workshop unless he meant to go there.

Like all lonely people, Brother Laurence talked a great deal. And yet, while being led from bubbling pot to deep, clay keeping jar, to yet another interesting concoction of macerated herbs at the bottom of some mortar vase, Aramis thought of how useful Laurence was to his community. He'd come here in winter, sometimes in search of medicines for Bazin who was as likely as not to suffer from a weak chest, and he'd seen the little man bring relief to many suffering from colds or other infections of the head and chest.

Brother Laurence brought him, with a flourish, towards a bench and handed him a little container of some pomade, saying, "And that should hasten the healing of any wounds you get in your duels. I had the recipe from a Gascon monk who visited."

Aramis took the salve, wondering if it was the same not so secret Gascon recipe that D'Artagnan swore by.

"I thank you, Brother Laurence," Aramis said, holding the salve in his hand and contemplating what to do with it, since he wore no capacious waist-pouch which would ruin the lines of his elegant attire, and he surely had not enough space for this jar of salve within his sleeves. So he held the smooth ceramic pot in his hand, and turned it round and round as he said, "But what I've come to you for is . . . a little different."

Brother Laurence turned around and fixed Aramis with

an intent look of his simian-like eyes. "Different?" he said, his voice seeming to echo itself in various tones of worry.

"It is . . ." Aramis said. "A child. A friend of mine . . ."

The Benedictine's eyebrows rose. "My dear D'Her—Aramis. You probably know more of foundling homes than I do. You could not—"

"It is not a foundling. It is—"

"Oh, that. You must know my friend, that while there are herbal remedies that stop the life within the woman there are none that do not endanger the mother also, and you—"

Aramis shook his head. "Not that, Brother. Not that. I'm well aware of my sins of propinquity and unchastity." He raised his hand as he saw the little Benedictine open his lips to speak. "But it is not that. At any rate I've never had to face that trouble. If things had been different . . ." He shook his head. "As it is the matter concerns not me, but a good friend of mine, and the child involved is not his, but only a boy to whom he agreed to teach the art of fencing."

The little benedictine remained mercifully silent, possibly surprised by such an unusual problem for a musketeer, while Aramis poured out the entire tale of woe involving Guillaume, and the symptoms of the boy's death.

"Nightshade," the Benedictine said, rubbing his chin. "Aye, it might very well be that, for look here, the berries ripen around now. Yes, it might very well be that. And many householders grow nightshade beside their doors, as an ornamental plant. But . . ." He chewed the side of his lip. "All you tell me, so far, makes sense, as far as sense goes. The boy had a dry mouth, was red and dreaming awake, as it were. Yes, it sounds like nightshade poisoning right enough." He opened his arms, palm outward. "I don't understand what you want me to do in the matter though?"

"Oh . . . There are questions," Aramis said. "Other questions than the simple fact of how the boy might have died. You see, while it is true what you say, and I'm sure I've seen the bush around Paris, there are people, perhaps, who wouldn't be in a position to go out and lop off leaves from a bush to poison anyone. People who . . . it could be said . . . would want a more concentrated dose, and more lethal. People in a position of power who . . ."

The Benedictine's eyebrows rose again. "You mean, in sum, his eminence Cardinal Richelieu, I suppose?"

Aramis shrugged. "Someone of prominence, whosoever they might be," he said. "Someone who would not be in a position to run to the garden and cut leaves, or to bake a pie incorporating them. You see, if this child was as I suppose him to be, streetwise and capable, I don't think he would easily be tempted by a dainty full of poisonous berries. Doubtless he would have tasted them or known them."

The Benedictine spread his hands again, this time in a seeming show of helplessness. "I always think that you gentlemen in the King's Musketeers are a little too obsessed with the Cardinal, as though if his eminence were to achieve all his goals France would be lost by it. And yet, I'd swear the man, though he enriches himself a bit, is not even as corrupt as most of our noblemen. He doesn't seem to crave riches or women or . . ."

"It is power he craves," Aramis said. "Just power. Surely you understand that."

"But a craving for power doesn't mean the power is necessarily wrong. It seems to me the Cardinal's aims are as much for the good of France as anyone else's at court. He might have different ideas as to what that good might be, but that is about it. Surely . . ."

Aramis shrugged. He transferred the jar to his left hand and examined the nails of his right hand, something he always did when immersed in thought. In anyone else making this speech, he would have suspected a fatal sympathy for the Cardinal, such as might mean Brother Laurence was already the churchman's agent. But Brother Laurence wasn't like that. He was one of those creatures who go through life thinking more than doing—and more involved in his studies than in any human affairs. If the Cardinal were an herb, then surely Brother Laurence's opinion would be soundly and carefully reasoned. The Cardinal, and France and the court for that matter being either people or assemblies of them, the good brother's opinion would be slightly less well thought out. "I'm not going to dispute with you," he said. "Whether the Cardinal's ideas for France are correct or whether the King's or . . . other people's are. I'm just going to say that surely you don't doubt, in the pursuit of his objectives, the Cardinal would not spare the life of a child."

"In the pursuit of his objectives," Brother Laurence said. "The Cardinal would not spare the King himself nor the Queen, but truly . . . why would he kill a child?"

Aramis shrugged. "As a means of creating the appearance of a crime so heinous that even Monsieur de Treville would not defend one of his own musketeers?" Aramis said. "Besides, you must know if he manages to strike at one of us, myself or my three friends, the rest of us are bound to go into exile or otherwise disappear, for what credit and face would we have, when presented with such dishonor in our midst?"

The Benedictine's eyes watched Aramis, attentively, then the man shrugged. "You might have good reason there. Or more than good reason. And yes, his eminence is quite capable of such behavior where it suits him, and I won't dispute it might have suited him. I don't live enough in the world to understand such impulses and such crimes."

Aramis nodded. "There are other suspects . . . other people who might have done it. A nobleman, perhaps one who was the boy's father or at least whom the boy thought was his father." He shrugged. "People like that, at that level, unlike housewives or other plebeians, might find it hard to come by the berries and leaves, and might have had to disguise the poison in some other way."

The brother nodded. "Well," he said. "Nightshade is called belladonna, because its extract, when dripped in the eyes, makes the pupils huge, something that is accounted of great beauty by our court ladies. There are other preparations that use it. As a cream, it is said to make the skin smooth and even. You must understand I have no personal experience with it in that form, as my patients are rarely concerned with the appearance of their skins, and yet . . ." He shook his head. "There's many ways it can manifest itself and many people who make extracts of it."

"And if someone ate . . . either the berries or the concentrate of it? How long till death?"

Brother Laurence shook his head. "It might not lead to death at all," he said. "You understand, it is possible to have it in such a small dosage that it causes only dreams and hallucinations. In adults, at least, most of those hallucinations seem to be of a . . . sexual nature."

"Supposing a dosage large enough to kill?" Aramis asked. "In a boy about this height," he held his hand at below his shoulder. "And weighing very little, though most of it muscle?"

The Brother sighed, then shook his head. "Half an hour? An hour? Not very long at any rate. With that little flesh, it is easy for the entire body to become poisoned very quickly."

Aramis nodded. Porthos had just had the time to become alarmed at the boy not having shown up for his lesson. That meant an hour, maybe less. And the boy had died shortly after Porthos found him. "So it is not one of those poisons . . . It wouldn't be possible for someone to have poisoned him over weeks, or months? Or perhaps to have given him the poison the night before?"

The friar shook his head. "Oh, no. It's not a slow acting poison at all. If you take enough to poison you, you will die very quickly." He turned his back on Aramis and started rummaging amid his clay jars on a shelf. "Someone would have had to poison the boy, at the most, a couple of hours before he died."

"Well, that at least gives us something solid to ask—a person's whereabouts just before the boy died."

"Well . . . indeed. Except they could have given it to him in some flask of liquor or some baked something with instructions to consume it at a certain time."

Aramis tilted his head. "It is devilishly hard," he said. "I much prefer murders by stabbing or bludgeoning." And, seeing Brother Laurence look over his shoulder at Aramis with a startled expression, Aramis added. "I mean, I much prefer trying to solve such murders, not that I prefer committing them that way, for as I hope you know I do not make it my business to kill people."

"I should pray not," Brother Laurence said. "Except for your duels, of course."

"Those are hardly murder."

"Indeed. I suppose not." The little friar sighed. "My friend, surely it has occurred to you that having found such a relatively easy way to dispose of inconvenient people, the murderer is bound to murder again?"

Immersed in this gloomy thought, as he left the monastery, Aramis managed to walked all the way into the middle of a group of men, who were waiting a little distance from the door before he realized that they were all dressed in the blood-red uniforms of guards of the Cardinal.

"What can this mean?" he asked. "Were you gentlemen waiting for me?"

The leader, an ugly man with a scar, whose name, Aramis vaguely remembered as Remy, said, "Indeed, and if you just deliver the papers to us, we shall now be gone. We ransacked the house, you see, and couldn't find it. So one of you must have it. And since there's a woman involved, it must, perforce, be you."

Aramis was as baffled by this speech as could be expected. The only thing he could understand from it was that these men wanted some papers. Porthos's genealogy, he thought. Now that it had failed to incriminate the musketeer, its very existence pointed to the Cardinal. They wanted to eliminate proof.

Mentally he counted them. Five of them. Very well, he would die here, then. He pulled at his sword. "This is the only thing you'll get from me, sirs," he said. And then, though he didn't expect any musketeers to be in this far flung area of town, far from their normal taverns, he yelled. "To me, musketeers. To me for the King."

To his surprise, four men appeared running. And though one of them was de Termopillae, and therefore as good as half a man, if that, at the very least the odds were somewhat even.

Squaring off against Remy, Aramis thought that the day that four and a half musketeers couldn't beat five guards of his eminence would be a sad day indeed.

Accidentally Stepping on Bottles;
The Very Great Advantage of Knowing
One's Sphere; The Foal and the Lord

ATHOS called for Porthos early morning, and was relieved to find the giant dressed and prepared to go out, polishing off a roast chicken by way of breakfast.

Athos's stomach clutched at the savory smell and grumbled something to the extent that it had been far too long since Athos had eaten anything of the kind. Which was true. It had been far too long. The nobleman, who had grown up on game meat and, once upon a time, would have disdained the taste of tame fowl, now ate meat, of any kind, but rarely. Somehow, most of his money—and it wasn't much, as he didn't like to draw upon the domains he no longer administered for fear his cousin who was taking care of the land in his absence should ask too many questions—received from his musketeer's pay or the occasional reward for extraordinary service seemed to run away from his hands faster than he could contrive to get it in them.

Truth be told, he knew he played too many games of hazard. He always lost at them and, in his more sane moments, was as likely as the next man to admit that his determined gambling could only be another way of punishing himself—one with his having assumed the musketeer uniform, one with his having cut himself off from all his old acquaintance. He also knew there was too much wine. Far too much. In the last few years, he, who had before always been somewhat more moderate than even a moderate drinker, had swallowed enough wine to float several ships at harbor. And yet . . . And yet, for all the liquor bought him a certain haziness, and sometimes—rarely—the ability to sleep, it hadn't managed to erase his perfect recollection of his wife's look, of the way she'd smiled at him on that day they'd set out together on their last hunt. The same hunt that had ended with his finding that the Countess's shoulder was branded with a fleur-de-lis, and him hanging her from a low branch. The hunt that had ended her life. And his. In fact if he drank too much, he often thought he spied her ghost, just at the corner of his field of vision. He would turn and not see her, and yet when he wasn't looking he always knew she was there.

Between the gambling and the drinking, he rarely had much money left and though his excellent servant, Grimaud, who'd served Athos's family for many years, always contrived to turn bread and a thin slice of meat into some sort of meal, it was often too little and not very nourishing.

"Do you want some?" Porthos asked, looking up from his plate which was heaped with fully half the golden-roasted fowl, while the other half sat on its tray, waiting to be devoured. "*Holá* Mousqueton, bring a plate for Monsieur Athos."

"It is not . . . I mean . . ." But before he could fully formulate that he didn't mean to intrude on Porthos's meal and that he didn't require to be fed—all against the embarrassing and audible growling of his stomach—Mousqueton had set another place at the table, and put a napkin beside it, for Porthos observed, even in private, the careful etiquette of the greater houses. Quite defeated, Athos sat down and—with the knife provided—helped himself to the leg of the chicken, while Mousqueton returned to set a cup of wine in front of him.

One taste of the chicken confirmed what his sense of

smell had told him—that the meat was excellent and deliciously seasoned. Slow roasted, too, and kept moist by some art that exceeded not only the abilities of Athos's excellent Grimaud, but the abilities of Athos's erstwhile cook at La Fere, as well. "I didn't know—" he said, and realized he was about to say he didn't realize that Porthos's pocketbook ran to chicken these days, when all of them seemed to be subsisting on dried bread crusts and whatever they could manage to get in the way of invitations to dine. He stopped his words, but not in time.

Porthos, who so often had trouble putting his feelings into words, seemed to understand other people's feelings and thoughts, even when incompletely expressed. He shrugged, as though Athos had said what he meant to say. "Mouqueton got it," he said.

"I stepped on the poor creature by accident," Mousqueton said. "There was nothing for it, but to put it out of its misery. And since it had been in the middle of the lane, I couldn't quite tell to whom it belonged, so I thought it was easier to remove the source of dispute by bringing it home."

Athos swallowed a mouth full and frowned at the meat in his hand. "But Mousqueton," he said. "If the chicken was lying in the middle of the road, it might have been sick."

Mousqueton sighed. "Oh, no. It was very healthy. I had the devil of a time, running it down so I could accidentally step on it."

Athos marked the small smile on Porthos's lips, and shook his head. After all, Mousqueton had grown up on the streets, living from his expedients. He supposed, in the final scheme of things, the chickens that people turned out on the street to feed on what they could find, were not in many senses truly owned. And yet, though he could eat it, he could not have gone out and got it himself. Or commanded Grimaud to get it. He ate another mouthful and drank half of his cup of wine, which Mousqueton promptly refilled from a bottle in his hand.

"I suppose you stepped on the bottle also?" Athos asked, smiling so Mousqueton would not interpret his words as censure.

Mousqueton smiled. "It was the oddest thing, monsieur."

Porthos seemed quite untroubled by all of this, as he helped himself to more meat. Athos waited until Mousqueton left the room to say, "I hope you have gotten over your conviction that the boy was your son . . ."

Porthos shrugged. "It wasn't so much a conviction," he said. "But you have to admit, as a suspicion . . ."

"As a suspicion it seems insane, Porthos. I'm sure that Monsieur de Comeau, whom we are supposed to see today, was the boy's father. Or that, at the very least, the boy believed he was his father. Though it would have to have happened elsewhere than Paris. I have made enquiries, you see . . ."

Porthos looked up, saying nothing.

"I had Grimaud ask around. Monsieur de Comeau came to Paris about ten years ago, intent on a good marriage. That, he contracted seven years ago. Or at least what people term a good marriage, for the woman is noble and wealthy. Other than that . . . well . . . Grimaud tells me that local gossip has it Monsieur de Comeau goes in awe of his wife, and is perhaps a little afraid of her. It would not be considered a good marriage in my opinion, but this is how the world views it, and therefore . . ." Athos shrugged. "At any rate, after his marriage, Monsieur de Comeau lingered in Paris, presumably to get whatever other social advancement he could procure. He's attached himself now to one, now to the other greater household, but he has no definite patron, and the couple has no children."

Porthos nodded. "If she's cold . . ."

"Yes, perhaps that is so," Athos said. He was tempted to say that marriages were complex and just because she appeared to not have given birth it did not mean she was cold in private. But when he thought about it, Porthos probably knew a lot more about marriage—through his quasi marriage with Athenais—than Athos could claim to know through his failed marriage and his one other almost-relationship. He shrugged.

"Very well," Porthos said. "Then we should go and question them, should we not?"

Athos nodded. He'd finished his chicken leg and though he'd eaten far less than his friend, felt as though he'd dined better than he had in months.

They walked to the Comeau residence in silence. Athos was not very talkative at the best of times, and given Porthos's difficulties in making his words obey him, it was often easier to be silent.

The lodging of the nobleman was a two-floor house, with a busy bakery on the downstairs floor. The smell of warm bread permeated everything and Athos was momentarily regretful that his morals would never allow him to imitate Mousqueton. The bakery had the lease of the downstairs floor entirely, but no lease of the field at the back or the yard that abutted it, which was entered via an arched doorway ineffectually closed by a rectangular iron gate. The gate stood open as the musketeers approached, and in the yard horses and grooms seemed to have set up a welter of activity. Far more grooms and horses, Athos thought, than befit this kind of establishment and which bespoke a horse-mad lord or a horse trader. Since he didn't think it was the later, it must be the former.

It took a moment for people in the yard to notice the two musketeers at the gate—which spoke unusual absorption in their task, since musketeers normally caused the action to stop wherever they went. Or rather, they could very quickly become the center of the action if ignored.

At last a groom noticed them and, doffing his cap, loped over to them. "Monsieur Musketeers," he said, stopping just in front of them and bowing deeply. "How may we help you? What can we do to further the service of his Majesty, what—"

"We are here not on the King's business, but our own," Athos said, straightening and managing to convey that he was one of the noblest men in the land and that his every word should be listened to.

"Your own?" the groom asked.

"I need to speak to your master," Athos said. "About one of the . . . about a boy who was said to have come here last and who has disappeared."

The groom frowned. "A boy? I don't recall . . ."

Athos could have said the boy was not a noble boy. He was sure many commoners had come and gone in here who were less than full grown men. But he didn't wish to tell the groom that. He knew all too well that in most people's minds a plebeian boy's disappearance was unimportant. Indeed, it probably would have been unimportant in Athos's as well, if he hadn't seen the small corpse on the floor of their practice room. Because the boy was unimportant, because plebeian boys disappeared and appeared like the sun on a cloudy day, it begged the question of why anyone had found this boy important enough to kill. Not just kill, but poison and then let go, almost guaranteeing that the boy would die away from his murderer. This would ensure the murder must be discovered as such.

Surely most men, on finding they needed to kill the boy, would have hit him on the back of the head and left him for dead in some alley, or some forgotten building, or stabbed him and left the body with every appearance of having died in a brawl. Or . . . a million other scenarios.

So why kill the boy with poison, and at a time when he would surely be discovered by someone who would care about his death—someone, what was more, who was likely to be of a suspicious turn of mind, and to have access to the ears of those in power? It seemed like a mad thing to do. And in that moment, Athos had the fleeting feeling that he could almost sense something . . . Something.

As though he stood in a tall place, looking below at the

maze that was this murder, he felt as if he could almost see the whole thing, beginning to end and the bit in the middle as well. But the groom said, dubiously, "Well, if you would follow me. My lord is in the stables."

And Athos was back in the yard with the horses and the busy grooms putting the horses through their paces and brushing them and grooming them. He nodded to the groom, and started to follow.

Porthos grabbed at his arm. "Athos," he said. "I'll stay here."

Athos turned back frowning. "You will? Why? Don't you have questions to ask Monsieur de Comeau?"

Porthos grinned, flashing that smile that made people think him simple or mad. "No, Athos," he said. "You have questions to ask Monsieur de Comeau. I shall wait for you here. Between you high lords, you are better served if you speak alone. While I, myself, you know, since I have horse traders in my ancestry, will stay here and watch all these horses, and think to myself about a few things."

Athos was about to reproach Porthos with silliness and to tell him that no one cared about Porthos's ancestry but Porthos himself. Or at least, none of Porthos's friends cared. But Porthos's eyes were full of speaking mirth, as though he meant to say something else. No, as though he meant for Athos to understand something else that he didn't want to have to say.

Finding he had opened his mouth, Athos closed it, then nodded curtly. "There is, of course," he said, slowly, ponderously, looking for Porthos to correct him if he was guessing wrong. "A great advantage in knowing your place in the world."

Porthos nodded. "Is there not?" he said. "And I know my place exceedingly well, I assure you. I always feel more at home in these kinds of places, with working men . . . aye, and women, too, who know what to do and what goes on in the bowels of your great houses. You, on the other hand, should go talk to the gentleman who is your equal and who will doubtless receive you with equanimity."

If Porthos had smiled any wider or more blankly, he would doubtlessly have sprained his jaw, and Athos chose to relieve his friend's mind by saying, "I understand completely. I will be back in a few moments."

Porthos nodded and looked about him, till he found a large rock in the middle of the yard, in the full sun of late summer. He sat himself on it, watching horses and working grooms with every appearance of satisfaction.

As Athos turned his back on Porthos, Athos again wondered at Porthos's seeming simplicity and whether it was truly so, or a degree of cunning so high that even Aramis didn't fully understand it for what it was. Left in this situation, in the middle of grooms working at the horses, Athos would have sat there, the whole time, mute and wrapped in his own mantle of nobility. Not that he disdained the grooms, but he would have been just as unable to find anything to talk to them about as he would have been of sprouting wings and flying.

Even now, as he moved among them, grooms and servants stepped out of the way and bowed hastily to him, but none would be so bold as to greet him, or to utter a word to him, not even a reverentially whispered "milord."

However, Porthos would, by the time Athos came back, know the name and age of every groom in the yard, doubtless know if they were married and, if so, if they were faithful or had a girlfriend on the side. He would know the ages of their children, the places of their births and their dearest aspirations.

"Your friend, monsieur is . . . er . . . he was, before becoming a musketeer . . ."

"As noble a gentleman as you might wish to meet," Athos said and his eyes warned the groom not to pursue it.

Few people could challenge such a look from Athos, and the groom was not equal to it. He nodded and turned,

and led Athos down the length of the yard, past as many
fine examples of horseflesh as Athos had seen gathered in
one place, to the door at the far stable, where he left Athos
to wait, while—presumably—he was announced.

Athos waited a long while. From inside came a warble
of voices. The groom's muttered tones, answered by
louder, impatient tones from a male voice. And there
was . . . confused shouting.

Of course, etiquette dictated that Athos wait outside for
the groom to return. Athos quite understood that, having
been trained in etiquette by his father, who had been something of a taskmaster on the matter. And he quite understood that he shouldn't barge in. But when one was
investigating a murder in Paris, these days and under these
circumstances, with the Cardinal behind the scenes, possibly manipulating all, sometimes the best course was to in-
tervene, before dastardly deeds could be accomplished.

He hesitated but one second, while the voice of his formidable father, to whom he'd been a late and unexpected
son, boomed in his mind, telling him there were things a
lord simply did not do, one of them being to break etiquette
in such a crass way.

And then he plunged into the dark door, into the smell
of blood and hay, into the sounds of horses and two men
yelling at each other.

One look was all it took for Athos, the erstwhile Count de
la Fere and owner of a fine stable in his own, abandoned domains, to understand what was happening and why. There
was a beautiful chestnut mare, and there was a foal, which
was lying on the hay, while the two men rubbed it with
straw. Meanwhile, the mare had pinned her ears flat back
and the skin at the corner of her mouth had wrinkled—a sure
sign she intended to bite someone—which, Athos judged,
occasioned the screaming.

That the men were screaming and rubbing the foal at the
same time, and not getting out of the mare's way, seemed
to betray some disconnection between mind and body, of

the sort Porthos often complained of. Athos plunged forward and grabbed at the two men, pulling them away, just as the mare bit at air where the older of the men had been.

The mare gave them something that sounded uncommonly like a warning hiss, then nuzzled at the foal, who stood and tottered over to her. It seemed at a loss for where to find the tit, looking for it in quite the wrong place.

The older of the men started towards it, but the younger said, "You may leave him to it, my lord. He'll find the tit right enough."

The older man hesitated, but finally nodded. Turning to Athos, he gave him the once over, head to toe, then said, "Pleasure to meet you, Monsieur Musketeer," the man said, extending a bloodied hand to Athos. "I am Monsieur de Comeau. I believe you wish to see me?"

Foals and Lords; The Follies of Youth;
The Requirements of a Large Stable

MONSIEUR de Comeau was a tall man, as tall as Athos, and as slim of body and refined of bones as Aramis. Unlike Athos, he had the olive skin that is common with dark hair. Unlike Aramis—who would never allow himself to be seen by anyone, not even his servant, in less than fashionable clothing—he was wearing a serviceable suit of undyed wool and he didn't seem in the least embarrassed by his common and undistinguished attire.

He waved away his groom, telling him to mind the foal, then led Athos into the house, up a back staircase—from its look a servants' staircase, dark, narrow and the wooden steps below foot quite unpolished, save where the feet of those running up and down had polished them.

"You'll forgive me," Monsieur de Comeau said, as he led Athos up the staircase. "But if we go in through the main staircase and track stable muck into the house my wife will never let me hear the end of it."

The face that turned back to look at Athos over the gentleman's shoulder, was a neat oval, punctuated by a wisp of moustache and beard excellently trimmed to shape. It was all unremarkable, from the well-shaped nose, to the neatly arched eyebrows. Only the eyes—brown and impish—lent it any dignity. They were the eyes of a school child getting away with a prank.

Athos nodded his condescension of this unusual reception, and presently they wound around the staircase, to arrive at a door, which the gentleman leaned over to open. Inside was a comfortable entrance room, the floor tiled in yellow.

There, through foresight or training, someone had left a basin and several pitchers of water, as well as towels for the hands, and various rags on the floor, presumably to clean their footwear. Two footmen waited, in a corner, but didn't move to receive their lord, as he said, "You may clean yourself here. I must clean and change before going within, or my lady wife will have my head on a pike."

Hoping it was metaphorical, Athos examined himself by the light of the broad window that took up most of the far wall in this room. To his surprise he found he had somehow got blood on his hands, and a slight stain on the cuff of his shirt.

Cleaning it was quick work, with the water provided, and he cleaned himself using a corner of a towel, dipped in water, to remove the spot of blood from his cuff. While he was doing so, the valets stepped forward and helped the Monsieur de Comeau out of his suit. It was all Athos could do not to smile, because the gentleman seemed as careless of undressing before a stranger as any musketeer, used to sharing quarters with his fellows, or any commoner who'd slept in a bed with many siblings. In fact, for lack of modesty or self-consciousness, the Monsieur de Comeau could easily rival Porthos.

He removed his suit, till he was left in his underwear, by which time Athos had finished using the basin. One of the valets threw the stained water out, and rinsed the basin, after which the gentleman proceeded to wash himself with remarkable thoroughness, and to use a comb in his, relatively short—barely touching his ears—black hair.

Even while he was combing his hair—and removing a wealth of straw from it—his men were dressing him, with the aplomb of those who had been trained to this and were used to performing their task without the least cooperation from their subject.

So it was that, as he finished combing himself, one of his valets was lacing the front of a splendid doublet in fawn-colored velvet, while the other one was contriving—to his lord's considerable inattention—to get a pair of highly polished boots on the gentleman's feet.

Athos made use of a rag in the corner to clean the main muck from his feet which wasn't much, his having spent a very short time in the stables.

They were both presentable at the same time, when the gentleman smiled at Athos, "What did you mean to see me about?" He hesitated. "At least I assume you didn't come to see the newborn foal?"

"No." Athos said, mindful of the presence of the valets and not wishing to question the gentleman about what might be an embarrassing subject in front of them. "He seemed lively enough."

"Aye, it's a good bloodline. Part of the reason I might have been a bit foolish about it. Could have got myself bit. So . . . What did you wish to ask me?"

"It is," Athos said, not meeting the man's eyes. "A rather private matter."

"Oh, so?" The gentleman's eyebrows raised, but he nodded, and waved one of his valet's away. "Francois, go to the kitchen and bring us a bottle of the red and . . . some cheese?" He looked over at Athos. "You'll forgive me, but I missed my breakfast, dragged out of bed because the mare was giving birth. And while I doubt there's anything ready and cooked now, since the kitchen will be preparing for lunch, there should be cheese and bread, if you don't mind . . ."

Athos bowed.

"Very well, Francois, cheese and bread and a bottle of that red we got last week from my farm."

Francois bowed and disappeared, and the gentleman opened a door bordered in gold trim, onto a room set in a far more opulent style. It was a man's room—or at least it had been decorated by a woman with the intention that it should be a man's room—with yellow silk curtains and straight-backed yellow silk upholstered chairs. Against a window, a small table had been pushed, which was piled high with documents, a welter of writing quills and a few pots of ink.

The gentleman led Athos away from that table and towards where two chairs sat almost side-by-side. He took one, and waved Athos onto the other.

"I don't have the pleasure of your acquaintance," he prompted.

Athos smiled. "I am a musketeer, and I am known as Athos."

The eyebrows went up. "Ah. I have heard rumors, in fact . . . It matters not, but there are those who say that half of his Majesty's corps of musketeers are noblemen in disguise."

"Not half," Athos said smiling.

The gentleman opened his mouth, and it looked for a moment as though he would say that surely Athos was a nobleman in disguise, but then he seemed to think better of it, and shrugged. "Well . . . It matters not. For some people the birth is evident in feature and movement."

Athos wondered if that was true. He very much suspected what was evident in him, other than a certain beauty of feature and form, which he knew he had inherited from the Countess his mother, was his father's excellent and relentless training.

At any rate, his host was disposed to wave this away and deal as though with equals. "You meant to speak to me of . . . ?" He prompted.

Athos nodded, even as he studied exactly what to speak to the gentleman of. "There was a boy, sometime back," he said at last, speaking slowly as he weighed the best way to phrase it all. "A child of about eleven, with auburn hair, who might have sought employment with you?"

Monsieur de Comeau looked at Athos a long time, his eyes seeming to look inward. Not a guilty expression, nor exactly a puzzled one, more the look of someone who is listening to another person speak in a foreign language and can't make heads or tails of it. At last, the fine dark eyebrows drew together and he said, "I beg your pardon?"

Athos sighed. "I'm putting it very badly," he said. "I know. But I don't know how else to put it. I'm not in the habit, commonly, of questioning noblemen about their private life or their private decisions, or even the street urchins who might have pestered them." The gentleman frowned as though not sure what Athos might mean by that, and Athos continued. "There is this boy who came to my friend Porthos, some time ago, and begged him to teach him fencing. He presented himself as a young man of birth, but we have reason to believe that he was a mere plebeian. He lived—and indeed was born at the Hangman—"

At the name of the inn, Monsieur de Comeau's expression changed, shifting so fast through various changes from astonishment to shock, to surprise, to . . . anger? At the back of it all there was something else, something in his eyes. It was a familiar expression, but one that Athos was hard put to place.

"Ah," the gentleman said and leaned back in his chair as though to appraise Athos from a long distance. "Ah. Guillaume."

Athos nodded. "I see you know him?"

"Know him?" the gentleman asked. "I have often been tempted to strangle him with my bare hands."

Athos was conscious of inhaling sharply before he could stop himself, and he saw the gentleman look surprised at this, then shrug. "My dear sir, I don't mean that literally. Surely . . . But Guillaume needs at least a very sound thrashing."

"If you pardon my asking, why?"

The gentleman shook his head and opened his mouth, but at that moment his servants came in with wine and bread, a plate of cheese, and a bowl of butter. While they disposed it on the table, the two men held their tongues.

Once their cups were filled and bread broken, and the servants had left, they resumed talking.

"Guillaume," the gentleman said, pronouncing the name as if it tasted wrong to his tongue. "Guillaume is . . . Well . . . I suppose no better could be expected of him, growing up as he did at the back of a tavern and with a . . . well . . . a common slut for a mother, but . . ."

"His mother was . . . a bawd?" Athos asked.

Monsieur de Comeau shrugged. He took a sip of his wine. "Oh, mind you, I don't know if she charged, save, of course that her admirers were likely to give her gifts, but she was known not to be too attached to her virtue. She would drink a little and she would . . . well, give in to the advances of whoever . . ."

Athos's eyes had grown big, and he said, "I can't ask if—"

"Oh, of course man. Not . . . Not in the last seven years, since I've been married. But before? Yes, of course. I was . . . in Paris, alone. That was when I used to frequent the tavern and I daresay Pigeon made herself agreeable half a dozen times." He frowned. "That's how the boy knew me, and that is, I fancy, how he came to me. But how come you—" He tore a piece off the bread and favored Athos with an evaluating once-over. "A man of quality, to concern yourself in the brat's affairs?"

"My friend was teaching him fencing," Athos said, conscious of how little explanation that was, in fact. "And he has disappeared."

"Oh, depend upon it, he has cast about for another father."

Athos, in the middle of swallowing a mouthful of wine was surprised enough by this to stare. "Another father?"

The man nodded. "He'd got it into his head that I was his father. How, I don't know, since even the tavern keeper tells everyone that when she arrived in Paris, and at his establishment, she was already big with Guillaume. But he was convinced of it, or at least pretended to be." He took a broad bite of the bread and shook his head. "It is quite possible that he simply feigned this belief because I was the most noble of his mother's clients and he knew so."

"And what did he wish of you?" Athos asked. "Not . . . recognition?"

The man shook his head. "Not . . . as such. Guillaume is not deluded. He is a sharp boy, actually, is our Guillaume. What he wanted of me was an allowance, or, as he put it, enough money to go on with, so he could set up as a young gentleman in town, after which—he assured me magnanimously—he would make his own way in the world."

Athos listened, astonished both at the daring of the boy and the casual way in which the man told him this.

"And you?" Athos asked. "If you pardon my asking, how did you react to such demands?"

The gentleman laughed, loudly. "Why, as anyone of sense would react. Well . . . and at that perhaps not, because I think most people of sense would be more outraged by it than I was. You see, the thing is, I nurtured a fondness for the rascal. Very bright boy, though the conditions of his birth perhaps not all that could be desired. I wanted to . . . I didn't wish to quell his enterprising spirit completely, no more than I wished to pay, so that his false accusation should not be carried to my wife. And so . . ."

"And so . . . ?"

"I had him thrashed and thrown out the yard."

"And you haven't seen him since?"

Monsieur de Comeau flashed a bright smile between bites of bread. "Oh, I've seen him. He's come around again. He's knowledgeable of horses and quite good with them, you know. Probably a result of having grown up in a stable. He's come around now and then to help the grooms, but he has not bothered me. In fact, he takes care to stay as far away from me as possible." He shrugged. "Someday he'll grow out of his ridiculous pretensions and make a fine groom whom I'd be glad to hire."

It was on Athos's tongue to ask about the horses and the vast establishment, all out of proportion to the lodging and the perceived wealth of the owner. It was none of his concern, and truly he had no excuse for even thinking about it. Other people's finances had nothing to do with Athos. He'd been taught that money was nothing next to nobility of birth and even now, he felt guilty thinking about it.

And yet, wouldn't it be possible that a gentleman as fond of horse flesh as Monsieur de Comeau, and as yet having failed to achieve any particular royal sinecure, would have been paid to attract the child here or to poison him? By the Cardinal, or even by Monsieur Coquenard, the husband of Porthos's mistress?

Just because Monsieur Coquenard was old, it shouldn't be supposed he was deaf, dumb and blind. And he certainly had cunning and money. In many ways, in fact, this plot bespoke more of him than the Cardinal who would have more ways in which to ensnare Porthos—and would probably target Aramis and not Porthos for his wrath. But Monsieur Coquenard . . .

Athos couldn't think of any way to question Monsieur de Comeau on the matter that wouldn't have brought about a duel, a duel in which he would almost certainly kill the man. And because Monsieur de Comeau had no fame—no reputation at all—as a duelist, it would be rumored far and wide that Athos killed the innocent.

It couldn't be tolerated. He made a correct bow to Monsieur de Comeau and walked down the stairs to the sun baked yard filled with horses. Porthos was waiting by the gate, as though all his own enquiries were done and he had nothing more to do with it.

A sudden feeling of being watched, and Athos looked over his shoulder and at a window high on the facade of the house, where he'd swear a woman was watching from. Just a hint of long hair, an impression of an oval face.

Truth be told that a woman should watch Athos was nothing new. They often did, noblewomen and maids alike.

And yet, this one's glance made the space between his shoulder blades prickle.

He determinedly turned away from that window, and joined Porthos by the gate, only casting a final look over his shoulder at the horses and grooms in the yard. Monsieur de Comeau had joined them and was inspecting the back leg of a nervous grey.

And Athos wondered if the extravagant pastime had been purchased with murder.

Horses and Memories; Guillaume's Trip;
Porthos's Subtlety

❧

"**D**IDN'T the grooms talk to you?" Athos asked.

Porthos looked startled, as if, Athos thought, he never expected such a question. He frowned slightly as he said, "Oh, they talked."

"Then why had you left to stand by the gate?" Athos asked.

Porthos shrugged and looked away, at the facades of the houses they walking past, as though something riveted him in the stone fronts, the tall windows.

"Porthos!"

A deep sigh answered Athos frustrated exclamation. Slowly, Porthos turned to look at Athos. "Athos, I think the boy was my son."

"Oh, not this again, my friend," Athos said. "Surely no one needs to explain to you that there are many girls who come from the provinces and who are with child. Surely you understand that just because Guillaume—"

"It's not that." Porthos's voice, loud even when controlled, had burst forth from him like something torn out against his will. Its echoes reverberated off the walls. He shook his massive head, the red hair glinting under the midday sun. "It's not that, Athos. I have reason . . . I have . . . reason." His throat worked, as he swallowed, convulsively.

Was that the shine of tears in Porthos's eyes? Athos was afraid of looking too closely. He'd seen Porthos angry and happy. He'd seen Porthos drunk and confused. He'd never seen Porthos cry. He didn't want to see it now.

Looking away from Porthos, he waited, but from Porthos's breathing, from the way he stomped as hard as he could, each foot hitting the cobbles as though they'd done him personal injury, he guessed that not only was something working at Porthos, but the something was of a kind that made his words tie in knots within the giant musketeer and refuse to come out.

If he demanded that Porthos explain himself now, he would only make Porthos more inarticulate and more angry at himself for being inarticulate and eventually that anger would spill over onto Athos, as if it were all Athos's fault—because it had to be someone's fault, after all. If Athos pushed now they could come to one of those awkward situations in which Porthos challenged Athos for a duel, then apologized for doing it, and then did it all over again. It would be an hour before he could get any sense out of him, unless he proceeded very carefully indeed.

Normally this was a task better left to Aramis who, for all he enjoyed teasing his giant friend and arguing with him over minute things, knew Porthos better than anyone else did.

But Aramis was away, at some alchemists or chemists or physicians, and not here, to talk sense to Porthos. So Athos tried. "Porthos, start at the beginning. How did you approach the grooms? What did they tell you?"

"I started by looking at the horses," Porthos said. "And making comments, all the while making out like the only thing I wanted was to wait for you, and like I couldn't figure out what was taking you so long or why. A touch of impatience."

Athos nodded, without looking at Porthos, but guessing that Porthos was looking at him.

"It wasn't difficult," Porthos said. "They have some fine

Arabians there, and an Andalusian beast, freshly imported, whom they hope will stud their mares. I tell you, I never saw such a stable in the city. It would rival some of the best ones even in the provinces that are known for horse rearing."

"Indeed," Athos said, soothingly, hoping to spin the whole tale out of Porthos by starting with this unassuming, unthreatening gossip, the same way that Porthos had discovered whatever he'd discovered from the grooms. "Monsieur de Comeau has exceptional taste in horses." He chose not to tell Porthos about how he couldn't understand where the money for the horses was coming from, nor to vent any suspicions of Coquenard's involvement. Not yet.

"Yes. And so we talked about horses for a while and then I said I knew a boy who used to work . . ." He stopped, his voice failing. "A boy who used to live at the Hangman, and how his name was Guillaume."

Porthos paused, a long pause and, for a moment, Athos was afraid that Porthos had, once more, become lost in his own thoughts and that he wouldn't find his way out. But after a silence, the musketeer burst out with, "Athos, all of them knew him. I think he spent most of his day there."

"But we knew this, Porthos, or suspected it. The hosteler, Martin, said that he'd tried to find employment . . ." Looking up, out of the corner of his eyes, he saw Porthos shake his head.

"Oh, no. That was not the sole thing. That wasn't even the most important thing," Porthos said. "I can't verify that he tried to find employment at all, in fact, unless you count as employment that he came and helped the grooms at all their tasks, in exchange for a crumb of bread and a drop of wine. I don't think he ever tried to attach himself to Monsieur de Comeau or wear his livery. And . . . Athos, he had him thrashed."

"Yes," Athos said, sensing the passion behind his friend's words and making his own words as calm as possible. "Yes. He told me so himself."

"God's Blood, why?"

"Because the boy imposed on him," Athos said. "Tried to tell him that he was his bastard son. Tried to get Monsieur de Comeau to make him an alliance and to—"

"Are you sure?" Porthos asked.

"It's what Comeau told me," Athos said. "In this case, of course, there is always the question of someone telling the truth."

"In every case, ever, there is the question of whether people tell the truth," Porthos said, speaking with the gravity of an oracle. "Guillaume never asked me for money and never told me he was my son."

"And yet you think he was?"

There was a long and sharp intake of breath. "I think it very likely he was," Porthos said. "Very, very likely. I don't know how to . . . You see, there are too many coincidences." His voice trembled, part in grief and part in frustration, and once more he showed a tendency to become snared in his inner thoughts and unable to express himself.

"Just tell it as you came to it," Athos said. "Slowly."

"Well," Porthos said. "All the grooms praised Guillaume. They thought he was very smart, and of course, he knew a lot about horses, because he was probably looking after travelers' horses since he was old enough to stand and hold a bridle."

"Probably," Athos conceded.

"And he never asked for payment for his work, though the grooms did take him out to . . . other taverns, when they went. I gather they didn't drink at home. And they would buy him food and drink. And they gave him things, you know . . . a used pair of breeches, a mended doublet."

Athos nodded thinking that such clothes as the boy had died in would not have been come by through gifts from grooms or other people of like quality. He didn't say anything, but Porthos's mind must have been running on the same path, because he said, "Of course, they said he must have found someone else to give him clothes, recently, because he showed up in fine violet velvet, the likes of which they'd never seen. Or rather, he wore his normal clothes but he would change into fine violet velvet before leaving. I think he was coming to me for lessons then."

Athos nodded. He thought so too.

"And they said," Porthos said. "That he'd come by money too. You know, throwing money around and demanding to pay his share of the drinks and the meals."

Athos didn't say anything, as there was nothing he could say to that. Where money was coming from in this matter was something that he would very much like to know. It seemed to him, that alone might solve the whole thing, and for a moment was tempted to tell Porthos to ask his Athenais whether she could trace it.

But Porthos was going on. "And then," he said. "About a month ago Guillaume was gone for a week. He told them he was going to a village, where his mother had come from." A struggling breath, as though Porthos's head where breaking above water after a long dive. "And the village was St. Guillaume du Vallon."

Porthos looked at Athos as if he had made some dramatic revelation, but Athos had absolutely no idea what it could be. So the boy had gone to the village his mother had come from. What did that mean? "Were you teaching him fencing then?"

"Had been," Porthos said. "For a few weeks. And he did tell me he was going to be absent for a week, but I had no idea where he went. I thought . . ." He shrugged. "If I had known. If only I had known."

"But why Porthos?" Athos asked. "What would it have signified? So the boy was named after his mother's village. What can it mean to you?"

"What can it mean to me, Athos? How can you be so calm? What would it mean to you to find you had a son, already grown to half man, and you not knowing him, not having any idea you had him?"

Athos blinked. "His name was Guillaume, and his

mother's village was St. Guillaume of something or other.
How does this tell you that his mother . . ." And then Athos
remembered. It had been stupid of him not to think of it
earlier, only of course, when he'd met Porthos he already
called himself Porthos. And yet he'd seen Porthos's name
but recently, in the genealogy in the boy's pouch. "Du Vallon," he said. "By God, Porthos, du Vallon."

Porthos sniffled, and Athos couldn't tell if he was doing
it to control tears or in annoyance at Athos's slowness of
mind. "I told you she was my Amelie. There's nothing of
her in that wench at the tavern, nothing I can tell you, at
least, but I think there has to be . . . a turn of the head, a tilt
of the brow. Something about her made me think of
Amelie. And it was Amelie, Athos. It was. And Guillaume
was my son."

Biting his lip, confused, Athos thought how this would
look now if the crime were found out and not a murderer
ready for it. The boy had been Porthos's bastard. The boy
had already demanded money from Monsieur de Comeau
on the pretext that Monsieur de Comeau was his father.
What would people think but that he'd also demanded the
like tribute from Porthos, and that Porthos had killed him
instead of paying.

It wasn't possible. No one should think it. Porthos was
more likely to fell someone, anyone, with a blow of his
huge fist, a quick strike of his nimble sword. What was
more, he could easily have killed the boy—if he'd wanted
that—and looking at Porthos who swallowed convulsively
in an effort to control his tears, Athos knew he'd never
wanted it. But if Porthos had wanted the boy dead, it
would have been the work of a few seconds to strike out
with his sword during one of their practices and claim it
had all been by accident. Who could gainsay it who hadn't
been present? Who was there in the world who could have
sworn otherwise?

And if Athos said that, if . . . If the crime were discovered and Porthos taken for it, and Athos were to say that

striking by stealth, with poison, was all out of Porthos's character, people would only tell him that Porthos was stupid and that he would think that a poisoning would never be found. Of course, Porthos wasn't stupid, but few beyond his three most intimate friends would know that. Very few.

"Porthos," he said. "It is a damnable situation."

"Yes," Porthos said. "Oh yes. If I'd known he was my son, Athos . . . If I'd known . . . I'd have . . ."

"Yes?" Athos asked.

"I'd have recognized him," Porthos said. "I'd have . . . Why, in a few years we could have found him a guard post with some nobleman. We could . . ." He swallowed and was silent.

And in his mind's eyes, Athos could see Porthos doing just the things he said he'd do. Porthos was no fool, but neither did he, unlike Aramis or Athos, care for the opinions of the world. He would have set the boy up in a proper position and introduced him to everyone in the world.

He would have withstood the pricks of mockery and the smiles of the world and the titters behind their hands at proud Porthos's recognizing the son of a common whore. And he wouldn't have cared two figs for it all, save that it would have given him the opportunity to fight some more duels with just cause.

And yet, what connections did Porthos have? What relatives that might mind what they would view as a humiliation for their whole line? And did Porthos have any relatives in Paris who might somehow have seen to the heart of the plot.

When Athos had told D'Artagnan that the great noble houses were all related to each other, he'd been speaking nothing but the truth. But the fact is, so was the lower nobility. In fact many people at about the same level married and married again, till their families were an interconnected web of affinity.

Of course Athos wouldn't know much about families at Porthos's level of nobility. Too young a line; too newly come to wealth and name. Athos could very well imagine what his father would say of Athos's even deigning to greet such in the morning, much less be their close friend.

This meant Athos didn't even know if Porthos might have near cousins in Paris, much less distant ones. And they were so secret about their identities—which Monsieur de Treville knew, and probably other people in Paris, but about which they never talked, not even to each other—that there had been no talk of family. He knew that Aramis and D'Artagnan were only children simply because they'd volunteered the information. But as for the others . . . For all he knew Porthos was the seventh of ten brothers, all of them living in Paris, and at least half of them resentful of the idea of a bastard nephew, and one born in a barn, yet.

"Porthos," Athos said, turning his head to ask his friend about all this. But there were glistening trails down Porthos's face, running from his eyes to his beard.

And then men appeared before them. They were dressed like guards, perhaps. Certainly their bearing was military. But they wore black breeches and doublets, and no insignias.

The one in front was blond and looked like he was doing a pale imitation of de Termopillae, who normally tried to copy Aramis. He stood in the path that Athos walked and he spoke, with a slight foreign accent. "You will give it to us now."

"It?" Athos asked. "I don't have the pleasure of understanding."

"It. You know very well what it is. And you will give it to us," the foreign man said, stomping his right foot.

Athos had absolutely no idea what they wanted. But he knew he was not about to give anything to anyone with such poor manners. "Perhaps," he said. "I need to teach you how to speak to a musketeer." He put his hand to his sword, but as he did, the man's eyes enlarged.

"There is really no need to fight," he said. "Just give it to us."

"Monsieur, we don't give anything to anyone, unless we know what it is and we're asked properly."

"Well, no," Porthos said, drawing his sword. "We easily give them a fight."

The expression on the man's face was pure panic. His friends, behind him, gibbered something that appeared to be English. And then they belied their military bearing by turning and running.

Porthos stood, sword in hand, open mouthed with surprise. "Should we chase them?" he asked Athos.

Athos frowned. "Not today. We have other things to do. But it is very odd."

"It's the air of Paris," Porthos said. "It makes even ruffians strange in the head. What they need is a good vacation in the country."

As happened so often, Athos had no idea whether Porthos was jesting or not.

Dreams and Reality;
The Unreasonable Behavior
of High Noblemen;
Going to the Source

D'ARTAGNAN had scarce slept the whole night, and waking to go to guard duty, he'd been less than alert. Now, after a long morning standing in the doorway of Monsieur des Essarts, without even the company of his friends to relieve his boredom, he was even more sleepy. So much so that he thought he was dreaming when he found all his friends assembled in his entrance room, around the table.

Only, their presence didn't exactly surprise him, since he'd suspected today would be spent in enquiries surrounding the death of the child. Also, it was easy to know this couldn't be a dream since his scrubbed pine table was as bare of all provisions as it had been this morning when he'd left, and the three didn't even have wine in front of them.

D'Artagnan pulled a chair and sat on it, and then he wasn't absolutely sure he wasn't dreaming, because as soon as he'd sat, Aramis said, "Now we're all here, and, D'Artagnan, you look like the dead, let us have something to revive us. *Holá,* Planchet?" And at the appearance of D'Artagnan's servant, Aramis tossed a coin in the boy's direction. "Get us wine. Decent stuff. And some bread and whatever meat you can find."

As the boy caught the coin overhand and grinned, doubtless thinking of his share of the largesse, Athos smiled and asked Aramis, "Another theology book."

Aramis shook his head. "Not as it would happen. I went to visit Brother Laurence who, as I told you, is a master of herbs and plants and the properties thereof. While I was there and asking about nightshade—of which I've brought a sample of its extract, so you can know the smell which Brother Laurence says is characteristic—and he gave me this new formula he's had from a Gascon and which is rumored to have a miraculous effect on wounds." He looked at D'Artagnan, whose eyes had widened. Aramis's own eyes were merry with mischief. "Since we have our own source of that excellent curative, and my having found that de Termopillae had suffered a grievous wound in a fight with the guards of the Cardinal last night . . ." Aramis grinned. "He was very glad to empty his purse to get his hands on the specific. As it chanced his purse was quite fat."

At this time, they were interrupted by the arrival of Planchet with an abundance of food and two bottles of wine, which he proceeded to serve. In addition to the bread there was some very good roasted mutton. Three of them ate in silence for a while, but it did not escape D'Artagnan's notice that Porthos was merely nibbling on a little bread without much appetite.

It wasn't, however, till they were done eating, and sat in front of newly refilled cups of wine, that Athos said, "I think we must speak of what we found this morning."

He spoke in carefully measured sentences, of Monsieur de Comeau's obsession with horses, of his vast stables and many grooms, then frowned. "Before I was done there," he said, and looked towards Porthos as though worried about the result of his revelations, "I was wondering about the horses, and where money for all those horses comes from. For you must know that feeding that large a stable in the city cannot be easy. They can hardly turn them out to pasture. Even if the lord has a country estate, to which he sends horses in spring and summer, the expense has to be enormous." He looked around the table, and then Aramis looked back at him with eyebrows raised, saying nothing. Porthos seemed to be lost in some sort of dream or nightmare of his own mind.

"You think he's being paid by someone," D'Artagnan said. "That this is the only way he can afford such a large stable."

Athos inclined his head. His eyes showed that expression they often wore around D'Artagnan—an expression of curious amusement, as though the workings of D'Artagnan's mind couldn't fail to amuse him.

"Do you have in mind who could have done it?" D'Artagnan asked, feeling sure that Athos did. It was in Athos's expression, in the way he was looking at D'Artagnan, as though willing D'Artagnan to voice something he didn't wish to.

"Many people could have done it." Athos said. "To begin with, the Cardinal, of course."

"You mean," D'Artagnan said. "That he might have done it to implicate Porthos in a crime? It has always seemed a little fantastic, though perhaps it is because I don't have as much experience of Paris as you do."

Aramis shrugged, one of his fashionably elaborate shrugs. He glanced at Athos, then turned to D'Artagnan. "Not that it's impossible. He's made other plots, just as elaborate, against other people. But normally, when he goes through this trouble, it is against crowned heads and those in power, not . . ."

"Not Porthos," Athos said. "This has occurred to me. And yet, if he's taken on a particular animosity . . ." He shrugged.

"There is still another objection," D'Artagnan said. "That if the lord had that many horses and had it all before the boy first approached him, surely he can't have been thinking of such a plan."

Athos shrugged. "It is possible," he said. "That he has

been in the Cardinal's pay all along, and that the boy coming along merely provided the opportunity for him to render his eminence a service."

D'Artagnan inclined his head. It was possible. Perhaps it was even likely. Sometimes it seemed that half the court was in the Cardinal's pay. "But if so," D'Artagnan said, "how convenient should it be that he found just the right boy to convince Porthos to teach him, and how cold-blooded to seize on any boy—"

"It wasn't any boy," Porthos said, in what was for him a roar, and which must have been heard loud and clear by the neighbors on either side. Then he lowered his voice to say, "It was my son." His face had gone pale, his features wooden.

"Your son?" D'Artagnan asked, now fully convinced this was some bizarre dream. It was all tied with Porthos's outburst yesterday and none of it made a wit of sense and he—

"Guillaume," Porthos said, "was my son." And proceeded to lay the story before them, in what was, for Porthos, almost an eloquent manner. His lost girlfriend, and the something of her he'd detected in the girl, Amelie. And Guillaume, named after the saint who supposedly protected the village at the center of Porthos's domain, the village in which his manor house was located. "It is a very small village, you understand," he said. "It is a very small manor house as well. Just a little place at the butt end of nowhere, and nothing like any of you would trouble yourselves with, but . . . small and humble as it was, it was my father's domain and yet he thought we were that much better than the peasantry that he would not allow me . . ." He opened his hands, as though to signify his helplessness. "He said Amelie was common as muck, with no name and no ancestors and no fortune either, and I needed someone with fortune, someone, he said, with something in her stocking foot. He said if I left the domain, he would not do anything to her. Only find her a marriage, and be done with it. But if

I didn't leave, he was going to send her parents from the land, for, you see, they only held the land from us."

"And so you left," D'Artagnan said.

Porthos opened his hands in a show of helplessness that, in its way, was a more eloquent demonstration of grief than any number of elegies. "And I'm guessing she came after me, instead of taking the marriage offered," Porthos said. "I swear by the Virgin and all the saints that I never thought she was that attached to me. If I had known . . ." He was silent a long time, chewing on the corner of his moustache. "But I would say the chances are very high, if not absolutely sure—and I'd hold it to be absolutely sure—that the boy was mine. And if the boy was mine, my son . . ." He shrugged.

"If the boy was yours, the wish to injure you might very well have gone beyond a wish to have you taken up for murder," Athos said, "to a wish to hurt you personally, which brings me again, forgive me Porthos, to the possibility that someone with money . . ."

Porthos looked blankly at Athos, his hands still open on the table. Athos opened his hands, in turn, looking as if he couldn't quite express himself with voice only. "Look, Porthos, Monsieur de Comeau is living well above his means. That usually means one is in the hands of the moneylenders. And if he's in . . . If the moneylender has a call on him, he might very well have set Monsieur de Comeau the task of . . . well . . ."

Porthos stared for a long time. D'Artagnan's understanding, of course, had leapt ahead to Athos's meaning, but he thought Porthos hadn't understood it, and he knew that Athos's delicacy would forbid him from saying it more bluntly. "He means—" he started.

Porthos waved his hand, commanding him to silence. "I know very well what he means," he said, and frowned. "He means that Monsieur Coquenard might well have given money to Monsieur de Comeau for his damned horses, and that as a result he was able to ask him to kill my son, in

such a manner that he would die near me and even, perhaps, get me taken in for his death." He made a face. "And
I don't say you might not have a point. After all, it is true,
very true, you know, that cuckolds can have the weirdest
turns. And while I don't think Monsieur Coquenard cares,
as such . . . Well . . ."

Athos nodded. "You can't be sure. It's quite possible he
knows of the going ons. In fact, given the way you gain access to her house, and how often, I'd be shocked if he
doesn't. And if he knows . . ."

"He would hardly make an open fuss," Porthos said.
"Of course he wouldn't. Because, you know, their kind
doesn't. They might starve their servants, and they might
make the most distressing economies, but all in the secret
of their houses. What they present to the world . . ." He
shrugged. "And so, you see, I think it is quite possible he
would do something like that, by stealth. But . . . that is not
of any great significance. I can ask Athenais, you know?"

"And will she know?" Aramis asked. "It is my experience that often ladies don't know anything of what goes on
under their own roofs, save only if they have enough for
their paint pots and their face creams."

Athos smiled at this—one of his odd, secretive smiles
that D'Artagnan had learned meant a secret amusement
he didn't wish to express aloud, either because it would
forever blight his friendship with someone or because he
thought of it as something best enjoyed in secret and
silence.

Porthos, on the other hand, was never a man to keep
anything to himself. At least not anything he could berate
one of them for. He glared at Aramis. "Aramis," he said.
"You've met Athenais. If you think she doesn't know all
the accounts and everything that goes on in her husband's
firm and household, you're a greater fool than I've ever
known you to be."

Aramis opened his mouth to reply. Even in the few
months that D'Artagnan had known the three musketeers,

he'd become accustomed to these quarrels between Porthos and Aramis. They'd arrive suddenly, progress alarmingly fast, and end with one or the other of them calling out for a duel before the offender apologized.

D'Artagnan felt they didn't have time for it now, and it was entirely the wrong thing. He glared at Aramis, who seemed so surprised to encounter censure from such a quarter that he stopped with his mouth half-open.

Porthos waited for the answer for a second, and when it didn't come, he got up, shrugging. "I suppose I'll go to Athenais, then," he said.

"Wait," D'Artagnan said, getting up. And having said it wondered what he was thinking. The words had come out of his mouth so fast that he had no time to decide what had impelled them. It was much, he reflected, with chagrin, like Porthos saying that his mind didn't know what he knew.

"Yes?" Porthos asked him.

And on that D'Artagnan's sleep-befogged mind cleared. "What I meant," he said. "Is that doubtless your Athenais will take some time to look through the books and discover whether Monsieur de Comeau has been receiving money from her husband. And even if she discovers it, because the matter is of such long standing—judging by the lord's stables—how are you to prove he was involved in killing the young man?"

Porthos's hands closed, on either side of his body. "If he killed Guillaume, I shall kill him."

"How?" D'Artagnan asked.

"You can't challenge him to a duel," Athos said.

"Indeed, no," Aramis put in. "His extreme old age protects him from such. And what are you going to do if you can't challenge him to a duel? What do you intend to do?"

Porthos's hands unclenched, then clenched again. "If he killed my son, I'll kill him."

Athos shook his head. "Indeed no."

"We'd be very poor friends if we allowed you that

course of action," Aramis said. "It is one thing to kill someone in a duel, but another and quite different thing to kill him by stealth and in the dark, or to kill someone of such markedly inferior strength as Monsieur Coquenard. If you kill him it will be murder, and they'll execute you, Porthos."

Porthos was quiet a moment, then frowned and asked, as if the question were difficult to formulate, "I am to allow him to live, then? To go on as though nothing had happened? I know that the Cardinal has many such debts to his conscience and yet goes on living and, such as it is, ruling France. But surely, you don't expect me to take the murder of my son in the same manner and to—"

"No," D'Artagnan said. "No. We wouldn't expect it and, indeed, wouldn't look for it. Only that . . . to get your revenge, you will need to involve the law and that will necessitate more proof than the fact that Monsieur de Comeau was indebted to Monsieur Coquenard, because I fancy that hundreds of people are, and are not, for all that, murderers."

"But—" Porthos said.

"What this means," Athos said, his voice serious. "What D'Artagnan is trying to say is that we must gather more proof of his guilt."

"How?" Porthos asked.

"Well, that was what I was thinking of," D'Artagnan said. "And why I thought I could not allow this meeting to end before I had established it. We must find out why Guillaume had your genealogy, and indeed if it was him who gathered it or if someone gave it to him, and if he got it, at whose request."

"How can we find out if he was the one who gathered it," Porthos said, "when he's dead? And you're forgetting he went to St. Guillaume du Vallon."

D'Artagnan inclined his head. "I'm not forgetting it, Porthos. Indeed, I'm not. But just because he went there, or was persuaded to go there, doesn't mean he was the one

who researched your genealogy—a difficult labor for a lad.
And tedious, besides."

"True, but in any case, he's dead. How will we find—"

"If he went to the village, he stayed with someone and
might have talked to someone," D'Artagnan said. "We
should go, all of us, and talk to people and find out what he
did."

"In my lands?" Porthos asked. "In my father's lands?
You want me to go and question my father?"

"Your father," Athos said, with a speculative tone.

"Athos, it would be monstrous."

"No more monstrous than things that happen daily,"
Athos said.

"But . . ."

"We must," Aramis said. "Go, as the Gascon says. We
will ask leave of Monsieur de Treville."

"And I will ask leave of Monsieur des Essarts,"
D'Artagnan said.

"And before all of that, I shall go and talk to Athenais,"
Porthos said.

At the Top of the Ladder;
Accounts and Accounting;
A Wife's Loyalty

༄

THE Coquenard home slumbered in silence. All but the mistress who, having responded to a hail of pebbles on her shutter, had opened the window and let down the rope ladder to admit Porthos.

Porthos had come into the small room—barely large enough for the one narrow bed and the small wardrobe at the foot—and there stood, holding his hat. He'd never felt so awkward in this place as he now did. Or at least, not since the first time that they'd conceived of this way of meeting. He was no longer sure which of them had suggested it, but the first time he'd climbed the ladder and found himself here, he'd been half in thrall of her and half in fear of doing this in a full house, with servants waiting.

Like that first time, this time, he stood by the window, his back to it, silent and still. Athenais faced him, her hair loose down her back, her simple nightgown hugging her body and revealing that despite the white threads in her hair, the fine wrinkles at the corner of her eyes, she was still more beautiful than half the painted misses at court. Her face went from a welcoming smile to a look of alarm. "Porthos," she said. And after a pause, in which he didn't answer her, "What is wrong?"

Porthos shook his head, trying to figure out how to begin and how to tell Athenais so many momentous things. Not for the first time, he wished he had Aramis's facility with words, his ability to ease his way into serious subjects with a quote, a scrap of Latin. But it wasn't part of him. He looked up, and his eyes met his lady's serious gaze. "Athenais," he said, only the word came out more as a lament, than just a saying of her name.

And now Athenais was alarmed, crossing the distance between them, taking his hand in hers. "What is wrong?"

"I don't know how . . . I don't know if . . . How can I tell you? How can I ask you?" Porthos said, hearing his voice out of control and trying to keep it low so no one in the nearby rooms would hear him. What if Monsieur Coquenard had already heard him? What if it had cost him his boy's life? "I don't . . ." He swallowed hard.

Her hands, holding one of his, squeezed tight. "You must know," she said. "You must know that there is nothing you can't tell me. While we have not had the benefit of having our hands joined in church, surely you know that our souls have long been joined, that . . ."

Porthos sighed, a heavy sigh, and said the only thing he could think of, "You will be angry at me."

"I? Angry at you? When have I been angry at you?"

"All the time. When I brought Athos over. When I do something you think is stupid. When you hear I fought a duel. When I make too much noise trying to get your attention at the window. When . . ."

She smiled. "I do get angry at you, don't I? Enough, I suppose. But I don't get angry at you in truth, Porthos. Irritated, perhaps. Annoyed. Particularly when you fight needless duels. But I don't hold anger against you for any time, Porthos. I don't resent you for hardly any time at all."

Porthos blinked. He knew this was true. Oh, in truth of fact, many times he'd climbed that rope ladder to find his Athenais fully dressed, with flashing eyes and stern countenance, ready to read him the riot book for, what she called, his mad behavior and his foolish disregard for his own life and nature. But there was never a time he'd left the room without their having made up, without her having at last smiled at him, even if she told him he was a very great fool as she smiled. And he'd never left without sharing her bed or, time not permitting so much, without holding her in his arms.

He took a deep breath and stepped away from the wall, and across to the bed, on which he sat. It creaked under his weight, as he looked up at Athenais's worried face.

"Are you ill?" she asked him, anxiously. "You know, you could stay in that little house down the way, and I could come and nurse you often enough and—"

"I'm not ill," he said. "I know I must look ghastly, but it is not illness. I wish it were, as it would be easier to cure. But it's not. Alas. No physical illness, at least. My heart . . ."

She searched his features with an anxious gaze. At last she knelt at his feet, and took his hands in hers. "My dear, what are you afraid of? What happened? Did anyone tell you I played you false? For if they did, they were wrong, you know? I never even look at other men."

It hadn't ever occurred to him she might play him false, and even now it didn't occur to him. Although now they were seasoned and used to their clandestine love affair, he remembered how many pangs of conscience it had, at first, cost her, and how difficult it all had been, even discovering some means to be alone together.

He shook his head slowly. "I never thought you'd play me false, Athenais. I know your heart. No. That never crossed my mind."

"And yet you say your heart has been wounded. Surely, Porthos, you don't mean really. Was it a wound, or—"

He smiled at her. Her alarm was so far from the mark. And yet he felt his own smile fade as soon as it appeared.

"No, no. That isn't it. It's just that . . . Athenais, he was my son."

"Who was your son? The boy who—?"

"Yes, yes. The very same." He let the words pour out of him, as he told her the whole story of their discoveries and what he had contrived to deduce.

Athenais listened to the story with an attentive air, and then at the end of it, it seemed as though her face, which until then had shown only attention and nothing else, melted. "Oh, Porthos," she said. "Oh, Porthos, I am so sorry."

He nodded. He didn't know how to take anyone's condolences. "But Athos and D'Artagnan and Aramis say that we must prove for sure why the boy was killed because . . ." And he realized where he was going with this, and this was not how he wished to break it to Athenais. "So that whoever killed him . . . so that . . . So we can prove it to the law." He realized he'd made a circular argument and took a deep breath. "We must go to the village and see if he was truly there, and if he talked to anyone, and what he might have said."

"It seems logical," Athenais said.

"Yes, but . . . Athenais . . . I haven't seen my father since I left to come to Paris."

"Well," she said, stroking his hands, gently. "Well . . . perhaps it's time you spoke to him, then. Perhaps it's time you went and saw how things are in the domains."

"I can't return, you know," Porthos said. "I don't want to, at least." He flashed a smile, realizing he was lying to himself when he said he simply couldn't go back. "I don't want to leave my friends, or . . . or you."

"Then you don't need to," Athenais said. "But you should go, and perhaps make your peace with your father. He can't be very young, is he?"

"All the men in my family live forever," Porthos said, shrugging. "But listen, Athenais, there's something else. Something I'm afraid of telling you."

"Something you think will make me angry at you, yes, I perceive, since nothing you've said up till now could even remotely upset my feelings."

"The others think . . . that is . . . Monsieur de Comeau has too many horses for his establishment being such as it is, for his fortune being such as it is. They think he's getting financed by someone and they think . . . In short . . . They think that someone paid him to kill my son."

"The Cardinal?" Athenais asked.

"Well, no . . . Or perhaps the Cardinal but it could also be . . . someone could have lent money to Monsieur de Comeau for years, and could have offered to forgive him his debt in return for giving the poison to the boy."

"What do you . . . Oh." Athenais's hand flew to her mouth. "You mean . . . Monsieur Coquenard," she said. "My husband?"

"I told you you would be angry," Porthos said.

She swallowed, then shook her head. "Not angry, but Porthos . . . no. The . . . He's still sharp, that I can't deny, in the business way. Still sharp, though he trusts me with more and more of it every day, but he's still in control of his business, but . . . but no. Not about me. I don't think he cares about me. I don't think he . . . He hasn't, you know . . . in years, and as long as I appear to be a good and faithful wife to him, as long as I manage his business and look after his household, I don't think he cares, in the normal way of things whether you . . . you visit me, or what . . ."

"I'm not sure he doesn't mind, Athenais. Just that he can't do anything about it. If he could, if an idea presented itself . . ."

Athenais had gone pale. She nodded. "I can't say . . . Oh, I wish my loyalty permitted me to say that he would never do that. I wish . . . I wish I had the very proper feelings of a wife, and that I could rely on those feelings to say that nothing, ever would persuade Monsieur Coquenard to try to kill anyone." She put both hands in front of her mouth, then lowered them slowly. "Oh, I am an unspeakable wretch. The only thing I can't believe—the only thing, Porthos—is that my husband would have the resources to find out about your son, or to know that your son was spending time at Monsieur de Comeau's. But he might have found it by accident. We get a lot of information in various ways. Whispers in the dark, you know, conversations that happen in here, behind closed doors. It is possible. It is possible he has somehow found it out." She shook her head. "The only thing I can think, Porthos, the only thing I can say is that my husband being who he is, and my having lived with him for these many years, he's not a . . . convoluted man. For someone in his work, he's not a devious man. He wouldn't think of killing the child, Porthos. He'd be more likely to kill you." She smiled, a nervous smile. "He would be very likely to kill you, probably stealth or with poison, of course—or even more likely to pay someone to challenge and kill you in the street." She held up a hand to forestall any possible protest of his. "Porthos, I know that no normal fighter could have killed you on the street, but Monsieur Coquenard wouldn't know this."

"Except, perhaps," Porthos said. "If he were very angry at our . . . involvement, he truly wanted to punish me. Perhaps he wanted to kill one of the two people I would have died to save, and in such a way that everyone would think I had killed him. Perhaps he was looking for me to be killed in the gallows. Perhaps that would be his great revenge."

Athenais paled, then blushed, then paled again. She sighed and shook her head. "I wish I could say . . ." she said.

"I know," Porthos said. "I don't want to believe it of him, simply because I know it would sully your name, and leave you alone in the face of the world . . . only not really, because you know I would be ever ready to protect you with my name and my honor . . . but . . ."

Athenais, who had been staring at Porthos with a horrified expression, as if she were looking onto her own doom, now giggled. "Porthos," she said. "Did you just tell me that should my husband be a murderer, should he go to the gallows and leave me penniless and lost, you'd marry me?"

Porthos opened his hands as he did when he didn't know what else to say. Didn't Athenais know this? How could Athenais not know this. "We'd go hungry, sometimes," he said. "And you might have to follow us on campaign. The life of a musketeer's wife is not an easy one, but, Athenais, of course I would marry you. Do you think I'd abandon you in your hour of need? Do you think . . . ?"

"Oh, Porthos," she said. "Don't say any more. Don't say anything else . . ."

"You're angry at me," Porthos said, trying to read her expression which was odd in the extreme. She was smiling, but her eyes were full of tears and half-closed, as though something hurt her.

"No," she said, and shook her head. "No. I'm not angry at you."

"Irritated, then," Porthos said.

But Athenais giggled. She giggled and covered her mouth, and then she giggled again. And Porthos hoped she wasn't hysterical because what he'd heard about curing a woman's hysteria involved slapping her hard, and he couldn't even imagine slapping Athenais, not the least of which because he had a serious suspicion that Athenais would slap him back.

However, Athenais's giggling didn't escalate. Instead, it stopped all together, and when she removed her hand from in front of her mouth, her smile was something of wonder, the smile of a child faced with a new toy, the smile of a woman on her first ball.

"Don't speak, Porthos, don't speak." And before Porthos could think or move or protest, Athenais surged forward and put her arms around him. Her warm lips met his, and she kissed him with passion that had happened rarely in their accustomed, comfortable relationship.

Caught between confusion and Athenais in his arms,

her warm body against his, her tongue in his mouth, Porthos did what any gentleman would do and kissed her back with all the passion he could muster.

It was a while before he could collect his thoughts again, enough to speak rationally. "But Athenais, why are you so . . . Why are you so . . . What did I say that was so good?"

Athenais smiled. She sat down by his side, looking composed, with her hands on her lap. "When you get to be my age," she said. "And never having been a beauty." She smiled at Porthos. "I know what you'd say, Porthos, but you have no need to be gallant. I was not beautiful enough to be sold to a higher bidder than an aged accountant. I know my price."

"Your father was a fool," Porthos said.

"Perhaps. Or perhaps you see more beauty in me than I actually have," Athenais said. "It signifies not. Until this moment I never fully believed you could want me for me and not for the substantial inheritance I'll receive when Monsieur Coquenard dies."

"Athenais!" Porthos said.

"I'm sorry, Porthos, did I—"

"I have a good mind to be angry with you," Porthos said, but looked at her, staring at him with her eyes still flooded with tears and her mouth still smiling. He reached out and grabbed her, and kissed her again, wildly.

Afterwards, as both were recovering their breath, Athenais said, "I'll look at the accounts, of course. Set a couple of my husband's clerks to trace things for me. If we've ever loaned anything to Monsieur de Comeau, I'll find it."

"Good," Porthos said. "I'll be gone for some days, perhaps you'll have an answer for me when I return."

"Where will you be going for some days?" Athenais said, then shook her head. "Oh, wait, you told me. Your father's home."

Porthos nodded.

"Good. I think it's time you went home. You don't have to stay but you should know . . ."

"Athenais, the only thing I want to know is whether Guillaume went there and to whom he might have talked."

The Domains of a Provincial Lord;
A Paternal Welcome;
When Winning a Duel Would
Be the Worst Thing

THE travel to Porthos's domains was unexceptionable; the horses Monsieur de Treville had loaned them were swift and even their servants, riding somewhat behind, had been provided with fast horses. Still, by the end of the second day—having overnighted and changed horses—for horses of like quality—in a hostelry of dubious cleanliness—Athos was wondering if Porthos's domains were mythical, or perhaps placed so far from the capital that they might as well be mythical.

Most of the ride, Porthos had taken the lead in silence, and the others had held still, till Athos wished highwaymen would attack them for the sake of creating a diversion. But as night fell, on the second day, Porthos announced, "St. Guillaume du Vallon."

Athos looked around in confusion. They had been riding for some time along an increasingly dark country road. Light was just enough to let him perceive the time-polished stones of an old Roman road underfoot, and the glimmer of a farm house, here and there, amid the thickets of trees that lined the path. "Here?" he said, thinking Porthos joked. "In this wilderness?"

Porthos laughed, the first time he had done so, in their entire voyage. He'd slowed down, so they could catch up with him, and he took his horse at a measured walk, so they could talk. "Indeed," he said. "I told you it was a little place."

But as they got farther down the road, they could see the smoke of a half dozen houses, dark against the evening sky. And farther on still, past what looked like no more than miserable hovels and a bit down a winding road, there appeared what seemed to be a pile of ruins in huge, golden stones.

It was only by squinting at it that you could see that only the sides and a part of the front were ruined, but at least a quarter of the house was kept in reasonable repair, and smoke climbed from a vast, central chimney.

Porthos dismounted in front of the entrance door—a huge door of what appeared to be age-old oak, inset in a carved stone arch that looked to be even older—and tied his horse to an iron ring firmly embedded in the stone.

Though Porthos would rather die than admit to it, Athos could guess his friend's reluctance—from a certain hesitant step to his walk, a certain diffidence in the set of his shoulders. He hastened to dismount and tie his horse besides Porthos's and to stand beside his friend. With no more than a moment's pause, Aramis and D'Artagnan stepped up on either side of them.

Their servants, riding behind, had stopped behind a ways, and huddled in a group, talking in low whispers of who knew what, but keeping their distance.

Meanwhile Porthos applied his huge fist to the door, making it shake and groan under his pounding. It seemed like an eternity before dragging steps were heard from within and, at long last, a woman opened the door. She was small and withered and grey haired, attired in a dress of undyed wood. For a horrified moment—given their different sizes—Athos wondered if this was Porthos's mother.

But then the little colorless face set itself in an expression of disbelief, and the pale blue eyes, which also gave an impression of colorlessness opened wide. "Milord," she said. "Monsieur Pierre."

"Marie," Porthos said, and smiled, pulling the little woman to him. Then he turned to his friends and said, "This is Marie, who was my nursemaid. My mother died at my birth, so Marie raised me. You may blame her for anything you don't like in my behavior."

"Your behavior," Marie said, looking up, horrified, as though thinking that anyone who had anything to say to her nursling's behavior must find it unexceptionable. "You were always the best child and the best of young men. Raised him as my own, I did," she said, turning to the others and smiling. "And he never gave me any trouble, really, but Pierre . . ." She looked at Porthos with real worry. "Why did you come back? Your father has declared that your name shall not be mentioned in this house."

"My father has?" Porthos asked, puzzled. "But . . . why? When I left I only did what he told me to, and I've done nothing to shame him or—"

The woman shook her head. "It is the boy, Pierre. Your boy. When you sent him here, how could you think that he would be well received, and by your father, yet? But you always were a bighearted fool."

"The boy? He came here? He . . . ?"

From within came a thunderous voice. "Who are you speaking with at the door, you fool of a woman? Who would you occupy yourself with that way?"

Marie shrieked and stepped back and the door was fully thrown open. In opening, it revealed a hall such as Athos had only seen in the oldest of manor houses—a vast, resounding, echoing space, paved in stones, with a vast hearth burning bright at its center, vast enough for the hundreds of knights and thousands of vassals who would cower in here when the enemy threatened and rounded on the fields outside. But this hall was empty and echoing dark, except for the fire in the center which seemed to cast more shadows than light into spaces one felt had been little used.

Out of that darkness, pierced by fiery reflections from the flames, a man strode. He was as tall as Porthos, white haired, with flashing grey eyes, and he might have been the fire god of some forgotten mythology. As he advanced on them, his gaze found Porthos, then slid away from him, while his features set in seething rage.

"What do you want, gentlemen?" he asked. "This is not a hostelry, nor a common house, such as you might be used to. It's a manor house and a poor enough one that we can't put up strangers as our guests. Go and find yourself some place to spend the night. It won't be here."

Athos had only to look to his right to see Porthos standing still, pale, as though struck by a thunderbolt, and no more able to defend himself than a child when confronted by an adult. That his father had, assuredly, been Porthos's size once himself, was obvious. The past strength was still there, in arms knotted with muscles protruding from what looked like a short-sleeved peasant shirt. The breeches below ended just beneath the knees leaving equally muscular legs exposed. He wore what Athos could only presume to be some sort of hunting boot, in a style that hadn't been fashionable for centuries. But such as he was and such as he stood—his feet apart, his arms crossed on his chest, his gaze threatening to call down Olympian thunderbolts— still, he had lost mass and probably strength. He stooped. The hair was all white save where the reflection of the red fire gave it back lost color. And Athos suspected that if the hall were better lit, it would show the man was wasted and weak.

But this light didn't show it, and besides, he was Porthos's father, the recipient of respect inculcated in those distant days of childhood when the reason for respect need not be rational, and the simple fact that his father was such, and a lord, and stronger than Porthos would have been enough to control the wayward boy's rebellion.

"I do not mean to disturb you," Athos said, putting on his best and haughtiest manner, his coldest and most polite air. "But we were under the impression that friends of your son, and your son himself might very well be allowed to shelter in your home for a night's sojourn."

The grey eyes that turned to meet Athos's gaze might be the same color as Porthos's, but the resemblance stopped there. Beyond the grey color and the same shape, there was nothing of Porthos's warmth in that look. Only cold, icy resentment and a soul that knew its own truth and cared not for anyone else's opinion. "I don't know how you could be so imposed upon," the lord said, his voice cold. "But the truth is that I had one son only and he died, years ago. I don't know who the imposter in your midst is, pretending to be my son, but he's none of mine. Go. Leave me alone with my old age and my grief."

"Oh, this is too much," Aramis said, from the side, in the tone of voice that sounded like the words had been torn from him by irritation. "He looks like you, just like you, and your servant knows him and—"

"I beg your pardon?" Porthos's father said, turning to stare at Aramis. "Did you call me a liar, sir? Will I have to call you out on an affair of honor?"

Athos, frozen with terror that Aramis would accept and kill Porthos's father, or worse, that he would accept and manage somehow to get wounded by the old man who must have taught Porthos all he knew, couldn't find the words to speak. And then Porthos spoke. He removed his hat, and held it in front of him, as if he had been a plebeian petitioning his lord, or a child petitioning his guardian, "I beg your pardon, sir," he said, his voice slow and exact, in that voice he used when he wished to appear dumber than he was. His appeasing voice, Athos thought.

"I beg your pardon, sir," Porthos said again and bowed very slightly. "I see now that we came to quite the wrong house. I don't know how I made that mistake, but it is easy in the dark of night, in this place in the middle of nowhere, or certainly nowhere civilized people would want to be. I beg your pardon most heartily and we will go."

And on that he turned, and walked to his horse to loosen the ties that held him to the wall. "But, Porthos!" Aramis said.

"*Shh*" was Porthos's only reply. "*Shhh.*"

He untied his horse, but didn't mount, instead starting to walk slowly down the path they'd come. Athos thought this was one of those times he would have to trust that Porthos knew what he was doing and follow Porthos's lead in his actions. He untied his horse and took him by the rein and started after Porthos down the path through what was either wilderness or very neglected gardens. The other two joined, on either side of them. Looking to his side, Athos could see that D'Artagnan looked wholly puzzled. He wondered what the boy's home life was and if an unreasonable parent was so wholly unexpected.

"You, stop." Came from behind them, in a scream.

Athos looked to Porthos, who shook his head slightly and continued walking down the path, as though nothing were the matter. They heard running steps after them, and an irate voice say, harshly, "Are you such a coward, sir, that you do not understand a challenge? I should have known that anyone who thought himself a friend of my son would be craven and—"

Porthos turned, and Athos turned also, just in time to see his friend intercept the old man who had been running straight towards Aramis. Porthos's father's left hand had been raised as if to strike a blow, and his right hand had been tugging at his sword. Porthos had grabbed both hands, holding them in their positions, immobile.

"I told you I made a mistake," he said. "And my friend, too, made a mistake in trusting me to identify my childhood home. It's clear to me you're wholly a stranger and not my father. It is obvious to me that I do not know you. Go back to your house, please. And be at peace."

It was clear to Athos, who was near enough to see the

exchange, that Porthos was exerting some force in holding the old man, and that his father was forcing forward, still attempting to carry out who knew what mad attack on Aramis. For a long time they were locked like that, and Athos was sure that the second Porthos let go of the old man he would come running, madly, to attack one of them, to seek the fight which he seemed to believe was essential to his honor or his well being.

But instead, after a long while, the man shook his head and shrugged. "If you're all such cowards that you won't duel me, then it is obvious I might as well go inside and eat my supper."

At the word "coward" Aramis stepped forward, but Athos held him, and the one small step must have been invisible in the dark, because the man turned and went back to the manor house.

"Athos, that was vile," Aramis said, turning to Athos. "And Porthos also. Why wouldn't you let me take up his challenge. Surely you're not going to tell me filial duty held you in place, when he treats you in such a disgraceful way?"

Porthos shook his head slowly, like one in a dream. "Not . . . not duty exactly," he said. "But Aramis, if you dueled him and killed him, it would be murder. He's not the man I remembered. Time has not dealt kindly with him, and he was already old when I was born. You'd have killed him far too easily and once having killed him, you'd have accounted yourself a murderer the rest of your life. He's not worth it, Aramis."

Aramis looked like he was about to say something, but he must have seen Athos's warning frown, because he stepped back.

It wasn't till they'd come within sight of the village again, that Athos said, "And now what? Where will we sleep, Porthos? Is there a hostelry, hereabouts?"

Porthos, who had seemingly been immersed in thoughts of his own, now turned to look at Athos. "There is no hostelry," he said. "Not for another two hours riding and that if we're lucky, as I don't remember very precisely. And that," he said, "was a vile accommodation, fit only for the lowest of villains. You wouldn't want to lodge there. It wouldn't please you."

Athos didn't know whether to laugh or cry. "I know this is all very well for you young people, but I'm past the age where I find it comfortable to sleep under a tree rolled in my cloak."

"No need for that," Porthos said, mounting his horse. "There is still one place around here where I may be sure of my welcome."

They mounted, and the servants who had stayed fixed on the road behind them as they passed, mounted also, and followed them.

The Mill House; Childhood Friendship;
Improvements and Fortune

PORTHOS led his friends, unerringly though the night, up a narrow path beaten in the surrounding forest probably centuries before by cows making their way from some forgotten field to some forgotten stable.

It had gotten almost pitch-dark, save for the curdled-milk glow of a distant quarter moon, and the path wound disastrously amid tall trees that obscured what residue of light there might be. At the place where it forked from the village street, Porthos dismounted again, and led the horse apace, telling his friends, "There are roots underneath and riding would lead to injury. Just follow me."

Halfway into it, climbing a steep slope, Aramis hissed from behind, loudly enough for Porthos to hear, "Are you sure you know the way, Porthos?"

"Oh, sure and sure," Porthos said. "Many times did I take this way in the dark of night or the sun of noonday. Many times as a child and as an adult."

"Where does it lead," Athos asked.

"To the home of my best friend," Porthos said. And even as he said it, he wondered whether that was still true. He'd been gone for years, and so many things had changed. He'd left St. Guillaume as an obedient son and he now seemed to return as a proscribed criminal.

What else might have happened in the village. For all

Porthos knew Rouge might well be dead, or could have turned wholly against Porthos by rumor or innuendo, or even by the long silence to which Porthos had subjected their standing friendship.

When Porthos had left, Rouge, a young miller's son had just been married to his childhood sweetheart. The contrast between their romances—started the same way and almost at the same time—could not have been greater. When Porthos had left, Morgaine, Rouge's wife had just been increasing. He wondered what the child was and what it had grown up to be. And did they have more? Thoughts and memories long forgotten rushed to his mind. Amelie and himself attending Rouge and Morgaine's wedding and drinking far too much to celebrate the pledging of their troth.

A knot grew in his throat. He would have given a great deal to be back there. He was not normally given to fantastic dreaming nor to weaving fantasies of what could never be, but this, this he wished he could manage—to wind back time, like a string on a spool, to that point at which his father had convinced him to leave St. Guillaume and go to Paris. The point at which his father had promised, and promised faithfully at that, to make sure that Amelie found herself a husband and was happily bestowed.

Had his father failed on his promise? Had he lied all along? Or had Amelie braved it all for the love of Porthos?

Porthos could not know. He'd written a letter to Rouge and Morgaine when he'd changed his name and gone into the musketeers, but he'd not given them his address, and they'd never tried to find him. Thinking back, he believed he'd been afraid if they wrote back or visited him, they'd tell him that Amelie was happy and the mother of a brood. Why that had scared him then, he didn't know. He'd now give half his life to know just that.

It was with a knot at his throat, a prickly feeling in his eyes that he got within sight of the mill house. And stopped. When he'd left, his friend's house had been a small, low building—one large room, where the whole family—six children, five dogs, and the parents—all slept and cooked and lived. Above it on a hill kept clear cut and so situated that it enjoyed almost continuous breezes from the sea, stood the windmill proper—a wooden building equipped with blades as large as sails, beating continuously against the sky and propelling the stone grinders inside to produce flour. The miller had bought the wheat from everyone around here and ground it and sold it at market to people in other places—as well as renting the use of his mill to grind the flour the farmers themselves used.

It had been one mill, small and perhaps mean, befitting the surrounding countryside and the small horizons of St. Guillaume. Now, on the hill above there were five mills. Five of them, arrayed, their blades beating at the sky. And beneath the hill, sheltered, was a sprawling building, probably as large as the manor house, though built of brick instead of stone, and in far better repair.

Porthos felt, all of a sudden, a misgiving. This could not be Rouge's home. It had all changed. Something must have happened. Rouge and his family had died, perhaps, leaving some stranger to buy the home and to exploit the mills and the region, who knew to what purpose.

He tried to look as self-assured as ever as he walked up to the house. He would be turned out again, and now his friends would have nowhere to sleep. It truly was dealing badly with Athos to force him to sleep under a tree.

Not that Porthos thought, for a moment that Athos was too old for it. In his midthirties, Athos was fond of telling them how much older he was and how his body was decaying, but, faith, Porthos saw no evidence of it. In fact, he had seen Athos go from duel to guard duty to brawl, fighting as well as men ten years his junior and making himself a formidable opponent to all who crossed swords with him.

No. It wasn't Athos's age that made Porthos flinch from the idea of making his friend sleep under a tree. It was

Athos's nobility and the way he had of looking around at a house others would consider well appointed—even Porthos's own manor house—with a faint look of distaste, as though someone had suggested he lie down with swines.

With this in mind, Porthos walked his horse up to the door, and knocked. The door was new, smooth and painted a dark red. The brick walls were whitewashed. From inside the house came the smell of wood smoking and the scent of cooking which made Porthos's stomach growl.

He knocked on the door again, almost timidly. Of course, he was aware that with his size even a timid knock sounded like the clapping of doomsday. From within came the sound of broken crockery and a peevish female exclamation. And then steps to the door.

Porthos steeled himself so that he was not at all surprised when a total unknown opened the door. She was a young woman, in an immaculate cap, shabby but well-laundered clothes, and an spotless apron over it all. She looked at Porthos with the stare of complete nonrecognition. "Yes?" she said.

"I beg your pardon," Porthos said. He removed his hat, since he was talking to an unknown female. "Only, I used to be a good friend of the owner of this place, a certain Rouge and his wife, Morgaine? I guess they must have sold and I'll disturb you no—"

But at this moment the young woman's eyes went wide and shocked. She looked at him and dropped a hasty and awkward curtsey. "Monsieur Pierre du Vallon!" she said. "I beg your pardon, Monsieur, only I was just a child when you left, and I didn't immediately recognize you with your uniform. Well, my master keeps us entertained morning to night with stories of your adventures when you were young men." She smiled broadly, and stepped away from the door. "Come in, come in."

Porthos handed the reins of his horse, blindly, to Athos, and stepped through the door, into warmth and light.

It took Porthos only a moment to realize it was the same

room that had been a whole house in his childhood. Only now the broad hearth had been redone with all, what seemed to be, brand-new brick work, and the walls were newly whitewashed. Against the walls, where there had been various contrivances of cots and tables to provide for the necessities of the family, there were trunks, some of them painted—and Porthos would have bet, in his day, that the family didn't have enough provisions for all those trunks. Some of the trunks were draped in cloth and outfitted with cushions, ready for use as seating, but there was also a broad scrubbed table, and several long benches in the center of the room.

Doors led out of that central room, in several directions, and the young woman scurried through one of them. The other three men crowded at the door, but did not come in. From somewhere in the now cavernous entrails of the house, came a masculine voice calling out, and a female one answering, and then the sound of running.

Before Porthos could quite take stock of anything, a woman came running out of one of the doors. A small, slim woman with dark hair ineffectively encased in a white cap and swirling skirts of what appeared to be a rich gown. Porthos could see no other details because she was running full tilt towards him, and, halfway through, jumped towards him, launching herself into his arms. "Pierre," she said. "Pierre you fool."

She smelled of fresh bread and herbs, and as she hugged him fiercely, he realized she was his childhood playmate, lately Rouge's wife, Morgaine. He remembered when they were all small how all the old people in the village used to talk about how her parents had given her such an unchristian name and what it must mean for the poor waif growing up.

But now, looking at her, as she stepped away from him, her dark eyes twinkling with amusement, he realized that Morgaine was the most appropriate name, as there seemed to be something enchanting and otherworldly about her, and indeed, it was easier for him to believe in the transformation of Rouge's abode through the simple means of magic than through any earthly agency.

"Morgaine," he said.

And on that, Rouge came running into the room. He was built on the same scale as Porthos, and had the same red hair but in a more startling red, from whence his name came. When Porthos had gotten older and thought about it, he'd realized there was a high prevalence of redheads in the village, and it hadn't taken him very long at all to imagine that all his ancestors must have been very close to their serfs and servants and farmers.

He was wearing a doublet and hose in dark brown velvet and no one—no one would have thought that he was anything but at the very least minor nobility. Of course, Porthos was used to this, to the bourgeoisie and businessmen of Paris putting on airs that dwarfed the nobility. What he wasn't used to was seeing it in his native village and amid his own friends.

But he had not a moment to feel awkward, as Rouge was grabbing at both his hands, and presently pulling the unresisting Porthos into a joyous embrace and pounding on Porthos's back in a transport of excitement. "Pierre, you fool," he said, in turn.

Porthos stepped back and blinked. "Rouge," he said. And with a look to the side. "And Morgaine. You haven't changed."

"Neither have you," Morgaine said saucily. Her tongue had always overrun her. "Despite that uniform of the musketeers, which I must say becomes you very well."

"Uh . . . Your clothes become you well too," Porthos said.

And at this, Rouge let out a peal of laughter. "Indeed. Everything has prospered since my father died, Pierre, everything." He looked behind Porthos's shoulder at the men standing in the doorway and said, "But we are being veritable rabble, not bringing your friends in." He called

behind his shoulder, "Jean, Francois, go and get these gentlemen's horses, and take them to the stable."

"We've brought our own servants, Rouge," Porthos said.
"If your boys show them the stables, they'll take care of the
horses from there."

"Certainly," Rouge said. "Oh, certainly." He turned to
two teen boys who'd appeared running. "You heard that,
you rascals? Go and help my guests' servants. And you,
gentlemen, come in, do come in."

Porthos turned to see his friends enter the house, removing their hats. "Rouge," he said, "allow me to present
you my friends. Athos and Aramis, his Majesty's Musketeers, and D'Artagnan, a guard of Monsieur des Essarts."

Rouge bowed. "My home is honored by your presence,
gentlemen. Please, sit, sit." He gestured towards the table
and they took their places around it. "Morgaine, get them
some wine and some bread and whatever meat we might
have cooking. Quick, my dear."

Morgaine scrambled off to obey—which mostly
seemed to entail calling to various wenches and helpers.
Soon there was a flurry of young females setting plates and
food and mugs of wine on the table.

"You've done very well for yourself," Porthos said.
"You astonish me. I thought for sure the house and mill had
been sold and strangers come in."

Rouge smiled. "Oh, no, not at all. It's just, when my father died, and as Morgaine was then with child for the third
time, I thought I would need to keep my family better. And
perhaps arrange for something better for my sons than
tending a mill in a small town. And, you see, I had the idea
of arranging for the mill to—besides grind the grain—
bring up water from the stream and irrigate our fields. And
then, you know, farmers paid me for the service of getting
water to their more distant fields, and they could suddenly
cultivate many lands that had lain fallow. And then they
needed more mills to grind the increased grain. St. Guillaume is doing very well indeed, Pierre. Very well indeed."

Porthos thought it was true, and he'd often heard that the commoners were rising in lifestyle and power even as the old nobility sank. But he'd never thought to see it here or to see it so clearly. "But," he said. "I saw no signs of all this when I was crossing the village."

"Well, you wouldn't, would you? Those are mostly serfs and . . . well . . . directly under your father's authority. The changes and the prosperity are mostly in the outlying farms and those claiming new territory from the forest. Pierre, when you inherit—"

"I'm not likely to inherit any time soon," Porthos said, dolefully. "We just went to the house, just a few moments ago, and the way my father . . . well . . . He challenged Aramis for a duel, which I obliged him to decline, because what if he killed him."

Rouge looked like he was going to say something, then sighed. "This is the strangest thing of all, Pierre," he said. "You showing up unannounced, like this, and your father furious at you."

"This I've experienced," Porthos said. "What I don't know is why."

"Well, when your son came to town, your father said . . . He said you were dead to him."

"My son?" Porthos said. "You saw him? How did you know him for mine?"

Family Resemblances and Family Burdens;
A New and Dreadful Code

"**H**ow could we not know he was yours?" Morgaine answered. She set a loaf of bread and the knife to cut it on the table, then sat down next to her man and held his hand while she looked at Porthos with wide and astonished eyes. "He looked exactly like you did at that age."

"He did?" Porthos asked, with some surprise, because it had never occurred to him that Guillaume had looked like him. And he'd never thought of himself as the boy had been—a gracile stripling, agile on his feet.

"But yes," Rouge said. "Same body type, same features, the same way of speaking, even. Well . . ." He grinned. "He is perhaps a little more fluent than you were at his age, and not a surprise, since you lived in the dreadful expectation that your father would violently disapprove of anything you might say, while he surely didn't grow up with such a fear."

From Rouge's smile, from his look, it was clear that he thought he was making Porthos a compliment. It was clear he didn't know that the boy was dead, much less what his upbringing had been. Part of him longed to tell Rouge all, just as he had told him everything as a child. Rouge had often been the sounding board for Porthos's discontents and confusion. Though he was only a miller's son, Rouge had been sent to the local priest for his first letters and from

that point had found much to read and write—scraps of
this and bits of that—around which he wove stories and ex-
planations for their lives and their difficulties. All of which
meant that he could usually better express himself and express Porthos's own discontents in terms that Porthos
could never find. He had, in fact, been much as Aramis now
was to Porthos. And yet, Porthos knew that he must not tell
Rouge anything. Not yet. First, he must ask questions,
while Rouge was unaware of what was happening.

"I never thought of his looking like me," he said, simply.

"I daresay," Rouge said, thoughtfully, "that you didn't
spend much time looking at yourself when you were growing up, so it would be more readily noticeable to us. But
trust me, Guillaume will look just like you when he grows
up and grows into his height and muscles."

Porthos thought of Guillaume, lying cold and dead in
Athos's cellar, and his throat knotted up again. Aramis,
who was looking at him, must have perceived this diffi-
culty, and his thought must have been parallel, because he
charged into the breach with his considerable aplomb. "So,
Guillaume came here, did he? You saw him?" he asked, ca-
sually, as though it were all one thing.

"Oh, yes," Rouge said. "He came here. He got a ride
with a peddler who was headed this way, and really, Pierre,
if I didn't know you, I would have been shocked. No other
father would think to let a young man of some address, let
alone nobility, travel on the back of a peddler's cart like a
tramp. Surely . . ."

"I didn't know what he was up to," Porthos said. "He
came of his own accord, on his own head. You know how
boys are."

"Aye," Rouge said, and grinned. "I remember some
scrapes we got into ourselves, and I daresay our fathers
would have given us a good hiding if they knew the half of
them."

Porthos nodded.

"So he came in," Aramis said.

"Well, I thought Pierre knew," Rouge said, confused, looking around the table. Then he looked back at Porthos. "Is that why you came? To find out what he did while he was here? Is anything wrong?"

Porthos shrugged. "Not as such. It's just . . . I can't get him to give me an account of his adventure," he said. "And considering the results I've already seen in my father, I thought . . ."

Rouge inclined his head. There was a small smile on the corner of his lips. "Ah, yes, your father came to Paris and gave you a piece of his mind. I guessed as much when he left last week. I thought after having stewed for over a month in his rage over the boy's visit, he'd finally broken down and gone to Paris to make you suffer for it. Was I right?"

Porthos opened his mouth to answer, but could find none. His father had gone to Paris last week. There was a pretty kettle of fish. His father was as likely as any other of the villains around to commit murder and to want to murder Guillaume. Slowly, he said, "He was very upset, I guess?"

"Upset? He was breathing fire. What he gave out was that you were dead, that you'd died in a duel and that he refused to recognize your brat by that . . . well, pardon me, Pierre, but he called Amelie a slut and said he could not believe you had married her . . . A lot of other things."

"He told this to Guillaume?" Porthos asked.

"Oh, to him first, and loud enough that all the servants heard and soon spread it to the village. But you know your father. He also told this to every trader, every peddler, every two bit friar to cross the village, and slowly worked himself up to greater fury."

"Of course," Porthos said, because that much was a given for someone who had grown up with his father. He wondered what Guillaume had thought of it all. He'd clearly made up a story about Porthos's having married his mother. And of course, he clearly meant to claim his place as Porthos's heir. Was all this before he'd actually located Porthos in Paris? Had he thought that Porthos was dead, as his mother was? Did he think that his grandfather would be happy to see him, glad to know he had a scion? How grossly he'd underestimated Monsieur du Vallon. "And what of Amelie's parents? What did they think?"

"Ah . . ." Rouge shook his head. "Have you been by there, Pierre?"

"Not at all," Porthos made an effort to eat the slab of meat on his plate, knowing that Rouge would know for sure something was very wrong if he didn't. "Not at all. I only just arrived and went to the manor house, only to be turned away."

"Ah," Rouge said. "They turned Guillaume away too. They were less . . . less kind than your father, if it's possible. Amelie's father had his grandsons beat him and turn him out."

"Beat him?" Porthos asked.

"Oh, yes. When he came to us, he was bruised and battered."

"But . . . why?" Porthos asked.

Rouge shook his head. "They've grown prosperous, Pierre. They're one of those farmers who've grown rich. And with the riches came a certain sort of respectability. The poorer people around here look up to them, and they are hard pressed to admit . . . you know . . ."

"That they were common as muck, or that their daughter slept with the lord's son?" Porthos asked.

"To own the truth," Rouge said. "Though they never intervened when it was happening, perhaps they didn't know it, or perhaps they thought you would marry her. But when Amelie started showing, they were very quick to turn her out of doors and disown her, you know?"

"They disowned her?" Porthos said, feeling his anger rage. Oh, his Amelie had been abominably treated, even by her own parents.

"Oh, Lord, man. She never told you, before she died? I

thought Guillaume said she only died two or three years ago. She never told you that her parents turned her out and that this was why she came looking for you in Paris?"

"Besides her loving you, which I'm sure she did," Morgaine said.

Porthos shook his head, dazed.

"Well, her parents did turn her out," Rouge said. "So I'm guessing even then, though they still hadn't any riches, they were already looking to their stern respectability. And since then her father has become very . . . rigid. All his granddaughters dress like nuns and behave like prudes. I guess it has worked, though, because all of them are marrying above themselves, but Lord, what a dreary life it is in that house."

"Though perhaps we shouldn't judge them too harshly," Morgaine said. "Because truth is that they turned him out and beat him, but their conscience must have hurt them because in the next month, first Amelie's father, then his mother, have gone to Paris. And her older brother just last week. Did you or Guillaume see either of them?"

Porthos shook his head. Amelie's parents had gone to Paris too . . . Oh, what might it all mean? Was he obliged, now, to suspect everyone of the murder of Guillaume? And yet, if they were so jealous of their respectability, wasn't it right to suspect them? Surely they would want to protect themselves against the rumors that they had an illegitimate grandson, even if that grandson was the lord's grandson as well.

There would have been a time when any peasant would have been proud to say that their daughter had had the son of Monsieur du Vallon—even if illegitimate. There was a time, and it wasn't far distant, when even Porthos's father wouldn't have viewed Guillaume as a young man's mistake and nothing much to talk about. At worst, the boy would have been taken from his mother and reared, discreetly, by some order of monks or something. He would have been an acknowledged bastard and, failing of a legitimate successor to the name, the acknowledged heir. His existence would no more have shocked anyone than it would have surprised them.

But the times were changing, as was clear by all this newfound prosperity all around Porthos. He chewed on some excellent mutton and thought it over. In the changed world, the lord couldn't afford a bastard, because he had no way to support him, or any others with similar claims. And if you couldn't support them in style, you might as well deny their existence.

By the same reasoning, the newly wealthy peasants should have been glad to embrace an offshoot of noble blood. But it seemed impossible for this new class that was forming, these peasants with money, these merchants with connections, to view morality the way noblemen had once viewed it—as something to be aspired to but, enfin, too demanding for fallible man to achieve in this lifetime, without special grace from the Almighty. In this new class, as he knew from Athenais's own life, respectability was everything, even when it was just a respectability of semblance without true content. And in this new class, it would be worth throwing your pregnant daughter out for having marred the family honor. Wouldn't it be equally likely that they would kill their illegitimate grandson, before he could embarrass them before the world?

Porthos felt a headache coming on, but there was nothing for it. Rouge and Morgaine paraded before him their eight children—seven boys and a girl, the youngest, as pretty as Morgaine and full of graces that had once been reserved to the daughters of the nobility.

And it wasn't until they, all four of them, were shown to the guest room at the back, with its warm-burning fire, its beds with sheets aired and turned and warmed by the fire, that Porthos dared speak to his friends. "It's hard," he said, "not telling him the truth."

Athos—always understanding—inclined his head. "I guessed it would be," he said. "But Porthos, you may come back and tell him the truth, if you wish, once we know the whole thing. For now, do you really want everyone in the village to know it? Do you want Amelie's family on their guard before we ever meet them?"

Porthos shook his head. "But Rouge is trustworthy. And though you, Athos, would say that no woman is trustworthy, I would guess that Morgaine is also reliable."

"Oh, it's not your friends that frighten me," Athos said, lowering his voice. "But with all the servants and possibly young relatives—I never understood exactly who all the servers were—coming and going around us at table, I would bet every single thing we said, and every expression, will be all over the village in no time at all."

Porthos nodded. It would be hard to dispute that. He knew it for the absolute truth. Soon everyone in the village would hear everything they had said.

"But the boy came here," Porthos said. "And told them that Amelie and I had married before she died and that . . ."

"It is my guess," D'Artagnan said, speaking quietly from where he was sitting on the bed and removing his boots. "That he came here before he had found you. It is my guess that he came by in the full assumption that you had died—"

"That I had died?" Porthos asked, with some confusion.

"Yes," D'Artagnan said. "I would assume he thought you were dead, because his mother had looked for you so long in Paris, and yet hadn't found you. What would be more logical than to think you had somehow died?"

"Oh."

"Indeed," Athos said. "And everyone in the provinces knows that life in Paris is full of dangers for those who live by the sword. You might have been killed in any of a dozen duels, any of a hundred skirmishes."

"Oh, nonsense," Porthos said. "Why would I die of something like that. It would take a fool to be killed in Paris. Or at least someone luckless or unable to fight ably with the sword. Neither of which I am."

"But Guillaume wouldn't know that," Athos said. "To him you would be nothing more than his mother's recollection of her childhood friend and lover, someone who had come to Paris and disappeared. He probably thought you dead."

"And thinking you dead, he thought the most logical thing was to claim that you'd married his mother. Who could trace among the several parishes in Paris, whether you'd actually married or not? Any parish priest might have married you," D'Artagnan said.

"And the records might easily have got lost afterwards," Athos said.

"And as such," Aramis said. "He could claim to be your legal heir and claim your portion."

"It must have shocked him," Athos said. "When Rouge and Morgaine told him you were still alive. Fortuitous they got it across before he'd given himself away by proclaiming you dead." He gave Porthos the weary eye. "Did you write to them and tell them you were joining the musketeers?" he asked. "They seemed to know it."

Porthos sighed. "Yes. It seemed like someone should know."

"But why not write to your father?" D'Artagnan asked, puzzled.

"Because my father doesn't know how to read," Porthos said.

"Oh," D'Artagnan said, looking somewhat shocked.

It was something that Porthos thought his friends would never fully understand, the difference between their upbringing and his. His father thought a lord should care about war only. While Aramis had been brought up for the church. And Athos had grown up with the examples of the men of Greece and Rome, who had left dialogues and memoirs and who knew what else. As for D'Artagnan, from what he said, his life had been half lived in books filled with sagas and legends of heros.

"That's why I wrote to Rouge and Morgaine," he said.

"So if I came to a bad end in Paris, and somehow word made it out, or Monsieur de Treville sent word out, someone would understand. And so if they needed anything . . . If anything happened to my father . . ."

Athos nodded. "Provident, almost. But I wonder how much they told the boy, and further how he contrived to get it out of them without ever giving away the fact that he hadn't grown up with you and hadn't, in fact, the slightest idea where you might live."

"I think," Porthos said. "That he was very cunning."

"Certes, he must have been," Aramis said, his mouth set in something that might have been humor or regret, or a bit of both.

"And then, after learning you were alive and in the musketeers, and, having seen your father, and perhaps having heard from your friends how much he himself looked like you and how much you, in turn, looked like your father, he decided to approach you. I wonder if he got the parish records of your family before or after finding out. If after, it was clearly with intention of approaching you."

"By God's Blood," Porthos said. "I swear he never brought it up. He never told me I might be his father or tried in any way to extort money or protection."

"No," Athos said. "No. And like you, I wonder what that meant."

"But surely," Porthos said. "If he didn't even know I was alive, he couldn't be part of the Cardinal's plot against me. Surely if the Cardinal plotted . . ."

"It was without Guillaume's connivance?" Aramis asked. "Using him rather than enlisting him? I was thinking the same."

"But then who could have done it?" D'Artagnan asked. "Other than Monsieur de Comeau. Would your father . . ."

Porthos sighed. "In the old days, I would tell you no. My father would be more likely to fell someone with a blow to the head, or attack them with the wood chopping ax than to use poison against them. But then, I don't think my father ever went up against a boy child. And then, you know, my father despised cunning—the same way he despised reading and all those other arts he called effeminate. And I don't know how he would choose to counteract someone he'd perceive as cunning and . . . sly. Plus there is the fact that my father is older than he was, and might not have known much about Paris or how to set about things in Paris. He could not have challenged Guillaume to a duel, at any rate."

"No," Athos said. "But would he resort to poison?"

Porthos shrugged. "He probably would not, still. Father is . . . a direct thinker. But he might have hired . . ."

Athos nodded. "Indeed he might. As might Amelie's parents. Or did you not think of that?"

"I did think of that," Porthos said. "I think we should talk to them tomorrow."

The Comforts of the Bourgeoisie;
Bees and Dogs;
Where a Daughter Might Not Exist,
but Her Shame Remains

ARAMIS had to admit that the comforts of this mill house were perhaps greater than the comforts of his mother's house—a noble manor that was, granted, far more comfortable and cheerful than the abode of Porthos's father, yet far from this world of fluffed sheets and blankets that smelled of rosemary and other herbs, as if they'd been rinsed in aromatic water.

Early morning the smell of baking bread pervaded the abode, as well it should have, he supposed, since its owners dealt in flour. But their trade did nothing to diminish the credit of having servants who brought warm water for washing and shaving as they did, with all the promptness and politeness that could be managed. And Aramis found himself thinking that perhaps he had been born entirely to the wrong class. He should have been born in a bourgeois household, growing prosperous and full of comforts. There wouldn't then have been the idea of sending him to the church for the atonement of his mother's youthful sins.

But then it occurred to him there just might have been. After all, these people seemed to have more of a care for their honor and more of a hidebound honor than even

Aramis's mother could manage. And that reflection of that thought on Aramis's face seemed to cause a chill in the graceful smile of the wench who delivered the water.

Aramis summoned Bazin who had slept in what he described as a very adequate room at the back, a room shared between the musketeers' servants and a group of young men who were either servants or young relatives of the master of the house—Bazin was not sure which.

Bazin had helped Aramis shave and brush his hair and dress with the efficiency of long experience. Afterwards, Aramis had read his breviary and said his prayers while the other three rose and proceeded to wash and shave and dress—though Aramis suspected D'Artagnan's shaving was still more hopeful than necessary. Oh, the boy had a neat beard and a small moustache, but their very neatness, their appearance, was characteristic of hair growth that hadn't fully come in yet, and not of hair that was carefully trimmed everyday.

At the table, over soup and bread, and honey—apparently the millers had their own bees—and while his wife struggled to keep a semblance of order amid their children, Rouge had said, "I suppose you'll be going to Amelie's parents, now, to see what the boy might have done there?"

"Yes," Porthos said. "Yes. I must find out why they've been going to Paris and what they've been doing there."

Rouge nodded. "There must have been a reason, if they didn't go to reconcile with you and Guillaume. Though perhaps they visited Amelie's grave."

"That is possible," Porthos said, suddenly melancholic, wondering where that pauper's grave would be and if the sad parcel of ground was even marked.

The rest of breakfast passed with desultory conversation, before Rouge saw them out, with his best wishes, and Morgaine flung herself into Porthos's arms for one last embrace before leaving. "You take care of yourself, Pierre," she said. "And that boy of yours. And bring him to visit us soon, will you?"

Looking at Porthos, Aramis was amazed at how his un-subtle friend managed to keep a straight—and even cheerful—face through this, amazed that Porthos did not break down at these words. Oh, he understood his friend enough to know how the words must cut at him. But there was no way Morgaine could have guessed it.

It wasn't till they were on the main road of the village again, riding into the morning sun, that Porthos permitted himself to wipe his face with the back of his hand, all the while complaining of the sun in his eyes and how it was making them tear. Aramis chose not to divest him of his disguise for his emotion.

They followed Porthos for a while, till they came to a road leading off the main road with its miserable hovels. Down amid fields they led the horses slowly because the road was too rocky and prone to sudden turns. Porthos made pertinent observations as they went. "This was all woods, or maybe sometimes pasture, when I left," he would say now and then, when passing some verdant field, or some just-harvested one, or rounding the corner of a well-grown orchard. "All woods, and not very good land. I guess Rouge really did make a difference with his mills that pull water from the stream."

None of them answered. It was doubtful whether their servants behind could even have understood a word of their exchange or what it all meant.

At the end of the road with its border of fields, they came upon a compound that rivaled the houses in Paris—with two pillars supporting a tall iron gate, and the area walled high all around. "*Holá*," Porthos said. "And this wasn't here either."

However, Porthos's view of gates was always—in Paris or the country—that he would pound upon them till they, presently, opened up.

These opened up—once more proving that rumors flew wide and fast in any village—to show a group of young men, villainous and scruffy, holding pitchforks and various farm implements. Aramis handed the reins of his horse to Bazin and stepped forward, his hand on the pommel of his sword. He'd rarely had to fight this kind of crowd, and he knew that they would obey no rule of combat, and yet, if the day had come that three musketeers of the King—or rather four, since D'Artagnan was a musketeer in all but his uniform—couldn't take on ten undisciplined youths, then it was time to relinquish the country to the untutored rabble.

"What do you want?" one of the boys, in the front asked, glaring. Behind them there were several dogs, barking and showing teeth. Mutts all of them, none showing the sleek lines or the careful discipline of hunting dogs. Mere brutes, trained to do violence and nothing more.

"I wish to speak to the owner of the house," Porthos said. And then, focusing on the boy nearby. "My word. Aren't you Evrard's boy?" he asked.

The lout who had spoken, a straw-headed creature with flat nose and all the marks of a brutish nature, glared, but was silent, as though disarmed.

"Let me see if I remember your name . . . You are . . . Mathis, are you not?"

The young man looked to the side, to another boy so similar to him that for sure he was a brother or a cousin, and the other boy glared at Porthos in turn. "Grandpa said we were not to open the door to you, and that he had nothing to say to you. He said you've done enough harm."

"Have I?" Porthos asked, mildly. He looked at the boy, frowning slightly. "You'd be Lucas, would you not?"

The young man glared and made some frantic gesture with his hand and, as though at his command, all the other boys started forward, to close the gate. They were a little too slow. At their movement, which took a little time to coordinate, Porthos moved forward and placed his foot in the way of the closing gate.

Aramis stared only half believing. Many times in the past, he'd seen Porthos engage in feats of strength which other men could only watch openmouthed. However, even he was shocked, as Porthos, his foot firmly planted, withstood the ten youths attempting to close the gate by brute force. The gate creaked and trembled, and Porthos's foot and leg seemed to tremble, also, with the effort, but the gate made no progress towards closing.

One of the pack of boys called out something inarticulate and whistled, and suddenly all the boys scrambled away from the opening while a dog—or at least Aramis assumed the blur was a dog, for in the circumstances it could have been a giant wolf—charged towards Porthos, growling.

Before Aramis, or Athos, or D'Artagnan, could do more than take a step forward, the creature was on Porthos. And it took Aramis a blink and a deep breath before he saw Porthos was in no danger. Rather, having bent down, he had grabbed the animal by its collar and now held it aloft, scrambling and suffocating.

"Let my dog down, you pup," a man's voice said, loudly from within. "Let him down, I say. Would you kill my best guard dog?"

"Do you promise not to send your dogs or your boys at myself or my friends?" Porthos asked.

"Yes. Let him go," the man said, his voice betraying that he must hold this dog in some peculiar affection.

Porthos immediately let the animal drop, and it proved to have no lasting damage, as it first fell heavily, but then struggled onto its legs and, whining, crawled away.

The man who stepped forward to examine it and pat it was perhaps in his late fifties, a tall and spare man, with white hair and a face marked by the creases of a farmer who lived most of his life outside. His beard was wild, and his eyes glared above it. "You had no right," he said. "This is a respectable house. You have no right to come here, lord or no lord."

Aramis judged this had gone far enough. He stepped forward. "Old man," he said. "You have no right to address one of the King's own Musketeers that way. For it would be disrespect to the King himself, and that in turn would force all the King's Musketeers to fight you."

The old man looked at Aramis, and his mouth dropped open. Aramis judged that in these heathen parts they'd never seen a man wearing the latest in soft over-breeches of finest velvet, and perhaps not the looser doublets that were now fashionable. At least everyone he had met here, even the better dressed, tended to favor the tight-fashioned clothes that Athos relished wearing, in the fashion of ten to twenty years ago.

At this moment, as though to increase the man's confusion, Athos stepped forward. He was doing his best grand seigneur impression, his head thrown back, his hand on the pommel of his sword, and, despite his worn and faded uniform, he managed to look far more the nobleman than Aramis knew he'd ever look. Aramis wanted to glare at Athos, but he knew that would be fruitless, as they'd had this contest many times before and each time Aramis had lost. So, instead, he glared intently at the man.

"My friend came to ask you some questions," Athos said. "By order of the King. Questions pertaining to the youth who called himself Guillaume and who—"

"I never met any youth named Guillaume," the farmer said, glaring back at all four of them, since D'Artagnan had taken this opportunity to step forward and stand on the other side of Porthos.

"Oh, surely you jest," Athos said. "For you see we have accurate information that the youth came here, and we are on his Majesty's orders to find all we can about his visit and about what he might have said and done."

Aramis was briefly, breathtakingly impressed by Athos's capacity to lie. And then he realized that Athos was speaking nothing but the truth. For, after all, they were here on the orders of Monsieur de Treville, and it was doubtless that Monsieur de Treville was speaking on behalf of the King himself. Therefore, since they were investigating the murder at the behest of their captain, they were under the King's orders to investigate whatever Guillaume had done on his visit to the village of St. Guillaume.

The farmer frowned. "The boy weren't nothing but his whelp. His whelp and that of the abandoned slut who—"

"Enough," Porthos said. He stepped forward. "Enough." His hand went up and closed around the farmer's neck. "You will not speak of her that way. You—"

"I'll speak of her as I please. And you know she was a slut, since you was the one who debauched her," the farmer said, glaring up at Porthos, unafraid of the giant's hand at his throat.

"Porthos," Athos said. "That solves nothing."

"God's truth," Porthos said. "And I know it doesn't. But I would feel better for knowing there was one less villain in the world. How could anyone send his own daughter out into the world, alone and with child, just because they think she marred their precious honor!"

"Oh, it's very easy for you to speak of honor that way," the farmer said, stepping back from Porthos's hand, back from the reach of Porthos's fingers. "You have lands and papers that prove your family is noble. We have nothing but this farm and what we can make grow with the sweat of our brows. If I allowed the slut to live here, I could only give my other girls in marriage to the poorest of the poor. No respectable merchant or attorney would trust a woman who came from such a tainted background. And why should they, when she had no dowry, either? Now I have made some, and my granddaughters shall leave the house with enough money on their stocking foot to see them to a good marriage. But back then I didn't. In corrupting my daughter—"

"I didn't corrupt her," Porthos said. "I loved her."

"Funny love, then, that runs off to Paris, leaving her embarrassed. I figured I'd send her to Paris and she could find you and marry you. Or not. It's not my fault she didn't find you."

Porthos opened his mouth and closed it. Aramis wondered whether the telling words in that sentence had had any effect on him. Porthos was both complex and astonishingly simple. It was quite possible he had taken no more notice of those words than any others. As it was possible, too, that he had remarked them all too well and knew precisely what they meant. Whichever way that went, he seemed, for the moment, struck speechless.

"I had the boy beat and thrown out of doors. I don't know what he wanted, but I know that it took me a devil of time to convince the other boys he'd been some mad fool with nothing to do with them. He came in claiming to be your son and . . . hers. And hers. And now, how I'll undo the damage of your presence . . ."

"There is no damage," Athos said. "If only you'll tell us why you, and, yes, your wife, then visited Paris several times, including I believe last week?"

The farmer seemed to choke on something. "Why we visited? Oh, to do business, for as I told you, we are prosperous now, and we can travel to Paris on business. If you care to ask, you'll find we visit Paris several times a year. Is this forbidden to the likes of us?"

"Not at all," Athos said, though his entire demeanor proclaimed he didn't believe a single word from the man.

As they walked away—without turning their backs, because Aramis judged these were just the sort of people who would do them an injury if they could—the gate slammed forcefully and there was a raised din of men's voices and dogs, but no one came out.

After a while they turned around and led their horses away.

"He wasn't telling the truth, you know?" Aramis asked Porthos.

"Aramis, I know you have no high opinion of my intelligence, but pray believe me, I am aware that he wasn't telling the truth about merely visiting Paris on business. I would bet he went to ferret out Amelie's whereabouts. And Guillaume's."

"And found them," Aramis said, piqued at being told that he considered Porthos stupid, which was not true. "For else, how would he know you never married Amelie? That would take more than merely looking at parish records. You would have to find Amelie and know how she was living."

Porthos face darkened at this. "If he found her," he said. "Then he found his own granddaughter, of the same name, living under pitiable conditions. And he did nothing to rescue her."

Aramis opened his mouth, but did not know what to say to this.

Porthos turned around, "I have half a mind to go back and—"

"No," Athos said. "No. Now let us find who is guilty of murdering Guillaume. And then we shall worry about Amelie's situation. Come, Porthos. You must be patient. For the sake of completeness, let us find what Guillaume told the curate in this parish, that allowed him to copy your family's records. And then we shall be on the road to Paris, where we'll endeavor to trace the movements of Amelie's father and mother."

Recognition and Identity; Ancestral
Tombs; Cousins and Confusion

IT didn't surprise D'Artagnan that Aramis took the lead when they reached the church. Among the four of them, they would easily have agreed that churches were Aramis's special domain.

None of them would have disputed that an occasion that called for Latin, or candlelight, for theology or musty disputations against the number of angels, should, by necessity, involve Aramis. It was like saying that any occasion that caused for an intimate knowledge of the functioning of great noble houses or ancient Greek history would call for Athos; or that a facility with border Spanish and an ease of melding amid those common as muck should be left to D'Artagnan; or even that anything needing the application of Herculean strength and the sort of mental disposition that cut through all sorts of rhetoric would belong to Porthos.

That the church was a small building of huge stones with almost no windows, built in the Roman manner—the sort of church where an entire village could pile in during a war or a a a sack and survive well enough—didn't seem to matter. Aramis advanced, in his fashionable clothes, his soft, loose venetians, his fashionably cut doublet with hanging ribbons and satin trim. When he removed his plumed hat of the musketeer—with which, at any rate, he could never have entered the low door of the church—and

advanced into the shadows, his golden hair glimmered like
sunlight.

The church smelled of must and long-enclosed spaces,
in which generations had crowded and sweated and prayed.
The altar was no more than a small cube of time-darkened
boards. Upon it, a cloth lent an air of grace, only barely
spoiled by the fact that the cloth itself was dusty with time
and fraying at its edge.

Behind the altar, a crucifix displayed the hanging
Christ, with the curiously distorted proportions of earlier
centuries and a profusion of wounds and blood on His
pale-painted limbs. The face, anguished above the mis-
shapen body, looked strangely human and realistic, con-
torted with a rictus of suffering beneath the head, crowned
in thorns.

Aramis walked in, and genuflected to the Christ, before
clearing his throat loudly, causing echoes to chase each
other into the small church. A small man, brown like a
nut—the curious brown of small people shrunken by age
and tanned by the sun—and crowned with silver hair,
emerged from within a little chamber to the side, doubtless
the sacristy. He looked at the four of them—all of them
clutching plumed hats to their chests—as though he'd
never seen such hats or such men. In fact, as though he
lived in a completely different world, populated perhaps
with angels, or perhaps with more humble creatures who
lived day to day, and more close to the land.

"Oh, Father, we've come on an errand of enquiry,"
Aramis said. "We wish to know—"

But the priest was looking past them, to the giant
Porthos, standing taller than any of the others and looking
as if he wished he could shrink his bulk to the church's
proportions. The priest's glance slid over Porthos, clearly
not recognizing him, and looked away, and back at Aramis.

"Any way I can help you, my son," he said, and continued looking at Aramis as though Aramis were an amazing
creature, perhaps an apparition of miraculous nature.

"There was a boy who came," Aramis said. "No more than a few weeks ago. Looking for information about the lord's family."

"Oh," the priest said, and smiled. "The lord's grandson. He told me. He said the lord didn't receive him, which is a pity. Very proud all that family. Very proud."

Porthos had sidled away from the group to where a tomb stood, carved in rock, displaying, atop its bulk, a knight, crudely carved, lying with his hands joined at the chest. Though the carver who had executed the work displayed no more skill than would have been needed to shape stones for construction, something about the knight—its massive proportions, its huge hands—seemed to speak of a familial relation with Porthos.

D'Artagnan hedged after him, even as Athos and Aramis followed the priest into some back room of the church.

Porthos was running his finger, pensively, around the carved boot of the knight, presumably his ancestor. He looked up to meet D'Artagnan's gaze, as D'Artagnan approached, and D'Artagnan was surprised to see the grey eyes glisten with tears.

"The priest doesn't know you," he said, in a casual tone. "Was he installed after you left?"

Porthos shook his head, and something very much like a small smile twisted his lips. "Oh, no," he said. "He's the priest who baptized me, but I daresay he rarely sees my father. He would be more likely to recognize me if he saw him."

D'Artagnan was sure his features reflected the purest confusion, because Porthos chuckled. "D'Artagnan when I left here I was just seventeen. Oh, I was large, for my age, as I could be. But my body lacked the bulk of muscle it would later acquire. And my features had not yet set, fully, in their adult form. My father looks more as I do now than I looked when I left here."

D'Artagnan nodded, understanding, but the expression of affliction and confusion threatened to return to Porthos's face and sometimes it seemed to D'Artagnan he would rather do anything—anything at all—than face a serious Porthos or a Porthos who tried to seriously think through something as difficult as his own feelings. So he said, quickly, "Your father didn't attend church?"

Porthos shrugged. "Oh, he did and didn't. He had not been much of a church man after my mother died. I never knew my mother, so I can't tell you much, but Marie told me that she was a beautiful woman with hair like gold and I . . ." He blushed a little. "In my mind she looks a lot like Athenais. Marie said that she and my father had a child every other year for years, and none of them lived to take the first breath. And then I was born and my mother died. Marie said my mother was tired of giving birth to so many children and didn't stay to hear whether I was alive, because she couldn't bear to hear I had died, also. I think . . ." He shrugged. "I think it was rather the size of my head and of my shoulders. The du Vallons kill wives. And mothers. A wonder that Amelie didn't die of Guillaume." He frowned. "And perhaps not a mercy."

And here, he was going again, back to Guillaume, which D'Artagnan guessed was the source of those tears glistening in his eyes, and of that expression of desolation on his features. D'Artagnan opened his mouth, but Porthos lifted a hand. "Leave it be, D'Artagnan, leave it be. It is well enough. Some grief must be felt, sometimes. Else, it damns up inside and bursts out as rage. Look at our friend, Athos." He shook his head. "I will mourn Guillaume. I will reconcile myself to his death, but . . . D'Artangnan, I wish I could bring him back to du Vallon for burial. Out back there, in the general cemetery there is a small plot, enclosed in a wall. There my ancestors lie. There my mother rests. I would like Guillaume to lie there, under the name du Vallon. I couldn't give it to him in life, but I think at the end of it all, when we're ourselves, he deserves to rest under it." He stopped and swallowed and looked away, at the narrow window on the wall, and at the light shaft that came through it to illuminate a confusion of dancing dust motes.

"Why shouldn't he?" D'Artagnan asked. "We'll travel back with you and with the coffin. Surely it can be made ready for travel. Surely. You know that people bring bodies back from war to rest in their homeland."

"Oh, it's not that," Porthos said. "It is my father. He'd never allow it." He smiled, a brief baring of teeth with no joy at all. "If it comes to that, I'm not sure he'll allow me to rest there, when my time comes."

The curate and Aramis emerged from the little room at the back, followed by Athos.

"To be honest, I never understood why the young lord was so excited. And of course, he was the young lord, whatever the old lord might have said. He was one of those young men who had his paternity written on his face. Looked just like his father when I taught him his prayers. But you see, he said his father was dead, and therefore he would surely have inherited when his grandfather died." He frowned slightly. "Not that several cousins and others, who have been looking to the inheritance as already theirs wouldn't take it upon themselves to challenge it, but with both parents dead, and the child so clearly young master Pierre's son, I don't think anyone could have carried a challenge very far."

"There are cousins, then?" Aramis asked, all gentle and detached interest. "Who might have an interest in the land? But surely until you got word from the lord's grandson no one would have thought the lord's son had died, would they?"

"Well . . ." the little priest shrugged, which seemed more like an all-enveloping movement of too-bony shoulders enclosed in a voluminous black garment. "Ah," he said. "That. You see, the lord's son was sent to the capital . . . thirteen years ago, it would be. And for a long time there were no letters, and then, five years ago, a single letter from him to Rouge, as runs the mills. And you see, it's not natural to be gone that long without sending word."

"But surely," Aramis said. "The first letter came after seven years absence. And besides, I understand Lord du Vallon can't read or write."

"No he can't," the little priest said, and grinned, the happy grin of a small man who nonetheless holds something over a much larger one. "He thinks that reading and writing effeminates you, he says. He says it would turn him into a priest or a cleric and make him less than a man." He shook his head. "Nor could the younger lord, but yet, I hear it's not all that difficult to get someone to write a letter for you, in Paris. Nor is it that hard for the lord to get one of his servants to read it. But there hasn't been word for years and years, save that one letter . . . and who knows if that was even true?" He shrugged again. "The letter, they said, said that the Lord Pierre had left his name and this very successful school of fencing and dancing he'd funded in the capital, and had become a musketeer—" he looked around at them. "As you are, monsieurs. But the truth is, people from St. Guillaume do go to Paris. Not often, it is true, but they do go. And those that went and asked around said there was no du Vallon in the musketeers. And see . . . I think that letter was sent by someone for some purpose I can't but guess." His voice climbed, into reed-thin registers, as he said. "They say Paris is all plots and counterplots and it would drive a man mad to live there and try to understand them. And I say someone wanted us to believe that the Lord Pierre was still alive in Paris. Perhaps one of the lord's cousins, waiting on the inheritance and hoping that no one would dispute it till then?"

"There are many cousins then?" Athos asked. "And is the domain of du Vallon much disputed?"

The priest shrugged. "There are many cousins. The current lord had five sisters and each of them went off and married a neighboring lord and raised families. And they all want the domain. Oh, not for what it is now, though some of the farms are getting very prosperous indeed. But those farms tend to be on freeholds, and therefore do not pay the lord as they normally would. But the cousins, all of them think that with a little investment and a little attention, and something else than the lord's unbreakable pride, it would be possible, quite possible, to make Du Vallon a profitable domain. At least profitable for those who don't want more than a little country place to which they may retire and in which they may live a quite life."

"And do you know if any of these cousins lives in Paris," Aramis asked. "Who could have sent the letter?"

"Now, that," the priest said. "I only have on hearsay, you see, because it's not in the records of this parish, and I only know what I hear people say, after Mass of a Sunday. But I heard from some people who went to Paris that there's a cousin of the young lord who lives in Paris and even is in the musketeers. I can't remember his name, now . . . except it reminded me of something Greek." He frowned. "Yes. Something Greek. Some great battle. Some pass. Yes, some pass, because for the longest time I've thought of the man as Milord Pass."

"De Termopillae?" Aramis asked, his voice full of disbelief.

"The very one," the little priest said, now looking at Aramis more than ever as if the young musketeer were a magical apparition, with all the miraculous powers that implied. "The very one. How did you know, lord?"

"Termopillae pass," Aramis said, and shook his head. "I know de Termopillae. A very well recommended, very well-connected man."

"That and poorer than a church mouse," the priest said. "And church mice are what I know something about." He grinned, as if he'd made high humor. "You see, his mother married a neighbor lord but it turned out the whole thing was all eaten up from the inside, all in the hands of the moneylenders. And then the man she married killed himself." The priest made the sign of the cross, as though to keep away the taint of such an evil event. "And there was nothing left for it but for their son to go and serve in the musketeers. Yes, I would say he would be quite happy to come in for a tidy domain like Du Vallon. And so I shall tell the young Lord Guillaume, when he comes to collect his inheritance. He needs to watch his back every minute and be on his guard all the time, as there are many who would do him in for the sake of his inheritance."

"I see," Aramis said, and cast a worried glance towards Porthos and D'Artagnan, who stood by the tomb. "Thank you, Father. You've been very informative. We must leave now, but you've solved all our problems."

"Not a bother at all," the priest said, and smiled again. "I get lonely here, sometimes in the shadows. The children come for their lessons, and the women for their prayers, but I rarely talk to anyone outside the parish. By the time the four of you ride away, there will be people coming in to ask me who the strangers were. I shall be the center of attention for weeks."

He blessed them all and sent them out of the church to the bright sunlight outside. Blinking, D'Artagnan received his reins from Planchet.

Porthos had already mounted. "We'll go," he said. "If we set out now, we'll make the hostelry by the time it grows dark."

None of them argued. It wasn't till they had stopped, to buy some food at an isolated farm house, and sat under a tree to eat a country repast of roast chicken and ham that D'Artagnan said, "This problem grows more charming by the second. There are your cousins—namely de Termopillae, our very own comrade, who might have seen the boy come to you, and who might have traced the boy's movements, or, who knows, may have been treated to a glimpse of that recording in his pocket. He might have decided that by killing Guillaume and implicating you, he was clearing his way to inheriting Du Vallon. It pains me to think that of a musketeer, but—"

"But de Termopillae isn't so much a musketeer as a rat in a musketeer's uniform," Athos said, and frowned. "You might as well say it, D'Artagnan, as there are a few of them. There are always those with the connections and the knowledge to get a musketeer's post from the King with no real desserts. Most of those die early, of course, but some are actually careful with their lives. Barring a call to war, de Termopillae might survive to embarrass us all . . ."

"I hope it wasn't him," Porthos said. "I would hate to have to kill a fellow musketeer."

"Indeed," D'Artagnan said, "but the other prospects are just as charming. There's your Amelie's parents—and I have to tell you that I didn't like the man at all and wouldn't disdain seeing him swing at the end of a rope."

Porthos frowned, a dark frown. "No. Nor would I. Honor or not, I still think anyone who turns their daughter out . . ." He shook his head.

"And then," D'Artagnan said, thinking he'd best not even mention Porthos's father. "There's Monsieur de Comeau who was getting money from who knows where."

"And it might have been Athenais's husband," Porthos said. "I know. Though I must say that I consider that far too unlikely. Only because, you see, Monsieur Coquenard would be more likely to want me dead, myself, and it wouldn't be so hard for some assassin to creep up behind me, some night, when I'm drunk."

"Except that when you're drunk we're all likely to be with you," Athos said. "And drunk or sober we, the King's Musketeers, are more than a match for any would-be assassin."

"Yes, yes, but still," Porthos said. "Monsieur Coquenard wouldn't be likely to know that. He doesn't set great stock in the work of the sword."

"Oh, yes, but doubtless he has informants," Aramis said. "All merchants do. And you know, it might give Monsieur Coquenard greater satisfaction to see you killed on the gallows than to have you murdered on the streets. Can't you see?" He looked at Porthos, who shook his head, at Athos who shrugged, and then at D'Artagnan who was aware of looking blank. "Oh, do none of you understand women?" Aramis said, in a tone of great exasperation. "A lover killed in a duel, or a lover killed in an alley, by stealth, would remain in any woman's mind and heart for the rest of her life. But one who was put to death by the King's justice after having killed a child? A woman would be likely to recoil and repent from such an unworthy attachment and turn back to her husband all the more faithfully for feeling she had wronged him."

"So, Monsieur Coquenard," Porthos said.

"Yes, yes. And of course the Cardinal."

"Why would the Cardinal concern himself . . ."

"Who knows?" Athos said. "Perhaps he wants de Termopillae to inherit. The Cardinal seems to spend half of his time disposing the noble families of France as though they were chess pieces on a tray. If he disposed of you for that reason, it would not surprise me in the least."

"And the fact remains," D'Artagnan said. "That there is no other way to explain all the attacks we've suffered from men who are clearly sent by the Cardinal, a lot of them guards, not wearing uniform, but guards nonetheless."

"We've not been attacked in very long," Athos said. "Not since we came out to Du Vallon."

Aramis crossed himself. "That is the sort of thing you should never say aloud, Athos."

But Porthos was looking past all of them, at the countryside which, though half a day's ride from his home, must still look much like that in which he'd passed his childhood. "And let's not forget my father in that list of suspects," he said. "Let's not forget my dear father."

He wiped his hands on some grass by the wayside and got up. "Let's go," he said, preparing to mount. "I want to be in Paris. The countryside is even more confusing than the city, and I fear that there are more plots brewing here than there."

Where a Roadside Ambush Is Not In Fact a Roadside Ambush; The Effect of Country Air on Parisian Ruffians

*T*HEY arrived to the hostelry late in the evening. D'Artagnan longed for nothing so much as a bed, and a respite from the continuous bounce of the saddle. While their servants took the horses to the stables, the four of them entered the inn.

The first impression D'Artagnan received was that it was full. Very full. Which struck him as odd since, on the way out, they'd found the place empty, its tables dusty and half its candles unlit, two of its three cooking hearths cold.

Now every table was occupied and not only the wenches who had helped serve them, but also three or four stable lads were circulating amid the tables carrying food and drink.

That was his first impression, and second upon it a more startling one. Half the people in the inn were dressed in good attire that yet bore no marks, no shield, no note of any particular house or patron. And the other half wore doublets and plumed hats of bright blaring red. D'Artagnan stepped back, straight into Athos, and said, "The guards of the Cardinal," as he took his hand to his sword.

A look over his shoulder showed him that Athos was already drawing his out, and he jumped aside and drew his, even as Aramis stepped fully in, his demeanor as elegant and composed as ever, although his lips tightened in an expression of displeasure and his hand went to the pommel of the elaborate sword at his hip.

And at every table, the men were standing, drawing their swords.

Counting the opponents and passing thirty, D'Artagnan was aware of Aramis, composedly and with great aplomb, crossing himself. He knew, without looking, that Athos's face would be composing itself into the mad expression of half resignation but mostly fury that distorted the noble features when Athos was sure that he must die, and took pleasure in the mayhem he would cause before death.

And D'Artagnan closed his eyes and opened them again. And all the men stood, hands on swords. Only, here was a saving grace, that there were two contingents of them—the red-attired one looking suspiciously at the secretive one—and the foes eyeing each other with as much animosity as they showed the three musketeers and D'Artagnan.

The lead of the guards spoke first—he was a tall man, with a scarred face, and it seemed to D'Artagnan they'd met before in the many skirmishes that marked the life of musketeers and their allies in Paris—bowing, and removing his hat. "You led us a good chase gentlemen, and I admit you do the Cardinal credit as foes, but if you think we are going to allow you, here and now, to mock us and confound all the Cardinal's plans, you are very wrong. Give yourself up to us, now, and we shall go easy on you."

"That is nonsense," a pale-haired man with a vague foreign accent said, from the other side. "I'm sure these men had no more intention of doing the Cardinal a wrong than they had of anything else." He looked at them all and fixed D'Artagnan earnestly. "Sir," he said, "if you give me a few minutes of your time I'm sure that all will be solved to the mutual advantage of both us and our friends."

D'Artagnan would very much have liked to believe him, only he remembered this same face all too well, and he remembered this man as one of the dark-attired attackers who had attacked him in Paris. Between these and the guards of the Cardinal there was little to choose and indeed, little certainty that they weren't acting in concert.

D'Artagnan dared a look over his shoulder and to the side, to see Porthos looking aggrieved, Aramis looking mulish and Athos looking almost gleefully bellicose. There was no doubt in his mind that his friends, too, had recognized their attackers.

"I thank you for your kind words, sir," D'Artagnan said. "But I find talking to people who have attacked me before, under cover of darkness, extremely distasteful. You will, therefore, do me the honor of crossing your sword with me. En garde!"

The fixed scene of the tavern broke into a panoply of violence. If both their enemies had converged on the musketeers and D'Artagnan, the four of them would have been quickly overwhelmed. But the two factions seemed as intent on fighting each other as on fighting the four of them.

It was not something that D'Artagnan had much time to understand as he found himself fighting, at once, the blond man with the foreign accent and the scarred man who was the leader of the guards of the Cardinal.

The guard—whom D'Artagnan remembered was called Remy—pressed D'Artagnan the hardest, pushing close, and speaking between his teeth, "Come, come, Monsieur D'Artagnan. You're little more than a child and you can't think you'll survive getting involved in such dealings that far surpass your ability."

D'Artagnan didn't answer. He had no idea what Remy meant by dealings. He had some vague notion he had displeased the Cardinal and he was not quite sure how. Perhaps by escorting Constance Bonacieux to her mysterious rendezvous or perhaps by interfering with the Cardinal's plan involving Guillaume and Porthos. In either case, he would fully agree with Remy that these plots surpassed his ability to comprehend. All of which meant nothing. He was honor bound and duty bound to defend his friends, and Remy attacking him like this, pressing him across the bar as he defended himself, crossing amid other duelers, didn't predispose him to cooperate with whatever the Cardinal might want.

Across the bar, Porthos roared, a sound followed by the noise of breaking crockery and the scream of several people. Through the corner of his eye, D'Artagnan could see that Porthos had grabbed a tray full of drinks from one of the serving wenches and flung it in the face of several of his opponents, in what seemed to be an attempt to clear the path to the bar. What Porthos wanted with the bar, D'Artagnan could not say, except that, knowing how Porthos's mind worked, he rather suspected that it had something to do with getting himself a drink.

Closer at hand, Athos jumped on top of a table, from which position he could more easily battle six determined opponents four of whom wore the red guards' uniform.

And to the other side, Aramis was battling half a dozen opponents, all the while lecturing them. "It is an interesting theological question," he said, between brilliant parries and fulminating lunges, "exactly how—and when—violence is allowed in defense of self, or of a cause deemed just. The very concept of just war, as exposed by St. Thomas de Aquinas in *Summa Theologicae* . . ." Aramis's voice went on and on, and D'Artagnan was sure that if he paid attention to Aramis he would presently feel dizzy and be unable to continue defending himself. And, despite his long theory in fighting, he had never, in practice met two such seasoned fighters as these foes.

While the two leaders of the attackers didn't cooperate, neither were they as foolish as their followers, that is, stupid enough to fight each other. Instead, they each pressed for advantage with him and might, occasionally, bare teeth at each other but without, ever, allowing their enmity to distract them from the task at hand.

He was having a hard time keeping his place, and guarding his back, in case either of the two got ideas.

Hearing Porthos yell from the corner of the room, nearest the counter, "Five roast chickens and four bottles of wine, host, now," did not exactly make him feel better. Oh, Porthos was the best of friends and a man who had, countless times, helped D'Artagnan out of tight binds. But what could he mean by ordering dinner in the middle of this devilish situation?

D'Artagnan, fighting as hard, as fast, as cleverly as he'd ever fought, half expected to hear Aramis rebuke Porthos, as he often did in these situations. When Aramis's voice didn't sound, D'Artagnan wondered if the blond musketeer had perhaps died in this fray. A fine sweat beaded D'Artagnan's forehead at the thought. Would any of them make it out of here alive?

"Athos, catch," Porthos's voice called and something— something white and large sailed over the heads of the combatants.

D'Artagnan, half turned away from the door where Athos was fighting, had the impression Athos had indeed caught whatever it was, but before he could think, Athos sounded out the call that so often resounded in Paris, "To me, Musketeers."

Normally that call, sounded out by a musketeer who'd just been attacked on the streets of Paris, called to the victim any number of willing swords, ready to join the fray. Here, in the middle of nowhere, in a tavern filled with enemy combatants, the call could only mean one thing, and that was that Athos expected D'Artagnan, Aramis and Porthos to flock to him.

More by sound than by sight, particularly since by then most of the candle flames had been extinguished by the candles being used either as projectiles or weapons, he started retreating towards Athos. He was aware of Porthos's progress in the same direction, from the other side of the room. As usual, the giant made use of whatever he could get hold of as weapons. In addition to the heavy blows of his nimble sword, his progress was marked by sounds of furniture breaking, crockery being flung, and always, the startled screams of those who were not ready for such unorthodox means of combat.

Aramis, on the other side, seemed to still be alive and also moving, in the same direction. At least, D'Artagnan could hear the polished voice of the musketeer who insisted he was practicing for the priesthood, calling out, "May God have mercy on your soul," just before an opponent's death scream.

D'Artagnan managed to wound Remy, and had only the blond man to contend with as he approached Athos. He heard Aramis ask Athos, "We retreat?"

"Against such odds," Athos said. "Only rational option."

"Besides," Porthos said. "I want my dinner. Let's hope that Mousqueton has the horses of Monsieur de Treville ready to go."

D'Artagnan, still engaged in a fight with the blond man, felt Porthos drag him backwards through the door of the hostelry at speed. Outside, fire and smoke were thick in the air, as well as the screams of men and the terrified sounds of horses, many of whom appeared to be milling free in the yard, or running scared through the open gate of the hostelry and the streets below.

The cause was easy to see, as the stables, a vast edifice that used to be opposite the hostelry, across a well-appointed yard, were on fire, their red glow lighting up the area like the setting sun, and the heat from the conflagration making the late summer night feel like full summer day.

And coming towards them, at speed, were their servants, each of them leading a horse alongside the one on which they were mounted. Athos jumped onto the saddle of the horse led by Grimaud, while Porthos climbed onto the saddle of the horse that Mousqueton led, and Aramis mounted the horse led by Bazin.

Before D'Artagnan could do more than reach for the reins of the horse that Planchet led, there was a sharp pain at the back of his head, and darkness descended over him.

He woke up mounted, somehow, in the front of Athos's horse, being firmly held. He felt seasick, and his stomach pulled, and there was a devilish weight on his eyelids that seemed to prevent them from climbing fully up.

Some inarticulate sound must have escaped his throat because Athos, whose arm was firmly around D'Artagnan's middle, holding him in place, said, "Oh, you're awake. Easy now. I will be very upset if you vomit. I don't have a change of clothes just now. Easy. We'll be stopping soon."

And indeed, even as he spoke, there was a feeling of their turning down another road, and then a narrow path, all eight horses thundering as though through well-known territory.

That the territory was well known at least to one of them, became clear as they came to a stop and Porthos came to help D'Artagnan down from his horse. "We'll be safe here," he said. "It's little enough known. A convent that got burned in the wars of religion in my father's time. It was a ruin when I was young and I used to stop here, sometimes, overnight, when I was hunting away from home. But the path, though once a Roman road, is almost all overgrown, and those fools are unlikely to find us, at least in the dark of night. Not that I could hear any attempt at pursuing us, but you never know."

"Easy with the boy," Athos said, letting go of his hold on D'Artagnan, even as Porthos lifted D'Artagnan bodily and set him down, gently, upon a fallen stone which, from the way another stone had fallen across its back, made a perfect seat.

His eyes clearing, by the light of the moon, D'Artagnan could see they were in what remained of a ruined chamber, four walls remaining more or less intact and half the ceiling missing. The chamber was vast, and retained its stone floor as well as many conveniently disposed stones.

"You'll be happy to know," Aramis said, "that I delivered what might very well have been a killing blow to the dishonorable canaille who hit you from behind."

D'Artagnan tried to swallow, but really felt very dizzy.

"Here, you'll be the better for this," Porthos said. He'd uncorked a bottle of wine, and pressed it against D'Artagnan's lips.

D'Artagnan dimly remembered some lecture from his mother about wine being the worst possible thing to drink when one had been hit on the head. And yet, it seemed only logical and he was thirsty, so he drank. And miraculously, little by little, his head cleared.

Presently he became aware that the servants had lit a small fire and were tending to the horses, and that the musketeers were eating roast chicken and drinking wine. When they realized D'Artagnan was awake, Porthos pressed some chicken upon D'Artagnan saying, "I think this is the last of the money Aramis made selling that salve to de Termopillae, and since the salve is a Gascon recipe, surely you're entitled to some of it."

"Your cousin de Termopillae?" Athos asked.

"Devil take him," Porthos said. "Truth be told I never knew much of my family. For you must know that my father managed to quarrel with all his sisters save the one that died in childhood. And that one, perhaps, too, except he no longer remembers it. So I don't know any of my cousins."

"He's much younger than you, at any rate," Athos said. "But I wonder if he's concerned in this."

"I don't like wondering," Porthos said. "Any more than I like wondering why the guards are so intent on being rid of us, or who the other agreeable gentlemen might be."

"So, the ruffians of the country are feisty enough for you, Porthos?" Aramis asked, teasingly.

"Undoubtedly too feisty, Aramis. I can't wait to get back to Paris, even if it must bring with it all the questions about Athenais's husband and all the rest. I must warn you that if her husband is guilty, I mean to marry her as soon as I can."

"Marrying is folly, but in this case it is the only thing you can do," Athos said.

At this moment their servants came forward, to share in the chicken and the wine with remarkable equality that didn't usually attend their relationships with their masters when in the capital.

They looked, D'Artagnan noted, embarrassed, as though they expected to be scolded for something. The musketeers, meanwhile, seemed to have no intention of scolding them. It wasn't until they were seated and eating that Planchet ventured, "I'm sorry for the destruction we caused and for setting fire to the stable, but you see, we found that there were several men ready to ambush us, and we—"

"I don't resent you for that at all, my good Planchet," Porthos said. "The only thing I resent is that you didn't somehow manage to find a few coins in the pockets of those you had to lie low with cudgel or tree branch in order to escape. Now the money of the Gascon pomade is gone, we're going to be in devilish straights back in town."

Mousqueton sighed. "As to that . . ." he said, and putting his hand inside his sleeve, he brought out a handful of leather purses.

"I suppose," Athos said, a smile on his face. "You had to put them out of their misery?"

"I thought they owed it to us, monsieur. For putting us through such a devilish uprising."

"Very just," Porthos said. "And for all the trouble you've gone through in cutting these," he said, turning the purses over onto his hand and counting coin, which he distributed to his friends, "you are very well entitled to the other five or six purses you're keeping to yourself."

Mousqueton blushed dark, and the musketeers—and their servants—laughed. All save Bazin who looked sour and shocked.

To D'Artagnan, perhaps because of the knock on his head, everything seemed foggy and dreamlike. It wasn't till he was falling asleep, rolling in his cloak, upon a mass of grass and dried leaves which the servants had gathered, that he reached within his sleeve for the perfumed handkerchief of Madame Bonacieux. And found it gone.

"It's gone," he said, sitting up. "It's gone."

"What is gone?" Athos, who was sleeping nearest him asked, his hand on his sword.

"The handkerchief Madame Bonacieux gave me."

Athos relaxed and let go of his sword. "Ah, that. She will undoubtedly give you another. I doubt you will be wise enough to have nothing to do with her?"

"It's the first time a woman has given me her handkerchief," D'Artagnan said, feeling unaccountably bereft.

"Ah. And we must all learn from our own experiences."

A War Council; What the Servants Said;
A Wife's Loyalty

BACK in Paris, and after a night slept in their respective beds—a night, for the first time in many, not interrupted by strange attacks—the three musketeers plus one gathered early morning to break fast and talk at D'Artagnan's lodging.

Porthos judged that the young man looked peaked. Perhaps it was the knock on the head. You never knew how it would take someone, and though the boy had survived worse scrapes before, perhaps this one had truly undone him. On the other hand, it might be the loss of the handkerchief.

Porthos, who still remembered very well the heady rush of being seventeen, and who, unlike Athos, had not managed in his life to conceive of much distaste for feminine company, found himself smiling at the boy's disappointment as D'Artagnan announced, "Madame Bonacieux seems to be at the palace."

Athos had merely frowned, and Aramis had grinned. "She will come back, young fool," Aramis had said. "And probably rather soon."

Planchet, having served them all with bread and cheese and wine, had retreated to enjoy his own meal in a corner. Porthos thought it was as good a time as any to bring the other ones up to date on his movements since coming back to the capital. "I went to see Athenais," he said. "Late last night, after her household was asleep."

"And?" Athos asked. "What is her word on her husband's dealings and on Monsieur de Comeau?"

Porthos frowned. "Well . . . Those are . . . complex. To begin with, as far as she could find, Monsieur de Comeau is not now, nor has he ever been in her husband's debt. On the contrary, perhaps, since Monsieur de Comeau seems to deal . . . in horses. He has bought horses from Monsieur Coquenard and sold them to Monsieur Coquenard. And he has bought and sold other horses with Monsieur Coquenard acting as intermediary. In the whole of their exchanges, Monsieur Coquenard is probably the debtor."

Athos raised his eyebrows. He looked more shocked than Porthos had ever seen him look. "A horse trader . . . ?" he said in shock.

Porthos laughed. Even though he still felt as though he were in mourning for Guillaume, and even though their situation remained dire, his amusement at Athos's shock dragged the laughter from him. "Athos," he said, gravely, "it is not as though he were a murderer. You must allow that horse trading is a lesser offense."

Athos sat back on his chair, his mouth half-open. "Yes, yes. But . . . horse trading? Zounds, man. He's a nobleman. And married to a woman of even higher pedigree."

"Well . . ." Porthos said. "As to that, Athenais said she doesn't think his wife knows anything of his . . . trading activities. She was, Athenais believes, married to him in the expectation of his having a greater fortune than he did. And she thinks he's drawing money from his estates. Which he is, in a way—since he cycles the horses through his estates."

"Horse trading," Athos repeated, as though both words were in some arcane foreign language and he had trouble understanding them.

Aramis looked just as shocked, but D'Artagnan, for his

still not fully focused looked, seemed more amused than anything else. He traded a look with Porthos, across the table.

"So, we can cross Monsieur de Comeau off our list?" Aramis asked.

"Well, perhaps," Athos said. He frowned at them.

"What do you mean perhaps?" Aramis said. "If he's making his money from horse trading, he's not receiving it from either Monsieur Coquenard or the Cardinal."

"True, but we know that Guillaume had a lamentable tendency to try to extort money from people based on the things of which they were ashamed and—"

"He never tried to get money from me," Porthos protested. "I think you are jumping to conclusions."

"Perhaps," Athos said. "But Porthos, he did try to extort from you something he wanted—sword fighting lessons— based on his knowledge that you were hiding your true name under an assumed name in the musketeers."

Porthos inclined his head. "I would have taught him sword fighting anyway."

"But he didn't know that," Athos said. "What I don't understand is why he would lie and tell Comeau he was his son, when it should be obvious Comeau would know he wasn't. I wonder why he didn't use Comeau's horse trading as the true string on which to draw the lord's purse."

"Or perhaps he did," Aramis said, raising an eyebrow.

"Or perhaps he did," Athos said, and sighed. "And Comeau lied to us."

Porthos frowned. "Well . . . perhaps, at that . . . but you know, I went back there and I asked around this morning before coming here."

"You went back there?" Athos said. "You didn't tell us."

"I'm telling you now. I was going to tell you, but you were so shocked at the horse trading . . ." He shrugged. "Well . . . You see . . . I went back, on the way here, and I talked to the servants and maids at the house. And all of them agree that Monsieur de Comeau tossed the boy out on his ear and gave him short shrift on his attempt to blackmail him."

"Yes, but did he intend to kill him, perhaps so that he couldn't talk to his wife."

"His wife," Porthos said, remembering. "Well, the thing is that the maids tell me Guillaume continued coming to the house, you know, and that he went and talked to his wife too."

"He I assume being Guillaume?" Athos asked.

"Yes, of course," Porthos said.

"And were you so enterprising as to go and find out from his wife what exactly Guillaume had talked to her about?" Athos asked.

Porthos shook his head. "What I hear, from the maids and everything," he said, "is that his wife was of higher birth than him, and . . . you know, a true lady, full of her own importance. As such, I figured she wouldn't want to talk to someone like me any more than she would want to go out in public in a stained gown, you see . . ."

Athos stared, eyebrows raised. "I suppose we should send Aramis to talk to her?"

"Indeed no," Aramis said.

Athos looked at Aramis and Porthos could tell that Athos was surprised, which was not a very common thing with him. "No?"

Aramis sighed. "It turns out that Madame de Comeau is the friend of a lady who . . . well . . . she wouldn't hold me in esteem." He looked at his nails, which he usually did to disguise embarrassment or to hide confusion. "The thing is, at any rate, that she doesn't consider me aristocratic enough to be part of her circle."

"You?" Porthos asked, and sat back on his stool so heavily he almost caused it to overturn. Only a quick grasp of the edge of the table saved him. "You? Who were the lover of a duchess and who are routinely courted by princesses. You are not noble enough?"

Aramis sighed. He flecked away some imaginary dirt from his doublet. "Well, you see, Porthos, it is like this, that princesses and duchesses don't care how noble you are and are likely to consider you noble enough for them if you are noble at all. But people like Madame de Comeau who are in the lower degrees of nobility . . . indeed, at about my level, like to flatter themselves that they are far more noble and of more ancient family line than they are, and thus they wouldn't dream of associating with me." He looked up. It was hard to tell if his green eyes were sparkling with something that might be annoyance or amusement or both combined. "I'm afraid, Athos, that you'll have to talk to her. You, with your looks and every appearance of being descended from crowned heads, she might be willing to talk to."

Athos made a face, and seemed to be about to refuse, but finally nodded, his expression still grim. "Very well, if I must talk to the woman, I will. Though I can't imagine what you expect me to find."

"Only what Guillaume told her, and what she might have answered," D'Artagnan said. "Always taking in account her expression and reactions, of course. You must rely on your sensible examination of the circumstances."

"But what do you hope to find?" Athos said.

"Anything, nothing," Aramis said. "I don't know. But if her husband did the boy violence, then she might know it."

Porthos nodded. "This leaves as suspects Monsieur de Comeau, Amelie's father and mother, my . . . father and, I suppose, my cousins."

Aramis nodded. "I should mention," he said, "that I talked to some people I know this morning."

"People, you know?" Athos said.

"Mostly people of the female persuasion, I assume," Porthos said, unable to resist ribbing his friend.

Aramis turned to him, his eyes oddly serious. "I can't determine that either of Amelie's parents approached the boy," he said. "But both of them asked around enough about their daughter. And your Amelie's father stayed at the Hangman for a while."

"How did you find this out?" Porthos asked.

"Ah . . ." Aramis shrugged. "You'd be surprised what mendicant friars see and hear. I simply asked some whose normal station is near the tavern. It was easy enough, by description of her father and mention of where her mother would be from, you see . . ."

"And my father?" Porthos asked. He wasn't sure he wanted to know. Oh, there was no love lost between himself and his father. There hadn't been for many a year. But the thing was that no matter how much Porthos told himself his father was a boar and a madman with no manners and worse morals, he was still Porthos's father.

Porthos could remember being a little boy in Marie's care and thinking his father was the biggest, the strongest and the most wise man in the world too. He remembered seeing everyone in St. Guillaume du Vallon deferring to his father and thinking that he was truly the most important of men. Somehow, the old, cantankerous man who had sent Porthos to Paris and now refused to admit Porthos existed inhabited the same body as the idolized giant of Porthos's childhood. And he didn't wish either of them to have committed murder, much less murder of Porthos's son.

Aramis shrugged. "Your father also looked around, though he must be credited with looking for you first, and then Guillaume. I think he spoke with Amelie. Guillaume's sister. Other than that, I haven't found much."

Porthos closed his eyes and hoped his father hadn't done anything stupid, but then he had to open his eyes again and go on hoping. He drank the wine in his cup, and nodded, all around. "I shall talk to de Termopillae," he said.

"I shall go with you," Aramis said.

"And I," Athos said, speaking as though he were being asked to sacrifice himself to some unknowable pagan deity, "shall go and interview Madame de Comeau."

"And I think," D'Artagnan said, slowly. "That I shall go back to sleep."

Porthos wondered if the boy was truly still addled from his knock on the head, or whether he wanted to stay home to see if the beautiful wife of his landlord would put in an appearance. Either way, it was a temporary affliction and would surely pass.

A Lady's Boudoir; The Commerce Stain; The Matter of the Jewels

❧

"**W**ITH Madame de Comeau?" the little maid asked Athos, giving him the once-over with a shrewd evaluating air.

Athos had dressed in his best and least-patched uniform, brushed his hair and tied it back. He held his best hat—the one with the plumes still feathered out and in good condition—against his chest as he spoke. He was aware that he looked, if not regal—it was hard to look regal in a patched suit—at least noble and dignified. He was also aware—had been aware since he'd reached manhood—that there was a certain air he could put on, a certain way of moving, that gave people the immediate impression he was highborn and much too good for his surroundings and their company. He now threw his head back, with just that expression, and the maid gaped at him.

"Does the lady know to expect you, milord?"

Athos shook his head. The woman ran up the stairs, leaving him in a small entrance room. This was a different entrance than the one he'd used with Madame de Comeau's husband. Athos suspected that this was the main entrance of the house, and the one that normal guests would use.

The entrance room was narrow but long, fashionably tiled in dark green marble. The walls were a pale yellow that looked, rather, like the paint in some Italian noble houses that Athos had visited with his father, in his youth—freshly applied over still-wet plaster and looking, for that, whitish and faded. On the walls hung what looked like very good portraits, cast about with that look of familiarity that denoted ancestors. Athos, noticing one of a cavalier of the time of Francis I—as least denoted by the man's attire—was quick also to realize that the painting was far superior to the quality then obtaining and, in fact, so different from his own portrait of his own ancestor of that time that the two couldn't be from the same era.

He would not expend the time needed to walk around and examine all the portraits, but he permitted one of his small smiles to slide across his lips. He thought he understood, and very well, too, that Madame de Comeau's sin, like Porthos's was vanity. Only hers rested on a far less stable foundation than the musketeer's who, for his continued certainty of superiority, required only his own strength and handsome appearance.

From this small room, a staircase climbed, broad, up to a door that had been painted yellow and studded all over with golden nails. Through that door the maid had disappeared and from that door, there now sounded a cackle that reminded Athos—conscious of being ungallant—of the sound of a disturbed henhouse.

Presently, the door opened a mere sliver, and there was a suggestion of someone peeping through the opening. Athos, suspecting it was the lady of the house, trying to decide of his eligibility for an audience, straightened himself and squared his shoulders. The door closed. And a few moments later, it opened again, to let a smiling maid through.

"The lady," the wench said, curtseying, "will see you now, monsieur."

She led Athos up the staircase and, at the top, opened the door and announced, "Monsieur Musketeer," as if this were some sort of title.

Athos entered the room to find it handsomely outfitted with a profusion of chairs, settees and a reclining couch in the Roman manner, upon which a young woman was lying daintily, holding silken embroidery upon which she seemed to have worked an intricate pattern of very diminutive flowers.

Not a man to judge others by their material worth and—being descended from an old and noble house—even less accustomed to thinking of objects as displays of good breeding, Athos was not yet so unworldly that he didn't recognize, in the large, gilt-framed mirror on the wall, a Venetian masterpiece worth a king's ransom. This, taken with the new yellow velvet covering the sofas and chairs, and the newly painted walls with their profusion of just-too-new, supposedly ancestral portraits made Athos think to himself that horse trading might be the way to go.

But he said nothing of the kind. Instead, he bowed, with every appearance of respect, and said, "Madame de Comeau. It is a pleasure to make your acquaintance. I am, as your maid said, a musketeer, but my name is Athos."

This so provoked her that she sat up, from her reclining position, and fulminated him with an almost glare from very fine, honey-colored eyes. "Oh," she said. "But that's not a person's name. That's no one's name. That is a mountain, isn't it? In . . . Armenia?" She was petite, rather than small, designed on a small frame, but with everything that the most lavish sculptor could want. Her oval face, with its slightly too prominent nose, betrayed more than a hint of Roman blood.

It was a face well adapted to frowning, and while she frowned at him, he bowed hastily. "Madam," he said. "Few women know that. Few men, even."

"Oh," she said, a sound of peevishness, not of surprise. "My father had all of us excellently educated, boys and girls alike. He said a well-trained mind was the best weapon in the world and he did not intend to send any of his children out unarmed." She frowned at him, dark eyebrows brought low over golden brown eyes. "But it is very provoking of you to call yourself after a mountain. What is your real name?"

Athos thought that, had he not enough reason to be weary of women, reason that had trained him as a dog or a horse could be trained, through severe pain instilling aversion, he would be in some danger now. There was to the woman a combination of peevish childishness and sharp reasoning which would doubtless prove the downfall of better men than himself.

As it was, and because he knew better than to court Madame de Comeau's—or indeed any woman's—favor, he permitted himself to grimmace and bow again. "That, madam, is known to my confessor and to very few other people in this world."

She set her embroidery aside and stared at him. "It is a noble name, that much I know," she said. "From your way of standing and your address. So why would you hide it? Have you done something to so displease the King that . . . But no." She flicked the thought away with a careless gesture of her fingers. "No, of course not. If you'd displeased the King, you'd not be in his musketeers." She frowned again. "But it is some great wrong here, something you very much wish to hide."

He bowed again, in silence.

She slapped the sofa by her side, with some energy. "Oh, you are a very trying man. Why wouldn't you tell me? It's not as though I'm trying to interrogate you so that I can babble it at court."

He bowed yet again and she sighed. "Very well," she said, and from the tone of her voice she might have been a queen dispensing a high favor. "Very well, if you must be that way. Please sit down."

He chose an armchair not too far from her, and sat down. And she sat primly now on her original reclining perch. Her hands folded on her lap spoke of a careful upbringing, as did the attentive glance she bent upon him. "You wish to see me," she said.

"Yes," Athos said. "Very much. I've asked your husband some questions, but I wish to ask them of you as well. Your husband . . . might not have apprehended the situation as well as you will." He'd meant to say this all along, knowing that flattery was a good part of questioning people about things they might not, otherwise, wish to share. But in this case, it might very well be true.

"Oh, my lord . . ." She shrugged, a gesture that effectively and tactfully dismissed her husband's discernment. Then she looked at Athos, giving the impression of turning her whole mind to his speech. "Very well. Tell me what you wish to talk about."

It had an odd effect of his being interrogated but, lacking Aramis's interest in and ability to speak to women, Athos felt it was just as well if he progressed quickly to the matter at hand. "I don't know if you ever even heard of this person, though your maids, apparently think you talked to him. However, there was a young boy, thirteen or so, with auburn hair, who used to come and—"

"Guillaume," she said, quickly, with no attempt at disguise. "From the Hangman."

Athos inclined his head, partly to avoid showing her his expression of surprise. "Your husband told me that Guillaume tried to get him to give him a stipend and claimed that he was your husband's natural son."

Madame de Comeau put her head a little sideways, a clear expression of doubt that didn't necessitate her saying anything about her husband.

Athos smiled a little. "I don't know if he told you the truth."

The little hand rose and fell in what seemed to be her peculiarly dismissive gesture again. "Oh, as to that, he might very well have. The whole thing is the sort of foolishness that Guillaume would contrive and that Monsieur de Comeau might even find amusing. He has a soft spot for rogues and cheats." She shrugged. "But you know, he never could be my husband's bastard. There are plenty of those around my lord's domain, and they are all, like my lord, small and dark. Guillaume is, as you say, auburn haired, and tall and rawboned enough that you know he's going to be a great hulking man when he's done growing."

Athos, amused by her attitude towards her husband's profligacy, nodded. "No. He isn't your husband's siring. But your husband had him beat and thrown out nonetheless."

She nodded, approvingly. "Well, it wouldn't do for him to go about thinking he had the power to force my husband to dance to his tune, now would it?"

"But he didn't prevent the boy from coming and hanging around the yard again."

"Which was his folly," Madame de Comeau said, her gaze merry. She seemed to view all of this as much of a game. "Because he found out my husband's secret."

"That your husband trades in horses?"

At this she raised her eyebrows. "If it is an open secret, then my money was ill spent. Or did Guillaume tell you that? Are you perhaps his attempt to extract more from me? Have a care sir. I neither have the money to give you, nor the disposition to submit to constant fleecing."

Athos shook his head. "I have no intention of fleecing you." This idea actually got a smile from him, but it vanished as soon as he realized what she had said. "You gave Guillaume money?"

She shrugged, a very expressive gesture. "What else was I to do?" she asked. "Otherwise the horrible boy would bruit it all around town that Bernard . . . Monsieur de Comeau deals in horses. And while I couldn't care much where our money comes from, the rest of society is so tiresome about it."

Athos raised his eyebrows. "Indeed. How much did you give Guillaume?"

She shook her head slightly. "Tell me, first, how did you come to find out about Bernard's dealings?"

Athos smiled. He guessed very well that there might be

some wifely loyalty there. In fact, thinking of the Lord de
Comeau, with his single-minded interest in horses, his tolerant deference to his wife's attempts at civilizing him, he
guessed that the man might, very well, be a good match for
this woman who seemed to observe social proprieties as
some other people said rote prayers—something done for
the others, not oneself. "My friend Porthos found out," he
said. "And please, don't alarm yourself. I don't think he'll
be in the least likely to divulge it to people." Not the least
because to divulge it, Porthos would need to explain how
he'd come by the knowledge, which would involve con-
fessing Athenais's husband's profession. Athos was so sure
of this that he was able to meet the lady's eyes square on,
with every expression of reassuring honesty.

. "Oh, but it is vexing," she said. "What if . . . Why is
your friend Porthos concerned in this at all?"

"For Guillaume's sake," Athos said.

"What's the brat to do with it? With the money the
wretch got from me, and a good velvet suit besides, which
he forced me to choose, and only secondhand, he should be
admirably provided for. Why would anyone concern himself with him?"

"He's disappeared," Athos said.

"Ah," Madame de Comeau said. "As to that, the brat
seemed intent on becoming a gentleman or a counterfeit of
one. I wouldn't put it past him to have gone to quite a different area of Paris and there impose on some unsuspect-
ing nobleman to become his squire or what not." She
shook her head. "He's a bright boy and seems capable of
any degree of deceiving and extortion. He'll do well for
himself."

"Well . . . perhaps," Athos said, and here he couldn't
meet her eyes. "But . . . you see, he disappeared a few days
ago and we are all very anxious for him."

"All?"

"My friend Porthos and I and a couple of other people
in our close acquaintance."

Madame de Comeau wrinkled her perfect brow. "Athos . . . Porthos . . . Oh. You're two of the inseparables. You must be, for no one else would have such odd names."

"You rub elbows with musketeers, ma'am?"

She smiled, an impish smile. "No, but to tell you the truth, my little maid rubs elbows with musketeers servants. Or at least the servant of one of the inseparables, whose name I can not now remember . . . Oh! The boy is a Picard, and she says he's amazingly clever, though to me he only looks pimply. I believe his master is a Gascon."

"I believe I know of whom you speak, madam," Athos said, once more marveling at how easy it was in Paris to have connections with practically everyone, or at least everyone in a certain circle. Though it could also possibly be said that musketeers and their servants, much like tomcats, covered a wide territory.

"Well, I'm pleased to have met one of you. All the ladies speak of the four of you, you know?"

"You do me great honor, madam," Athos said, rising. "But before I go, I don't suppose you'd tell me how much money you gave young Guillaume?" And as she started to speak, he said, "Don't be offended. If you tell me at least the general amount, I shall be able to guess, easily enough, how far he might have gone with it and what folly he might have taken upon his head to commit."

"But . . ." Madame de Comeau said. "But what business is it of the four of you? Oh, I've heard you often concern yourselves with . . . well, with the King's work that can't be entrusted to anyone else." She fluttered her hand desultorily. "Secret things. But what can the boy have to do with it."

"Why nothing, madam," Athos said, though not absolutely sure he told the truth. There were, after all, the repeated attacks by the Cardinal. And yet, he was almost sure . . . almost absolutely sure that whatever that was, it involved something quite different. "It is that my friend Porthos is the boy's father."

"Oh," Madame de Comeau said, and put her hand in

front of her mouth. "Oh. Of course. No wonder the boy
was so intent on being a gentleman. Of course. Though it's
unhandsome of your friend not to supply him the means
to do so."

"My friend," Athos said. "Didn't find out until . . ."

"Until Guillaume had in fact vanished?" Madame de
Comeau said. "Oh, it's just like a story. I do hope you find
the boy."

"I do too," Athos said, and inwardly told himself he
hoped at least they found the boy's murderer and gave both
Guillaume's memory and Porthos some measure of rest.
"Only, if you'd tell me how much money you gave him?"

"Well, I didn't have very much money on hand," she
said. "Not as such. But I had jewelry. Bernard is a great
fool and always buying me some trinket or another." This
was said in the complacent tone of a woman who knows
she is worth any tribute her husband might bestow on her.
"So . . . I sold some pins and a necklace I didn't like very
much." She made a little dismissive gesture with her hand.
"I believe it all came to five hundred pistoles. Not that
much at all."

Not that much. Athos wondered in what class the lady
had been reared, exactly, that five hundred pistoles was not
that much. A hundred pistoles could keep the four of them
in style for quite a while, and their needs were greater than
most. Five hundred pistoles would certainly have bought a
lot for both Guillaume and Amelie. Perhaps not enough to
make her a lady, as he had promised her, but enough to see
them lodged in some comfort and without daily drudgery.

But there had been no money at all on Guillaume, when
he had been found. Where could the money have gone?

Athos bowed to Madame de Comeau and made his
good-byes in his most correct fashion, somehow thinking
the only way to deal with this very unconventional lady
was with the utmost civility. She responded and rose as he
turned to leave.

And then by the door, he noted a small table, piled with

perfumes and creams, and he turned to look at the lady. "Milady, do you use belladonna?"

She blinked. "Not very often. Only now and then on my eyes. Why?" Her reply was quite innocent and devoid of guilt.

"No reason," Athos said. Hat in hand, he bowed low. "Madam, your most humble servant."

She smiled at him. "Do come back when this is all resolved and you've found the scamp," she said. "I'd like to know how the story turns out."

So did Athos.

Family and Familiarity;
The Complications of an Inheritance;
The Lot of the Youngest Son

$\mathbf{D}$E Termopillae got up from where he had been, sitting on a low stone bench, casting dice with his fellow guard.

Aramis suppressed an irritation he was very aware of being hypocritical. It was all very well to fume at de Termopillae for playing the dice while he should be guarding one of the many entrances to the royal palace, but the truth was that every musketeer did it, and Aramis not least of all.

"Porthos," de Termopillae said, as the redheaded musketeer stepped in front of him and then, with a more pleased tone, "And Aramis."

The truth was that de Termopillae was, for lack of a better explanation one of a few young musketeers who idolized Aramis and tried to copy his style of dressing, his manner of speaking and his gestures, down to the careful examination of their nails when in a tight spot. What none of them could imitate, of course, was Aramis's intelligence and his ability to find his way through complex situations.

At least, this was what Aramis liked to think. But none of this helped him feel better about de Termopillae who, to own the truth, was the most successful of Aramis's imitators, and for that the one he detested the most. Just looking at de Termopillae, who combed his blond hair exactly like

Aramis and who wore venetians in a shade of grey that exactly matched some that Aramis often wore, and who tied his doublet in the exact same way. And—what was most galling—he pinned a lovelock to the side of his hair in the exact same way as Aramis, with a pin that looked almost exactly like Aramis's save for being of cheap construction. This made Aramis's blood boil, and something like a shade of rage fall in front of his eyes.

Porthos was looking at de Termopillae with a frown. And when Porthos frowned people were likely to pay attention. Oh, Aramis knew that frown. It was Porthos's confused frown, and Aramis would bet he was trying to imagine in what way this foppish man, almost half his size and looking very much like a dandy, could be related to the du Vallons.

But de Termopillae, clearly, had no idea why either of them had taken an interest in him. He took a step back, and then another. "I . . . er . . ." he said, and stared at them. "I . . . er . . . used the balm you sold me, Aramis, and it has worked wonders. You'd never know I was stabbed almost clean through the arm. It is almost completely healed."

Porthos made a sound deep in his throat, and then rumbled something half under his breath. De Termopillae jumped and stared. "I beg your pardon?" he said.

"I said," Porthos said, making each of his syllables a small work of art, polished and perfectly set out for examination, "that it is a characteristic of the family. I never need a salve. I just heal."

"The . . . the family?"

"My family," Porthos said.

De Termopillae's throat worked. He was looking up at Porthos, his eyes wide, and he had lost color so that what was normally a triangular and catlike, impish face looked like a tallow sculpture or the face of someone about to die of blood loss. "You know," he said, his voice low.

This, Aramis could have told him, was the most stupid thing he could say. He clearly didn't know how Porthos's mind worked. Porthos was here about Guillaume's murder, and though Aramis very much doubted that by "you know" de Termopillae meant to confess to it, to Porthos's direct mind it would seem exactly like he had.

Porthos moved forward, a siege engine slipping its moorings. Aramis made an ineffective grasp for his sleeve, but it was all for nothing.

Porthos's huge hand caught de Termopillae on the chest and lifted him, under the sheer impulse and force of its own movement, pressing him up against the wall. "Why did you do it, wretch?" he asked.

"Porthos, I don't think—" Aramis said.

"I . . ." De Termopillae, his wound healed or not looked like he was about to lose consciousness. "Do what? I couldn't help being born to whom I was, could I?"

"What does your birth have to do with this, sirrah?" Porthos asked. "How does your birth make you a murderer. And a child, yet?"

From the other side of the gate, la Roselle, the musketeer who was standing guard with de Termopillae, stared. He stood, transfixed, his leather dice cup in his hand and looking like he was not sure whether to run for help or just to run, since Porthos had, clearly run mad.

De Termopillae stared at Porthos. "What child?" he asked.

"My son," Porthos said. "Why would you murder my son? Did you intend to dispatch me as well? And fat good it would do you. The manor house is a pile of stones, and I would bet you none of the fields about, none under my father's care, are worth any more than the largest farm in his domain. Bless me if any of them are worth as much, considering how the farms go around there."

De Termopillae, pinned against the wall by the force of Porthos's hand, half bent over the stone bench, blinked. "I don't know what you're talking about," he said. "I don't know anything but that we're cousins. Or at least, that's what my father said when he visited last year. He said you had the mark and body of my mother's family, and that bet it, you were my cousin. Other than that, I don't even know your real name, much less that you have a son. And I couldn't care less for your father or your son."

"You don't?" Porthos looked puzzled. He pulled his hand back, and de Termopillae fell, nervelessly upon the stone bench, and leaned against the wall.

"What did you think I had done?" he asked. "You have a son? Or did you say someone killed your son?"

Porthos glared. "It is none of your business," he said.

"Granted, granted," de Termopillae said, in the voice of someone who, just at that moment, would have granted anything, half the world included, if only Porthos would leave him alone.

Porthos seemed done with him, and ready to go, but Aramis was not quite of the same opinion. Instead, he held Porthos's arm, now the giant looked as ready to retreat as he had been, first, to press de Termopillae to the wall. "Porthos, stay," he said. Then, to de Termopillae, "Your father visited you in town?"

De Termopillae looked at Aramis. Aramis could tell, the way his gaze measured him that de Termopillae was totting up all the similarities and the differences between them, trying to decide how to make himself look more like Aramis, if that were possible.

"My father came," he said and ducked his head, then started brushing at his collar in a gesture so reminiscent of Aramis's own that it made Aramis seethe. "To talk to me of my affianced wife, who is but waiting to marry me, as soon as it is safe to go back to my home."

"Why should it not be safe to go back to your home?" Aramis said. "And you have a wife waiting for you?"

"She is my cousin," de Termopillae said. "On my father's side. An only daughter set up with extensive lands and property, and wanting only a man's hand on the rudder of her ship."

Aramis bit back a terrible impulse to ask which man de

Termopillae meant to find for the task, and instead said, "Then why can't you go back home and be married."

De Termopillae sighed. "I killed a man," he said.

"I knew it," Porthos said, starting forward towards de Termopillae again. "You are a vile murderer."

Aramis put an arm up in front of his friend, without even looking. He knew very well that should Porthos not choose to stop—should he push forward—he could push Aramis's arm and overturn Aramis too. But he also knew, with the comfort of long-accustomed friendship that Porthos would stop, and he did, even though de Termopillae, who had no such assurance, was doing his best to knit himself close with the wall.

"How did you kill a man?" Aramis asked.

"In a duel. Just a duel," de Termopillae said. "And because of the edicts . . ." He shrugged.

"How likely would you be to get any inheritance from your mother's side?" Aramis asked.

De Termopillae blinked in confusion. "I beg your pardon? My father describes his marrying of my mother as rescuing her from some forsaken place in the middle of nowhere where people lived still as in the time of Charlemagne. Why would I want to inherit any of it, even were any of it worth inheriting?"

Aramis felt the pressure of Porthos against his extended arm, as if Porthos had almost taken a step forward, doubtless eager to defend his domains. "Never mind that," he told de Termopillae, quickly. "Just tell me—if there were no heir on that side, would you inherit?"

De Termopillae stared at Aramis as if he thought the musketeer likely to grow a second head. "No. How could I? My mother was the youngest sister, and all her three sisters have children. And then there's my brothers who'd inherit before I ever did. You see, the reason that my father arranged me a marriage with an heiress is that of my three brothers, Charles will inherit my father's land, and Felix will go into the church and Henri, enfin, is well in his way to become a general. That leaves me, and Father thought the best thing to do with me was marry me to my cousin, and I do not mind, only Father thinks we need to wait another year, till the scandal of the duel dies down."

"Very well," Aramis said, and turned to Porthos. "You see, it is all explained."

He could tell from Porthos's blank expression that nothing was explained, or at least not to Porthos's satisfaction. But Porthos, used to trusting Aramis took a step back and nodded.

And Aramis said, "Thank you for answering our questions, de Termopillae. You've been very helpful."

De Termopillae nodded, somewhat dazed looking, still casting a suspicious glance at Porthos, as if he suspected the huge redhead of who knew what. But he said nothing—being a wise man and intending to live—and Aramis turned as did Porthos, and they started to walk away, before Aramis turned back. "Oh, one last thing."

"Yes?" a shaken de Termopillae asked.

"Where were you . . ." Aramis calculated mentally. "Five days ago, early morning?"

"Here," de Termopillae said. "I was keeping guard from midnight till almost high noon, as I was taking my shift and Firmin's on account of Firmin being pickled."

"And did you see a skinny auburn-haired lad, named Guillaume?"

"I saw no one, really, except a veiled lady who went out. One of the Queen's maids and the goddaughter of Lavalle. No one else. Right, la Roselle?" and, in an aside, "We stood guard together."

"There was no one unusual, and certainly no lad," la Roselle said.

"Right," Aramis said, and bowed gracefully. "Thank you very much for helping us."

Counting Cousins Out; Playing
the Blame Game;
The Mercy of Enemies

❧

"**S**o, explain it again," Porthos said. He knew that he wasn't stupid. At least, oftentimes he saw things that escaped the other musketeers, even Aramis with his theology and rhetoric, and Athos with his classical learning. But whatever had happened back then had left him completely baffled.

They were now some distance away from the royal palace, and preceding at a good clip towards D'Artagnan's place where, as Aramis had assured him, Athos was bound to head himself, once he had talked to the lord's wife.

"Tell me why it is that it couldn't possibly be de Termopillae."

"I'm not saying it couldn't be de Termopillae," Aramis said. He was frowning slightly. "It could of course be him if two conditions obtain." He counted it off on his fingers. "One, if he is a consummate liar and lied to us about his circumstances. And two if he managed to make la Roselle lie as well." He looked at Porthos and added, "About where he was, on the morning Guillaume was poisoned."

"And are those two so hard to obtain?" Porthos asked, lowering his eyebrows over his eyes and glaring. "I'd say all musketeers are consummate liars, and that getting two of them to lie about the same thing, well . . ."

Aramis grinned. "Liars perhaps, but not consummate liars. I don't think poor de Termopillae could lie convincingly. And if he could normally do it, he certainly couldn't do it after you'd scared him within an inch of his threatened life."

"So you don't think he was lying?" Porthos asked.

"No," Aramis said. "I don't, and at any rate, it would be stupid of him to lie about such simple things as the number of children in his family or which of your aunts is his mother, because how did he know you didn't have some idea? Or, how did he know you hadn't talked to someone about it?"

"Still he could be bluffing it," Porthos said.

"Not, with you there, so near, and ready to slip the leash and hurt him at the slightest excuse," Aramis said. "Not likely. I'd say not possible. Most sane people don't want you turned on them in a rage."

"You speak," Porthos said, "as though I were some kind of war machine."

Aramis grinned but said nothing, as there was nothing to say. They walked their way past the broad streets filled with imposing houses, their doors guarded by dogs and menials, and wended into the more populous quarters of town, towards the Rue des Fossoyers where D'Artagnan lodged.

"Mind you, if we're going to cross out people who might have done it," Porthos said. "Our list is getting mighty scant."

Aramis nodded. "I suppose there's little hope," he said, "that Monsieur Coquenard might have done it."

"Just as well," Porthos said. "Much as I love Athenais, if I had to marry her in order to look after her, she would be very ill looked after." He opened his hands in a show of helplessness. "I am in no condition to support a wife."

"No," Aramis said, smiling slightly. "Besides, I fancy

your Athenais would drive poor Mousqueton insane if she started minding his housekeeping."

"More likely he would drive her distracted with his unerring ability to step on chickens and bottles of fine wine."

Aramis nodded. "And I suspect Monsieur de Comeau didn't do it. Though of course, it is possible that Athos will find his wife did."

"You don't sound as if you believe it."

"Well . . ." Aramis sighed. "I've heard something of the woman, and I daresay if she thought it was of some real advantage to her to kill a child, she's the type of woman who would, quite likely, do it. However . . ."

"However?" Porthos asked.

Aramis opened his hands. "I must own to having lied to Athos."

Porthos smiled a little. "That," he said, "is very bad of you."

"Indeed. The truth is I know the lady somewhat by reputation, and I know that she can wrap any man she wishes around her finger."

"Oh. Which is why you set Athos on her."

"Well, if a man can interview her and be undaunted by her charms, it is our friend."

"Our friend," Porthos said, "is not indifferent to women, particularly beautiful ones."

"Oh, no. Not indifferent. There are such men, and if that were merely the case, then he would have no more trouble interviewing her than interviewing any man. Athos is more like a man who having nearly perished of a terrible disease—say, small pox—has developed such a reaction against it that he never will catch it again. Immunized, rather than indifferent."

"So in practical terms, that people like me can understand . . . ?"

"Well, it means that she will be less likely to convince him of her innocence by sheer charm, but . . ." Aramis frowned. "She is charming. And though there are, I've heard and read about, charming women who are famous criminals, and often famous poisoners, I don't think it is her type of charm. From all I hear of those in her circle, she is a kind woman with a good sense of humor. And there, I must own, Porthos, that I don't think poisoners do very often laugh."

Porthos nodded. "Though I bet they do, I know what you mean. You mean you don't feel her to be guilty, though you'll wait Athos's judgement."

"Exactly," Aramis said.

"So, this leaves whom still to be suspected?"

"Oh, the late Amelie's mother and father," Aramis said. "Though my mendicant friar could find no evidence that they'd ever been near the child himself. Or not near enough to poison him. Certainly, they established no relationship with him that would allow them to offer him food and have him eat it."

"This doesn't mean that they couldn't have paid someone to . . ." Porthos frowned and sighed. "You know I don't like to say it of my own father. Proud as the devil, of course, but bastards who don't impinge on him and his land, provided they aren't made legitimate by my marrying their mother . . ."

"Exactly," Aramis said. "I would say it would not concern him. And indeed his main work in Paris seems to have been to make sure that you hadn't married Amelie."

While speaking, they'd arrived at D'Artagnan's neighborhood and started, through dint of long habit to walk along a normally deserted alley between buildings. It was normally deserted because it was not in point of fact an alley, but only a space left when buildings had been put up. Musketeers and other big men not scared by the darkness cast by the tall buildings nor by the odor of urine caused by the many men who chose that place to relieve themselves cut through that space. But few other people did.

Porthos sighed. "I don't suppose we can pin it on the Cardinal after all?"

"I don't see why we shouldn't," Aramis said. "There's also that group of anonymous ruffians who seems to fall on us out of nowhere. The leader sounds distinctly English, and I'll be cursed if I know—"

"Stop in the name of the Cardinal," a voice said.

Aramis and Porthos looked at each other. Porthos had thought for a moment that the voice came out of his own thoughts, and doubtless Aramis thought the same. In the time it took them to realize that both of them had heard it, five men had emerged from the shadows, blocking the alley ahead of them.

"If you'll just give us what we want," one of them said—and Porthos was sure it was Remy, the same ugly, scarred fellow from the hostelry on the road back to Paris. "You've led us a chase long enough."

"We have not," Porthos said, "the slightest idea what you want." He bowed gallantly, while saying so, because that was what Athos would do. "And so we will just have to fight you."

"With pleasure. And then you must give it up, or tell us which of your friends has it."

"I say," Aramis said. "The guards of the Cardinal must have run insane. I wonder if his eminence himself has lost his reason."

"Canaille," the scarred man said, charging Aramis. "You shall pay for that.

In no time at all, the alley resounded with the noise of crossed swords.

A Rude Awakening; A Lady in Distress;
A Monstrous Idea

∽

D'ARTAGNAN slept. At the back of his mind, in the part of him that was somewhat conscious, there was the idea that he had slept too long. But there was also another feeling, a feeling of needing rest and of relishing it, which was quite unusual to this young man of seventeen and of an active disposition.

And then upon his deep, dreamless sleep there impinged a sound of crossing swords and a couple of exclamations that he knew for a fact to be uttered in Porthos's voice—well, either to be uttered in Porthos's voice or to have been shouted right by his bed, because that was the only way a voice could be that loud.

Adding insult to injury, a hand seized rough hold of D'Artagnan's shoulder and shook it. "Monsieur D'Artagnan, Monsieur D'Artagnan." The voice was undoubtedly Planchet's and yet it couldn't be, because Planchet was not fool enough to wake his master from a deep, dreamless sleep.

Without opening his eyes, D'Artagnan half turned and muttered as much through his teeth, though he might have taken the time to add a couple of choice swearwords to make Planchet understand the enormity of what he was about to do.

"Monsieur," Planchet said. "You'd never forgive me if I

let you sleep. If what I can see from this window is true, then it's Monsieur Aramis and Monsieur Porthos and as many as half a dozen of the guards of the Cardinal."

At these words, D'Artagnan was instantly awake and sitting up. He'd had the foresight of lying down to sleep fully attired and as he stood, he found Planchet with admirable promptness, helping him strap on his sword. The boy would make an excellent servant yet.

Fully attired, D'Artagnan started down the stairs to his front door two at a time. It was a measure of how much better he felt that he did not misstep a single time. He pulled his door open and ran out, fully intending to run across the street to the alley, to help his friends.

Only instead he careened full force into a warm, soft body, and both of them fell. It took him only a moment to realize the person he'd toppled, and atop of whom he was now lying, smelled of some soft roselike perfume. Another moment to realize it was undoubtedly a female. And a blink of his disbelieving eyes, to take in blond hair, oval face and amazed blue eyes, and to realize he was lying atop Madame Bonacieux.

"Monsieur D'Artagnan," she said, and the two of them did a creditable job of springing up and apart.

She blushed and he blushed, and only the sound of swords from across the street could force him to move. He reached for his hat, and started to remove it and to bow, when to his confused mind there came the thought that he had lost the handkerchief she'd given him. And in his befuddled state he said, "Only . . . I've lost your handkerchief."

She blushed a dark, dark pink, and lowered her eyes, then looked back up at him, and sighed. "Don't worry about the handkerchief," she said. "It is safe."

He couldn't understand why she looked ashamed, nor what she might mean by it, but he only bowed again, and then he ran into the alley, screaming "To me," and calling the attention of two of the opponents who had engaged

Porthos and Aramis. He could perceive he had arrived just in time, since both Porthos and Aramis—each of whom had been fighting three enemies at once, for who knew how long—gave the impression of being very tired.

The problem, as D'Artagnan realized, is that this still left each of them defending himself from two enemies. Except that at that moment, from the entrance of the alley, there echoed in Athos's most resonant voice, "To me, musketeers."

A moment later, Athos claimed the attention of one of D'Artagnan's opponents, whom he discharged in very short order, just as D'Artagnan managed to dispatch his own. Which left both of them in the position of being able to relieve Porthos and Aramis, just as three more musketeers, called by Athos's yell, charged into the alley. Moments later, another two arrived running from the other end.

The two guards of the Cardinal who were still unscathed made the rational decision of running full tilt towards the newly arrived musketeers, while the two who were wounded leaned against the wall and surrendered their swords.

Leaving their comrades to dispose of dead and wounded, the four inseparables walked towards D'Artagnan's home. D'Artagnan led them, of course not expecting to see Madame Bonacieux anywhere. And indeed, she was gone, and he didn't have time to look at the windows of her house, to see if she might be watching him. Besides, what she had said really troubled him.

What could she mean by saying the handkerchief was safe? And by looking so guilty?

D'Artagnan led the other men up the stairs to the room where they normally had their councils. They each took his accustomed place at the table.

"So, Athos, what's your verdict on Madame de Comeau?" Aramis asked.

"I don't think she had anything to do with the boy's death," Athos said. He was frowning, as if something were troubling him. D'Artagnan could interpret the expression accurately because it mirrored his own puzzle over Madame Bonacieux's words.

"Why not?" Porthos asked.

Athos shrugged. He spoke lightly, though his forehead remained knit in a frown. He spoke as though all of this were less important than some puzzle he must solve. "Because . . . well, she said her husband was very fond of rogues and imposters, but I think she nurtures a fondness for them herself. Or at least for the boy. His audacity in threatening to denounce her husband for horse trading seemed to delight her."

"So . . ." Porthos said slowly. "We are coming to the conclusion no one killed Guillaume. Perhaps it was just a seizure?"

"No," Aramis said. "No. It was definitely belladonna poisoning. And while it's possible it was eaten by mistake, Guillaume didn't look so hungry that he would eat any leaf or berry that . . ."

"No," Athos said. "But . . . something is puzzling me. Something different. There is something new—something Madame de Comeau told me—and which we have not yet accounted for."

"Oh?" Porthos asked.

"She gave the boy five hundred pistoles."

"Five hundred pistoles?" D'Artagnan asked, his eyes opening wide. "How? And why?"

"Oh, he threatened to reveal that her husband dealt in horses. And though she knows of it and doesn't seem to mind, she says that appearances have to be kept for the sake of society."

"But then . . ." Porthos said. "Perhaps she killed him to recover the money. That's quite a sum."

Athos shrugged. "She didn't seem to think that was quite a sum. It was just some jewelry, she said. And, Porthos, I don't think she was lying because I don't think she had the slightest suspicion of the child being dead. The way she talked of him . . ." He shook his head.

"But then . . ." Aramis said. "There was no money in his pouch when he was found."

And all the while, while the others looked at each other and tried to reason it out, D'Artagnan was thinking—how would Madame Bonacieux know that the handkerchief was safe? She'd given it to him the night of the day they'd met. It said "CB" on it. And then, almost immediately a series of anonymous rogues that D'Artagnan had never seen before had started attacking him, demanding he give them *it*.

"Are you saying the boy was hit on the head and robbed?" Porthos asked.

"No," Athos said, shaking his head. "No. He wasn't hit on the head, and indeed, who would poison him to rob him? Unless . . ."

"Unless?"

What could *it* be but that handkerchief? But why would a band of ruffians and—D'Artagnan frowned—the guards of the Cardinal want Madame Bonacieux's handkerchief? It made no sense at all.

"Unless it was given to him by someone he trusted."

Trust. He had trusted her. But the leader of the ruffians had an English accent. Constance Bonacieux. Charles Buckingham. CB. The same initials on that handkerchief.

Constance Bonacieux worked for her Majesty the Queen whose rumored lover was the Duke of Buckingham. In fact, it was a current joke at court that the Queen might yet give France an heir if only Buckingham would visit more often. But then . . .

The King and, more importantly, the Cardinal, forever anxious to catch the Queen in some faux pas that allowed him to have her divorced and exiled, often made it very difficult for the Queen to communicate with Buckingham at all. Even if her communication with him was often meant to tell him to stay away.

CB. A handkerchief sent as a signal. Had Constance Bonacieux, on first meeting him, thought him such a young . . . dullard, that she'd thought she could entrust the handkerchief to him as a love token and get it stolen from him without a problem, and no one would suspect?

He remembered how he'd protected her to take her important message somewhere. It had all been a sham. She had used him. She had . . .

D'Artagnan got up from the table, vaguely aware that his friends were also standing up. He had no idea why they were standing up. It had been some time since he'd stopped paying attention to their conversation. He rushed down the stairs, to the front of the house, where he looked up.

The window which she'd opened before to talk to him, now opened again. She looked out, her features full of guilt. "I'm sorry, monsieur," she said. There was something other than guilt in her gaze, some deep appreciation, something he couldn't quite read. "I thought it would be very simple. You are so young. I thought they could take the handkerchief again from you, without a problem. I thought they would never know and you would never know. They were under orders not to hurt you."

"You used me," D'Artagnan said. "You used my admiration for you." His all too open admiration. "Oh, Athos is right. Women are the devil."

Madame Bonacieux nodded gravely. "Perhaps we are, monsieur. Perhaps we are. But . . . she is so lonely. My lady. She had a friend, but her friend was killed. She is so lonely and there's no one she trusts. She thought, a handkerchief with the initials . . . Well . . . They're the same as mine. Even if I were searched, the Cardinal would never guess that was the message. And words written upon it by a cunning ink that looks invisible till he uses the right chemical to deliver it." She shook her head. "He wants to come to Paris, you see. He said he would come and see her unless she sent a note to deter him. And my lady, she can't . . . She can't risk her position, her crown, her whole life for love. Even if she loves him."

"You used me," D'Artagnan said. This single fact, persistent, in his mind, would not go away nor would it allow him space to think of anything else.

"Oh, monsieur. I thought it would be quick and easy."

"Guards of the Cardinal attacked me. And my friends."

"But none of it should have happened. I don't know how the guards, how his eminence got word of it. They can't have seen it, because they had no idea which of you had the handkerchief. Or even that it was a handkerchief. They just thought you or your friends had been given . . . something. But the palace is rotten with plots. You can't trust anyone."

"Yes," D'Artagnan said, heavily. "Yes. I begin to perceive that."

"Oh."

At that moment D'Artagnan became aware that his friends had come out his front door and stood, looking like they were waiting for him.

"I bid you good afternoon, madam," D'Artagnan said, removing his hat and bowing low, as he turned to accompany his friends.

He was young enough, though, that he couldn't resist a look over his shoulder, just a glance, to see how she was taking his rejection. But her window had closed.

How One Speaks to Girl Children;
The Advantages of Not Being Easily
Convinced; The Vanished Coin

PORTHOS didn't want to go into the Hangman. Everything else aside, he remembered the unpleasant face of the host's wife and it seemed to curdle bile in his stomach. Besides, he imagined that if he tried to speak to the girl child again, she would only be called a whore and attacked by her unkind guardian again.

But the thing of it was that Athos was right. If anyone still alive in the world knew where Guillaume might have put the money or to whom he might have given it, it would be Amelie. So they must steel themselves to going into the Hangman.

Porthos had been talking to himself in stern terms, as they crossed the few blocks that separated them from the tavern. He had, in fact, been nerving himself up so much to go into the place that he did not realize that Amelie herself had just come out of the tavern. Barefoot and hurried, she was running in their direction and, in the way of a street urchin, moving back and forth, trying to spy an opening between the approaching men.

As she made to run between Porthos and Aramis, Porthos put a hand out and grabbed her little arm. The girl squealed in fright, but Porthos said, "Shhh. It's us. We're friends. We mean you no harm."

Amelie looked up, her eyes searching. "Oh, you," she said. "You asked all the questions about Guillaume. Have you seen him, monsieur? Because I think he might have got sick, something might have happened to him. He was acting funny when he left, five days ago, and he hasn't come back."

Porthos took the girl's hand and led her to the side of the road, where he knelt in the dust, not caring if it marred his fine velvet suit. "Amelie," he said. "Listen, you must tell me . . . Did Guillaume ever tell you he had money?"

Amelie looked at Porthos, then behind Porthos at the other three. "No. No. He said he was going to get money, and I would be a lady and dress like one."

Porthos was aware of Athos kneeling beside him. A glance sideways revealed Athos looking grave, more serious than Porthos had seen him in a long time, but with a soft look to his eyes. And when he spoke, his voice that could make adults tremble came out very gentle. "Amelie, don't lie to us. It is very important that we find out about the money. Whoever took the money probably hurt Guillaume, and might hurt you."

The girl was silent, a long time. She looked away from them, at where her hand was twisting the frayed edge of her cloth dress. "Why do you say I'm lying?" she asked, at last, her eyes serious and her voice full of the businesslike aplomb of a much older person.

Athos answered just as seriously, seemingly making no allowances for his interlocutor's young age. "Because I know Guillaume got money. I also know he didn't have it with him when . . . when he left here five days ago. At least I don't think he did. Did he, Amelie?"

The girl looked at him a long time, then, after a while, nodded. "No," she said. "He didn't take the money. There were two double handfuls"—she showed with her little hands—"of gold coins. His hands, bigger than mine. And he hid them in the stable. There's a place in the upstairs where a board is lose, and he hid them there. But, you know, he must have come back for them, because when I went up there and checked yesterday, it was gone. I didn't want you to know in case you thought he had done something bad with the money. Only he wouldn't, you know? He wouldn't do anything but what he said, and get a better life for us. And if he did something you don't like—"

"He didn't do anything I don't like," Porthos said, feeling tears come to his eyes. He wished Guillaume had grown. He wished in the course of a long life there would have been the time for him to disagree with Guillaume on some of Guillaume's choices—his choice of profession or his choice of attire or his choice of bride. As it was, there was nothing, nothing, now for him to disagree with Guillaume on.

And the money was gone. Who could have known the money had been there at all? "When did you see the money last, Amelie?"

"At night, when I went into the stable to sleep," she said.

"Could anyone else have heard it or seen where the money was?"

"No," Amelie said. "No. Guillaume made sure all the grooms were asleep. They slept elsewhere, anyway, in a room at the back. All of them were asleep, and we were all alone."

"No one could have come or gone?" Porthos asked.

Amelie thought. "No. No one. The part of the stable we sleep in is a division at the back. The hay is kept upstairs, and that's where we sleep. On the bottom there's only one horse, and that's Martin's own horse."

"And could Martin have come in?"

"No, because when Guillaume showed me the money, the horse wasn't there yet, and the horse still wasn't there when we went to sleep."

Porthos looked at Athos and Athos back at Porthos. Athos was frowning. "Was it very late?"

"Oh, yes. So late."

"Does Martin often stay out very late?" Athos asked.

The girl nodded. "He'll leave after he's done serving in the tavern, and he'll stay away for hours and hours and hours." She frowned. "Madam says he goes to the whores, but then she calls me a whore, too, so I'm not sure what she means or if she knows where he goes."

Madam. In Porthos's head, an idea was forming, but he didn't know how to prove it, even if it were true. He looked up, meeting Athos's gaze and realizing that both of them were thinking the same thing.

Aramis and D'Artagnan, the cunning ones, looked blank for once. Perhaps, Porthos thought, it was that he and Athos were the two older ones here, and had had more time to observe the workings of unhappy marriages.

"Softly," Athos said. "Softly, Porthos. I'll go and get mine host out on some pretext."

"But . . . how can we prove it?" Porthos said and it came out half as a complaint and half as a wail of protest.

"With luck," Athos said. "With a lot of luck."

A Husband's Knowledge; A Wife's Rage;
A Daughter's Duty

❧

"**B**UT . . . I don't understand any of this," the hosteler, Martin said, as he stood before them, in the afternoon sun, rubbing his head as if it hurt him. He looked from one to the other of them. "I'm sorry, but are you gentlemen amusing yourselves at my expense? It is a fantastical story."

"And yet it is true," Porthos said.

"But . . . Guillaume . . . dead?"

Porthos looked down at Amelie, who had given a sudden shout at first hearing of her brother's death and who was now crying silently. He put his hand on her head, and his hand more than covered her small head. He petted her gently, as one would pet a disturbed animal. He looked back up at the hosteler, and nodded.

"And what's all this of five hundred louis d'or? It can't be. How could he gets his hands on that much money?"

"It was—" Porthos started to say.

"A legacy," Aramis interrupted. He looked at Porthos. "A distant relative who had no need for them any longer had her jewels sold and left the money to Guillaume."

"Oh. But then . . . Guillaume found his family?"

Porthos sighed. He transferred his hold from Amelie's head to her shoulders, and rested his hand there. "I was Guillaume's father," he said.

"Oh," Amelie said, looking up. "He said you were a

musketeer and the most wonderful sword fighter in the whole world. And he said you could never support him in style, but he was sure you would recognize him, because he'd been to your native village and you . . . not all your . . . uh—" she came to a sudden stop and blushed dark.

"Not all my—?" Porthos prompted.

"I'm afraid you'll be angry," Amelie said.

"With Guillaume's sister?" Porthos said. "Never."

"Oh. Then. He said not all of your grandfather's grandfather's were noble, and that you would recognize him even though he was the son of . . . even though mother wasn't noble." She looked at Porthos, attentively. "Would you have?"

"Yes," Porthos said. "Yes, I would have." On impulse, he picked the little girl up. She was, he was sure, the hosteler's daughter. At any rate, being years younger than Guillaume, she could never be his own. But she was all he had left of the love of his youth and of his son. The daughter of one, the sister of the other.

"I still don't understand," Martin said, looking from the little girl to Porthos, then back at the little girl. "You say someone poisoned Guillaume and took his money, but this I can't understand. Because the stable boys wouldn't have given Guillaume any food, save maybe if they put the poison in his drink when he went drinking with them, which I think he did once or twice."

"Not that day or the night before that day," Amelie said. "He didn't go anywhere. He talked to me and that was all."

"But then . . . who can have killed the child and stolen the money?" Martin asked, scratching at his head, his face the picture of astonishment. He looked at them, one at a time again. "Are you sure this is not a joke you're playing on me?"

"*Sangre Dieu*," Porthos said. "How can it be a joke when a child is dead? No. It is not a joke and none of us is laughing."

"Perhaps . . ." Athos said. "Perhaps you can do me a very great favor?"

Martin blinked. "Anything, Monsieur Musketeer, but . . ."

"Is there a place your wife hides money? A place she thinks you don't know about?"

Martin looked blank for a moment, but then a fleeting smile crossed his lips. "Oh yes," he said. "Provided I remember not to take too much or too suddenly, she just thinks she forgot how much she had."

Porthos had seen this sort of arrangement many times and now kicked himself for not having thought of it before Athos did. Of course the wife would have a place to hide money that she considered secure. All the wives of profligate husbands given to drinking and consorting with women of easy virtue did. And of course her husband would have found it out years ago. All the husbands did. As long as you were careful to only milk the cow a little, the game could go on for years.

"Have you taken any money out of there recently?" Porthos asked.

Martin shook his head slowly. "Oh, not in a month, at least," he said. "I try, you see, not to hit it too often, or she would find out." He sighed. "It's not that she's a bad woman, you know, but she is, of herself, so cheerless and so little in need of company that she doesn't understand that I require every once in a while to go elsewhere and to be with people who laugh and drink." He frowned. "But what can any of this have to do with the boy and his money?"

"I would like you to go to that place now, with all of us attending, all of us watching," Athos said.

"But . . . why? It's in the tavern, you know? If she sees me go there and sees that I know her place she'll only change it."

"That . . ." Athos shook his head. "It won't matter. Trust me. It's the only way for you to understand and the only way for us to know for sure what happened."

At this, Martin's eyes flew wide, and he stared at Athos.

"Here, what are you saying? Are you saying that Josiane murdered the boy? For money? It's monstrous. She's been my wife for twenty years. She would never—"

Athos straightened his back, his face a mask of perfect gravity. "If we go to the hiding place and you find nothing, I will accept I was wrong and I will apologize for having slandered your wife."

Martin's face hovered between shock and anger, but anger won out. "Oh, you will, by God," he said. "You will beg my pardon and Josiane's too. I know she has a temper and that, for reasons I don't understand, she doesn't like poor Amelie, but just for that, it is no reason to think that she would murder Guillaume. And Guillaume, yet, whom she didn't care about one way or another, save that he helped bring heavy things into the tavern and looked after the guest's horses."

Martin wiped his hands to his voluminous apron. "You will be proven wrong, by God, follow me and you'll see." And full of his own righteous certainty, he marched towards the tavern.

The tavern was almost empty. Only one table—at a corner—was taken by a group of four strangers who were eating their midday meal in silence. Martin's wife, behind the counter, was wiping it with vigor.

As they came into the tavern, with Porthos still carrying Amelie, she darted the girl a venomous look. "There you are, you laze about," she said. "Again in the company of men. I don't suppose it has occurred to you to go to the laundress as I sent you, to find—"

Her recrimination stopped, mid sentence while Martin walked in and walked straight towards the fireplace. When her voice resumed, the tone was the same, but the target different. "Martin, what are you doing? What do these men want?"

Martin, on a righteous mission of his own, ignored her. He marched straight to the fireplace, and grabbed at a certain brick that didn't seem to protrude any more than any others. The sound of brick scraping on brick could be heard, as he moved it slightly back and forth.

"Martin, what are you doing?" his wife asked and, leaving the counter, came running towards them to grab onto Martin's arm. "What are you doing? Have you gone mad?"

But he only shook his head and continued pulling. From where Porthos was, he could see that his face was set in an expression of anger, still, and his eyes burning with the certainty of his own righteousness.

"Martin!" his wife said, and now started raining blows on his arm and shoulder, blows he ignored as though they were no more than the sting of a wayward mosquito.

And then the brick came loose, and there was a sound of metal, and a rain of gold came spilling out of the hole in the wall, to tinkle on the floor, calling even the attention of the guests in the corner.

The woman wailed, and Martin stood, staring at the hole and at the gold. He put his hand into the hole in the wall and brought it out covered in coins, which he allowed to fall between his fingers to the floor, as though they didn't mean anything or he wasn't sure exactly what they were for.

Then he turned to his wife, his gaze still angry, but now burning with something else. "You," he said. "You killed the boy. I could take your coldness. I could take the fact that you don't love me. But you killed the boy? Why, Josiane, why?"

She looked at her husband, her face rigid, and then broke suddenly in a deep sob. She stumbled towards the nearest table and dropped onto a bench next to it. "You only married me because my parents owned the tavern," she said. "I saw even then, how you looked at every pretty woman who passed by. And I thought it didn't matter, because we'd have children, and I'd be the mother of your children. But it never happened. And then you had your whore come and live here, already with child, and then you had this other one"—She pointed at Amelie—"with her.

And then Guillaume was just as bad as you are. That brat, always looking here and there, and knowing everything . . .

"I poisoned the slut. Five years ago, I poisoned the slut, and everyone thought she had died of a fever. The nightshade out back, my mother always said not to get any leaves in anything by accident, because it makes you burn up inside, and I gave it to her, because I knew you were visiting her every night, there, in the stable, like animals, and she was swelling up with another of your bastards, yet again. And I gave it to her and she died, but then you just started going to other women. And you wouldn't come home till near morning, and drunk, and I thought, I thought . . ." She shook her head. "I got up, on Sunday, late at night, and I went into the stable, to see if you'd taken your horse, or if perhaps you'd gone out on foot, and I saw your brats with all this money, and he was talking about how they'd live like royalty. And I was sure it wasn't money come through in a good way, and all I could think is that you'd leave with them. There was enough gold there to buy another tavern, if you wanted. And I thought you'd leave with them, and I'd be alone, and I didn't even have any children. So I poisoned your bastard."

Martin was staring at her, his mouth half-open in complete astonishment, his eyes filled with horror. But all he said was, "The children aren't mine. I'd never laid eyes on Amelie when she first showed up here, and she was already big with child. That man says Guillaume was his son."

The woman looked at Porthos, then back at her husband, and then at Amelie. "Oh, perhaps, but the girl has your face and your gestures, so I was justified in thinking they were both yours. And I was justified in killing him, too, and taking away his ill-gotten gains."

She got up from the table, suddenly calm. "Put the money back in the wall. I don't want to speak of this ever again."

When the constables came to arrest her, she was busily polishing the counter, and seemed surprised anyone would want to punish her, after she confessed to murdering two people, in the sight of her husband, three musketeers, a guard and a group of honest merchants who'd found this a very strange entertainment provided for their mealtime, and who'd listened to everything very attentively indeed.

A Daughter Found;
Legacies

༄

"AMELIE, bring the gentlemen some wine," Martin said, and dropped everything he was doing—which at that moment was picking up dirty mugs and delivering them to tiny Amelie behind the counter.

The girl already looked different. She was wearing different clothes for one. Squinting at her, to see her better against the early morning sunlight, Athos was sure the clothes she had on were the woman's, inexpertly altered to fit her much smaller size. But they were better clothes than the rags she'd worn before, and her hair was combed and loosely tied back. And she looked . . . happier.

She nodded to her father, and expertly drew the wine from the barrel and brought cups she put in front of each of the men. Then she hurried to serve another table that was clamoring for something.

"I don't have much time," Martin told them. "There aren't many heavy drinkers in the morning, but the guests like to break their fast before they go, and Amelie is filling in valiantly, and of course we have a cook in the back, but still, we might need to hire a wench or two to help, till Amelie is older."

"You sent for us," Athos said. "You sent a note . . ."

Martin nodded. "What I want to know is this—is there someone to whom we need to return the gold?"

Porthos started to open his mouth, but Athos shook his head. "No one. It was given with good and free will. Only, I hope you're not intending on spending it on drink and—"

The man shook his head. He looked, Athos noticed, more serious than he'd looked before. "That's all behind me now. I don't even want to marry again. Not till Amelie is settled. You see, I have a daughter." He shook his head as though at the wonder of it. "It turns out everyone around here knew she was my daughter and thought I knew. Only I . . ." He shrugged. "When I . . . When Amelie came here, I'd already been married to Josiane so many years, and we had no children. And, you know, there had been other women and I had no children. So I thought there was something wrong with me. I thought . . ." He shook his head. "But I have Amelie. She's quite a little worker, and if I keep the gold for a dowry for her, who knows . . . She might even marry an accountant or an attorney."

Athos gave Porthos a sideways glance, to see how he took that, but Porthos only nodded. Sometimes Porthos could be very sensible, and see, as well as they all did, that an attorney's life was a step up from this.

"Or she can inherit the inn and make it the best and largest inn in Paris," Martin said. He looked grave. "At any rate, I wanted to thank you. You'll always have a meal or a drink here if you need it."

Athos, knowing that they would save that for when they needed and not for when they wanted it, which would save Martin growing tired of them very quickly, nodded. "And Amelie will always have four protectors," he said. "Should she need them."

"We would like," Porthos said. "To take her with us, for four days, leaving tomorrow, if you will let us?"

To the man's look of startled surprise, he explained. "We're having Guillaume buried in my family plot, where all my ancestors sleep. And I'd like Amelie to be there. I think he would have wanted it."

A shadow passed over the man's eyes, and then he nodded.

For the Sake of a Lost Handkerchief

D'ARTAGNAN was asleep. It was not a dreamless sleep, rather a sleep filled with dreams in which a beautiful, blond woman ran just ahead of him, laughing lightly and calling out in the voice of Madame Bonacieux, "You fool. You poor fool!"

Into this dream there intruded a sound like a scratching. It wasn't enough to wake him. Instead, he thought it might be a mouse and there was a momentary dream of being a mouse in the wall—a mouse taunted by a beautiful blond woman.

But then the mouse whispered, back and forth in two voices; there was the sound of a door closing; then of steps, and then of the door to his room—the innermost of the two rooms in his lodging—opening and closing, and a smell of roses seemed to fill the whole room, overpowering.

Light steps approached his bed, and it was too much for D'Artagnan to hold on to his shreds of sleep. He opened his eyes, and he knew he was dreaming.

Madame Bonacieux stood there, in the moonlight.[4] She

---

[4] Here we see one of the many instances in which Monsieur Dumas tampered with the timeline of acquaintances and events. And, of course, there have been hints dropped over the years that Madame Bonacieux's actions were not quite those portrayed in the book. Here we see her much longer acquaintance with D'Artagnan and the reason for his great attachment to her and their relationship.

was dressed in only a very flimsy shirt that covered to her knees. Beneath it, one could see the rosy forms of her breasts, swelling gently, and guess at the narrow waist. Her blond hair was loose down her back. In a pile at her feet lie those accoutrements of respectability—her over dress, her cloak, her bonnet—which she'd clearly just discarded.

D'Artagnan raised himself on an elbow, to look more closely at this apparition, which might be a dream and insubstantial, but was, nonetheless, the most beautiful thing ever to grace his room.

"Don't say anything," she said, rapidly. "I don't do this." Her hands went up to cover her face, and when they came away, revealed she was blushing dark. "I've never done this before. Not with just anyone. But I want you to know that if I used you abominably, it was at least in part to lie to myself, to tell myself that you didn't matter. I could tell you were overcome at first sight, but, monsieur, I was overcome too."

She stepped towards the bed, moving—where D'Artagnan was concerned—as if on a cloud of dream. "But then I saw how you behaved when you realized I'd used you, and I thought I'd betrayed myself, too, and there was only one way to make it right. My husband doesn't know I have this night off from the palace. Your servant says you're leaving tomorrow on a trip. So, you see, that leaves us tonight. Please, don't say no."

"I wouldn't dream of it," D'Artagnan said. The dream was now close enough that he could extend his hands and touch it. To his surprise, it was very corporeal and warm and human—female flesh, pliant to his touch. "I wouldn't dream of it," he said again.

He pulled; she tumbled onto the bed.

And then there was warmth and softness and the diffuse smell of roses.

Fathers

PORTHOS'S pounding on the door of the manor house at Du Vallon brought an almost immediate response. There could be no other way, since they'd been traveling slowly, with the sealed coffin in a cart among them, and there would have been talk and comment about it.

The door was opened by Monsieur du Vallon, himself, in a towering rage.

"Good morning, Father," Porthos said.

The old man half-flung the door. "I have no son," he said.

"How strange," Porthos said. "For you had one."

"He's dead."

"No," Porthos said. With his massive hand, he forced the door open wide, so his father could see the cart, with its black-draped bundle. "No, Father. My son is dead. And my son is going to be buried in the cemetery of Du Vallon, next to our ancestors. And the name on the tombstone, which I brought with me is Guillaume du Vallon. Do you understand me, Father?"

For a moment it looked like his father was going to flare up and scream back at Porthos. But he looked at Porthos, and at the cart, and at the other three silent men, and the dark-dressed little girl with them, then back at Porthos. "Do what you want and be damned," he said. "Why should I care where a pile of bones rests?"

Which was how, a few hours later, they came to be

standing around a small grave, newly filled, while Porthos
carefully set the tombstone over it. The stone read *Guillaume du Vallon, son of Pierre du Vallon.*

In death, at least, Porthos thought, Guillaume had come
home. Even if all the paternal care that Porthos could give
him now was a father's tears.

Turn the page for a preview of
the next Musketeers Mystery

The
Musketeer's
Inheritance

Coming soon from Berkley Prime Crime!

Where the Musketeers Are Good Samaritans; Springing His Eminence's Trap; An Unwelcome Summons

"**E**N garde," Monsieur Henri D'Artagnan said, as he danced back to a defensive position, and lifted his own sword. "Unsheathe your swords."

Facing him, under the pale yellow sun of early autumn, outraging him with their presence on the outskirts of Paris, just outside the convent of the Barefoot Carmelites, three guards of Cardinal Richelieu pointedly did *not* unsheathe.

Instead, the lead one—a middle-aged blond—looked from D'Artagnan to the three musketeers who stood behind the young guard, staring at the scene with varying expressions of amusement.

"But, monsieur," the guard of the Cardinal said, lifting his hat and scratching at the sparse blond hair beneath. "All I did was remind you of the edicts against dueling. How would this justify *dueling* with you?"

D'Artagnan hesitated, his internal conflict visible only in a straightening of his shoulders and a sharp look up. Seventeen years old, with the lank dark hair and bright, dark eyes of his native Gascony, D'Artagnan was muscular and lean like a fine horse. And like a fine horse, every one of his thoughts was obvious in movement, in stance, in a tossing of the head or a quick glance. He was aware of his body betraying his impatience.

"It seems to me," a mannered, cultivated voice said from behind D'Artagnan. "That you have offered our friend a great insult, monsieur guard."

It was a voice that would have sounded very well coming out of a pulpit and explaining in rounded phrases some obscure point of theology. The gentleman who spoke, so far from looking like a priest, was a tall, well-built blond, whose wavy hair shone from brushing.

His clothes, in the last cry of fashion, boasted a doublet that was only vaguely that of the musketeer's uniform. Though blue, it was made of patterned satin and crisscrossed with enough ribbon to adorn several court dresses. More ribbons adorned sleeves and hung in fetching knots from wrist closures. A profusion of silver buttons shone like the ice that sparkled from the ground on this cold November morning.

His name was Aramis and despite the languid speech and the intent gaze he now bent upon his perfectly manicured nails, he was known as one of the most dangerous blades in the King's Musketeers and a breaker of ladies' hearts. It was said he was pursued by princesses, courted by duchesses, and that a foreign queen had sent him the expensive jewel that dazzled from his exquisitely plumed hat.

D'Artagnan knew Aramis well enough that he did not need to turn to know that his friend's bright green eyes shone with mischief. That Aramis enjoyed this. His enjoyment did not help D'Artagnan calm down.

"Indeed," another of the musketeers said. He was as tall as Aramis, but of quite a different type. For one, he did not wear fashionable clothes. Rather, his clothes were in the fashion of decades ago—a tightly laced doublet and old-fashioned knee breeches that displayed, below the knee, a muscular leg encased in mended stockings.

This musketeer's curly hair—a black so dark as to appear blue in certain lights—was tightly pulled back and tied roughly with a scrap of leather. His pale skin revealed the slight creasing around the eyes, the lines around the mouth that showed him the oldest one of those present—and as not having lived an easy life.

Looking back over his shoulder, D'Artagnan saw that his friend's smile was guarded, but that his dark blue eyes sparkled with as much mischief as those of Aramis. His name was Athos, though D'Artagnan had found that in another life—before he'd joined the musketeers to expiate what he considered his unforgivable crime—he'd been the Count de la Fere, scion of one of the oldest families in the realm.

His nobility showed now, as he advanced a foot and tossed back his head. Despite his mended clothes, he was very much the grand seigneur as he said, "I think these gentlemen owe you an apology, D'Artagnan."

"What I don't understand," the third musketeer said, his voice booming over the landscape and making the guards jump. "Is why they assume we were dueling, I mean . . ." He paused struggling for words.

This enmity with language was the trademark of Porthos and despite his present outrage D'Artagnan couldn't help smiling slightly at hearing it. It often made people think him stupid, but very few would tell him to his face, because Porthos looked like a Norse god. Much taller than his companions—or indeed than anyone else—with broad shoulders and a muscular body capable of feats of strength to rival those of mythology, Porthos could not be made more splendid by wrapping himself in finery. This didn't stop him trying.

Norsemen had dreamed of such as him in the guise of Thor, beating an eternal forge. They probably had failed to imagine his gilded baldric, the rope of gold that surrounded the brim of his hat, or the multiple jewels that flashed from each of his powerful fingers. Most of them glass, if D'Artagnan knew his friend, but splendid looking nonetheless.

Porthos shook his head, giving the impression of utter bewilderment, as he asked the guards, "*Mon Dieu*, can't four friends meet to go to a dinner without bringing you down on them with your edicts and your . . . your . . . I know not what to say . . . Your regulations? The precious orders of your . . . Cardinal?"

"But, monsieurs," the guard pointed out reasonably. "Surely . . ." He shrugged, not in a show of lack of knowledge, so much as in total bewilderment. His bewilderment, his meek pose were an affront to D'Artagnan's mind and heart. "Monsieurs, surely—" He looked around at the immediate surroundings, where the scuffed ground, two broken swords, and a trail of blood leading, speakingly, to the door of the convent, all spoke a recent fray. "Surely you see . . . There's been a duel here."

"Oh, and if there's been a duel, we must be to blame, eh? Very pretty reasoning that," Porthos boomed. "That's the musketeers. Always dueling. Easy thought. And wrong. We were going to a dinner."

D'Artagnan, who found none of this funny, and whose blood lust was rising at the guard's refusal to face him, spoke only through clenched teeth, to repeat yet again, "En garde."

"But—" the guard said, and opened his hands in a show of desperation. His companions, two smaller, darker men, stood with hands on the hilts of their swords, but did not draw.

Aramis sighed, heavily—the sort of world-weary sigh that could be expected from a man who claimed that he was wearing the uniform of a musketeer only temporarily, until he could attain his ambition of becoming a priest. Hearing it, no one could guess that his seminary education had been interrupted years ago when a gentleman had found Aramis reading the lives of saints—at least that was what he swore he'd been doing—to his sister and challenged Aramis to a duel, thereby forcing Aramis to kill him.

"If you must know," he said, looking up from an intent

examination of his nails and speaking in a voice that implied that no well-bred person would push the point so far. "We heard the moans of the injured and we stopped to render assistance. I am, as you have probably heard, all but in orders, and I thought perhaps I could give some comfort to the dying."

The guards looked from one to the other. "You're telling us that you came to help other men?"

"Very good of us, it was," Porthos boomed. "In fact we behaved like true Philistines."

The guards looked up at him with disbelief, and even D'Artagnan was forced to look over his shoulder at his giant, redheaded friend.

"I believe you mean Samaritans, Porthos," Athos said, and coughed.

"Do I?" Porthos said, then waved airily. "All the same, I say. All those people were the same, anyway. Always giving their aunt's wife's donkey in marriage to each other." And with such a cryptic pronouncement, he said, "D'Artagnan, if they apologize, will you let them go?"

D'Artagnan shook his head. No. No and no and no. Their very apologies would only enrage him. The truth was that the guards had come, of course, just at the conclusion of a duel arranged by the musketeers the day before. They'd arrived just after the musketeers had dispatched their opponents and helped the wounded carry the dead to the convent.

And now they persisted in their nonsensical quest to arrest the musketeers—without drawing sword, without raising their voices, without in fact, even calling attention to Porthos's blood-smeared sleeve or the noticeable tear that rent the sleeve of Athos's doublet on the right side.

They not only had found out that the musketeers were going to duel—in itself this was not a great mystery, since the duel had been called in a tavern over a handful of noblemen's refusals to drink the King's health—but they refused to fight.

D'Artagnan's scornful gaze accessed the guards' middle-aged countenances, their pasty faces, the fact that each of them carried the sort of extra weight that a few duels a month burned off and judged them to be nobodies. The sort of nobodies given a post in the guards to appease some family connection or some powerful nobleman.

They wouldn't fight because they couldn't. And if D'Artagnan slaughtered them all, the best to be hoped for would be that he would be everywhere known as a killer of the defenseless. There was no honor in a killing such as this. There would only be shame in winning, and losing was unthinkable.

Sending them was, in fact, not only an insult, but a cunning ploy of the Cardinal's. The sort of ploy the snake that ruled behind the throne of France was well known for. And D'Artagnan's friends didn't even see it.

D'Artagnan stamped his foot, in hatred of the Cardinal and in fury and frustration at his friends. "Draw, or I slaughter you where you stand," he said, knowing only that to back out would be shame and to continue forward would be disaster. He was caught in the Cardinal's trap.

The sound of running feet didn't intrude into his mind. He did not look until a well-known voice called, breathlessly, from the side, "Monsieur, monsieur."

D'Artagnan turned. Planchet had been left safely in D'Artagnan's lodging, at the Rue des Fossoyers. Planchet would not come here, like this, much less think of interrupting a duel without very grave reason. Reason so grave that D'Artagnan couldn't even imagine it.

All this was in his mind, not full thoughts, not fully in words, as he turned, sword still in hand, still lifted, to see his servant—his bright red hair standing on end, his dark suit dusty and stained as if he'd run the whole way here—leaning forward, hands on knees, a respectful distance from him. "Planchet, what is it?"

And the guards attacked. D'Artagnan heard the sound of swords sliding from their sheaths and turned. He was barely in time to meet head-on the clumsy rush of the blond guard.

"Ah, coward," he said, only vaguely aware that Porthos and Aramis had joined the fray on either side of him, taking on the blond's assistants. D'Artagnan parried a thrust and made a very accurate thrust of his own, slitting the man's doublet from top to bottom and ending by flipping his hat off his head. "Would you duel with a real man?" he said.

The blond had a moment to look aghast at his torn clothing, cut with such precision as not to touch the flesh beneath, and to bend upon D'Artagnan a gaze of the purest horror. His lips worked, but no sound emerged.

And D'Artagnan, his mind viewing the man and his fear as only a move in his chess game with the Cardinal, thought he glimpsed an opening, a way out of the trap of honor in which he found himself. He lunged forward, saying, "You think you can stand up against the musketeers? Don't you think it will take more than that to face the men who have so often proved superior to his eminence's best guards?"

"That's right," Porthos said. He had, with easy bluster, inflicted a minor wound on his opponent's arm and was grinning as he prepared to parry a counterattack that might very well never come. "That's right. We'd rather die. Be cut to pieces right here, than allow you to arrest us."

"At any rate, monsieurs," Aramis said, from D'Artagnan's right. "It would be a more merciful and quicker way to die to allow ourselves to be killed here than to face the wrath of Monsieur de Treville." There was still a tremolo of amusement to his voice, and D'Artagnan wondered if Aramis had begun to glimpse both the trap and the way out. Or if he, cunning as he was, had seen it all along, and before D'Artagnan did. "So we die here, monsieurs, but you cannot arrest us."

And in that second something broke in the leader's eyes. He looked down at his torn doublet that showed a dubiously

clean linen shirt beneath, then he looked quickly up at
D'Artagnan. And then his sword clattered to the ground
and, before D'Artagnan could gracefully accept his surrender, the man had taken to his heels, running fast over the
ice-crusted fields, slipping and standing and slipping again.

His men, clearly treasuring following their leader over
value, dropped their swords so fast they seemed like
echoes of his, and did their best to catch up with him.

"Well played, D'Artagnan," Aramis said. "I was wondering when you'd see their surrender or preferably their
flight was the only way out of this for us. The only way
with honor." His lazy smile, the paternal tone of his words,
implied that he'd seen this all along. D'Artagnan wondered if it was true. With Aramis it wasn't easy to say.
Aramis himself might not know.

"Poor devils," Porthos said, looking after the fleeing
men. "They were as set up for this as we were. And the
wrath they face from the Cardinal makes what we'd face at
Monsieur de Treville's hands seem almost gentle." He took
a deep breath, straining the expanse of his broad chest.
"The affront is the Cardinal's. I wish it were possible to
challenge him to a duel."

"He was a good enough duelist in his youth," Aramis
said, his tone deceptively light.

And D'Artagnan wondered if his mad friends, who
hated the Cardinal for many good reasons as well as many
foolish ones, would suddenly decide to challenge the Cardinal.

He opened his mouth to remind them that men such as
his eminence didn't fight with their swords but with the
might of the kingdom, when Athos spoke, "D'Artagnan,
attend. This is grave business." He held a letter in his
hand—its seal broken—and waved it slightly in D'Artagnan's direction.

"Grave?" D'Artagnan asked. He sheathed his sword
and stepped towards Athos. "What is it? From whom? And
for whom?"

But the words died on his lips. He'd got close enough to recognize his mother's hand, the rounded, convent hand that she'd been taught as a young girl. His mother? Writing to him? Normally his father did.

And Athos was alarmed, as doubtless had been Planchet to run all the way over here. With shaking hand, D'Artagnan plucked the sheet of paper from Athos's unresisting hand and brought it up in front of his eyes, focusing on the writing.

"Dear son," the letter started primly. "I regret the obligation of it, but I must call you back from Paris at a very short notice. You see, there is no one else to claim the name or the domain. There is no one else to take up the care of the lands, or even to look after me." D'Artagnan blinked in confusion at the words, wondering what his mother could mean, and almost had to force himself to read on. "Your father departed this world on Monday, a week ago. Today is the first time I've had the time and solitude"—*Solitude* was heavily underscored—"to write this letter to you. For you must know that though they say it was a duel, I cannot be easy about your father's death. He had, after all, been looking into your uncle's affairs and I think he was doing it at the behest of that great man, Cardinal Richelieu. Of course, no one else knew this, either that he was looking into things or about the Cardinal, but a woman knows these things." *Knows* was, again, deeply underscored. "You know how your father valued you and trusted you. I can't tell this to anyone else. Please, hurry home, son, and take up your rightful place in this household." It was signed in a tremulous hand with what read like Mauvais D'Tortoise but D'Artagnan could guess to be his mother's signature— Marie D'Artagnan—distorted by emotion.

But . . . what emotion? D'Artagnan could barely absorb the contents of the letter.

His father dead? From a duel? Impossible. Monsieur D'Artagnan, père, had taught his son to such effect that even the most famous fighters in Paris could not best him.

A murder disguised as a duel? Impossible again. D'Artagnan's mind ran over the place of his childhood, those domains that he'd described often as smaller than the Cemetery des Innocents in Paris.

D'Artagnan's father had grown up there and, save for the brief time at war, lived there, in those villages and fields. There was no one there who'd raise a hand against him. It would never happen.

And yet . . . His father was dead. And his father had been working for the Cardinal?

Every feeling revolted, and the print seemed stark and cold upon the page. D'Artagnan felt a sob trying to tear through his throat and fought it back with all his might, with greater strength than he'd ever had to employ against a human enemy.

He took a deep breath. His voice came out reasonably controlled. "You are right, Athos. This is grave. I'd best attend to it."

"Of course," Athos said. "When do the four of us leave for Gascony?"